HIS BODY SPOKE FOR ITSELF.

Francesca grabbed a digital camera from her desk, focused, and began clicking. As she worked her way back to the most excellent front view of Reese, she knew even though she had more to interview, this was *the man* to launch her magazine into the ranks of *Playgirl*. He was perfect. He had an edge to his features that inspired women to want to tame him. His tan skin and deep-set crystal-blue eyes contrasted, giving him the predatory look of a lone wolf. A faint thin scar ran behind his right ear down his throat stopping just above his collar bone, giving him an air of danger. She needed to capture that danger on film and sell it to delirious women across the country. Her smile widened behind the camera.

ALSO BY KARIN TABKE

Good Girl Gone Bad

SKIN

KARIN TABKE

POCKET BOOKS

NEW YORK   LONDON   TORONTO   SYDNEY

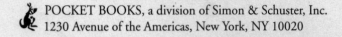 POCKET BOOKS, a division of Simon & Schuster, Inc.
1230 Avenue of the Americas, New York, NY 10020

ISBN-13: 978-1-4165-2492-2
ISBN-10:   1-4165-2492-4

This Pocket Books trade paperback edition April 2007

10 9 8 7 6 5 4 3 2 1

Manufactured in the United States of America

For information regarding special discounts for bulk purchases, please contact
Simon & Schuster Special Sales at 1-800-456-6798 or
business@simonandschuster.com

To my mom, Iyone Stanton, the bravest lady I know. Stay strong, stay healthy, stay just the way you are.

To my other mom, Marlene Tabke, the best mother-in-law a daughter could ever wish for. Never change.

Acknowledgments

To Sheryl Rowland, the woman who makes it possible for me to write. Without your willingness to run the business, I could not follow my dream. Thank you one thousand times over.

Thank you to everyone who has purchased one of my books, then read it, liked it, and smiled.

To Allison Brennan and Natalie R. Collins, thank you for spending a great weekend at my house and breathing life into the tag line: jaded cop vs. mafia princess.

To my CP's, Michelle Diener, Liz Krueger, and Edie Ramer, much thanks for putting up with my manic revisions.

Rae (Monet), thanks for the emergency plotting sessions and whining phone calls when these characters just wouldn't listen to me.

Lauren, once again, thank you for the heavy editor's hand. You made this story so much stronger.

And last but not least, to Gary. Baby, you know without you, my *hot cops* would never have been born. xoxo

SKIN

CHAPTER ONE

"Strip."

"I beg your pardon?"

"Drop your drawers, take off your clothes, *get naked.*"

Reese hesitated. The woman sitting behind the desk stood, the movement slow and fluid. Her expression, though, screamed impatience.

"Look . . ." She glanced at the file he'd handed her when he was ushered into her office. "Reese, *Skin* is an upscale chick rag. How the hell can I tell if you have the goods if I don't see them first?"

He'd never been shy about shucking his clothes for a woman, but he'd never been commanded to do it in the middle of the day in the downtown office of a very attractive and very irritated female. He stood.

Miss Donatello had legs long enough to wrap around him twice and a waist he bet he could span with his hands. Her full breasts bobbed in rhythmic sensuality with her every move under the fitted white shirt. His gaze dipped lower, admiring the way her black

1

leather skirt hugged her lush ass like a second skin. His taste usually ran to tall, lithe women, but this voluptuous drink of water would quench his thirst any day. He warmed to his assignment.

"Reese, I'm a very busy lady, I need to see your package, *now.*" Her eyes narrowed. "If you can't drop your drawers for me now, how the hell are you going to drop them for my camera?"

Too much was riding on him being picked as *Skin's* first centerfold.

He grinned, a rare gesture given his generally antisocial demeanor. He'd gladly reveal more skin than she could handle. Slowly, he unbuttoned his 501s, his eyes catching her hazel ones.

Reese held her gaze as he slid the denim down his thighs, his muscles slowing the process. Like a stunned rabbit, her nostrils flared. He knew she was more than curious. His eyes continued to hold hers, daring her to look before he was ready to extend an invitation. He'd lay odds she didn't normally allow a model to control the show-and-tell stage of this type of interview. His black boxer briefs followed his jeans to his knees. Reese grinned big.

Warily, Frankie's eyes dipped. She gasped, for a moment unable to control her female response to his male. Her reaction was one of basic attraction, and she was having a hell of a time breathing normally. She'd seen a lot of the male anatomy in her business and more cocks in the last twenty-four hours than she could count, but she'd never seen a package this beautiful, this complete, and never so eager to salute her. The models she'd interviewed the previous day and this morning shriveled up in shyness. Not so this guy. She racked her brain for his name. She was lousy with names. Oh, yeah, Reese.

She cleared her throat. "Nice salute you have there, sailor." Leaning a hip against the edge of her desk, she crossed her arms over her chest. She wanted to touch him, to see if his tan skin was as warm as she suspected. His erection bobbed and she wondered what he was thinking.

Collecting herself, she pursed her lips. Resisting the urge to smile, Frankie silently thanked God for this blessing. "I'm so glad you're not gay."

"What makes you so sure?"

Frankie laughed and cocked a brow, inclining her head toward his impressive erection. "The fact that you haven't shriveled up or failed to rise to the occasion." Her eyes locked with his. "And the fact that your boy there keeps growing."

"He likes what he sees."

Her skin warmed, and while she didn't want to admit it, she was glad on a personal level he was very obviously heterosexual. She allowed her eyes to ravage the smooth, hard planes of his belly and lower to the smooth thickness sprouting from his thighs.

He would do very nicely for what she had in mind.

"Well, tell your little man the only job he's being interviewed for is to perform for my camera. Nothing more."

But Frankie began to think she did want more. She knew if she touched him he would be warm, and she'd feel the thick surge of blood course through him. She squirmed in her heels and quelled the urge to brush her fingertips down his shaft. This was business, and with the one exception she'd paid dearly for, she made it a hard and fast rule not to touch the models, except to position them on a shoot.

"Is there a hands-on segment to this audition?"

His deep, husky voice sent chills cascading along her neck. The guy had trouble stamped all over his arrogant face.

She nodded. "Maybe. Let's see what you have upstairs."

He cocked a dark brow. She smiled when he pulled his form-fitting black T-shirt over his head. "You learn quick, sailor."

His chest was almost as irresistible as his astute cock. Hard, defined, tan. Several pale slash-mark scars tattooed one side of his rib cage. Her imagination ran wild with scenarios of how they got there. Instead of detracting from his maleness, they intensified it.

Thick arms rippled with the slightest movement, his biceps bouncing softly as he smoothed his dark brown hair back into place with both hands. She swallowed hard, the image of his arms up over his shoulders, his chest flexed, and his cock growing inches by the second burning in her memory banks. Warmth infiltrated the moist spot between her thighs. Dormant desire roused deep inside her. Crap. She might run a skin rag for chicks, but she wasn't one to sleep around, especially with her models. Goose bumps coursed down her arms. Even if she was attracted to this guy, she wouldn't go down that road with him. One time had been more than enough. Since the Sean incident two years ago, her knees were welded together when it came to mixing business with the obvious pleasure Reese was capable of giving.

"Do I muster up?"

She gave in to a rare smile. Crossing her arms over her chest, Frankie slowly walked around him. "Very nice glutes." He did have a fine ass. Smooth, muscular cheeks screamed for her hand to test their hardness.

"How'd you get the scars on your chest?"

"Old girlfriend. Really sharp nails."

"Are you Italian?"

"I am if you want some Italian in you."

Frankie gasped. "For someone who's looking for work, you sure are cocky." She snorted. "Pun intended."

She grabbed a digital camera off her desk, focused, and began clicking. As she worked her way back to the most excellent front view of this man, she knew even though she had more to interview, this was *the man* to launch her magazine into the ranks of *Playgirl*. He was perfect. He had an edge to his features that inspired women to want to tame him. His tan skin and deep-set crystal-blue eyes contrasted, giving him the predatory look of a lone wolf. A faint, thin scar ran behind his right ear down his throat, stopping just above his collarbone, giving him an air of danger. She needed to capture that danger on film and sell it to delirious women across the country. Her smile widened behind the camera.

His body spoke for itself. She could see the handwriting on the wall. The entire staff would want to be in on his photo sessions. An idea sparked. They'd go with location shots. A day in the life of Mr. Skin. She quickly warmed to the idea, then scowled. Time was limited and his agent wanted top dollar—she was short on both. Unk had hinted there were some accounting issues; so had her father the day before he died.

Her lips drew into a firm line. Since her father's death two weeks prior, she'd been off balance, unsure—afraid. The turmoil in her personal life and here at *Skin* sent her control-freak nature into a tailspin. Yesterday, her first day back at the office, she'd forced herself to produce and not lament what she could not change. And the winds of change blew hot and heavy through the family. She always knew her family was dysfunctional, but now they were downright scary.

A shiver skittered across her skin, and her belly flip-flopped. Papa was dead now and playing the rebellious daughter was a moot point. But God, how she wanted to best him, to prove to him she had what it took to be involved in the family business, to change his perception of her after the Sean debacle. Now she couldn't, damn it, and worse, their last words to each other were harsh.

Frankie shook off the malaise. She had a job to do. Pushing past the pain, she gave Reese her undivided attention. She focused and shot, getting every conceivable angle she could of the man who would launch *Skin* into the stratosphere.

"Tell me about your last job," Frankie said, working her way around him, taking advantage of every angle.

"I spent the last few months in Europe. I did a spread for Mercedes, then hung around and soaked up the local culture."

She bet he soaked up more than historical landmarks. And bet he didn't do it alone.

"Why come back?"

"I need cash."

"You want more cash than I can afford."

"I'm worth it."

For a brief moment Frankie lowered the camera. Her eyes swept him his from boots to the top of his head. He was worth more.

"I have a budget."

"Once my issue comes out, you won't have to worry about budgets."

Raising the camera, she smiled. She would always worry about budgets. For all of her father's money, he was frugal when it came to business. What would Papa do?

Emotion welled when she thought of him. She had so much she wanted to prove to him. So much to make up. She'd not only lost what little respect her father had given her as a businesswoman, but she had become the laughingstock of the family—proving once again that women were not worthy of the same respect as the male family members. The hot sting of tears caught her off guard. The trauma of the last two weeks caught up with her, realization hitting her hard. She was on her own now, in more ways than just business. She took a deep breath and exhaled slowly. A deep chuckle jerked her out of her musings.

"I have to admit, you're the first, Miss Donatello."

Lowering the camera, her eyes focused on Reese. "First what?"

"The first woman I've brought to tears without laying a finger on her."

Her eyes narrowed and warning bells sounded. The man was too intense, too bold, too distracting. She'd worked with models like him before. She didn't play well with other dominant personalities. Was he worth the hassle and the money? She had a tight window of time, and wrestling with the likes of this man would put her behind schedule.

"I—" The door to her office flew open with a bang and Reese and Frankie started.

"Son of a bitch, Anthony, do you know how to knock?" Frankie demanded.

Anthony stopped in his tracks and gave Reese and his erection a cause for pause. "Back to your old tricks, sis?"

Frankie set her camera down on her desk and stepped around toward the door. "Excuse us . . . ?"

"Reese."

"Sorry—Reese," she apologized, then pushed her brother out the office door and into the crowded anteroom of her offices, where Tawny, her assistant, sat surrounded by hunky male models. A dozen sets of eyes looked expectantly at her. Frankie smiled and continued down the hall with her brother in tow until she came across the office recently vacated by one of her father's accountants. She hustled Anthony in and shut the door behind them.

"What the hell, Tony?" she demanded.

His dark brows shot up. Good looks ran in the family. Expressive, olive-skinned features accentuated Tony's Italian heritage. Lucky for her half brother he didn't inherit much from his maternal line. Instead he was a miniversion of their handsome father, Santini "Sonny" Donatello, and his older brother, Carmine. Santini wasn't known as Don Juan for nothing. He was a ladies man until the day he died, much to the chagrin of Tony's mother, Connie.

"You're asking *me* what the hell? What the hell was that naked guy doing in your office?"

"I'm interviewing for my centerfold."

"The hell you are!"

"The hell I'm not!" He might be the heir apparent for all things nefarious, but *Skin* was legit and it was hers.

"You are not going through with that."

"I sure as hell am. *Skin* needs a shot in the arm and the anniversary edition is launching our first centerfold."

"Father forbade it!" Tony shrieked. He sounded like a teenage girl on a roller-coaster ride.

"Father is dead."

"And you have no more respect for him dead than you did when he was alive. No wonder he disowned you."

"He did no such thing." *He only threatened it.*

"That's a load of shit. I talked to him before he left Carmel."

Frankie chewed her bottom lip. They had quarreled, she and her father. She wanted complete creative control over *Skin,* and that meant giving her permission to go with the naked centerfold. Santini was violently opposed to his only daughter—a daughter who in his mind had proven to be naive, emotional, and impetuous—taking pictures of naked men and then publishing them for the world to see. He had his honor, he told her.

"But, Papa, you own strip joints and peep shows!"

"That's different, Francesca. It's what men do. I will not have my daughter, my flesh and blood, take pictures of naked men. I'll lose respect in the family. My answer is no!"

When she refused to be swayed by him, then threatened to enlist the aid of her uncle, his older brother, his last words to her were, "Then you are dead to me."

The next afternoon he was dead to her.

Frankie tilted her head up to look at her brother. He wasn't much taller than her. She read no affection in his black eyes, only cool disdain. It had always been that way. "Papa promised me *Skin*. He didn't change his mind."

"As soon as father's will is located and dissected you'll have legal proof, everything he owns including *Skin* will be mine."

"Unk will have something to say about it."

"I'm sure he will, and he can say all he wants. But the documents will stand on their own. I win and you lose." And that was always how it was with Anthony. A game. He played hardball. This time he was in for a big surprise. Not only was she stepping up to the plate, she was coming out swinging.

As angry as she and her father had been with each other, she didn't believe he would go to such drastic lengths to cut her out. Or would he? Santini Donatello was old-fashioned to the core. If he believed she was going in a direction he was opposed to, would he reach out from the grave to control? Flicking her hair off her shoulder, she shrugged. It didn't matter. *Skin* was hers. "Give it your best shot, little brother."

Tony flashed his sister a narrow-eyed glare. "You'll lose. You always have."

"Not this time."

He nodded as if contemplating an offer. "I'll be around, Frankie—watching, keeping my eye on you and the family's interests."

"Watch all you want, Anthony. Despite your delusions, at the very least, I'm still creative director here. Go back to running your strippers."

Anthony's features hardened. "My girls turn a profit every night. You haven't turned a profit since you gave up all your secrets the night Sean humped you dry." Frankie gasped at his crudity.

Anthony continued, "It makes me wonder what else you've done to drive this place into the ground." He walked to the computer sitting on the bare desk. He ran his hand across the top of the monitor, then turned to look at her with a thoughtful, narrowed gaze. "Father finally woke up to your schemes, and lucky for the family he did it before he died."

Frankie fisted her hands at her sides. What she wouldn't give for just one sucker punch. *Skin is mine.*

He shrugged and moved to look out the window at the busy street below. "Maybe. For now." He slid his hands into his trouser pockets and smiled his best weasel smile. "But in the meantime, I'll take this office and make myself comfortable. Enjoy your job, sis, while you still have one."

"Like I said, Tony, give it your best shot," Frankie said, and moved to the door. She was done with her brother. She'd made dozens of overtures over the years to close the gap between them, but he consistently refused. The gloves were off now. She'd fight tooth and nail for what was rightfully hers.

Anthony laughed. "I play for keeps, sister."

"So do I. Now, if you'll excuse me, I have my magazine to run." And oh, shit, she had a naked man in her office!

CHAPTER TWO

Frankie sprinted down the hall, dismissing her brother's threats and ignoring the hunks sitting impatiently, waiting to show her their stuff.

She opened her office door just enough to slide in and shut it behind her. She pressed her back up against the smooth wood and her gut somersaulted when a very sexy Reese turned from her window to bestow her with a million-dollar smile. While her heart did a giddyup thump, she frowned, disappointed. He'd dressed. Not that this view was bad. Far from it.

She'd dealt with scores of models over the last five years at *Skin*, and she was used to pretty faces, but Reese was more. He possessed that certain je ne sais quoi that only came along once in a blue moon. It could get a girl in trouble—big trouble. Trouble that could push her disjointed life off the edge. She took a deep breath. Tony's reminder of her foolish behavior with Sean tore a festering wound wide open.

She wasn't a moron. She'd learned very early the opposite sex was more attracted to her father and his perceived glamorous life than to his daughter. The minute they met Santini Donatello, notorious don, their eyes glazed over with dreams of life as a goombah, the posturing began, and they were lost to her forever.

All of them—except Sean. He wasn't interested in her father, he told her, he was interested in her and her life. Yep, he was. That and getting her in bed to pump her for secrets. The more he pumped, the more she shared, until he had her blueprint of success for *Skin*. He took it, walked across town, and sold it to her competitor.

It not only ruined her standing in the business community, it ruined what little respect she'd managed to garner from her father, and it also emotionally devastated her. She didn't trust easy these days, especially her own instincts.

"I apologize for my brother's rudeness," she breathlessly said, then strode past him to her desk. "He never grasped the concept of manners."

Reese shrugged it off. "No big deal. Every family has its problems."

He had no idea.

"So when do I start?" he asked.

Frankie sat down at her desk and looked up from the file she just opened. The intensity of his gaze nearly undid her. Warning bells shrilled in her head. "You don't." Her words startled her as much as him. But she'd learned a dear lesson after being so impulsive with Sean. *Skin*'s survival depended on the model she hired and how well she could or couldn't work with him. She promised herself two years ago she would always without fail take slow, deliberate, *informed* steps the next time she felt a spark with a potential employee. And as much as she didn't want to, she felt more than a spark with Mr. Hotshot Reese. He could wreck a woman with a smile. The man she chose to launch her magazine into the company of *Cosmo* and *Play-*

girl would have to not only fit her stringent physical requirements, which Reese more than did, but also be a safe bet on all other fronts, which Reese definitely was not.

Besides, she couldn't afford him.

She and her model would be spending too much time together, and most of that time would be her instructing him to take his clothes off while she got very close and very personal with her camera.

Reese's eyes widened in surprise. "I'm out because . . . ?"

"I don't owe you an explanation."

"Because you don't have one."

"Consider my decision a calculated risk."

"So you calculate I'm too big a risk?"

Reese walked to the edge of her desk and leaned against it. His warm, woodsy scent drifted below her nose. Her nostrils twitched. His moves stiffened her resolve.

"What do I have to do to change your mind?"

Not be so male? Frankie's nether parts warmed. She snapped the folder shut, pushed back her chair, and stood up to face him on an equal plane. "Nothing."

He smiled slow and easy. "Are you afraid of me?"

Her jaw dropped before she caught it. "Afraid of you? How?"

"You must have ice for blood if you don't feel the connection we have. Isn't that a must between a model and his photographer?"

Frankie couldn't deny it in her heart. But she would deny it to his face. She'd made the right decision. The man was lethal to her senses, and she wasn't up for more drama in her life. *Skin* meant everything to her, and part of taking it to the next level was having a model she felt comfortable with. She felt the complete opposite with this man.

"I don't mix business with pleasure," Reese said. His eyes glowed and a playful smile toyed with his lips.

Frankie's lips twitched in response. And she felt a rush, a rush to rise to that challenge, to hire him just to break him. She moved away from him. She could hear her father now. *There you go again, Francesca. Have you learned nothing from your mistakes? By allowing your emotions to dictate business, you lose respect. You're too much of a woman to rule with the iron hand of a man.*

"Neither do I," Frankie said. Setting the file down on her desk, she walked to the door and opened it. "Thanks for coming in, Mr. Barrett. If we choose to go with you, we'll call you."

Reese headed for the door but stopped beside her. His blue eyes gleamed at a private joke. She fidgeted in her heels. He smiled and bent down to her ear and whispered, "Don't take too long. Once I leave here, I'm on my way to *Stag*. I hear they're launching a couples centerfold issue."

Frankie's skin warmed, but she dug in. Her back stiffened. She'd heard that too, and what made it worse was *Stag* was the rag Sean sold out to. It was also where he was employed as editorial consult. She pulled the door open wider. "Good day, Mr. Barrett."

He gave her a short salute.

"Frankie, that guy was gorgeous," Tawny said, barging into her office the minute the door closed behind Reese Barrett's very nice ass.

Her instinct was to run after Reese just to keep him out of Sean's hands. But she curbed the impulse. She might be a female, but she had the guts and tenacity of any male in her family. If there was one lesson she took to heart from her father, it was the virtue of patience. *Skin* was her priority, and she would make calm, cool, collected decisions to ensure its success.

"Hello? Earth to Frankie." Tawny waved her hand in front of Frankie's nose.

"He's no one we're interested in."

Tawny's brown eyes widened. "Are you telling me that hunk has a Mini Cooper?"

Frankie made a lame attempt to smile, her energy suddenly drained. "Quite the opposite."

"Then what the hell are you thinking?"

Frankie scowled. She wasn't thinking, she was reacting. Her brain warred with her emotions. Her gut screamed Reese Barrett was trouble—too much of a distraction, a distraction her upside-down, inside-out life didn't need. There was a room full of models waiting to jump through hoops, and if none of them mustered up, there were scores more in the wings.

Rubbing her temples, Frankie groaned. Her father wasn't dead two weeks, the family was coming undone, everyone pointing fingers at everyone else, and if she didn't act now, *Skin* would go down the proverbial toilet.

His words echoed in her head. *"It's just business, Francesca, never forget."*

Skin was not only her business, it was her passion. She wanted to prove to herself and to the family that she, a woman, could take *Skin* from modest to record-breaking circulation. To do that, she needed the right centerfold. She was back to square one.

"Did you see anything out there that did it for you?" she asked her trusty assistant.

"Not like what just walked out of here."

Great. Frankie stepped out into the anteroom. A dozen sets of hopeful eyes zeroed in on her. She forced a smile and began her scan of the room. From left to right, her gaze paused at each hopeful, their smiles promising to deliver, but her radar instantly dismissed them. When she came full circle, she made another round, this one cursory.

Nothing.

"I'm sorry, gentlemen, if I've wasted your time, but you're all excused."

Before any one of them decided to take their frustration out on her personally, Frankie ducked back into her office and shut the door. She turned to wide-eyed Tawny.

"Call Images and find out who else they have. If they're dry, go to Models, Inc. If they can't come up with the goods, find me an agency that can. We need a centerfold like yesterday. I was hoping to start shooting tomorrow."

"I'm on it, boss." Tawny scurried out of her office, leaving the door wide open.

Frankie shook her head. Tawny wasn't the brightest bulb in the chandelier, but she could type, trash talk, and cajole a fish out of water. She was also loyal in a business that didn't recognize loyalty.

Getting up, Frankie closed her office door. Impulsively she picked up her phone and pressed a number. She needed Anthony off her back, and there was only one person who could deliver that.

"Donatello."

Just the sound of her father's COO (the PC word for consigliere) warmed her. "Unk, I need your help."

"Anything for you, *cara mia*. What do you need?"

"Get my brother off my back."

Deep laughter filtered through the airwaves. "What has he done?"

Unk never gave Tony enough credit. Maybe now Tony was looking for some payback?

"He thinks he can fire me."

Silence.

Alarms rang in her head.

"Unk?"

"I'm here."

"Talk to me."

"There seems to be a few gray areas with some of your father's business."

Frankie felt as if her stomach just thudded to her feet. "Such as?"

"*Skin.*"

"*Skin* is mine!"

"*Si, cara,* I know. I'll settle things, do not worry."

A modicum of relief soothed her. She had complete confidence in Unk's word. It was gold. However, she didn't share his tactics in making it a done deal.

"Look, I want what is mine because it's right, not by default—or any other means."

"Of course, *cara,* I would expect nothing less. The last thing we want is more family distress."

By that, she knew he meant blood on his or her hands.

"Any word on Father's will?"

"Aldo hasn't produced it. But of course I can't produce Aldo."

Another mystery. Her father's personal attorney, Aldo Geppi. Gone. Disappeared. But then, with her family, nothing struck her as mysterious. People disappeared all the time. Some returned, but most didn't.

"But there *is* a will?"

"There is a will. We'll have to be patient a little longer."

And she could rely on her uncle to keep Anthony under his thumb. She needed time. "Can I meet you later?"

"Of course. My office around five."

She chewed her fingertip. "Five is too early." Knowing Carmine Donatello never left his office before eight on any given weeknight, she asked, "How about if I bring some of Gina's cannoli for later. We'll have dessert."

Rich laughter poured through the phone. Frankie smiled. The man she loved most in the world had returned. "You know I can never resist Gina's cannoli."

And he had the belly to prove it. Since her first memory, Unk filled the shoes her father refused to step into. He was also the man who bridged the gap between father and daughter and brother and sister. It was Unk who stood quietly in the background in case she needed a hand up when she fell too hard. He had been a godsend after the Sean debacle, when her father fired her.

It was Unk who threatened to divide the family if Santini didn't reinstate Frankie as creative director. It was also Unk who stood by her decision to transform *Skin* from a women's health and beauty magazine to a women's eye-candy magazine. Sex sold, it was basic economics. And even though her father ran the family, it was his brother, Carmine, who was the quiet mastermind.

She would be forever grateful for the round Sicilian's protective arms and deep, soothing voice reminding her she was a Donatello and, with that, part of a long line of Italian aristocracy.

She knew what that meant too. Her father was up to his eyeballs in nefarious business, and her brother relished following in his footsteps. More than once over the years, she wished she could blink and be a member of the Brady Bunch instead of the black-sheep daughter of the Sopranos.

"*Cara,* have you gone to see your father?"

Fear of breaking down paralyzed her. Somehow, Frankie knew if she hadn't defied her father, challenging him as she had, he would have stayed in Carmel as he planned and would still be alive. Frankie let out a long breath. "No, I haven't. We never got along in life, what makes his death different?"

"He loved you."

"He loved Anthony. I embarrassed him."

"No, you challenged him." Carmine chuckled, the sound comforting.

"He fired me!"

"That's all water under the bridge. You learned the hard way to keep business and family secrets to yourself."

"No kidding." She'd paid dearly for what her father called her "hormone-induced stupidity."

She had big plans for *Skin* the day she walked into the mail room as an intern. She worked her ass off, putting in fifteen-hour days and doing the grunt work no one else would touch, and asking more questions than anyone had patience for. But gradually she gained the respect of those in power. She found her niche behind the camera. Cello Margolise, the creative director at the time, took her under his wing. She was a quick study. When he retired, she was the obvious choice. It was also when she hired Sean, a too sexy, too slick, charismatic model. She fell hard and fast.

The night he asked her to marry him, she confided in him. Then the bastard hung her out to dry.

She'd learned her lesson, but in the process lost her father's respect.

So when she came up with the idea to convert *Skin,* she shared it only with her father and her uncle.

"Francesca," her uncle said, bringing her back to the present, "changing a ladies' health magazine into a ladies' eye-candy magazine was more than his ego could take. He would have lost respect in the family. You're a good Catholic girl, maybe you shouldn't be taking pictures of naked men and printing them for the world to see."

She sighed. "I always knew in your heart you sided with Father. Why can't you understand for me it's just business? A means to an end. Just like the rest of the family. And for the record, I didn't approve of what Father did. At least *Skin* is legit." So now in her mind they were even. An eye for an eye. It was the way of the family.

"Listen to your words, Francesca, and try to understand your father. You claim *Skin* is just business, a business of selling sex."

"No, it—"

"Don't interrupt," he sternly said.

She pressed her lips together.

"You use naked or near naked men as a commodity. A means to sell magazines. You use the oldest angle. Sex sells. Your father didn't disapprove of the concept, he disapproved of his daughter's involvement. Turn the tables, *cara*. You didn't approve of your father's business endeavors."

"But my business isn't *illegal*."

"The family has many legitimate holdings."

"But his bread and butter wasn't." Frankie pinched the bridge of her nose with her fingers. Her temples throbbed. The feeling of walls closing in around her stifled her. "We can argue semantics later, I need a caffeine fix. See you at eight."

After hanging up the phone, Frankie called to Tawny through the open door. "I'm going to run a few errands, then hit Baccio's. I expect an office full of models when I get back."

CHAPTER THREE

"Houston, we have a problem," Reese said to his captain. He slipped into a chair in the field office of the San Francisco County organized crime task force. Propping his booted feet up on the desk, he not only met his captain's scowl but scanned those of his team.

"For Christsakes, Bronson," Ty Jamerson grumbled. "You have the biggest damn cock on the West Coast and you can't get her to take a picture of it?"

Ricco Maza, a hotshot from Montrose PD, hooted and slapped Reese's longtime partner, Jase Vaughn, on the back. *"Dios mios,* you couldn't get that little mafia princess to bite? Not even a nibble?" Both men doubled over in laughter.

Reese's eyes narrowed and he cast a quick glance at Andi Fuentes. The long-legged, darkly exotic So Cal detective gave him an equally narrowed look in return. He guessed he deserved it. While he'd made her no promises several years ago during a brief but intense fling, she apparently hadn't forgotten or forgiven him. Despite her glare, his body warmed. Andrea Fuentes was spicy hot. If he were a better man, he'd make an honest woman out of her. As he was, she was too good for the likes of him.

Besides, he knew she wasn't interested in growing roots either. It was one of the reasons they maintained a working relationship.

"It wasn't a performance problem, was it, Reese?" Andi asked, her thick, husky voice conjuring up wild summer nights, twisted sheets, and the hottest sex north of the border.

Jase chortled. "I always thought what happened between the sheets stayed between the sheets."

Andi stood and every eye in the room roamed across her ass. She walked past the men and poured herself a cup of coffee. She turned and leaned her backside against the coffee table. Reese admired the smooth curve of her hip. His gaze traveled up to her dark flashing eyes. He deserved her scorn.

Refusing to break her stare, Andi said, "Unless there's nothing going on between the sheets."

"Watch out, Bronson," Ricco, said between laughs. "Latinas are a vindictive lot."

Breaking his gaze, Reese scowled and rubbed his chest, remembering the sharp pain of her nails. "Tell me something I don't already know."

"Bronson, Fuentes, if you two can't keep your objectivity, one of you goes," Ty said.

Andi smiled and sipped her coffee. "I have no problem with Bronson, sir."

Ty cocked a dark brow at Reese. "I'm good," Reese said.

"Good, then let's get this show on the road."

Reese grinned and settled back into his chair and gave them the 411. "For your information, Miz D took a picture, all right. Lots, in fact. I had her too. Until her brother busts in and makes a smart-ass comment before she drags him out. They were gone for a few minutes. They must have gone at it, because she came back a different person."

"Fucking sibling rivalry?" Ty asked.

Reese shook his head. "No, it's more than that. I think Anthony isn't keen on the direction his sister wants to take the magazine. And we know from the street the old man put his foot down."

"So crying to the brother won't help?" Andi said, shaking her head. "I find it amazing that that pissant Anthony Donatello, who runs whores, loan sharks, and has a piece of every strip joint in three counties gets butt-hurt when Sis wants to publish pictures of naked guys."

"You could go back and plead your case," Jase said.

"And look like I need the job? No fucking way. I do my best work when they come to me," Reese said.

Andi snorted and mumbled something about pompous-asshole cops into her mug.

Reese flashed a grin at his ex and continued. "Besides, I told her I was interviewing at *Stag*. Word is a former love interest consults over there. Not sure what happened there, but I'll find out."

"Providing you get in," Andi challenged.

Reese's face tightened. "I'll get in."

"What happened when Tony showed up?" Ty asked.

"Instant tension," Reese said. "I thought she was going to tear him in half."

"So the lady has claws?" Jase asked.

"She has claws, all right, and a temper and guts."

"She's got more than that from the looks of her," Ricco said.

Reese eyed him and nodded. "She's a looker, a half-cocked one."

Andi shoved off the edge of the table, set her cup on the counter, and flashed an angry gaze at the men around her. "You talk like she doesn't deserve some respect. If you grew up surrounded by arrogant criminals, you'd have to grow some balls or die."

"Survival of the fittest. I think the lady has more going on under that sexy skin than meets the eye," Jase threw back. He looked hard at Reese. "She's the most worthy opponent. She makes you want her, then cuts your balls off when you least expect it."

Jase's words were not lost on Reese. He'd been doing this too long to get blindsided by a nice pair of tits and a petulant smile. "You think she ordered the hit?"

"I'm convinced of it," Jase said, his tone empathic.

Reese turned to his captain. "My read says, it's possible. But my money is on the brother."

"Okay," Ty said, "this is what we have. One dead mafia don, his daughter with over six million dollars in four buried offshore accounts, a pissed-off brother, and no will declaring the new don. Which leaves us with a war brewing. If I were a betting man, my money'd be on the daughter whacking the old man, for two reasons. One, he was opposed to her change of venue for her magazine, and two, I'll bet he found out she was ripping him off."

"Which leaves the brother out for a vendetta," Reese said. "It would explain his sudden interest in the magazine and their little tiff today. Brother is pushing to get in and sister wants him out."

"How out?" Andi asked.

"I'll lay odds enough to make him have an accident," Ricco said.

"She's up to it to her neck. Maybe she's looking to take over completely. What better way to prove she's one of the guys than to do like they do?" Jase asked.

"That'll buy her some respect, and from what I've read and heard, she has more brains then her brother." Andi smiled. "I kinda like that, a lady don."

"I don't know, my gut doesn't make her out to be power hungry. Driven, yes, but enough to kill her father?" Reese said.

"Just because she's a woman doesn't mean she isn't capable of killing," Ty reminded Reese.

"I get that, but my gut isn't buying her as the killer. Besides, the Donatellos are known for their tightness," Reese defended. And he wondered why. Was it his gut instinct or was it something else?

"They're like any other dysfunctional family, except these guys are a group of criminals," Ty said.

Reese nodded, agreeing. He knew about dysfunctional families. His family wrote the handbook.

"They're tight and they don't trust. Typical of the breed," Ricco said.

Reese gave a half smile. "The same could be said of us."

"Our lives depend on that code, Reese. No matter what dicks my brothers in blue turn out to be, they always know I have their back." Andi's eyes challenged his. Her words hit hard. He had been a cold-hearted bastard. If he had changed, he would reach out to her. But nothing had changed. His heart was forever locked.

Ty turned back to the case. "Last month we finally got a grunt into the front office of *Skin*. We're still working on the phone taps. In the meantime we need to nail this bitch before she whacks someone else, or worse, the families blow up on the street."

"Wait a minute, Captain," Andi said as she poured herself another cup of coffee. "Why are we assuming it's the daughter? I want to know why Anthony Donatello took a sudden interest in his sister's business."

"Boiled down, he has more to gain by offing the old man," Ricco mused out loud.

"I don't buy that," Jase said. "If the rest of the family agrees, Anthony is heir apparent. His sister, on the other hand, would be toast if the family thought she was ripping off the old man, or worse, that she offed him. She has the most to lose. I'll bet next month's paycheck little brother gets iced."

Ty nodded in agreement. "Francesca had means, and, if the whispers on the street are true and Daddy was about to cut her out of the business, motive. And she sure as hell had opportunity. She knew Santini hit that restaurant on his way back to the city. No witnesses? How fucking convenient for her."

Reese shook his head. "I'm not completely sold. After what I saw in her office today, I wouldn't put anything past Anthony Donatello. The guy walks around half-cocked."

Ty stood. He set a hand on Reese's shoulder. "Well, then, my man, you have your work cut out for you. You were handpicked—hell, you were cockpicked for this assignment. I don't care what you have to do to get that job, but get it. We need answers. There's too much trouble brewing on the streets. Wiseguys'll be coming out of the woodwork from every family in Nor Cal vying for power if this isn't settled. A war is the last thing we want."

Reese nodded, the seriousness of his task settling in. He would take this case on as he did every other UC case. With emotional detachment and a bite like a pit bull. Once he latched on, he wouldn't be shaken loose.

Too much was riding on his successful infiltration. If he didn't get in, not only would a Donatello get away with murder, but all hell would break loose over a power struggle.

Frankie stood in line, her arms crossed over her chest and her right foot tapping an irritated staccato on the black-and-white tile floor. She'd spent too much time out of the office. She was sure Tawny had come up with more models. She was anxious to resume her search. The long line moved at a snail's pace. At this rate it would be dinnertime before she got her latte.

"Are you following me, Miss Donatello?"

The fine hair on the back of her neck rose as warm breath caressed her skin. Although she'd only heard his voice briefly, it was imprinted in her brain along with the image of his cock. Reese Barrett's voice had an unforgettable husky timbre. "Considering you're behind me in line, I'd say you're following me."

She turned around. Her hardening nipples scraped against the broad hardness of his chest. She gasped, the sensation electrifying her skin. His deep-set blue eyes darkened and his lips turned up in one corner, crinkling his eyes in a way that reminded her of a very naughty little boy.

He didn't move away and she'd be damned if she would blink first.

"So, did you find your centerfold yet?" His warm, minty breath fanned her lips. She licked them.

"I'm still interviewing."

"*Stag* isn't."

Frankie stiffened. An unexplainable sense of loss hit her. Had she made a mistake not hiring Reese on the spot? Had Sean beat her to the punch yet again?

He brushed his chest against her straining nipples. Warmth pooled between her thighs. She looked up into his smiling face. Her stomach shifted. He had really long lashes. Thick and black like hers. His lips were full too. She liked the way they pulled to the left when he smiled. She imagined them slowly sucking and kissing the column of her neck, her most sensitive erogenous zone.

Holy hell, what was she thinking? He was pushy and insolent. Dangerous. She'd made the right choice. Sean could deal with him.

"Next!" the barista shouted from behind the coffee bar.

Reese nudged her with his chest, propelling her backward an inch. "You're next, Miss Donatello."

She could see it in his eyes. He wasn't talking about her coffee order.

CHAPTER FOUR

Frankie moved as far away from Reese as she could without actually exiting the café. Impatiently she sipped her latte and waited while Gina Sportaletti filled a few cannoli shells. Just her luck they ran out and she had to stick around. Despite her misgivings about the man, her skin warmed as she watched Reese charm the hell out of the reticent Beatrice, Gina's dried-up spinster aunt.

Reese glanced back at her and shot her that to-die-for smile. Her knees wobbled. He started toward her. She backed up, the edge of the counter biting her in the tush.

His eyes stopped her where she stood; his slow, lazy smile held delicious promise. Frankie halted the inevitable flood of warmth she felt every time he looked at her. She seriously questioned her sanity. The man was a stranger, and she reacted to him with the familiarity of a lover.

"Knock it off, Reese, the interview is over."

"Apparently I need to work on my convincing skills."

As men had so often led her to do over the years, Frankie smiled and raked her eyes across his chest. "If it makes you feel any better, the bottom line is I can't afford you."

"If you really wanted me, you'd find a way."

Her smile widened. She twisted a lock of her hair around her finger and cocked her head. "Maybe I don't really want you."

Reese moved in closer, his body heat radiating into her skin. He dipped his lips to her ear. "Who are you trying to convince? Me or you?"

Her smile waned and she let go of her hair. But she didn't move away.

His dark blue eyes turned black, his lips curled into a half smile. Even though she thought the man was intrusive and rude, she felt herself sucked in by his charisma. And it bugged her that in her vulnerable state she was so responsive to him. She was once again certain her decision to continue her model search was the right one.

Just as she reaffirmed her decision, a sudden thought struck her dumb. If she—a woman who had no use for a man, especially models—reacted to him so strongly, how would women desperate for a man, especially a prime specimen such as the one standing before her, react?

She sucked in a deep breath and took a step away from him. Was it fate? Meant to be, as her *nona* was famous for saying? Was Reese Barrett the *it* man? Like a deck of expertly shuffled cards, everything fell into place. Who was she kidding? He had that extra-special something, and more. She knew it in her gut just as sure as she knew if she didn't act soon, she'd lose her magazine to her brother.

Frankie chewed her bottom lip, indecision ping-ponging in her brain.

Unexpectedly, in her mind she saw their naked, sweaty bodies tearing up the sheets. Reese's long, powerful body over hers, commanding it to respond. She gasped and stepped further away.

Her father's words, "hormone-induced stupidity," rang in her ears.

"I know what's best for *Skin,* Mr. Barrett, and you aren't."

She grabbed the bag of cannoli from the table and ran out of the café.

"Shit, shit, shit," she muttered. Holding her latte in one hand and the bag of cannoli in the other, she weaved between the traffic on Post Street. What the hell was wrong with her? "Sex," she said out loud, "Sex with Reese Barrett."

"Holy Mother Mary, what am I doing?" She tried to cross herself with the hand holding the cannoli and nearly dropped the bag on the sidewalk.

As she hurried into her office, she noticed a half dozen studs perched around Tawny's desk. Sheepishly, her assistant looked up and shrugged her shoulders. "You told me pronto, so here's pronto."

"Give me a minute, then send one in."

Frankie sipped her lukewarm latte and continually forced Reese Barrett from her thoughts. Since the first model strutted in a half hour ago, she hadn't bothered to get up and take one picture. While the man standing in front of her had the required equipment—tight ass, hard abs, and substantial penis—his penis listed limply to the left and looked like it had a kink near the torpedo-shaped head. Like someone had stepped on it and broken it. She flinched at the notion. Not one of the four models she'd seen had become even semiaroused after her direction to strip.

Grimacing at her cold drink, she set the paper cup on her desk. She started to load the digital pictures of Reese onto her computer.

"So tell me a little about yourself"—she glanced at the file in front of her—"Enrique."

"I've been the top producing male model at Images for the last three years. You'd be stupid not to hire me." He grinned wide, showing two rows of perfectly capped teeth. "I guarantee I can get your circulation up."

So now the models were telling her how to run her business. She slipped on her reading glasses and peered at him from above them. She was a lot of things, but stupid wasn't one of them. Reese's grin darted into her thoughts. *If you're so smart, hire me.* She scowled and said, "As opposed to getting your cock up?"

His eyes widened.

Ignoring his surprise, Frankie stood and came around to the front of her desk. She leaned against it and spread her legs slightly, jutting out her substantial breasts. She could thank her Italian heritage for the breasts and her gypsy mother for her length of leg. Crossing her arms over her chest, she stared at him.

He nodded and smiled, his face morphing into the sexy Latin lover milieu. "I am very good at what I do, sexy lady. Give me a chance to show you my work."

He snapped at her, showing his big white teeth. She jumped, the edge of her desk cutting into her ass. She was going to be black and blue by the end of the day. "I find you hot, *mamacita. Mucho caliente.*"

Oh, for crying out loud. And she thought she'd seen and heard it all.

Beyond bored, she dropped her gaze to his flaccid penis. "Too bad little Ricky doesn't." She unfolded herself, walked back to her desk, and sat down. "Zip up, Enrique. We'll give you a call if we're interested."

As the door closed with a window-shaking slam, she clicked through the pictures she took of Reese. Her reaction was instant. Her skin came to life. Her earlier boredom dissipated. Damn, *he* was *mucho caliente.* The man wasn't bashful and she felt proud that he came to attention so quickly for her. There was no doubting Reese's sexuality.

Experience told her if she couldn't get even a slight wave from a cock, the guy sporting it was either gay or on drugs. She'd learned the hard way that while gay models were the crème de la crème in the looks and physique department, if her readers suspected or knew outright the model was less than hetero, they didn't buy. When it happened in the past, she'd received more than a few nasty letters and e-mails and even a few threats to sue her for false advertising. So now she went strictly with the real deal.

So, while she couldn't outright ask a model if he was gay, she had her hetero-meter. Herself. Reese came right to attention. In fact, she couldn't remember a cock saluting so nicely and so quickly. She clicked through the pictures again. Indecision flared again. Her instinct told her she was making a colossal mistake by letting Reese slip through her fingers. Her emotions told her to run as far away from him as possible.

She pounded her fists on her desktop and winced at the pain shooting up her arm.

How would her father make his decision? The answer was simple: with no emotion. Papa would do whatever was necessary to ensure *Skin*'s survival—even if that meant putting himself at risk, emotionally or financially.

Frankie unclenched her fists. What was best for *Skin* was a specific model who was guaranteed to be temperamental and manipulative, with the potential to disrupt her carefully controlled life. He was also one she couldn't afford.

Her mood darkened at the implications of hiring Reese. A war waged inside of her. Her gut instincts *versus* fear. *"Go with your gut, Francesca,"* her father had drilled into her. *"Your intuition will never let you down."*

Her gut told her Reese was the man to garner her magazine much-needed respect. And with that respect, respect for her personally in the industry.

Her gut also marked him as trouble. Big, bad, expensive trouble.

Reese's dark eyes making a statement words never could toyed with her. Was she woman enough to resist? To draw the line?

"Shit!" She stood.

"Tawny!" she called. "Get my banker on the phone."

As soon as her conversation with the bank was over she called Tawny again.

"Yes, boss lady." The perky little assistant poked her head into the office.

"Dig out Reese Barrett's contact info. Then call him and tell him if he wants this job, he'd best be here by eight tomorrow morning to sign contracts. If he's a minute late, we go to Plan B."

Tawny grinned and snatched the file from her boss's hand. "Gladly. And as your valued right arm, I expect to be in on the more candid shots."

Frankie shook her head, her hair swirling around her shoulders. Irritated, she swooped it back away from her face. "Yeah, you and every other person in this building."

Tawny clapped her hands like a three-year-old getting the biggest piece of cake. "I can't wait!"

"Me either," Frankie mumbled to herself, wondering why she wasn't more excited.

Just as she was going through Reese's pics again, Tawny knocked on the door and popped her head in. She was grinning ear to ear. Frankie cocked her right brow. "What?"

"Ah, yes, I just spoke to Mr. Barrett and he said he wouldn't accept unless he heard the offer from your mouth."

Frankie's jaw dropped. The audacity of the man! "Tell him to"— she cut off the words—"shove it up his fine ass."

Tawny squirmed and handed Frankie Reese's file. "He said he has a meeting to go to and if he didn't hear from you in the next five minutes, you were more than welcome to go to your Plan B and he would go to his."

Rage infiltrated Frankie's cells. The hell she would grovel. She didn't need him *that* bad.

Jesus, yes, she did.

"Thank you, Tawny."

The assistant appeared to deflate. "You're going to call him, aren't you?"

Slowly, Frankie shook her head.

"C'mon, Frankie, he's the hottest thing to hit this town since, since, hell, ever!"

"No one tells me what to do. You of all people know that."

Tawny entered the office and shut the door behind her. She lowered her voice to a high whisper. "I know you and Anthony don't see eye to eye and I can understand why. He's mean and you can't trust him, but I happen to like my job and just because you're being spiteful and, well, dumb, I'm in serious jeopardy of losing my job. If you can't swallow your pride for yourself, think about the rest of us who depend on this magazine for a paycheck."

Now it was Frankie's turn to deflate. Tawny was right, and shame on her for jeopardizing her employees' livelihoods because she was a pile of vindictive emotional mush right now. "I'll call him." Frankie plopped down into her chair and swung her legs up to the corner of her desk. She sat back and folded her hands behind her head just like she'd seen her father do before he inevitably screwed someone's life up, including hers and her mother's. "But on my time."

Tawny threw her hands up into the air. "I'll be clearing my desk."

Frankie stared at the number on the piece of paper in her hand. Five minutes came and went, stretching into fifteen minutes. Her money was on Reese's ego wanting the job as much as she wanted him to have it. Leisurely, she pressed the numbers on her telephone.

"You've reached Reese, leave a message at the beep—oh, and if this is Miss Donatello, your five minutes are up, and so is my price, but thanks for the call."

Beep.

Frankie stared at her handset. What the hell? Who was this guy? She hung up. Then she hit Redial. After his smart-ass message and the beep she said, "Tag, Mr. Barrett, you're it. My terms are the same. Either show up at eight a.m. sharp tomorrow for your original fee or we both go to Plan B." She hung up. She'd show him. She'd learned from the master how to make people squirm. Telling her that her five minutes were up and his fee as well? She snorted.

This guy had no idea who he was tangling with. *Five minutes are up, my ass.*

She sat up straight in her chair. Shit, what if he meant it?

Reality set in. Just in case, she dug through the remaining port-folios on her desk and pulled two distant second-and third-place candidates. She studied the shots of two very attractive men. Even with their well-muscled, well-endowed, and well-oiled physiques, their sex appeal didn't convey well from the photo. Not like Reese's did. His charisma jumped off the page. She pulled a pic from his portfolio and studied it. No contest. Setting the other photos down, Frankie stared at Reese's unsmiling face.

Odd, she thought as she looked into his deep blue eyes. He had no laugh lines around his eyes or mouth. For a man who seemed so comfortable with himself and with her, how strange he didn't come off as the sexy smart aleck he did today. Was he naturally so serious but putting up a front to get this job? She looked harder at the hooded eyes. Dark secrets hid behind them. Suddenly she wanted to know what they were.

Reese sat in a dark van across the street from the corporate offices of the late Santini Donatello and his cohorts. The nondescript three-story yellow brick building looked like any other building in North Beach. The only deviation was La Trattoria, the little Italian restaurant that took up most of the first floor. It was also the congregating place for the Donatello network of made men all the way down to runners. Reese whistled. If those walls could talk, what a story they would tell. Too bad the warrant for the wiretap was being held up. They were missing out. By the time they got in there and set it up, Santini's hit would be old news.

Old-man Donatello, known to his cronies as Santo Gabriel because of his uncanny ability to pounce on opportunity with no fear, was also the man the little people came to for protection. He never wavered in offering it, but always for a price. A price many ultimately paid for with their lives. There was nothing saintly about Sonny Donatello. He was a plague to society, and, Reese thought ruefully, his fruit did not fall far from the tree. While Santini had been old-school mob, his son, Anthony, was the new flash mob. A wiseguy with no rep except his father's name to back him. Yet he knew Anthony was smart—but could his sister be smarter?

Reese popped a toothpick in his mouth and chewed it. Time would tell, and maybe they wouldn't even have to make a move. The mob did a better job of cleaning up their messes than the cops ever could. They had no compunction when it came to taking out one of their own.

A chill swept across Reese's skin. How far had Francesca fallen from the paternal tree? Was she part of the family business? If so, how deep was she in? It was common knowledge she and her father didn't jibe. The word on the street was the powers that be were none too impressed with the son. The elder brother, Carmine Donatello, seemed the obvious choice to pick up Santini's fallen reins. Carmine was smart, and patient. Anthony was the polar opposite. The combination should be interesting. Would Carmine mentor his nephew? Or take him out and pronounce himself Santini's heir apparent? Or— Reese bit down on the toothpick, snapping it in half—if Anthony had given the word on his old man, would he do the same on his uncle?

Reese hunched down lower into the battered van. He jolted when his cell phone vibrated in his lap, then grinned when he saw the number that flashed across his LED. Frankie was calling. It took a fair amount of his willpower to resist answering the call.

He frowned when she didn't leave a message. It was even harder to ignore the second call from her. But he grinned like an idiot when his voice mail beeped. He grinned wider when he listened to her message.

He liked her spunkiness, and the way her body reflected the emotion flashing across her face. Francesca Donatello might be a cagey businesswoman, and quite possibly a murderer, but she did a lousy job hiding her emotions. Reese's happy face vanished into a scowl. Showing emotions was dangerous, especially in his line of work. He'd learned long ago it didn't pay to play out feelings, no matter how deeply felt.

Old hurts welled up, and despite his best effort to stuff them back into the darkest corners of his mind as he had done for years, they erupted, unwilling to be denied. For the first time in more years than he could remember, Reese wondered if his parents were still alive, and felt surprised as pain stabbed at his heart. He winced when the vision of his little sister Missy's smiling face flashed into his brain. She was riding June Bug, her prize pony, her face radiating happiness.

Reese's hands clenched and unclenched, his teeth ground, the sound grating. It would be so easy to blame his mother for his sister's death, but he knew it was he who was to blame. Even after all these years, the pain and guilt was as fresh as the day Missy died.

Anthony Donatello sauntered out of the building, and abruptly, Reese's thoughts cleared. He glanced at his watch and noted the time. He bet sis was still holed up in her office, cursing him. He smiled. So long as she was thinking of him, he didn't care how. A woman darted up the steps toward Anthony. The gangster feigned a smile. Reese knew it for what it was; after all, he'd mastered it. The woman looked familiar. She turned and snuggled into Anthony's arm as he ushered her toward a waiting car. Tawny, Frankie's assistant. Interesting. Only a few reasons for her to be hooking up with Donatello, and no matter which one he chose, it didn't bode well for his soon-to-be boss lady. He followed the black town car.

CHAPTER FIVE

Frankie glanced at her watch. Seven thirty. She needed to get to Unk's. Systematically, she shut down her computer, drew the window blinds, and threw a few things in her purse. For a long moment she stood at her desk, feeling like she was forgetting something. Reese's face popped up in her mind and she smiled smugly. Impulsively, she grabbed a contract from a file drawer, then jotted Reese's number down from the open file on her desk.

As she drove to her uncle's she called Reese.

"Barrett."

"It's Francesca. I want you to meet me at nine tonight at La Trattoria on Columbus."

"I have plans."

"Change them. I want this contract signed tonight."

"It can wait."

"No, it can't."

There was a long pause, then Reese said, "Fine."

She smiled and hung up.

• • •

A few minutes later, Frankie pulled up in front of the family building. Several minutes went by and she still sat quietly in the seat of
her ragtop Bimmer. Part of her wanted to run up the stairs to
Unk's—and what was once her father's—office and scream and
vent until she was hoarse. The other part wanted to contemplate
and scheme. She waved to old Mrs. Loguzzo, whose black suitcase-
size purse was no doubt loaded with bread and leftovers, her fifty-
year-old bachelor nephew, Phil, in tow as they exited La Trattoria,
another family-owned business, this one run by her cousins Della
and Louie.

Of course her father and now Anthony had their fingers in the
Trattoria pie, but it was how things were done. In the alley there were
two entrances to the restaurant. One frequented by delivery trucks
and employees, the second, the private entrance, reserved for her
father's men, who could usually be found sitting around their
favorite table, shooting the breeze, smoking cigars, or eating. It was
through the back door that much of the family business comings and
goings transpired. Frankie preferred to use the front door.

As she made her way down the hallway to Unk's office on the
third floor, it occurred to her how quiet it was, the usual boisterous
voices of Unk's entourage absent. Alarm bells shrilled in her head,
and she hurried to his office. The door stood ajar.

"Unk?"

"In here, Francesca."

Relief flooded through her. She was getting paranoid. Frankie
smiled despite her anxiety and urgency to get answers. Unk always
called her by her full name, never in anger, always with love. Why
couldn't he have been her father? She slowed her agitated gait and
decided she wouldn't unload on her uncle as she had intended.

"Francesca?" he called, a note of urgency raising his normally deep voice.

"Coming, *Zio*, coming." She picked up her pace.

The rich aroma of fresh ground espresso beans tantalized the air. She'd forgotten Unk had his own espresso machine, one of his few indulgences. The light from his small corner office lit her way forward. Her smile widened. That was Unk, hard at work after everyone else had packed it in for the day, the quiet, unpretentious force behind Donatello Brothers, Inc. Unlike her hotheaded father, who liked the trophy wives, custom suits, and hand-rolled Cubanos, Carmine was old-school Italian. Formal but loving, and as level as the horizon. She wondered why Unk wasn't the figurehead of the family and the business.

She greeted him as she always did, with a hug. For a long moment she held on to the man who had shielded her from her father and, on more than one occasion, herself. She inhaled his fine tobacco and basil scent.

Unk liked his pasta. He was the polar opposite of her father. Whereas Papa had been tall, dark, and angry, Carmine was short, round, and jovial. He pulled back just enough to take her face into his sausage-plump hands and smile down at her, his dark brown eyes glittering.

"*Bella, bella, bella, como esti?*"

"*Bueno, Zio.*"

He kissed her on each cheek and took her hand. "Come. Here, I have an espresso for you."

She raised the bag she carried in her hand. "And I have Gina's cannoli for you." His dark eyes beamed. He bustled around the little table that held the espresso press and poured her a cup of the thick, hot liquid. "Come into my office, it's too cold out here." It was a beautiful autumn evening, the temperature perfect. But she didn't argue the point. If he said it was thirty below zero, she would humor the man.

Like a mother hen, he pulled out a plush chair for her from the corner of his small office after setting her tiny espresso cup on his desk. His disheveled appearance didn't go unnoticed by her. "You look like you've been working too hard, Unk." He looked up from the napkin he spread out on his desk. "I have. With Sonny gone, it all falls into my lap." He quickly made the sign of the cross and said, "Sit, and *mange.*"

She wasn't hungry, but even if she had been, she steered clear of sweets. Her Italian heritage made her thighs subject to cellulite and she worked hard to keep from resembling her matronly cousins. She sipped the hot espresso, then set the cup down on its saucer.

"I didn't see any of the boys around, Unk."

The old man shrugged and waved a hand like he was the Pope in Saint Peter's Square. "They're downstairs having dinner. I told them I wanted some peace and quiet with my niece. Since the assassination, they've been worse than Nona Cece around her grandchildren."

"That's not a bad thing—"

"No, but it's annoying. I've never had the craving for people fluttering around me like your father and brother. You'd think they were Elvis or someone."

"You need to be careful. I don't think I could stand losing you too." The unexpected sting of tears pricked her eyes. From years of practice, Frankie sucked it up before her weakness could be detected. She wasn't quick enough.

Unk patted her hand. "We all need to be careful, especially in these times. Suspect everyone, Francesca."

Frankie nodded, but an icy shiver raced along her spine. In all of the years she had been alive, there had never been the dark tension hovering over the family like there was now. A war was brewing, and not for the first time she wished she was just a normal girl, living a normal life with a normal family.

"Do you miss him?"

"Sonny?"

She nodded.

"*Si*, I do. More than I thought possible. We didn't see eye to eye on everything, but our styles worked. We were a good team, Sonny and me."

Now it was Carmine's turn for melancholy.

She understood all too well his bipolar feelings for his brother. A part of her had so much bottled up anger, frustration, and, she admitted, love for her father that the cool indifference she'd worked so hard to perfect over the years had become the norm, no longer the exception. Had she become as callous as her father? Like him and Anthony, turning off emotions like faucets?

"Did you love him?" she asked.

Her uncle choked on his second cannoli. The dusting of white powdered sugar Gina used as a garnish shot into the air like tiny snowflakes.

"Of course." His eyes watered. Frankie stood and hurried around to his back and thumped hard. Carmine coughed and sputtered but raised a hand, signaling her to stop.

She hurried to pour him a glass of water, and he drank it down when she handed it to him. His reddened face slowly returned to deep olive. "Francesca, why would you ask such a question?"

She shrugged and picked out the chocolate chips from the filling of her cannoli, pushing them aside. "I didn't mean it like it sounded, I was just wondering if it's as easy for you as it was for my father and is for my brother to tune people out?"

He patted a napkin to the corner of his mouth. "I can tune people out." He smiled. "It's what the male of the species does."

"No, I mean, turn off your emotions. Like Father did when he took someone out."

Carmine's eyes widened. "Took someone out?"

She wasn't going to play coy. "I'm not talking about a hit, although I wouldn't put that past him, but taking out a friend for business, cutting them out of the deal, turning yourself off so you can make the deal, you know, just business."

He sipped his espresso and nodded slowly. "I can do it. To a point."

Maybe she needed to adopt that single-minded sociopath angle. If she played by the family's rules, she just might come out on top. Her stomach churned at the thought. It wasn't her nature to be cold and unyielding, to put business first. But she told herself that if she was to hang on to *Skin,* she would have to play like the pros. Her heart hardened a notch.

"Then you aren't like Father in that way."

Carmine cocked a dark graying brow. She continued. She needed to get her anger out on the table, to see if she was justified, to see if her uncle would turn on her in the end like her father and her brother. "I know Father had my mother's cousin Johnny Trino removed to pave the way for Anthony. Do you know where Johnny is?"

"What is really bothering you, *cara?*"

Everything. "Nothing."

"Come now, *cara*—remember who you're talking to."

He always could catch her in a lie.

"Anthony."

"I told you not to worry about him."

"How can I not? He barges into my office and starts throwing his weight around. He has some vendetta against me." Her hands shook, she was so angry. "He wants *Skin,* Unk."

Carmine's eyes narrowed and he sat forward, the fine leather of the chair creaking under his substantial weight. "What exactly did he say?"

"He claims Father left him *Skin.* Is it true?"

Carmine's features didn't flinch. "So Anthony claims."

Cold infiltrated her body.

Carmine brushed the powdered sugar from his hands and looked thoughtfully at his niece. "Your brother always cries for more than his share. I wouldn't worry about him."

Frankie folded her hands on her lap and looked down at her fingers entwined so tightly her knuckles whitened. On her right ring finger was her maternal grandfather's signet ring of bloodred rubies in the shape of a hawk's head. The hawk's diamond eye twinkled at her. Her grandfather gave it to her on her eighteenth birthday. *"Never fear the hawk,* cara, *embrace him, use him, look to him for strength when you feel the world is against you, and always know the family will protect you."* She laughed, the sound brittle. Maybe her mother's Calabrian family would protect her, but it was the other family, her half brother, Anthony, and his gang of Sicilian thugs she needed protection against.

"Is there proof Papa wrote me out of *Skin?*"

Carmine's hands fisted and he pounded the table, the rare show of anger surprising her. "Your brother is a fool."

"Did Father write me out?"

Carmine's eyes flashed. "So Anthony insists, but I have yet to see written proof. Sonny would have not only informed me of a change but he would have made sure I had a notarized copy. I gave Anthony ten days to produce this supposed new will, a week ago tomorrow."

"So he hasn't produced it?"

Carmine shook his head. His dark eyes flashed dangerously. "No, and if that remains the case, the last document recorded will stand."

"What does that mean?"

"I retain control—then dole out my brother's personal assets."

"*Skin?*"

"He had the lion's share, but the family has the other piece."

"Can Anthony gain control?"

"With backing—yes."

"I don't get Anthony's hard-on for *Skin*. It's totally legit." Her eyes widened and she looked at her uncle. "He wants to put his people on the payroll and pay out benefits and probably run his dirty money through it."

Carmine shook his head. "He has other ventures for blowing up the payroll, even laundering—"

"Does he hate me so much that he wants it out of sheer spite?"

Unk's dark eyes reflected his sympathy.

"I don't want your pity, Unk. I can handle how Anthony feels about me."

He reached across the table and patted her hand. "Your father was a bigger fool than your brother. You're a good girl, Francesca."

Emotion welled in her chest, and she quickly tamped it. There was time for tears later, now she needed to focus on *Skin*. She smiled and nodded, contemplating her position. In the event the will didn't surface, and if she had the time to prove to the family she had what it took to control *Skin,* then Anthony would lose support. "I need to position myself, Unk. To do that I need to get busy and I don't need distractions. I have *Skin*'s anniversary edition to launch. If it fails, then I lose with the family and I lose with our advertisers. Can you find something other than *Skin* to occupy my brother?"

Carmine shook his head and sat back into his chair. He pushed what was left of the second cannoli away from him. "I'm afraid, *cara,* Anthony is much like your father at that age. The difference being your father knew how to create allies. Anthony just plows through whoever stands in his way, and right now, the family dynamics are too volatile to issue edicts. I suggest we both lie low, and so long as Anthony is only making noises, we tune him out."

Carmine's reserved approach to explosive situations was his trademark. He never reacted impulsively. The complete opposite of her brother.

This was all the fault of Anthony's mother, Constance Vezzio. Santini Donatello bucked the old guard on most levels, especially when it came to philandering and divorce. After Connie, a stripper at one of her father's clubs, gave birth to a bouncing baby boy and blood tests proved the up-and-coming don the father, Sonny-boy pulled a Henry the Eighth and had his first marriage, the one to her mother, annulled. Everyone knew it was a polite way to say divorce. Her mother never forgave him. For that and a laundry list of other things. With a male Donatello and an annulment, Connie swooped in and made Francesca's life miserable.

Whatever Connie wanted Connie got. Including zero interference when her sweet little angel Anthony required discipline. Anthony learned at a very early age that all he had to do was run to Mama and his problems were solved.

"I heard his uncle, Sal Vezzio, is yucking it up with the family." She smashed a chocolate chip under her thumb. "They seem to be listening."

Carmine chuckled and eyed the half cannoli on his desk. He picked it up and plopped it in his mouth. He chewed slowly, a look of satisfaction caressing his full features. "Sal is an ass. His brains wouldn't fill a thimble."

"All the more reason to be wary, Unk. He's a hothead like his nephew. He scares me."

Carmine nodded and stood. "Good you think that way, *cara*. But don't worry. Your health and interests are safe as long as I am alive."

Frankie swallowed hard. Her skin flashed cold and she had the uneasy sensation of creepy crawlies scurrying up and down her back. She shook off the feeling. No one would dare touch Carmine. She caught her breath. She had thought the same of her father. Her heartbeat slowed. Carmine didn't have the enemies Santini did. Carmine always treated the family and foes with respect. In fact, over the past few years, Frankie knew many of the cousins bypassed hotheaded Santini in favor of Carmine's levelheaded advice.

As Carmine looked out his window, he said, "Come here and look, Francesca."

She stood and walked toward him, stopping past his shoulder. The city lights twinkled under the autumn moon. "You own this town, *cara*. By your name alone there is no one who would do you harm for fear of your father's wrath and now mine. Go out there and take your pictures. Anthony will come to heel. I have ways to make him see things from my perspective. Vezzio has another thing coming if he thinks I will allow him to have a say in what your father and I have worked so hard for."

He turned and took her face into his big, warm hands. She felt secure in the shadow of the dark, all-knowing eyes. "Thank you, Unk." She reached up to hug him. The sharp ping of shattering glass and a hot sting across her arm startled her.

"Down," Carmine yelled before she realized what the sound was. *Pfft-pfft.* Two more followed in rapid succession; more glass shattered overhead. They'd been shot at! She touched the heat on her arm, feeling the warm wetness there. She'd been hit! Her uncle's heavy body lay protectively across hers. "My God, Francesca, are you okay?"

She nodded, too stunned to form words. Someone shot her! He rolled off her and, surprisingly for a man so large, he scurried across the room on all fours like a crab running from a gull. He reached up and hit the lights.

Adrenaline pumped through her veins, and under the blanket of darkness her anger rose. Who the hell wanted her dead? She popped up and peered over the sill just enough to see the empty street below. Son of a bitch!

Ducking, she hurried toward her uncle, whose large frame was illuminated in the soft glow of the streetlights. His cell phone was open. "Are you hit, Unk?" A quick shake of his head set her mind to rest, then he spoke into the phone.

"Jimmy, get up here."

CHAPTER SIX

"I'm waiting outside of La Trattoria right now, she wants me to sign the contract tonight," Reese said into his cell phone.

"I don't know how you got her to turn around so quick, buddy, but props to you," Jase said.

Reese smiled and looked up to a lighted third-floor window. He knew it was Carmine Donatello's. He'd been quietly watching the comings and goings of the building for nearly an hour. If someone questioned him, he would simply tell the truth. He was waiting to meet Francesca for dinner.

He sat up straighter in his truck when he saw two shadows in the window. As they came closer, he saw Frankie's silhouette. His cock stirred.

"Like most women, she came to her senses."

The sharp sound of glass shattering had him out of his truck and on the street in less than two seconds. "Shots fired at 700 Columbus Street," Reese said into his phone. The screeching of tires followed by high beams flashing in his eyes had Reese jumping back and out of the way of the speeding car.

He hopped back into his truck.

"What the hell is going on, Reese?" Jase shouted.

"In pursuit of a black sedan, looks like a late-model Caprice."

Reese gunned his truck and went after the car. When he turned onto Mason he cursed. The street was empty. The car didn't have that much of a lead on him. He headed down the street, looking down each side street, and because of the traffic he couldn't see the sedan.

"Son of a bitch!"

He picked up his phone. "I lost them. It's like they evaporated."

"Any side-street garages?"

"Maybe, get some units down here to start looking. I'm going back to the restaurant."

And with that thought, the realization his main suspect might be wounded or, worse, dead sent the hair on his arms shooting straight up. He did a fast U-turn in the street.

"Unk, I'm fine, it's just a scratch," Francesca argued.

"You need to see a doctor," he argued right back.

Her initial shock quickly wore off. If they were gunning for her uncle, they missed; if they were gunning for her, they came too damn close. Frankie shook her head. Instead of fear, anger blossomed in her chest. "Son of a bitch, Unk!" She dabbed at the wound on her arm with a sodden tissue. The damn thing wouldn't stop bleeding. "Who wants me dead?"

Her uncle's dark brown eyes snapped in unleashed anger. "Not you, *cara*, me."

Her stomach rolled. Of course.

He pulled a fresh tissue from the box her cousin Jimmy "Peanuts" Tambouri proffered. Pressing it to her arm, he walked her down the hall to La Trattoria. Jimmy, and Unk's longtime bodyguard Leo Stazzi followed, watching every shadow, with guns drawn in the long hallway.

As they turned to enter the restaurant from the inside of the building, Frankie stopped short. "Leo, can you run back upstairs and get my purse?"

He looked at Unk, who nodded, and they entered the quiet restaurant. It closed at eight. All non-family diners had long since left.

"Del," Unk called, "get Sanzo on the phone."

Della came running into the dinning room, wiping her hands on her apron. Her gray brows crinkled in question. "Don't look at me like that, woman!" Unk commanded. "Francesca has been shot!"

Della gasped and made the sign of the cross, then hustled over to the maître d' stand and picked up the phone. A commotion from the kitchen caught all of their attention. Della stood with the phone half raised to her ear; Jimmy cursed, drew his gun, and ran toward the kitchen as Unk pulled Frankie to the alcove behind the coat closet.

A second after Jimmy ran through the bat-wing doors to the kitchen he burst out, back first, along with another cousin, Johnny, and his little brother Mikey. The three of them looked like bowling pins crashing in the alley under the wrath of—

Frankie gasped. "Reese!"

He exploded into the room like a bull on a rampage. Every set of eyes in the place looked expectantly from Reese's furious stance to her surprised face.

"You know this chump?" Johnny asked, rolling his meatball of a brother off him. Jimmy hurried to his feet, his semi trained on Reese.

"He's my model."

The old man scowled, giving Reese the hostile look he reserved for those on their way out. She swallowed hard. "What's going on here?" Unk demanded.

Frankie looked at Reese's angry face. "I—ah, Reese was supposed to meet me here at nine."

"I found him snooping around out back," Johnny said.

Mikey added the obvious. "Yeah, he coulda been the shooter."

The news didn't seem to affect Reese.

"The front doors to the restaurant were locked. I heard shots so I came around back," Reese said.

Unk looked at Frankie again for confirmation. "We have contracts to sign," she said.

Leo entered the room, gun drawn, Frankie's purse hanging off his arm. Frankie couldn't resist a smile at the absurdity of the situation.

"Let's just all calm down," she started. But the sirens echoing in the distance wrenched the tension right back up.

She grabbed her purse from Leo. "Unk, I'm not dicking around with the cops." She looked at Reese. "You drive, let's get out of here."

"One minute before you go, *cara,*" Carmine softly insisted.

She didn't dare argue. Reese stood rigid and silent beside her. Her heart thumped hard against her chest and her skin flushed warm. She felt on the verge of an anxiety attack.

"*Si, Zio?*"

His dark eyes trained on Reese. "What did you see outside before you came in here?"

Most men would have shown signs of discomfort, but not her dumb model. Nope, he stared back at her uncle, refusing to back down.

"Nothing, just heard three shots."

Carmine nodded. "If you happen to remember anything you haven't told me here, be sure to come to me with that information before you share it anywhere else."

Please, please don't let him argue.

Reese nodded. "Of course."

Oh, good model.

As she moved past her uncle, he called to her, "Go to Sanzo's, he'll be expecting you."

Not waiting for any more conversation or, worse, arguments from her uncle or cousins, Frankie grabbed Reese's hand and pulled him behind her toward the kitchen and out the back door of the restaurant.

"Don't ask," she said as they came around to the front of the building. Sirens wailed closer. She sprinted to her car, quickly unlocked the trunk, and pulled out her camera bag.

"Where are you parked?" she asked breathlessly, looking up and down the street.

This time Reese grabbed her by the hand and pulled her back across the street. "Black Tahoe directly ahead."

Just as the cops arrived, Reese pulled away from the curb, going the opposite direction.

Looking over her shoulder, Frankie said, "Faster."

Reese hit the pedal. "What's the rush?"

"I don't do cops."

Reese nodded and focused on the road ahead of him.

After several minutes he turned to look at Frankie, who looked at him through narrowed eyes.

"What?"

"How did you manage to manhandle all three of my cousins?"

"Didn't you read my bio?"

"Some of it."

"Did you miss the marine part?"

"Oh, I guess I didn't get that far. How long?"

"Four years."

"Why did you leave?"

He shrugged and glanced in the rearview mirror, and she turned to look out the back window. No flashing lights. Her shoulders relaxed a notch.

"I don't do authority. If I had reenlisted, I'd be in a brig somewhere."

"That doesn't surprise me. You're the most insolent employee I've ever hired."

Reese flashed her a grin. "You ain't seen nothing yet, baby."

Frankie rolled her eyes. That's exactly what she was afraid of.

Without looking at her, Reese said, "You're bleeding."

Her adrenaline rush continued to infuse her with energy. Glancing over her shoulder again, Frankie let out a long breath. "It's no big deal."

"What the hell happened in there?"

"Someone tried to kill my uncle."

"Why?"

"I guess someone doesn't like him."

"Will he talk to the cops?"

"My family takes care of their own business. They don't do cops."

"Do you?"

"Hell no, I don't do cops!" She touched the wound on her arm and winced, then said, more quietly. "Cops don't mix well with my family."

"From what I've seen of your family so far, they don't seem the type to mix well with many people." Reese popped open the console lid, pulled out a small pack of tissues, and handed it to her. Grateful, Frankie ripped off the plastic and pressed the entire mound to her arm.

"I don't trust cops. If I called them right now, they'd end up hauling my uncle in for some bogus charge, and me for not reporting a gunshot wound. Who the hell needs that?"

"Is your uncle a criminal?"

"He's a businessman."

"Then why not call the cops?"

Frankie snorted, the contempt of her action palpable. "Like I said, it's none of their business."

Reese mimicked her snort, and she shot him a glare. "You should hear yourself—"

"Butt out, Reese."

"Are you sure it was your uncle they were after?"

Frankie gasped and looked at him. A niggle of doubt tugged at her gut. "I'm sure. Now stop with the questions."

"I think I have a right to some information. We'll be working closely together, and if someone is taking potshots at you, I don't want to be around."

"If it's too scary for you, you can leave as soon as you drop me off."

"I need this job."

"I'll take that as a yes you're hanging around." Looking straight ahead, she asked, "Are you familiar with Pacific Heights?"

"Over off Jackson?" He glanced at her. "Do you live there?"

"No, my uncle Sanzo does."

"And we're going there why?"

"He's a doctor."

"Smartest thing you've said since you hired me."

Frankie didn't dignify his comment with a response. A long, heavy silence followed.

Reese glanced at the soaked glob of tissue she pressed to her arm. "You should go to the ER."

"And what do you propose I tell them when they ask who shot me?"

"The same thing you'll tell the cops."

"I'm not having this conversation with you." She winced when she crossed her arms over her chest, and thankfully he didn't push her.

Reese excused himself as Uncle Sanzo clucked over his niece. He walked outside to the sprawling backyard. The tranquil gurgle of a nearby fountain was the only sound disturbing the sultry night air.

He shook his head at Frankie's stubbornness. If he had thought her wound was even close to life-threatening, he would have had her in an emergency room faster than her Unk could order a hit. While Frankie might be connected to every Italian gene pool in town, Reese had a few connections of his own.

He dialed a number on his cell phone and waited patiently for an answer.

"Yo, Guido's."

Reese smiled. Jamerson's goombah impersonation wasn't too bad. If he'd had a landline, they could speak openly. "Wiseguy one here, Guido."

"Yo, wiseguy, wassa matta you?"

"Wassa matta is we need peeps on the little piece of shit we chatted about. I'll lay odds he just tried to reduce his family by two."

"We're on it."

"We'll compare notes when I have a secure line."

Reese hung up and walked back into the doctor's opulent house. Looked like crime did pay, and well.

"He said I need stitches."

Reese stopped in his tracks. Frankie sat quietly in the shadows of the large living room. He scanned the area for the good doc.

"I don't want stitches. I don't have time for stitches. Stitches hurt."

Reese felt a jolt of compassion. She sounded like a scared little girl. But he knew better. Francesca Donatello had the mentality of a barracuda, and besides that, little girls didn't have curves that made his hands itch. He watched her finger the ruby ring on her right hand. "You're going to rub those rocks right off."

She stopped and clasped her hands. Reese felt an urge to kneel down beside her, take her hand into his, and comfort her. He shook his head and stepped away. No fucking way.

"Who were you talking to outside?" she asked.

"Just business."

She rolled her eyes and sat back into the overstuffed chair.

Reese scowled down at her. This latest incident put a whole new spin on the investigation. He was more convinced now than ever that Anthony Donatello was working his way up the food chain. And apparently he had no compunction about killing off his family to get to the top.

Reese paced the room. He wanted to go back out on the street, back to the scene to look for casings, prints, anything. This was the hardest part of undercover work for him. The pretending to be a civilian, his hands tied, his patience tried to nearly breaking. He thrived on the street, where he could roll up his sleeves and get his hands dirty.

"You really should call the cops, maybe they can dig up something."

She shook her head adamantly, and he noticed the wound bleeding again. "My family takes care of their own business."

"Where's the doc? You're bleeding more."

"He went to his office to get supplies, he'll be right back."

"We should have just followed him over there."

Frankie nodded. "I didn't think to suggest that."

Heavy silence hung between them. He knew from experience that once the adrenaline started to wane, fatigue and pain set in. "Do you have somewhere you can stay tonight?"

Frankie flashed him a bright smile. "Yep, your place."

Reese stopped in his tracks, the implications of that statement racing through his mind. "I don't mix business with my personal life."

"Trust me, there will be no mixing. Purely business." She dug into her purse and pulled out several papers. "Speaking of business, sign this, now." She handed him the contract, then dug out a pen from her purse and handed that to him as well.

"I want to go over this with my agent."

"It's standard, and your exorbitant fee is so noted."

Reese gave the papers a quick scan. He was no fool, but he needed to play the model part. "If I find out you're screwing me, I'll sue you, saying I signed under duress."

"If I was screwing you, you'd know it."

He smiled. "That makes two of us."

Frankie's cell phone ring startled them both. She answered it. "Hello." He watched her expression soften. "Yes, Unk, I'm here now." She shook her head. "He said a few stitches, then I'm good as new. What?" Her brows knitted together. "I don't need a bodyguard, Unk. I appreciate the offer, but—"

Reese snatched the phone out of her hand. "Mr. Donatello, Francesca will be coming home with me."

Reese grinned down at an indignant Frankie. "I'm sorry, sir, if I give you that information, I'd have to kill you. Your niece is safe with me tonight. Good night." He hit the End button and Frankie looked like she was about to give birth to kittens.

"Did you just tell my uncle you would have to kill him? Are you crazy?"

"Maybe."

"What on earth for?"

"He wanted to know where I live. It's none of his damn business."

Frankie stared wide-eyed, her full lips parted. His body warmed. Why hadn't he been the one to suggest she stay with him? He wanted her in his bed. Tonight. Suddenly the imposition of her staying at his place evaporated. Maybe they could find a physical release to ease the tension of the evening.

"You really are stupid."

Reese grinned. "Isn't that status quo for us model types?"

"Really, really, really stupid. My uncle will hunt you down for this."

"No, he won't. More than anything he wants you safe. I can make sure that happens."

She opened her mouth to argue when Uncle Sanzo bustled into the room. "Come now, Francesca, let's take care of your arm."

As if she were going to her own funeral, Frankie rose by increments. Her feet dragging, she followed Sanzo. Reese followed behind her, and the old Italian doctor raised a brow and cocked his head at his niece.

"No sense in telling him no, Sanzo," Frankie said. "He doesn't listen."

Reese chuckled. "Smart girl."

Because she had an audience and because she refused to show weakness and because if she didn't put up a front, she'd collapse into a pool of bawling mush, Frankie sucked it up, ready to take the stitches like a soldier. Until Sanzo injected her wound with Novocain. The sharp prick of the needle into her skin made her see black spots. Nausea welled in her belly and she felt the blood drain to her feet.

Reese's strong hand gripped hers and he kneeled beside her. "It's okay, Frankie, he's done." He smoothed her hair back from her face and gently pushed her head down between her shaky knees. "Take a deep breath."

She felt clammy, and foolish, but she sucked air into her lungs and slowly exhaled. The trick worked. Almost instantly she felt better. Slowly he sat her back up. Their eyes caught and locked.

"Good girl, *cara,*" Sanzo crooned. "Now let me cleanse the area and three small stitches should do it. *Yo promiso,* no pain."

CHAPTER SEVEN

For the second time that night, Frankie settled back into Reese's SUV. The throb in her arm dissipated thanks to the pill her uncle and Reese insisted she take. At first she'd been wary of Reese's concern, sure he was out to take advantage of her, but she hurt, inside and out.

In less than nine hours, she's been threatened by her brother, shot at, stitched up, and now she was going to spend the night with a man she'd only met a few hours ago. A girl had the right to some narcotically induced help.

If she wasn't smack dab in the middle of the situation, she wouldn't believe it.

As if her eyes were the lens of a camera, Frankie looked over at Reese's classically honed profile. A shot of adrenaline in fused her system. Her artist's eye could find no fault with the image before her. She'd definitely use the sexy shadowed angle. An idea sparked with that thought. What about a lead-up? A teaser to the reader in the months prior to the anniversary edition? Could she play it out, and segue into the centerfold issue? Did she have the time? It would be close, very close.

"What do you think of us keeping you in the shadows for an issue or two, each time showing just a little bit more? We'll reveal you one scrumptious inch at a time."

Reese looked at her as if she'd just grown a second head.

Ignoring his expression, she grew more excited. "I can do shadow body and face shots, we'll let the ladies get a peek of you each month, whetting their appetite for more, until the February issue, when we'll go full frontal and full face!"

A new round of adrenaline pumped through her as the ideas formed. The idea of stripping Reese stitch by stitch sent her pulse racing. "It's genius! Why didn't I think of this earlier?"

Immediately she regretted her outburst.

"Look, Reese, I need to know up front if we're on the same page here."

Reese shot her a puzzled look before focusing back on the highway. "Be specific."

Frankie sucked the bottom corner of her lip between her teeth, then let go. If she told Reese she wanted complete secrecy, would he sell her out like Sean had, despite their contract?

"What?" Reese demanded. His harsh tone startled her.

"Per our contract, unless given specific written permission, you cannot disclose any information regarding this shoot or *Skin.*"

"I see we trust each other."

"The only trust we need is between model and camera."

He nodded but kept silent, his eyes on the road. In a show of truce, she reached over and touched his bicep, his hard muscles bunching under her palm. He cast her a scowl, and she withdrew her hand.

"It won't work," he said. "I'm not going to be around for months."

"You don't need to be. I have severe time constraints right now. I can get all of the shots I need in two weeks. We'll do location shots. A day in the life of Mr. Skin."

Reese groaned. "No way. No location. Studio only."

"Yes way. Your contract states very simply, you go where I want you to go and take off what I tell you to take off. Consider your ass mine for the next two weeks."

At his continued silence and obvious rancor, Frankie filled him in on a few more facts. "First thing tomorrow morning we'll get you into the studio and do some test shots. I want to nail a color scheme ASAP. Then we'll brainstorm locations. I'm thinking beach, maybe a ranch. Yes, slap a pair of chaps and boots on you—"

"Not without jeans."

Frankie laughed, the sound low and throaty. The drugs had mellowed her some and she was glad her arm didn't throb. "C'mon, now, Reese, do you have any idea how hot it would be to have you in just a pair of chaps and boots and a Stetson, standing next to a stallion? Maybe even with a slight erection. You, not the horse."

Peals of laughter erupted when Reese shot her a look that would have split a lesser person in half. "We can caption it 'Clash of the Stallions.' "

"I'm not a piece of meat."

Frankie's laughter died down some. "Yeah, you are. A big, juicy hunk of meat that is going to set my readers on fire." She laughed again. "A big, juicy piece they'll want to sink their teeth into."

At Reese's silence Frankie poked him in the rib with her index finger. "How about I pay you double and we go on tour after the anniversary issue releases?"

Reese shook his head.

"Think about it. You can make a fortune with endorsements afterward, not to mention all the freebies you'll get. Fiscally it will be a windfall."

"Yeah, for you."

"For you too. It could lead to all kinds of offers. Book deal, movie deal. I've got a feeling, Reese, if we play this right we'll both win big."

And the bigger she won, the stronger her position would be within the family to retain control should Anthony bend any ears.

She sat back into the comfortable captain seat, feeling smug. And that in light of her most arduous day.

"So what perks do I get for being at your beck and call?"

"Your face and nether parts splashed all over my magazine."

"I want more."

She knew where the conversation was leading. And a couple of years ago she might have bit. Turning in her seat to face him, she said, "Look, since we're going to be working very closely for the next couple of weeks, let's get a few things straight right off the bat."

Reese gave her a quick glance and a sly grin.

She inhaled deeply and despite the narcotic, her cut stung. She winced. "I don't do models. I don't do employees. I don't even do sex these days. Not that that is any of your business."

"What *do* you do?"

"I work."

"That sounds boring."

"It works for me. Make it work for you."

"If it makes you feel any better, I don't do models either. Or employees. And while I do do sex, I'm a self-proclaimed workaholic, so we should get along just fine."

"You forgot to mention you don't do your employers."

"I know."

He flashed her another grin. He wasn't getting it.

"You and I will not have sex."

"Define sex."

"Trading of body fluids."

This time when he grinned the gesture nearly split his face in half. "I think that can be arranged."

"I can almost see the wheels turning in your head. Don't try and trip me up, or I'll replace you so fast your head will spin."

"Sure you will," he said, then turned into an upscale condo complex. Security gates opened when he hit a hidden remote.

They parked in a secured carport. As she reached for the door handle, Reese put a hand on her shoulder. "Let me just make sure there's no one lingering who shouldn't be." He'd been watching the rearview mirror and felt comfortable they weren't followed, but with her family, who the hell knew?

Reese hopped out of the vehicle and gave the surrounding area a quick scrutiny. Ominous silence shrouded the night air. It was almost too quiet.

He came back to the truck and opened Frankie's door. "All clear."

"You sound like a cop."

He grinned at her. "I watch a lot of TV."

"You don't strike me as the couch potato type."

"There's a lot to be said for couch potatoes."

"I'm not buying it."

He shrugged. "I'm not selling it."

She eyed him suspiciously. There was more to Mr. Skin than a six-pack and a killer smile.

She let out a long breath, not realizing she was holding it. She needed a glass of Grandpa Donatello's Chianti and a hot bath.

Reese hustled Frankie up the steps to his brand-new condo, compliments of the task force.

"What has you spooked?" she asked.

He pulled her closer into the alcove that shielded his front door from the parking lot. Her body heat wrapped around him like a warm blanket. He could very easily find a reason to get her in his bed. In fact, he had a reason. A good one. Women were vulnerable in the afterglow of sex, and pillow talk took on a whole new meaning to him.

He dipped his head toward the top of her hair and inhaled her cinnamon scent.

"Considering what happened to your father and almost happened to you, let's just say I'm being careful."

Her spine stiffened, the gesture causing her breasts to press against his chest. Reese didn't retreat. Snapping her head back, Frankie's eyes flashed angrily. "What do you know about my father?"

"I know he was a mob boss and someone wanted his job enough to kill him. Now it looks like they want your uncle's and are willing to put you into the collateral damage category."

She tossed her long hair over her shoulder and put her hands on her hips. She moved into him, the gesture meant to push him back. He didn't move. "Don't believe everything you read in the paper or see on the five o'clock news."

Unable to resist, Reese swept a stray lock of hair from her face, his knuckles caressing the smooth skin of her cheek. He watched her eyes close for the briefest of seconds, as if she just wanted to melt into him. "Don't be so naive, Frankie."

Her quick flash of vulnerability didn't last. Her eyes, angry again, flashed open, and she stepped back. "Believe me, I lost my naïveté a long time ago."

Reese touched her shoulder. "You don't trust easy, do you?"

She yanked her head back. "I don't trust at all."

"You can trust me."

She laughed low, not amused. "I don't even know you."

"Sometimes you just have to go with your gut."

She smiled. "My gut tells me you're up to no good."

He traced a finger along her cheekbone, swerving upward toward her eye. "You have beautiful eyes."

"You have beautiful lines. Do they always work?"

He lowered his lips to hers. "Most of the time."

Frankie turned her head and laughed as his lips brushed her cheek. "Not this time, cowboy. What part of 'I don't do my employees' don't you understand?"

"It's just a kiss."

"That would be trading body fluids."

Apparently, those drugs she took hadn't loosened her up enough. Reese knew when he was beat. He unlocked the door and pushed it open, stepping back and allowing her to go in. He watched Frankie's eyes scan the Spartan apartment. Her eyes narrowed suspiciously.

"Just move in?"

He shrugged and tossed his keys on the small table just inside the condo door. "It works for me. For now."

"I'm surprised all of your women haven't femmed it up."

He headed for the kitchen without answering, flicked on the light, and opened the fridge. "Want a beer?"

Frankie shook her head and yawned.

"I want to go to bed." The minute she said it, he popped his head up from inside the fridge, the light illuminating his handsome face. "Alone."

He groaned, twisted off the bottle top, and took a long swig. "I only have one bed."

She walked out of the kitchen and said over her shoulder, "I'll sleep on the couch."

She dropped her purse and camera bag on the cushion. "I plan on taking shots at my leisure."

Reese walked out of the kitchen and leaned a broad shoulder against the jamb. His blue eyes danced, and Frankie knew that in a different place and time she wouldn't hesitate to slip between the sheets with this man. He was all things male and carnal wrapped up in one very sexy package. She couldn't wait to get him stripped and in her camera lens.

"If you keep looking at me like that, Frankie, you'll give me no other choice but to trade body fluids with you."

"Trust me, Reese, the last thing you want is to get tangled up with me."

He chugged the rest of his beer and set the bottle down on the coffee table. "I doubt that."

She cocked a brow and strode past him into the kitchen. "I changed my mind." She grabbed a beer from the fridge, twisted off the cap, and tossed it into the sink as he had done. She turned and tipped the bottle his way, then chugged almost half of it down. "The fact is, Reese, I'd rock your world, then walk away without giving you a second thought." She winked at him and strode past him into the living room.

He followed her, watching the gentle sway of her hips. His groin warmed.

Flopping down on the couch, she took another healthy swig of the beer. "And after I rocked your world, you'd be whining and crying for more, and I don't do more." She polished off the beer and set the bottle down next to his. She raised her eyes and smiled. "So, can I borrow a shirt and a pair of boxers to sleep in?"

Reese grinned. Her moxie impressed him. "Yeah, I've got something you can wear."

When he returned with a shirt and pair of boxer briefs, she was still smiling. He couldn't remember ever enjoying an undercover assignment so much. He lived for the hunt, and this particular prey, once felled, would be well worth the effort. His dick swelled and he muttered a curse under his breath.

Frankie raised a brow. "You okay?"

"Couldn't be better." Reese handed her the clothing. "Bathroom is the first door on the left and the bedroom is the last door on the right."

"So you're sleeping on the couch?"

He nodded. She smiled. He watched her walk down the hall, his skin warming at the sight. "There's an extra toothbrush in the cabinet," he called.

She turned and smiled at him over her shoulder. "I never doubted that for a minute. I'm surprised you don't have an entire ladies' wardrobe for your 'guests.' "

"I'm working on it."

While Frankie did what women did in his bathroom, Reese reassessed his game plan. She was dug in hard about the no-fraternizing thing. And he needed to get her into bed. One, to build lust; two, to build trust; and three, to get as much information out of her as possible. He was convinced that once he had her emotionally, she'd give up sensitive information. It wasn't the most gentlemanly ploy, but then she wasn't Emily Post either. At the very least, she was guilty of Lord knew what by association, and at the most, she was a cold-blooded killer. He felt no remorse for his means of generating information.

So to get her in bed, he had to make it her decision. Some reverse psychology. He'd play hard to get and see how she liked it.

He groaned audibly when she emerged from the bathroom ten minutes later, her skin scrubbed to a rosy glow, clad in one of his white wifebeaters and black boxer briefs that were too big for her and hung sexily off her full hips.

As she walked down the hall, she pulled her hair up and wound a rubber band around the thick mass. Her tits rode up high, and blood slammed to his cock. He could see her nipples under the thin white fabric and he knew she knew it. Instead of focusing on that very fine sight, his eyes traveled lower to her belly, then her long, tanned legs. He swallowed hard and raised his eyes to lock with her gaze. She smiled, and if he were a betting man, he'd say she blushed. The look became her.

"I'm hungry," she said.

Reese stood, not caring if his hard-on was noticeable. "So am I."

CHAPTER EIGHT

"I have frozen pizza, pistachios, and enough beer to float an aircraft carrier."

Frankie sighed, stepped into the kitchen, and poked her head around his shoulder and into the freezer. The chilled air swirled around her chest and she felt her nipples pucker. She smiled. Why she enjoyed rattling Reese's cage, she had no idea. But she did. Immensely. Maybe it had to do with the fact he seemed genuinely interested in her, even if it was on that most basic male-female level.

Grabbing one of the boxes, she read the ingredients on the front and gave it her seal of approval. "Right now I could eat cardboard and not complain."

Reese bent his head down to her ear and said, "Then don't complain when you bite into this."

She turned with the box in her hand and smiled. Heat swirled around them, tempering the cold from the freezer. His eyes dipped to her protruding nipples.

Grinning like an idiot, Reese took the box. "Go into the living room, I'll be right there."

A few minutes later, Reese joined her in the small room. Handing her a beer, he sat on the floor next to the coffee table. He propped up a knee and rested his elbow there.

"So, tell me, Frankie, what's up with your family?"

She shrugged and took a sip of her beer. "Nothing is up."

"So it's par for the course for your family to be shot at?"

She shrugged again. "It's—complicated."

"I guess. Who were those guys at the restaurant?"

Frankie sighed and settled into the comfortable cushions. It was common knowledge who was who in her family. "Tweedledumb and Tweedledee are Johnny and Mikey Buzzawini. My auntie Ada's boys. We call Mikey 'Meatball.' The other one is Jimmy 'Peanuts' Tambouri. My auntie Lola's son. His dad died in Vietnam. Didn't even know Lola was pregnant. Unk raised Jimmy."

"I can see why you call Mikey Meatball. Why Peanuts?"

Frankie smiled. "When Jimmy was a kid he always had a pocket full of pistachios. He left shells all over the place. Auntie Lola used to yell at him to clean up his trail. They were everywhere. If you ever wanted to know where Jimmy had been, just follow the shell trail."

"He didn't look like a nice guy."

"Jimmy? He's an angel. He had some trouble a while back. But he's cleaned up now."

"Who was the big guy with your purse?"

Frankie smiled and sipped her beer. "Leo. He used to be my father's bodyguard but now he's Unk's."

Reese shook his head and tipped the bottle back, taking a long drink.

"Why are you shaking your head?"

"Leo would be the last person I'd want looking out for my back."

Frankie squinted, not understanding. "Leo is loyal."

"He obviously isn't very good at his job."

Frankie sat up, the impact of what he said hitting her broadside. "I never thought of it that way. Do you think my uncle should hire someone else?" The minute she asked the question, she recanted it. "Ignore that."

"Why? Is everything such a big secret in your family?"

"No, it's just, well, we like to keep a low profile."

Reese laughed out loud, the rich timbre sending tremors across her skin. "C'mon, Frankie, how can a family like yours keep a low profile?"

"I don't know what you mean."

"Your family business?"

She shrugged and finished her beer. The second was nicely mingling with the painkiller Sanzo gave her. She felt warm and very relaxed. "My family is legit."

Reese shook his head again and finished off his beer. Without a word he rose, went into the kitchen, and brought back two more cold ones. He twisted off the caps and handed her one. She hesitated for only a second before she took it.

"Really? Name one legitimate business."

The need to protect her family welled. "I can name several. Finance. Import-export, and there is *Skin*."

Reese chuckled. "Is that the PC way of saying loan-sharking and contraband?"

"And you have the perfect family?"

Reese scowled. Frankie caught the look. "Tell me about them?"

"Who?"

"Your family."

"Nothing to tell."

"There is always something to tell."

"In my case there isn't."

Frankie laughed low. "I see how it is. It's okay for me to spill the beans but not you. I'll remember that. It's a two-way street for me that way. Not one-way."

"I don't have fond memories of my family, let's leave it at that."

A wave of sadness filled her. Her family was on a good day diffi-cult. On a bad day? Impossible. So she didn't have much room to talk, and there were more days than not she wished she'd been born to a normal family. But she'd also learned to accept her family for what and who they were. But still, there were those days when she longed for normalcy. Maybe that was one reason why she so much wanted *Skin* to fly. It was the only legitimate holding the family pos-sessed. As long as she had breath in her body, she would not allow it to turn into yet another nefarious family scheme.

The oven timer dinged. Frankie tried to stand up and the room spun. No food, drugs, and three beers collided. Reese grabbed her, steadying her. His long arms slipped around her waist and, oddly, she felt safe. She looked up at him and caught her breath. His features had sharpened in what she knew was hunt mode.

He smoothed back a lock of hair from her cheek. "You okay?"

"I just need to sit down."

His arms wrapped tighter around her waist. Her breasts pushed against the hard plane of his chest. His clean, woodsy scent tickled her nostrils. "You smell really good." Oops, did she just say that?

Reese lowered his nose to her hair and inhaled. "So do you."

He gently sat her down. Reluctantly, she slid her arms from around his waist. Then watched him go into the kitchen. Not for the first time, she felt something shift inside of her body. There was something very basic about this man that moved her. She shook her head. That was the drugs and alcohol talking. She needed to get a grip.

Frankie wrinkled her nose as she chewed the first bite of the pizza. "This is awful."

Reese nodded and chased a bite down with a swig of beer. "I told you."

Despite the cardboard consistency, she finished her piece and a second one along with her beer.

Reese helped himself to another beer but gave Frankie a glass of water instead. She frowned but nodded. "Thanks, I'm feeling a little too comfortable right now, another beer would kick my ass."

Reese grinned and took a long pull of his beer. "Talk to me about you."

Frankie's eyelids hovered over her eyes. She looked damn sexy sitting there in his wifebeater, her full breasts screaming for release and her sexy green eyes hooded behind her long, black lashes. His cock twinged and he knew having her once wouldn't be enough.

"I'm boring."

"Not to me."

"You're just saying that coz I'm your boss."

"I'd say it regardless."

She picked at a piece of crust. "Don't try and take advantage of me in my wounded state."

Reese laughed. "I would never attempt to take advantage of you. There would be hell to pay the next day."

"You've got that right."

"So, then, tell me about you."

"What do you want to know?"

He grinned wide, and Frankie shook her head. "It's always got to be sexual."

Reese warmed to the conversation. "I'd love to find out what a woman like you fantasizes about."

"I don't have any fantasies."

"Everyone has fantasies."

How could she explain to him her fantasy was having a normal family? Or rewinding her life back two and a half weeks?

"Look, Reese, even if I did, I don't think it's professional to divulge such intimacies to an employee."

He actually looked affronted. He quickly recovered. "I think we're a little past the standard employee-employer relationship, Frankie."

She nodded. "I'll give you that. But that doesn't negate the fact I'm paying you a lot of money for a specific job. The last thing I want is for gray areas to develop."

"True, but what better way to get into my head than by allowing me into yours? Don't we need that certain je ne sais quoi?"

He made a good argument.

"I mean, just you sharing with me about your family gives me more of an understanding of you. You don't come across as the hard-ass you did earlier."

"Don't fool yourself, Reese. The last thing I'll allow is for my emotions to interfere with my business."

"I can be a very demanding model, Frankie."

She stood, not comfortable with the conversation. He was right, to nail the shots, to be simpatico, they should be cultivating the natural chemistry they shared. But the thought terrified her. She didn't trust herself to remain in an emotional void. "I can be an equally demanding boss."

Reese stood as well. He moved close to her but not enough for her to feel his heat. She was disappointed. "Well, I guess we'll just have to play it out, won't we?"

Frankie turned and carefully made her way down the hall. "I guess we will. Good night."

Reese grumbled and finished his beer. Damn it, even drugged and liquored up she didn't budge. If he wasn't careful, his scheme could backfire. It was a tightwire act. One false move and he'd fall crashing to the ground. He needed Frankie in bed.

He'd learned long ago pillow talk was not only the most expedient way to get incriminating evidence but also the most pleasuable.

He'd simply reverse roles. Women always wanted what they couldn't have. He knew she wanted him naked as her cover model, and she would come to want him naked in her bed. He laughed softly. He'd make her work to get his soldier up. As she worked that angle, he'd work just as hard to keep the devil between his legs quiet, until he maneuvered her right between the sheets. Excitement heated his blood. He felt no guilt. It was just business, and there was more at stake than Francesca Donatello's feelings.

To build a case against the family, he'd use any means available. He chugged the balance of his beer and grimaced. He preferred Jack neat, but for this cover, beer would have to do. He grabbed another one from the fridge and shucked the lid.

He turned off the lights and slipped over to the living room window. With the tip of the bottle he pushed back the heavy curtains enough to see a dark colored sedan parked inconspicuously at the corner. It looked similar to the one Anthony and Tawny jumped into earlier.

He didn't doubt Carmine Donatello had them followed. But how the hell? He'd been careful.

The hair stood up on the back of his neck. "Son of a bitch." More than likely the good doc called Carmine and gave him a description of his car. The wily bastard planted a GPS device.

Reese drained the bottle. He'd take care of that first thing in the a.m. Carmine Donatello might be the new don, with muscle and money to buy him an army and loyalty, but he was playing a game Reese had mastered with his own inexhaustible supply of manpower.

CHAPTER NINE

Reese woke to the quiet whirring sound of a camera shutter. He opened his eyes and stretched in the pullout bed. Unhurriedly, he turned over onto his back, the white sheet falling to his waist. He grinned up into the surprised hazel eyes of his guest. Her eyes dropped to the tented portion of the sheet.

"Good morning, sunshine," he said, his voice low and husky from sleep.

Frankie quickly recovered. "Good morning yourself."

She moved closer to the bed. Crouching, she moved in close to the side of his face. "Close your eyes."

He did.

"Stretch, like a wild beast waking from a delirious night of sex with his fantasy woman."

He performed on cue and gave a low moan of pleasure to go with the action.

"Good, now slowly open your eyes and look at me like you're a starved dog and I'm a bone."

That was no stretch for him. Reese did as commanded. He didn't bother to try and curb his erection; it was a morning thing that now started to throb with want. He'd exercise self-control later.

Frankie inhaled sharply. Reese's blue eyes burned fire straight to the core of her. Electricity sizzled between her legs and warm moistness lubricated her slow throb. She'd been a fool to allow her fear of failure to get between this man and the success of her magazine.

Anthony had spooked her, undermined her confidence. It would not happen again. She would not allow Anthony to get between her and her magazine.

Despite the drugs and beer she'd consumed last night, several aspects of the evening with Reese sunk in while she slept. She'd made her decision to do everything in her power to keep Reese happy in order to further herself, and *Skin*. If that meant sharing a little of herself with him, so be it.

Frankie smiled. Yep, as she saw it, she would do whatever it took so that the ladies of America would get their world rocked, and she'd be damned if she'd let anything come between him and her readers. It was all or nothing. And she wanted it all.

And now, with such a compromising position presenting itself so nicely, what better way to hone her skills as an emotionally detached businesswoman.

"Turn over," she said, her voice just as low and husky as his had been.

Slowly, Reese did as commanded. "Tell me your fantasy."

"I told you I don't have one."

"Make one up."

"Be careful what you ask for, you just might get it." And so she would give him what he wanted. But he'd have to work a little harder for it.

"I can take it."

She focused and took a few test shots. "The lighting in here sucks."

"You're avoiding the question."

Frankie reached across Reese, her chest barely brushing his back, and turned on the table lamp. As she moved back, he rolled to his side and grabbed a hank of her hair, stopping her.

"Are you afraid of me?" Reese asked.

Her skin flushed warm under his regard. Maybe. Just a little. "You don't scare me."

"Then tell me your fantasy."

She pulled her hair from his hand and leaned back, focusing her camera. "Once, I was out at a bar, sitting by myself, minding my own business like a good girl." She took a few shots, then attached a different lens to her camera. "As I sipped my wine, a man walked in. A tall, dangerous-looking man. Immediately we locked eyes. I thought maybe he was someone my father brought in from out of town to keep an eye on me. And I didn't care, I wanted him."

Frankie knelt next to Reese and focused in on his face. His eyes shone bright, and she had his undivided attention. "I wanted him to come up behind me, to touch me, to whisper in my ear to meet him in the dark alcove in the corner. In my fantasy he does. His breath is hot against my ear and his hand slides up my thigh and then under my skirt. I'm so wet for him I can't stand it. 'I want to fuck you,' he says, and I almost come on the bar stool."

Reese's chest rose and fell, his breath coming out in short, hot bursts. "Do you?"

"Do I what?"

"Fuck him."

"Oh, yes. He slips his hands around my hips and gently pulls me off the stool and guides me toward the dark corner. He follows so close I can feel his hard-on against the small of my back."

Reese's hand slid to the edge of the mattress nearest to her thigh. "Sex with a stranger turns you on?"

"With this stranger it did."

His fingertips traced the skin of her knee, just enough to let her know he was interested. She shivered. "Tell me what happens next."

Frankie stood and stepped back. She smiled a half smile at him, liking his body on high alert. "Use your imagination."

Reese groaned and rolled over onto his chest, grinding his hips into the mattress. "Not fair."

"I never said I played fair."

Reese cocked a dark brow but said nothing.

"Don't move," she directed, and angled her camera, taking several shots.

"I'm about to impale the mattress."

Frankie laughed. "Oh, I won't keep you like that too long." She took a few angled shots. "Put your arms up and rest your head on them." In a languid movement he did just that. The muscles across his shoulders and arms rippled with the action. Something deep inside her moved. He had the grace and stealth of a leopard, and she was sure he possessed equal physical strength.

Primal emotions sprung up from nowhere. She envisioned what their children would look like and her body went rigid. Holy hell—she did *not* just think that! What was wrong with her? In all the time she'd been with Sean, she'd never considered giving birth to his children. Lord, she needed to see her shrink.

"You going to take the picture or what?"

Reese's abrupt comment jolted her out of her ridiculous revelry. He'd turned half on his side, his pecs bulging under his weight. She swallowed hard. "Yes, of course. Turn back around."

Just business, she repeated in her head. Just for business she grasped the top of the sheet and pulled it down his back, revealing a hint of his round left cheek. She wondered what he would do if she ran her fingertips down the curve of his ass, then slid them down between his legs and caressed his heavy balls. She imagined the sharp hiss of his breath, his body rising, him turning and pulling her down to him, kissing her so hard her lips would be bruised for days.

"Frankie!"

"I'm focusing."

She took the necessary shots and backed out of the room to her borrowed one. Minutes later she heard the shower running. She pictured him in the shower, hot water spraying his naked body, beading on his tight skin, steam rising in the tile stall. Her fingers itched and her blood quickened. She *had* to shoot him like that. She didn't bother to resist the temptation or opportunity.

Camera in hand she hustled to the bathroom, excitement zipping through her. Stealthily she turned the knob. Disappointment flooded her. Locked. Anger flashed. What the hell? She'd expected it to be wide open with a neon sign flashing for her to enter and join him.

Not to be denied the stellar hot shots she knew she could get, Frankie reached up to the top of the doorjamb and felt for the key. Dismayed when she didn't find one, she checked every jamb in the condo and came up empty. Had he removed them, suspecting she might try to get in? Or God forbid, had he caught a case of shyness? Refusing to believe that, and more determined than ever, she dug through her purse for a bobby pin. Instead she found a large paper clip. It would do. She pulled it straight and inserted it into the small hole in the knob. It clicked and she smiled triumphantly, turning the knob.

She opened the door to the hot, steamy bathroom, the thick air swirling around her. The semisteamed shower doors did little to hide the man on the other side. What she saw set her body on fire.

Reese lathered up.

With his head back and his eyes closed, ever so slowly his big hands rubbed the creamy lather across his chest, moving slightly upward as he slid across his pecs. His dark brown nipples hardened beneath the soft friction. His hand slid lower, across the hard tautness of his belly. Steadying her breath, Frankie raised her camera.

Reese's hand slid down to his burgeoning cock. His body flinched when he wrapped those long fingers of his around the thick shaft. His chest expanded when he caught his breath. Frankie's own breath echoed in her ear. In a slow, rhythmic slide he began to pump.

A heaviness filled Frankie's body, blood rushing to fill every capillary she possessed. Her hips rocked in silent approval with his. When his back arched, her back arched. Frankie bit her bottom lip and held back a cry of pleasure. For the first time in her life she understood what "in heat" actually felt like.

Her legs felt like waterlogged sacks of sand, making it hard for her to take a step closer. The sound of the pulsing water covered the low click of her camera. He was turned slightly away from her, unable to see her taking shots of him—unless he turned around. She gave no thought of being caught. All that mattered was the shot.

She watched, through her lens, spellbound as his hand pumped faster. Her heart rate accelerated and she licked her lips; her hips keeping their own subtle cadence. He was truly a magnificent specimen of a man. She'd been a fool to have considered another model. Pressure built at the apex of her thighs.

His hoarse voice called out her name. Frankie gasped, unable to keep the sound from escaping. Her hips jolted simultaneously. Heat flashed across her skin. Her blood vessels opened and filled. Her body throbbed. If she didn't get out of there, she'd break her cardinal rule.

Quickly she backed out of the bathroom, giving him time to clean up and her heart rate time to calm down. She leaned against the wall just outside the bathroom, the cool air easing her body's elevated temperature. Something too primal to name encompassed her. She didn't bother to examine it; instead, she allowed it to lead.

This time when she opened the bathroom door, she did it with fanfare, announcing her entrance. "Hellooo."

Reese stopped lathering his chest and smiled, slow and cocky, as if he knew a secret. Had he been aware of her presence during his little show? Had he done it knowing she found a way in? No, she suddenly realized, he'd made it painfully clear he didn't want her in the bathroom. And she felt a stab of shame. Was she stooping too low? Getting the shot no matter the cost?

Her gaze darted away from his and caught the four door keys sitting on the edge of the vanity. Anger surfaced but she quelled it. She had no right taking those pictures. Her business head kicked that notion aside. Maybe not, but he had agreed to whenever and wherever.

She focused back on Reese's lathered body. Her limbs warmed again. Reese Barrett had the body of a gladiator. Tall, ruggedly muscled, and scarred. She'd never really liked the perfect beauty of so many of today's models. She liked a man who had character, his body reflecting that. She was betting the masses of women out there felt the same way.

She wrinkled a brow at his indifference. While it appeared he could turn off his lust for her, her body parts still hummed.

"I'd love to get a few shots of you all lathered up. What do you say?"

He nodded and pulled back the shower door. Her eyes instantly dropped to his firm but fallen erection. She couldn't help it. He was just so damn attractive down there.

Reese gritted his teeth. It took every ounce of willpower not to spring back to attention. The fact that he'd just jerked off didn't seem to play into the mix. The way Frankie stood there staring at him, a mixture of surprise, wonder, and, damn it, lust on her face almost did him in. He was only human after all, and when the object of his own lustful thoughts stood so close and looked so interested, what the hell was he supposed to do?

Shit! His reverse psychology method was about to backfire in his face. He felt his cock twinge and watched Frankie's pouty lips form a silent *O.*

Gritting his teeth, Reese let his thoughts go to the cold, snowy planes of his home in Wyoming, and the way the wind would whip snow into mountainous drifts, how it made travel of any kind impossible. He'd damn near frozen more than a few times during his hours on horseback looking for stranded mustangs. He remembered Missy throwing a hissy fit one Christmas when he refused to allow her to make a round with him during a blizzard. His body tingled, but not with heat: this time the feeling was cold, frosty, chilling. Missy's laughing face floated into his thoughts and suddenly her eyes closed, and her laughter quieted, never to be heard again.

Reese squeezed his eyes shut. Even after all these years, he couldn't forgive himself his part in her death. All desire for sex drained like the spring thaw from his body. His muscles tightened and his brows drew tight.

Frankie watched Reese's face morph from sexy to hard, then bitter, in less time than it took her to snap a round of shots.

"What's wrong?" she asked, and she realized she really wanted to know. When had this man's feelings become important to her?

He turned the water off, his actions abrupt. He grabbed the towel from the rack and briskly dried off. Skin still damp, he wrapped the towel around his waist and shot her a dangerous look. "I'd like a little privacy."

Frankie nodded, and for the second time in the last few moments shame coursed through her. She turned and hurried out of the bathroom.

Pacing the living room floor, Frankie realized she was reverting back to her old emotional involvement habits. She reminded herself what mattered was getting the shot. Period. Feelings, emotions, whatever they were, had no purpose in getting "the shot." This was business, and her business was to launch *Skin* off the charts. To that end it was all about the shot.

The door to the bathroom opened and she watched Reese walk into his bedroom and shut the door. The click of the lock was not lost on her. That was okay. She didn't want any more pictures of him in the condo anyway.

She hustled into the bathroom, still steamy from the man who just exited it, and jumped into the shower.

She'd washed her bra and panties the night before. Without his permission, she borrowed a black button-down shirt. She'd change when she got to the office. She had an overnight bag and extra clothes she kept there in her little powder room.

When she strutted out of his bedroom, he looked her up and down. "Nice shirt," he drawled.

"I'll send it out to be laundered. You'll have it back by the end of the day."

"Polite people ask."

Bent on putting more distance between them, she picked up her camera bag and purse, careful of her stitches. "I'm not polite."

Few words were spoken as they drove to the studio. Reese's closed face and body language offered no opening for conversation.

Frankie didn't push it. She'd let her guard down last night and blabbed too much. It was retreat time. Professional-distance time. Time to be the bitch she needed to be to not only survive in this world she lived in but to succeed in it.

When Frankie walked into her office with her hair hanging damp down her back and Reese following close behind, Tawny raised a brow and choked back a smile. Frankie ignored her assistant's smug look and put the key into her office door.

Her gaze immediately zeroed in on the wrapped box on her desk. The gaily wrapped package beckoned her. Setting her camera bag down, perplexed, she picked up the box.

"Birthday?" Reese asked.

She shook her head and pulled the ribbon, then removed the lid. Just as she lifted it, Reese grabbed her hand. "Let me do that."

"Why?"

"Don't you think it's a bit unusual to have a gift on your desk in your locked office?"

Her gut lurched and she felt sick to her stomach. Her hand slid from the box top. Reese moved between her and the box and pushed her back with his right hand. "Do you have a ruler?"

"Top drawer."

Reese slid open the desk drawer and pulled out a plastic ruler. Stepping as far back from the box as he could while still touching it with the tip of the ruler he slowly lifted the lid. Frankie's muscles tightened, and the feeling of nausea swelled. What she expected, she didn't know. When nothing exploded or leapt from the box, Reese stepped closer and peered into it. His brows slammed together and he shot her a disturbing look.

"What?" Frankie asked, afraid of the answer. Her fear angered her. And what angered her more was the distraction. She didn't have time for this crap. She stepped over to Reese and looked down into the box. Her blood chilled. Son of a bitch! She stepped back, tripping on her feet. Reese caught her, then steadied her.

"What does it mean?" he asked.

Frankie's hand shook and she put it to her throat to still it. The alarm clock lay faceup, the glass shattered and the time set to nine o'clock. "It means my time is up."

"Who has access to your office?"

After the first wave of shock and fear swept through her, another wave followed, this one hot and filled with fury. Her office was her sanctuary, her private space, and someone had violated it.

"Anthony!" She grabbed the clock from the box and shoved past Reese, ignoring his calls for her to stop. She marched down the hall to the office her brother had claimed as his and without an invitation she burst in.

He started when the door slammed against the wall, then his eyes narrowed. "You never learned manners, Frankie."

She threw the clock at him, narrowly missing his face. He caught it. "If you're man enough to take me out, little brother, be man enough to tell me to my face."

"What the hell are you talking about?"

She pointed to the clock in his hand. "That was on my desk this morning."

Anthony looked at the clock in his hand. Realization dawned. He was pretty good, Frankie thought. He almost looked as surprised as she'd been.

Anthony set the shattered clock down on his desk. "I didn't put that in your office."

"Then who did you pay to do it?"

He sat back in his chair, relaxed, and didn't seem to give a shit she'd been told her time was up.

"I don't work that way, sister, and you know it."

"Why do you want *Skin?*"

"Because Father didn't want you to turn it into the smut rag you want to make it."

Frankie laughed. "I can't believe I'm hearing this from you! What do you call your peep shows in the Tenderloin. Sunday school?"

"That's different."

"Different because it's entertainment for men?"

He nodded.

"You're a chauvinist."

Anthony shrugged. "Sticks and stones, Frankie." He smiled, the gesture smarmy. "Have you spoken with our uncle this morning?"

"No. What does Unk have to do with this?"

"Then you haven't heard the news."

Blood drained to her feet. His lack of concern for her well-being and his cocky demeanor didn't bode well for her. "What news?"

"My mother found a codicil to Father's old will."

"You're lying."

Anthony smoothed his two-hundred-dollar silk tie. "Carmine knows Father wanted you out. No way was he going to be embarrassed by his daughter and the 'new look' you wanted for *Skin*. You should have remained the obedient daughter and taken the crumbs he threw at you."

Anthony's words stung.

"Father may have given me my first break here, but I worked my way up from interning to creative director on my own."

Anthony's eyes sparkled with mockery. "If you say so."

She said so because it *was* so. She'd worked her ass off. Spending sixteen-hour days for years working on one assignment after another. No one put more blood, sweat, or tears into the magazine than she did.

"Give our 'Unk' a call. He'll fill you in." Anthony picked up the phone on his desk, and when she refused to take it, he punched in Unk's number.

Fear ran icy fingers along her spine. What the hell happened since last night? And why did she have to find this out from her brother?

When Carmine answered, Anthony put him on speaker and hung up the handset. Her fingers twitched to slap off his smug smile.

"Unk? Is it true? Is there a codicil to Father's old will?"

"Francesca, I was going to call you—"

"Is it true?!"

"I have the codicil here in my hands. Connie brought it to me last night."

Why didn't that surprise her? What was Connie up to now? Constance Angelina Donatello was as transparent as a window. Everyone knew she'd maneuvered Sonny into her bed and gotten pregnant deliberately. She made no secret of her conquest. Now she suddenly comes up with a codicil? How convenient. "Where is the original?"

"Somewhere I'm sure Santini felt was secure. But never fear. I will find it."

Hope swelled. "Unk, is the copy notarized?"

"No."

"Then it's worthless. I'll contest it. I don't believe Father would cut me out." Uncertainty tugged at her thoughts. Her father had disowned her the day before he died. But the only one who knew that was dead. "What's the date on the document?"

"A year ago."

Relief flooded her. If he had changed his will, cutting her out of *Skin,* it would have been after he disowned her, which would have been the day before or the morning of his death two weeks ago. This one was a fake.

"*Cara*—"

"Unk, please, for now would you tell Anthony to stop drooling all over this place like a goombah over a stripper? Give me some time to locate Father's last will."

"Do you know where it is?"

"No, but when Mr. Geppi surfaces, I'm sure he can produce the original."

"Aldo was found dead in his office this morning," Unk said.

Frankie gasped loudly and watched Anthony's brow furrow. Her eyes locked with his. For a flash of a second she thought she read fear in his eyes. Not of her, but the person responsible for Aldo's death.

Frankie didn't ask if Aldo died of natural causes. It was too coincidental. Someone didn't want Santini Donatello's latest will to surface.

"I'll call you later, Unk," Frankie softly said, suddenly thinking of Maria and the kids. She'd go over later in the week. She hit the Speaker Off button and looked back at her brother.

"What's happening, Anthony?"

"Why don't you tell me?"

At a loss for words, Frankie felt as if the walls of her life were slowly closing in on her. If she didn't get out, the life would be squeezed out of her.

"What do you mean by that?"

"Figure it out." He pointed to the clock. "And hurry, sister. Time is ticking away."

The urge to argue with her imbecile brother drained from her. Instead, she picked up the clock and tossed it into his trash can. "You're wasting time with your games, Anthony. I'm not playing."

When Frankie entered her office she found Reese and Tawny engaged in a rather animated conversation. Reese clearly found Tawny's Malibu Barbie looks appealing. And Tawny obviously reciprocated the admiration. Her blue eyes sparkled and her long lashes batted coyly every time she touched Reese's arm. Or at that particular moment, despite the fact Frankie had just walked in, his thigh.

Frankie scowled. "Tawny, don't you have something better to do than drool all over my model?"

Tawny grinned, taking the question in good humor. "Actually, I can't think of anything better than this," Tawny answered, looking up into Reese's eyes like a lost puppy finding her master.

"Well, I can. Get out of here and make sure the studio is clear." Frankie held open the door until Tawny walked haughtily by, as if she were the Queen of Sheba. Frankie slammed it behind her.

Throwing Reese a scowl, she dared him to comment. She walked to her desk. Pulling her camera out of her bag, she hooked it up to her computer. She wanted to see the pics before they headed down to the studio.

"You should have the cops dust that clock for prints," Reese said.

Her head snapped up. She was about to tell him to butt out; instead, she shook her head, her attention on her monitor. "The only set of prints on that thing are mine and my brother's. It was his lame attempt to scare me. It didn't work."

"What if it wasn't Anthony?"

She clicked the mouse, bringing up a file. "It was. He's a cry-baby."

"Do you know who killed your father?"

Her head snapped up. "No."

"Do you think you brother had a hand in it?"

"Do you have any idea what you're insinuating?" she asked, not believing she was actually having this conversation with an outsider.

He came closer. Her skin flushed hot when he walked around the desk to look down at the computer screen, just as a shot of him holding on to his lathered rod in the shower that morning flashed up.

"You're a bad, bad girl, Francesca Donatello."

"You're worse. You knew you had an audience." He grinned and his warm gaze slid across her. She felt her color deepen. "You set me up."

"Like a row of dominoes."

"Paybacks are a bitch."

He chuckled. "I can't wait."

Frankie broke eye contact and watched the rest of the pictures load. As one flashed across the screen, she gasped. Quickly she hit the Back button. There she was, in almost full naked color, sprawled across Reese's bed, the covers twisted between her bare legs and a smile of satisfaction plastered across her face. For the second time that morning, heat rose to her cheeks. Taking matters into her own hands last night had been the only way she could fall asleep.

"It looks like I'm not the only sneaky one around here." She managed to keep her voice level.

Reese's eyes glowed in mischievous pleasure. "That wasn't the only one I took."

Frankie clicked the next button and her heat rose. The shirt of Reese's she'd slept in hung off her shoulder, and her dark nipples, clearly aroused, dominated the picture. "It's only fair I got to return the favor," he said.

She clicked to the next shot, this one innocent enough. It showed her snuggled up to Reese's pillow, her face still and soft in sleep. She looked peaceful, unlike how she felt at the moment.

Reese leaned over her, putting a hand on her shoulder. "That one is my favorite. I'll take Frankie the kitten over Frankie the hellcat any day."

"So you don't like your woman with claws."

"Only if they're in my back."

She turned and caught her breath; they were eye to eye, his warm breath caressing her face. She had planned to bare her claws and ask if he wanted a demonstration. Instead, she bit her bottom lip and closed her eyes, willing the heat that pooled between her thighs to chill and the sudden fullness of her breasts to evaporate. Her chest rose of its own volition toward him, her lips following. Santa Maria, this man was dangerous.

Reese backed away and stood straight. "Let's get this show on the road, shall we?"

"Frankie?" Tawny barged in as usual. "Oh, um, sorry."

Frankie smoothed her hair back over her shoulders and straightened. "Sorry for what? Barging in—again?"

Tawny blushed. "Um, yeah, sorry, I need to work on that."

"Start now," Frankie snapped. Her tone surprised both her and Tawny. The little blonde skulked out of the office. Frankie felt bad; she didn't normally chip off on her employees. Especially the loyal ones like Tawny. But for the love of God, didn't the girl have any manners?

Frankie walked to the door Tawny left open and slammed it shut. She turned to a bemused-looking Reese. "What's so funny?"

He shook his head. "You have more moods than a mood ring."

"Get used to it. I have a lot on my mind."

"Let me help you."

"You'll help me, all right. We start shooting today." She laughed. "Hell, I started this morning."

"Delete the ones you took of me in the shower."

"Are you kidding me? Those shots are going to quadruple my subscriptions."

"You're not going to print those."

"The hell I'm not! Those shots would heat up a corpse."

Reese stood his ground, just as determined. "I decide what goes to print. You invaded my privacy this morning, you had no right to do that, and I'll be damned if I'm going to have half the world seeing pictures of me jerking off."

Frankie stepped close. "Don't give me that, Reese. You wanted me in that bathroom, you made it so I had to break in. Don't tell me you didn't. Besides, I own your ass—you signed the contract last night. I took the pictures this morning."

Reese's eyes flashed bright blue; the color deepened beneath his dark skin. "You know as well as I do, that was for your eyes only. No one else's."

"They're going to production as we speak."

"I see how it is with you, Frankie. Just business, huh?"

"You learn quick."

He nodded, his anger seething just below the surface. "I'll remember that. And when I remind you when it comes back to bite you in that pretty little ass of yours, don't come crying to me."

"I'm glad you understand. Now, hopefully Tawny can keep her hands off of you long enough to take you downstairs to Stella to work out a color scheme."

He cocked a dark brow.

"You're a model, don't tell me you don't know about schemes."

"I'm a summer."

"The hell you are. Winter all the way. Now, I have a few things to do. I'll meet you downstairs in fifteen."

Reese didn't cotton much to being dismissed, but he played the obedient model, grateful for such a big break. Besides, he had a call to make.

He exited the office, told Tawny he had to make a quick call and then he'd be back up. He hurried downstairs to the front lobby and the pay phone there. He glanced around. All clear. Not wanting to be conspicuous, Reese turned his back and dialed.

"Guido's," a voice answered.

"Yo, Guido, I have a bug. I need an exterminator."

"We can kill whatever you got, mister."

"Dust my ride with powder, then get me a new one."

"You got it, man. I'll call you with the info on your new buggy."

"I also need a 24/7 shadow on Princess Daisy."

"Got it."

When Reese hung up, he saw Anthony standing by the front doors of the building, staring straight at him. Reese ignored him and jogged up the three flights of stairs to the offices of *Skin*.

CHAPTER TEN

Frankie stood, arms crossed and looked out the window up at the sky. White puffy clouds floated like sailboats on the ocean across the powder-blue plane. She wondered if her father was up there, watching, laughing. She scowled, and looked down at the ugly gray concrete sidewalk. If Santini Donatello was anywhere it was beneath that hard cement, not up in the clouds. The thought neither upset her or warmed her. She never kidded herself about her father and what he did. In his profession there was only one way: Down. Returning to her desk, Frankie sat down, her elbows on the surface, and stared hard at a crack in the ceiling.

As much as she wanted to locate her father's will, she resented the intrusion. If anyone had the latest will or at the very least a notarized copy, it was Mr. Geppi. First he was missing, now he was dead. She shook her head and groaned. When had life become so complicated?

None of this made sense.

Was her father playing with them all from the grave?

It wasn't like him to be so negligent. Or was it? The codicil dated last year was BS. She knew it in her bones. It made no sense. Not only was Anthony nowhere near ready to take over any of the family's business, he had shown no interest in *Skin* until last month. There would be no reason for her father to leave control of it to her brother. *He promised it to her.*

Santini knew how much the magazine meant to her, and despite their differences, he, along with Unk, had given her more and more responsibility. Besides, her father held no interest in the rag. It was Unk who acquired it for the family, her father not caring as long as he received his cut of the action. Had Father's sense of old-world honor driven him to take it from her? No—while Father hadn't wanted her to turn *Skin* into a skin rag in the truest sense of the term, she knew there had to be more to it than that. There was no fiscal reason to leave the magazine to Anthony. He knew nothing about publishing. He'd drive it into the ground.

A worm of a thought niggled inside her brain. What if Father didn't want Carmine, Aldo, or Anthony to know in advance of his death what was in the will? Maybe Aldo didn't have the will after all. But who would he entrust the document to? And why *not* his trusted attorney or brother?

The only reason he would do that was because . . . Her brain immediately rejected the thought. Reality pushed right back. Her skin chilled at the implication. Didn't he trust them with the content? The only feasible reason anyone would keep the contents secret was because there was something the main players would object to. What on earth could Anthony, Carmine, *and* Connie object so vehemently to?

"No," she said, "none of this makes sense." Not all of it anyway.

Okay, she could understand not trusting Anthony to handle the bulk of the family business at this stage, and maybe Papa wised up to Connie. They had seemed rather distant from each other this past year. Didn't matter. Papa doted on Anthony. And despite her brother's immaturity, Papa's eyes lit up like the proverbial Christmas tree when his only son walked into the room.

And Unk? He was not only her father's right-hand man, but his older brother and the one who always covered Santini's messy tracks. There was no one wiser or more trustworthy than Carmine. So, what about Aldo? The Geppis had been the Donatellos' personal attorneys since both families came to the States in the late nineteenth century. Hell, the families shared great-great-grandchildren. It didn't make sense for her father not to entrust his will to the older man.

Maybe Father did see Anthony for the lame-ass he was and because of that kept his will a secret. She dismissed that thought. Without a will, the business would fall apart. He would never leave the family in such turmoil.

She sat back in her chair and contemplated other possible reasons why the will hadn't turned up.

Obviously the contents. Anthony felt he was going to get their father's personal property and Uncle Carmine would be named interim don until Anthony proved himself. Or, she shivered, what if Unk, not feeling Anthony was ready, refused to step aside? Did Anthony suspect? Was it Anthony who took a shot at him? No. She couldn't see Unk preventing Anthony from stepping up. Well, as long as he proved himself. And he had a lot of proving to do.

Tears stung her eyes. She refused to believe her father had disinherited her! Sniffing hard, she looked up toward the door, relieved that for once Tawny respected her privacy. It hurt deeper than she cared to admit that her father gave so little of himself over the years to his eldest child. And her mother? Frankie's mood softened despite her mother leaving her to Connie and her father. Lucia had put up with Papa's women for years. Even when he had the audacity to bring them home to his table, Lucia endured. Frankie remembered watching her mother drop a plate of steaming spaghetti in her father's lap while his "friend" shrieked next to him at the dinner table. "I hope your balls fry," she'd said, and that was the last time Father brought a "friend" home.

It was when Connie the showgirl/stripper came into Father's life that Lucia realized she might lose what she had a tenuous grip on. Her husband, her daughter, her standing in the community, and her beloved home in Carmel.

In the years after the "annulment" her mother fought for her. Father refused to allow her mother in the house when Connie was present. And Connie had the uncanny ability to show up when it was Lucia's turn to visit. Finally, Sonny told his ex-wife she was disrupting his household and that she was no longer welcome. It wasn't until years later that Frankie understood you did not go up against Sonny Donatello, not if you wanted to live, and that included ex-wives who wanted to see their daughters. Lucia Donatello dried up and blew out of Frankie's life like an autumn leaf on a breezy day.

Frankie straightened her shoulders. If anything, her parents' abandonment made her stronger. She'd learned early on to look out for herself, understanding full well that in her family it was survival of the fittest. If you were born with a penis, the family smiled on you. If you were born with a vagina, you were a second-class citizen. It wasn't until the women of her family matured and took on matriarch status that they gained power, and only a precious few managed to do that.

With the back of her hand she wiped away a tear. The turmoil in her head mushroomed, spawning a headache. Something was very wrong, and she had no idea what it was.

On an impulse she called her mother. Lucia Analise Fazzio. Once a beautiful tigress of a dancer, now a former shell of herself. Santini did his work well. Once he forced Lucy from the family she came to love, she never recovered.

Her mother answered the phone on the first ring, her voice listless. "Hello, Mama."

A long silence followed Frankie's greeting. "Mama, I need your help. Someone shot me last night."

"*Bella,* no!" Lucia's voice resonated with shock—and life.

"*Si,* last night at Unk's. I took stitches in my arm."

Anger sizzled across the airwaves. "Who? And why? What has your father done, the putz? From the grave, no less."

What on earth had changed her mother from a reclusive divorcée into this spitfire? "Mama!"

"I'm over the bastard, darling, may he rot in hell."

Had Frankie been standing, she would have fallen over.

"*Bella,* I knew I should have called you earlier. I had a feeling something like this would come up. Get out of that town now. There's no telling what rats will chew themselves out of the woodwork and come after you. Santini had more enemies than Mussolini, and I don't want to see you caught up in it. Let them get hold of that rat-fink half brother of yours and his whore mother too! Come to Scottsdale with me."

Jaw agape, Frankie held the phone in front of her and blinked. Who *was* this woman?

"I was quiet all of these years while that bastard nailed anything that wasn't nailed down. Lord only knows how many little bastards he has, and no doubt they'll be climbing out of the sewer for a piece of the action. Get away from them, *cara,* they'll kill you like they did him."

Finding her voice, Frankie coughed, then said, "Actually, I think the hit last night was on Unk, and I just happened to be in the way."

"Another snake. Stay away from him."

Frankie shook her head. "No, Mama, Unk is my only hope to hang on to *Skin.* Connie produced a codicil leaving everything to Anthony."

"I doubt it's authentic. That family has been known to pull the bait-and-switch routine. It's how Santini ended up with my brother's two houses in there in the city. You'd think the prick would have left them to you instead of that whore's spawn."

Frankie coughed so hard that tears filled her eyes. Once again, she wondered who this woman was. "Um, Mama, are you okay?"

"I'm fine. I've kept my mouth shut all these years for your sake, to keep peace, to keep you in your father's sights, but he always put that bastard son of his first, not his legitimate daughter."

"He did marry Connie."

"*After* she gave birth to a son and he proved it was his through blood tests. I know for a fact last year he had a DNA test done to be one hundred percent certain."

"How do you know all of this?"

"I have eyes and ears everywhere, *bella,* and it pays for me to know these things. I can assure you if there was any doubt about Anthony, I would have made a big stink about it. Sadly, he is the bastard's little bastard."

"Mama, where would Father have put his will? Or at the very least a notarized copy?"

"Carmine doesn't have it?"

"No."

"What about Aldo? He did all of your father's personal paperwork."

"Aldo turned up dead."

"Ah, yes, how convenient for all parties involved. I smell a fish."

"You mean?"

"Unless Santini had a fallout with Aldo, someone made sure he didn't produce the authentic will. Francesca?" Her tone darkened. "Listen to me. Get away. Come to me, *bella*, and we can for once live a normal life. It is what you want, no?"

More than she realized. "I can't. I have responsibilities to *Skin*. And I refuse to run away and let Anthony ruin what I've worked so hard for."

"You were always as stubborn as your father. Thank the Holy Mother that's all you have of him."

Regret stabbed at Frankie's heart. How much she would have loved to have this feisty woman as a part of her life when she needed her most. There had been no one to give her advice on boyfriends, no mother to fuss over her prom dress, no mother to wipe away tears of fear and frustration. Frankie's transition from adolescence to womanhood had been awkward and terrifying without a mother to guide her. Yet, she had survived it. And she would survive this too.

"I must find his will, Mama. Where would he have hidden it?"

After a long, exasperated sigh, Lucy said, "Carmel, most likely."

The Carmel house. The last place she saw her father alive. The place where they quarreled. The place where he told her to never darken his doorstep again. Emotions welled in her belly and for the second time that day Frankie felt sick. She didn't know if she could go back there and face the ghosts.

"I'm sure my efficient stepmother has gone through the house."

"Maybe, but she never liked that house. She doesn't know it like you do. Remember, you grew up there. You know all the nooks and crannies."

"Grazie," Frankie softly said, and heard the hitch in her voice.

"Go *now,* and watch your back."

"I will."

"And Francesca? Do not tell a soul where you're going."

For a long minute after she hung up the phone, Frankie digested her mother's words. Words she never would have believed could come from her mouth. Amazing. Just when she thought she knew someone, they turn out to be a different person. She shivered. Flashes of Sean's smiling, handsome face flashed in front of her. She'd been so caught up in his laughter, his passion, his love for her. The way he announced it to the world. Hell, even Jimmy Peanuts liked him. How wrong she had been.

"Frankie," Tawny said, bursting into her office. "Anthony called. He wants to talk to you."

Frankie scowled. "I have test shots to do."

"C'mon, Frankie. He said he was calling me because he didn't want you to hang up on him, and that he'd really like to talk to you. He sounded sincere."

Frankie's scowl deepened. Using her mother's words, she said, "I smell a fish." She stood. "I think I'll pass. I have too much to do right now. Besides, he's just going to rub what he thinks he's getting in my face."

Tawny's color paled. "But Frankie, he sounded like he really meant it. Shouldn't you at least hear what he has to say?"

"Since when do you defend my brother?"

"Since he could very well be my boss. I want peace here, Frankie, and it takes two."

"You are quite right, Tawny, but you fail to realize one minor detail. Until I have indisputable proof I don't have a job here, I will not speak to my brother about working for him."

"But—"

"No buts. *Skin* is mine, and until I'm pushing up daisies, that will not change."

Tawny was smart enough to retreat. Head down, she backed out of the office, once again neglecting to shut the door behind her. Frankie shook her head in exasperation. Despite Tawny's occasional lapses in manners, she was grateful for her assistant. The girl did whatever Frankie asked, and did it well.

Frankie glanced at her watch. Shit, she needed to get to the studio.

CHAPTER ELEVEN

"Everyone scram. This is now a closed set," Frankie announced, striding into the studio.

Reese grinned. Frankie didn't mess around, and he was glad she knew her staff. He'd met more of them than he cared to in the last twenty minutes. And most of them still hovered along the fringes of the studio, hoping, he was sure, to get a glimpse of his naked ass. Stripping for Frankie was one thing, but doing it for an audience was a whole different animal.

Frankie looked around at the hangers-on. They stood like deer caught in the proverbial headlights. She clapped her hands loudly. "Scram. Now!"

Like startled birds off a wire, they flocked out of the studio.

Frankie's eyes scanned the room. "Where is Stella? I need your palette."

Reese shrugged. "Tawny couldn't find her."

"And you'da thunk she'd have told me?"

Reese shook his head. Frankie was on a tear. He grinned. Her color was up, and although he'd enjoyed her in his black button-down, the emerald-colored shirt she'd changed into suited her. He liked the way the smooth, stretchy fabric hugged her tits. She had great tits. He'd dreamed about them last night. Full and warm, overflowing in his hands, the nipples several shades darker than her caramel-colored skin. Overly sensitive to his touch, especially his tongue.

"Reese!"

Frankie's voice snapped him out of his erotic daydream. "What?"

"I said, let's get this show on the road."

She moved past him and pulled back a large, heavy black curtain. She stepped into the dark room and suddenly it was drenched in light.

Reese nodded in approval. Though compact, the studio was versatile. Large backdrops hung off rolls tucked up high in the ceiling. Several props, chairs, sofas, tables, wineglasses, and even a motorcycle were neatly stowed in the corner. Tripods of different heights and widths hung from hooks in another corner. Various floor coverings were rolled neatly one on top of the other in another corner. Large decorated vignettes were neatly arranged behind the backdrops. A wide computer screen sat on a sleek black desk, with a keyboard nearby.

"I use almost all digital now," Frankie said, noticing his interest. "I can add color, take it out, change the lighting, your hair color." She laughed. "Even your cock size."

"Then what was the point of hiring me?"

"Because the one thing I can't add is charisma, and you have that in spades."

Frankie strode to the backdrops and pulled down a white one, then she rolled out a white plush carpet, settling it over the cool linoleum floor. She turned to give Reese instructions but he beat her to it. Her body reacted of its own stead. Some things one just couldn't control. And for Frankie it was the automatic warming her body reserved for Reese Barrett.

He stood half clothed. The muscular planes of his chest gleamed under the harsh lights of the set. He smiled, catching her eyes as he had earlier that day and holding them while he unsnapped the top button of his jeans. "That's enough for now," she said, her voice suddenly husky. "Just come over here and lie down on your back. I'll show you the pose."

Obediently, Reese walked past her to the white set and sat down on the carpet. His dark complexion stood out in stark contrast to the brilliant white of the backdrop and carpet. "Lie flat on your back and put your hands behind your head like you're going to do a sit-up."

He obliged. "Like this?"

She glanced down at him as she attached her camera to a tripod. His abdominal muscles bunched in hard symmetry. He flexed his biceps, and the full, round sinew jumped. She smiled, and he wagged his eyebrows at her. "I can flex more than that."

She laughed and adjusted the lights and scrim. Back at her camera, she focused. "I bet you can, now lie back."

He did, and she pushed the tripod over on its rollers until she was nearly on top of him. She adjusted the lens downward. "Close your eyes." He did. "I love it. A man who listens." She clicked a few frames. "Now slowly, as if you're awakening from a very sexy dream, open your eyes."

"Why don't you take off your shirt and skirt," he murmured, "and it won't be a sexy dream."

"Do it."

He did, and her heart stutter-stepped. His eyes speared her soul through the camera. Tamping down a surge of emotion, Frankie clicked away, moving closer. "Unbutton the top button of your jeans." He did, his eyes never leaving her lens.

"Now the next one."

His long, thick fingers nimbly opened the denim. Her lens caught the growing mound beneath, and her body responded accordingly. Heat pooled between her legs and her breasts tingled, her nipples tightening. As he slipped the next button open, she realized she wanted him. Right there on the soft white carpet, under the ever-watchful lens of her camera. He slipped open the fourth, then the fifth button. Her imagination ran wild, thinking of all the hot poses she could stage with herself as Reese's prop.

Her father's scowling face swam in front of her. The impulse to stick her tongue out at him was overwhelming. There was no law that said a girl couldn't fantasize.

His fingers slipped between the denim and his skin. Her moan startled her. At first she wasn't sure which one of them it came from. She licked her lips. "Reese." She heard the rasp in her voice.

"Frankie?" His voice mirrored hers. Deep. Husky. Wanting.

If she set the timer on the camera, slid her skirt up and her shirt down . . . "Slide your jeans down just a few inches."

He slowly hooked his fingers on a belt loop at each hip, then pulled down. Dark curly hair against deeply tanned skin emerged. Her pulse quickened.

"That's far enough," she softly said. She loosened the legs of the tripod to lower it, and in so doing straddled him.

"What are you thinking right now, Reese?"

"Me inside you."

Her body hitched. She was thinking the same thing. And she needed to stop it. "That's good." She focused on his lower extremity.

"You have my permission to fixate on me, as long as it gives you a rise and that smoldering look in your eyes."

It was crucial she know up front how well her subject could take direction and how much energy was required to get the ultimate response from him. She was more than happy to discover he took direction exceptionally well and that getting him into the mood was a piece of cake.

She knew from the minute he dropped his drawers in her office that he would be highly responsive. During her career, there had been only a handful of times when she and her subject had a synergy that came across in the photos, and she desperately wanted the spark of their chemistry to jump off the page and into her readers' eyes.

She wanted Reese hot and eager in the palm of her hands. She wanted to show the world what she could do. In that second, she decided playing his sexy little cat-and-mouse game could gain her far more than would drawing the professional-discretion line.

And so the game progressed. Reese's erection strained for release. She bit her bottom lip. "Touch yourself," she whispered.

"Look at me," he commanded.

"I am," she whispered.

"At my eyes."

Slowly, she dragged her gaze from his beautiful body to his equally beautiful eyes. "What?"

His jaw tightened and his eyes flinched, and she knew his hand had slipped beneath his pants. He hissed in a breath and for a moment his eyes fluttered, and his jaw tensed. "Now what?" he asked, his eyes steady and piercing.

"Squeeze."

His eyelids flickered, and she knew he'd obeyed. "Does that feel good, Reese?"

"It would feel better if it were your hand. Touch me, Frankie, and take the picture."

Her breath hitched low in her throat and her vaginal walls constricted. Warm moisture seeped into her panties, and she could smell the sultry musk of her sex. His nostrils twitched, and she knew he caught her scent too. Excitement burned through her. With practiced self-control, she put her eye to the camera and clicked. "Do you trust me, Reese?"

"No."

"If we're going to work together, we need to trust each other." His hips rose, brushing her leg. Frankie retracted. "Ah, ah, don't do that. No inappropriate touching."

"Define inappropriate."

"Touching unnecessary to the shot."

Small beads of perspiration dotted his forehead. He ground his teeth. "You drive a hard bargain, lady."

Pulling slightly away from the camera, Frankie winked at Reese, enjoying his discomfort more than she should. She'd guessed from the very beginning, Reese Barrett wasn't a man used to being rebuffed by women. "That I do, but the sacrifice is worth the prize."

"Touch me for the shot, Frankie," Reese said.

"You read my mind. I actually have something in mind."

Moving from her straddling position to his side, Frankie set the timer for five seconds. Kneeling on the plush carpet to his side, she set her open palm on Reese's belly. His warm skin trembled beneath her touch. The heel of her hand brushed the full head of his penis hiding just beneath the denim. He hissed in a breath, and she splayed her fingers, turning her hand slightly to the left. The shutter snapped. She sat back on her heels.

"That's going to be the first picture of you my readers will see," she said. "They'll know what's beneath my hand and they'll wait with bated breath for the next issue to see more."

"How do you know that shot will work?"

She caught the mischievous glint in his eyes, then stood and viewed the shot on the computer screen. Her feminine hand was a sharp contrast to the rigid planes of his belly. The mound beneath prominent. As good as it looked, her trained eye picked up the fact her fingers weren't spaced just right and the lighting was a tad off. She adjusted the gobo. She grinned. "I think I'll need a few more."

"Yeah, shoot till it's right," Reese said.

Frankie nodded. "For a model, you have a good eye."

"I have more than a good eye."

"You're arrogant."

"You're a prick tease."

"It's part of the job. I need you up for the shot." She laughed and reset her camera. But before she pushed the timer, she got serious. "Look, Reese, just lie back and relax. I need to set this shot up and comments from the peanut gallery will only make it take longer." Time was of the essence.

"By the time we go full frontal with you, Reese, you'll be the fantasy of every woman and her mother."

"What's *your* fantasy?"

Frankie stared at him, refusing to go down that road.

Reese reclined against the white carpet. "I'll tell you mine if you tell me yours."

"I'm not interested in your fantasies, only your body."

"That's one of my fantasies."

She spread her hand across his lower abdomen and frowned. Though he was still aroused, his erection had lost some of its volume. Grinning, she told him, "Appropriate-touching alert." Then rubbed the palm of her hand up the outline of his shaft from the base to the tip. Reese's hips bucked and she felt the hot surge through the fabric beneath her hand.

"Good boy."

"Did your last man indulge your fantasies?"

Frankie looked Reese directly in the eye. "I think we need to revisit a few ground rules here." As if she were sizing up a bag of fruit, she spread her hand across Reese's reinvigorated erection. Maintaining her business mien, she couldn't help an inward smile for the perks of her job. Satisfied, she set the camera. Placing her hand in the perfect position, she said, "Flex."

He did and the shutter clicked.

She turned to look at the shot on the screen. Perfect. She turned back to Reese and his long, warm fingers caressed the side of her hand. She steeled herself.

"I'm not interested in a relationship with you, Reese," she said matter-of-factly.

"You've misunderstood my signals, Frankie. A relationship is the last thing I want."

"Then . . ." Her face warmed. Why did she always think a guy wanted a relationship and she was the last one to find out they really wanted an in with her family? She looked at Reese with new interest. His candor surprised her. "You just want to have sex with me? No strings?"

"If it works for you."

"Sex isn't part of my current agenda."

He stood and slowly buttoned his jeans. She couldn't wait to get him on location.

"Change your agenda."

"If I did that, I wouldn't get any work done."

He grinned, his teeth brilliant under the bright light. "I'll keep my hands to myself, then."

She frowned, not used to men rejecting her so early in the game.

"Here's Stella," Tawny blurted out as she pushed through the thick black curtain into the studio. Frankie's temper flared. She was going to kill the little blonde.

What if she had been in the middle of a crucial shot?

"Damn it, Tawny, how many times do I have to tell you to knock first?"

The petite assistant slid to a halt and had the decency to look chagrined.

"Not to mention I have the 'Closed Set' sign out."

"I—I'm sorry, I just thought you'd be happy to have Stella here."

Frankie let out a long breath. She was. "I am." Turning to Reese, she said, "I need a break, and you need your scheme done. I'll be back in about a half hour. Do you want anything from Baccio's across the street?"

"No thanks."

Frankie shot Tawny a glare. "I'll be across the street."

Tawny nodded but kept her eyes downcast. As soon as Frankie exited through the curtain, Tawny smiled at Reese. "I'll be back in a flash," she said, and disappeared through the curtain.

Looking over her shoulder, Tawny grabbed her cell phone off the clip at her hip and punched in a number.

"Yeah," a gruff male voice answered.

"She's on her way to Baccio's."

The phone clicked in her ear and she scowled at it. The prick. If it wasn't for her, he'd have nothing. She gave the phone a one-finger salute and snapped it shut, then inserted it back into the clip. She looked up to find Reese staring at her from a part in the black curtain.

"Ready?" she asked, her voice an octave too high.

Reese nodded, and she silently cursed under her breath while she manufactured a saccharine smile. "Well then, let's get busy!"

CHAPTER TWELVE

Frankie strode into Baccio's deciding her body needed a triple espresso to kick her brain into overdrive. She needed to pack up and get down to Carmel. She was taking Reese along. A two-for-one deal she couldn't pass up. She warmed as she thought of the shots she'd get down there. And during the downtime she'd tear that place apart one square inch at a time until she found the will.

She glanced around and scowled as the corner door to the street opened. Anthony.

Her brother strode into the café, his signature smug smile twisting his handsome lips. For a long moment she wondered why she didn't take her mom up on her invitation and chuck it all, move to Arizona and live the life of a normal person. She watched her brother approach. As a child he wasn't completely to blame. Connie had made sure there was no love lost between the siblings.

As adults it was too late for them now. Anthony was the son of a once powerful mafia boss. Those were intimidating footsteps to fill. There was no time, even if there was motivation, for him to resurrect a relationship with Frankie. She accepted it as fact and ignored the stab of pain that went with it.

He walked straight toward her. She stiffened. "Anthony, I have no intention of discussing *Skin* with you."

"Then how about Father's will?"

She narrowed her eyes with renewed irritation, stopping a few steps from the counter and turning to order. Beatrice scowled at her, and Frankie scowled back. Old biddy.

"Bea," Anthony said, "how about a triple for my sweet sis, and a mocha over ice for me?"

The old woman's gap-toothed grin beamed. Anthony smiled at Frankie, the gesture for once apparently genuine. Frankie's antennae shot up. Anthony, congenial?

"What do you want?" she asked.

"Peace, believe it or not."

"Or not. Please, Tony, you can't stand me and I can't stand you. There will never be peace until one of us is lying six feet under next to Father."

"Look," he said, lowering his voice and looking around for avid ears, "I think that codicil my mother produced is a fake."

Frankie gasped, shocked at his candor. "Why would you tell me that? You get everything."

"Not exactly. I get control of joint family business, but it's discretionary. Carmine and the capos have the ultimate say. I will not be don."

Ah yes, the ultimate power.

"I happen to want to live, and until the notarized copy of Papa's most recent will is found, it wouldn't surprise me if I have a price on my head."

"Who would want you dead? Why do *you* think it's fake?"

"The surrounding families have been very quiet these last couple of weeks. Too quiet. That means they have something in the works, and I'm figuring it's to get me out of the way. So it could be any of them. You can't tell me you haven't felt the tension."

Frankie nodded.

"Why do I think it's fake? Because it doesn't read anything like what Father told me he was going to do. It doesn't add up."

Exactly, because *Skin* was promised to her. "Why would your mother produce a document to the contrary?"

"She's afraid for me. And she's terrified of Unk. While I can't get her to admit it's a fake, she feels she's doing what is best for me."

Or covering her own ass. "What does she have against Unk?"

Anthony shrugged. "I'm not really sure, I've never been able to put my finger on it, but there is definite tension between the two. A mutual dislike."

"Here you go, *caro,*" Bea said, sliding the two cups across the counter. When Anthony went for his wallet, the old bat smiled and fluttered her lashes. "On me."

Frankie shook her head. She spent a fortune every month at the café and had yet to gain "on me" status.

Sipping her espresso, Frankie moved to one of the tables in the corner by the front window. "After last night I'd think you'd have an aversion to windows," he said.

"How'd you know about last night?"

Anthony raised his brows. "Everyone knows about last night."

She impulsively touched her fingertips to the Band-Aid on her arm. She'd been so caught up in her business woes, she'd completely forgotten.

"I wasn't the target. It was Unk." They moved further into the café and sat down at a table in the back, near the restrooms. "Who wants Carmine dead?"

"Everyone who wants a piece of the Santini pie."

Frankie's eyes narrowed. It was a very large, lucrative pie. "I only want what is rightfully mine."

"Would you consider co-owning *Skin?* Without the naked men?"

"No. Start your own magazine."

"Like Sean and Lindsey?"

Pain stabbed her heart. Not for Sean, but for what she thought they had and what she thought she lost. And for his ultimate betrayal. "Yes, exactly."

Frankie regrouped. This was her chance to appeal to Anthony in a civilized manner to back off. If he refused? Well, then she was her father's daughter after all.

Leaning toward him, she said, "Let's be clear here, Anthony. Father promised me *Skin.* I don't believe he gave you control of his share. It was and has always been understood that *Skin* was Unk's and mine."

"That might be true, but Father held the control in trust—"

"I'll take my chances, Anthony. If I have to plead my case to the family, so be it. You have no experience in this field, and you can make no valid case why you should be given control of the trust. I'll do what's necessary to keep what is mine."

"Are you threatening me?"

"No, I'm telling you if the will doesn't surface, the one where Father left me *Skin,* my gloves come off and I'll go to the family for their blessing." She set her cup down and looked hard at him. "Besides, why would you want to mess with a moneymaking venture? I mean come on, *Skin* is a cash cow and it's going to get even bigger with what I have planned. Isn't that the bottom line?"

"I won't have the family involved in your version of *Playgirl.*"

Frankie laughed, genuinely amused. "It's just business, Anthony, get with it."

"Is embezzlement just business too?"

His question stopped her laughter cold. "What?"

"The money you stole from Father."

"Are you crazy?"

Anthony's face clouded in disgust. "I knew you'd deny it."

A sudden realization dawned on her. And her gut roiled. Silently she cursed herself for ever believing Anthony would fight fair. "You're good, Anthony. I see what you're trying to do here, but spreading rumors so the capos will look at me walleyed won't work."

Anthony set his cup on the tabletop and stood. "Watch me."

Frankie quickly followed his lead. All signs of amicability evaporated. She nodded, leaned close to him, and softly said, "As usual, your true colors bleed through. I don't care how any will reads. I don't care what crazy accusations you come up with, but mark my words. You will *not* take my magazine from me."

She pushed the chair out of her way and strode toward the front door. Anthony hurried up behind her. "You're making a big mistake, Frankie. I hold all of the cards."

"Then I guess, Anthony, you need to produce a bona fide will to prove it."

The cool autumn air hit her in the face and she squinted against the sharp bites of rain. The weather had changed. Only an hour ago the skies sported white fluffy clouds. How quickly Mother Nature changed her mind. Without turning to face Anthony, Frankie continued toward the street.

She stepped out onto the asphalt, scanning both ways for oncoming vehicles. The street clear, she stepped between two parked cars and hurried away from her irate brother.

"Sleep with your eyes open, sister," he called.

Frankie wheeled around. "Are you threatening me?"

He strode toward her, his hair blowing in the chilly air. He looked like Satan's minion. And for the first time in her life, she felt afraid of her brother.

"A warning."

She tamped down her fear and laughed in his face. "Poor baby Anthony. He can't have his way and Mama isn't here to get it for him. So he resorts to juvenile threats of violence." She turned and strode away from him.

Anthony grabbed her by the elbow and spun her around in the middle of the street. "Don't force my hand on this."

She shoved him away, breaking his grip. "Don't force mine."

The sound of a revved engine drew her attention down the street. A black car rounded the corner behind Anthony. Dark tinted windows glinted at her.

"Anthony!" She grabbed his arms. He pulled away. She grabbed him again, this time twisting him toward her in order to push him to the side and out of the way of the oncoming car. "Anthony, move!" she screamed when he fought back.

He grabbed her back toward him, his face twisted in hatred.

"No!" she screamed as the car approached. An instant later she was hit from behind and propelled straight into Anthony's chest, the velocity of the hit sending them flying several feet into the air before they landed between the two parked cars she'd only moments before walked between. The black car sped by. Frankie lay stunned, her brother on top of her, trying to comprehend what just happened.

"Are you all right?" Reese asked from above her.

"What the hell happened?" she gasped, her body shaking violently. She'd almost been killed—*again*.

Anthony sputtered and cursed, pushing up off Frankie.

Reese reached down and pulled Frankie to her feet, bringing her close. He let Anthony help himself up. Frankie pushed away, her limbs wobbly. As she brushed debris from her skirt and shirt, she looked down at her brother through narrowed eyes, anger overriding her shock. "You idiot, I was trying to get you out of the street. That car was gunning for you."

Anthony stopped midbrush, realization dawning on him. "You thought that car was going to run me down?"

"Yes, and it would have if Reese hadn't pushed us out of the way."

Anthony's features hardened before his eyes darted nervously up and down the street. "You tried to save my life?"

"You're my brother." And God help them both.

Anthony stood silent for a long moment. From the back-and-forth play on his face, she bet he was talking himself out of thanking her. Typical. Their mutual dislike and the fact he'd just threatened her aside, she didn't want to see her brother dead.

She stepped to the curb and with shaky hands continued to brush the road dust from her clothes. She glanced at Reese, who didn't look the least bit disturbed. She leashed her body's urge to shake. Licking her dry lips, she straightened her spine and lifted her chin.

"I thought you'd be busy with Stella until closing time."

The fine lines around Reese's blue eyes crinkled. "I got bored."

CHAPTER THIRTEEN

"Do you really believe that car was after your brother? Collecting herself, Frankie nodded. "It came straight for *him.*"

And didn't he just admit to her that he felt the surrounding families were gunning for him?

"It came straight at both of you."

"Your imagination is running wild, Reese. *If,* and that's a big if, that car was looking to mow me down, it wouldn't have been so obvious. It's not how the family works."

"So you're saying if someone was trying to kill you, it would be your family?"

Frankie opened her mouth to deny what he said, but caught herself. Her subconscious knew he spoke the truth, but her heart refused to believe it. "No! You're confusing me. There is no reason for anyone in my family, including Anthony, to want me dead. And what if Anthony did? He isn't so stupid to almost get himself killed in the process of killing me."

Reese stared at her, incredulous. "You really should listen to yourself. A pattern has been established. You've been shot. A threatening box is put on your desk in your locked office telling you in no uncertain terms your time is up, and now you nearly get run over. Are you blind or too foolish to see it?"

Frankie shook her head. The clock prank was all Anthony. His way of giving her the jitters. He did that kind of crap. She considered explaining to Reese what was brewing in the family, and then he would understand that there was no one after her. Anthony and her uncle, maybe—okay, probably—but not her. But her family strife was just that, *her* family's strife. Sharing it with an outsider could get someone else hurt.

"I'm a realist, and I have my reasons. Anthony may be a lot of things, but he isn't a killer. He doesn't have the balls or the stomach for it. He's the type that likes to pull the wings off flies and watch them suffer. Just like he's trying to do to me right now. There's no fun for him if I'm not suffering."

"Maybe it isn't Anthony."

"Okay, Reese, I'll play devil's advocate with you." Maybe that would shut him up. "If my brother isn't after me, who the hell is and why?"

"Who have you pissed off?"

Without missing a beat, Frankie answered, "My father and he's dead."

"What did you do?"

"None of your business."

"Stop fooling yourself, Frankie."

"Anthony was the target."

Reese scowled down at her, slowing his pace as they entered her building so she could keep up. "Looked to me like maybe you both were."

She'd never hurt anyone. Unable to wrap her brain around the fact that someone wanted her dead, she continued. "Listen to me. Last night that shot was meant for my uncle. He's in an enviable position. He inherits my father's power and all that goes with it, even if it may just be temporary. Never mind Anthony will in all probability get it. Anthony has to prove himself to the family, then there has to be a vote. If Carmine is knocked off, then maybe another interim don—er, boss will be named. Maybe not. So I can see why someone would want Carmine out of the way. I can see lots of people wanting Anthony's head on a pike. He's made a lot of enemies over the years. With my father out of the picture, there won't be the retaliation for knocking him off like there would have been if my father was alive."

"What about the clock?"

"I told you. Anthony's scare tactic. He wants *Skin,* and for a second I was scared."

Once they entered the elevator, Reese stood quietly absorbing her words. She looked solemnly at him. "It's not me they want, Reese. I swear it."

"Who would gain with you dead?"

Frankie let out a long breath. "Anthony."

"Then I suggest you keep him close."

"I told you, Anthony doesn't have it in him. And he doesn't have the power yet. He couldn't even order a hit." When they reached her office door she turned to Reese. "And let me tell you this. If Anthony or anyone so much as looked at me wrong? You saw how Unk was last night. He's worse than ten *nonas.* He would hunt the bastards down and kill them himself. All of the Bay Area families know that, and a good many So Cal families."

Reese opened his mouth to comment but she put her hand up, halting him. "Am I so arrogant like my father to think I'm untouchable? No, but there would be nothing gained by my death. With the family, *there has to be gain.* They don't kill for pleasure."

She put her hand on the doorknob. "I've said too much already. I won't discuss this matter with you again. Now, please get down to the studio so we can finish up your scheme and get the hell out of here. I have plans for us."

Reese cocked a dark brow. "Care to share?"

"I will when I come for you."

She turned and entered her office, loudly closing the door behind her.

Making her way to her small bathroom, Frankie tidied up, her thoughts zigzagging. She refused to give Reese, an outsider, another word on the topic of Anthony ordering a hit on her. It was preposterous. She even pushed her worry over her uncle aside. He was a big boy and had plenty of muscle. Since her father's death, Carmine's men had made themselves very noticeable. Besides, she didn't have time to worry, she had business to take care of.

"Tawny!" she called through the open door. The spunky assistant popped in, her brows raised. "Make sure I have a key to Anthony's office. And have the locksmith re-key mine."

"Will do."

Reese sat patiently while Stella the wardrobe/hair stylist/makeup tech draped him with one swatch of colors after another. "My best color is naked."

The older woman stuttered and stammered, and he smiled. It was in his best interest to have as many *Skin* employees in his pocket as possible.

He heard the click of Frankie's heels coming into the room before he saw her tall, curvy body, her head held high, her stride confident.

Her energy filled the room. His blood quickened in immediate response. He might be there to work a case, but he found himself sucked in by her on more than one occasion and on several levels. He constantly reminded himself he was there to do a job, not get tangled up in an emotional quagmire.

His libido, however, had other ideas. Francesca Donatello had become an incessant itch he couldn't scratch.

"Stop pestering my employees, Barrett. I'd hate to have to slap you with a sexual harassment suit."

"He wasn't bothering me, Frankie." Stella draped a large swatch of royal-blue cloth across one of Reese's broad shoulders and down his chest.

Frankie stopped in her heels. "Perfect color, Stella. Matches his eyes." Crossing her arms across her chest to cover her suddenly hardening nipples, Frankie nodded at him. "I see a beach location in your future. I'd love to get a shot of you naked coming out of the surf, your hair all wet and those big hands of yours brushing it out of your eyes as the afternoon sun glistens off your hard, wet body." The picture she painted stirred every nerve south of her neck. Stella sighed and Frankie glanced at her, a wistful look softening the hard edges of Stella's face.

Frankie laughed. "Earth to Stella."

The old woman shook her head, her face pinkening.

"I know he's hard to resist, but you can do it," Frankie said.

Reese scowled as if embarrassed, which Frankie knew was impossible. The man ate up attention.

"He likes women, and that makes a big difference," Stella admitted.

Reese waved a hand in front of Frankie. "I'm here, so knock off the third-person dialogue."

Frankie laughed and stepped close enough to touch him. "Feel like an insignificant piece of meat, do you?"

He scowled hard.

Taking his chin in her hand, she wagged it. "Imagine how it is for all of us women."

He grabbed her hand and bit the tip of her index finger. When she pulled away he increased the pressure. His eyes sparked and she felt a hard rush of heat. He sucked her finger into his mouth and tongued it.

She yanked her hand from him and cursed the cool air as it crossed the warm moistness of her fingertip. Damn, he was distracting.

"Stella, can you finish up later? I need to have a chat with Mr. Skin here."

Stella nodded, giving Reese a longing glance. He rewarded her with a wicked smile. The old woman returned it, then scampered out of the room.

Frankie stood with her hands on her hips and tapped her toe on the linoleum floor. "Stop seducing my employees."

Reese stood up. "Stop being so naive."

Back to that again? "Stop trying to scare me."

"You don't get it, do you, Donatello?"

"Do you always call your lady bosses by their last name?"

"Only the stupid ones."

"You're fired."

"It's really a moot point, since at your current hit rate, you'll be dead by the end of the week."

Frankie stopped short. "Even if you are right, which you aren't, we're leaving town tonight, so whoever you think is after me will have to find me, and since you'll be the only person who knows where I'll be, I guess we'll be fine."

He swiped his hand across his chin. "I can't just up and leave town. And what the hell for?"

"I'm beginning to feel like a damn parrot with you, Reese. I own your ass. You go wherever, whenever. The when is tonight, the where is Carmel, and I would greatly appreciate it if you kept that information to yourself."

"If someone wants you, they'll find you."

He could worry for them both and in the end see that it was all for naught. Moving closer into Reese's personal space, Frankie smiled up at him. "It has occurred to me, I owe you."

Reese raised a dark brow and grinned down at her. "Big-time."

"Can I touch you?"

He nodded.

She wrapped her arms around his neck.

"Can I kiss you?"

He nodded again.

On her tiptoes, she pressed her lips to his—the force of the contact jolting.

Frankie meant to give him a thank-you peck on the cheek, but the meeting of their lips morphed into a wild moment. His arms slid around her waist, pulling her tightly against his hard chest. She opened her mouth, allowing her tongue to meet his. His hands slid down the small of her back to rest on the swell of her ass. The hard strength of him pressing intimately against her sent her senses reeling.

Her lips parted further and she rolled her tongue languidly against his. He tasted . . . dangerous. Excitement filled her and the realization she wanted to tame this glorious man hit her broadside. The thought sent a bolt of desire straight to her womb.

As abruptly as she started the kiss, Reese ended it. Stunned, she stood breathless, glad he didn't completely release her but kept her within the hot circle of his arms. "I don't do mafia princesses." He set her away from him, a rueful look on his face as he looked down to the obvious mound below his belt.

"I'm not a mafia princess."

"That's not what I hear. Besides, you have a price on your head. And if I allow you to make love to me, that might piss someone off, like your uncle or that crazy Peanut."

Frankie laughed. "It's Jimmy Peanuts and he's not crazy."

Reese's expression turned serious. "Kidding aside, Frankie, call the cops and let them get in on this."

"I told you, I don't do cops. I'll call my uncle *if* I need protection. My family can handle it." She turned and started toward the computer stand, where swatches lay in colorful disarray.

"Like they did for your father?"

She whirled around and faced him, an unexpected surge of emotion welling up in her. "Don't."

"Don't what? Speak the truth? Was he as arrogant as you? Did he walk around feeling bulletproof like the Pope did thirty years ago? Did Santo Gabriel think he was immortal?"

"How do you know that?"

"I read the paper."

"Who are you?"

"An airhead model can't read the newspaper?"

"And kick three of my cousins' asses at the same time, tell my uncle you'll kill him, and then save my life and my dumb-ass brother's?"

Reese shrugged. "I've been around."

"Around who? Rambo?"

"Nah. I was a nerd in school and decided I was tired of the bullies pushing me around. It's why I did the military thing."

"You, a nerd? I hardly think so."

He shrugged. "It's all about perception, Frankie. What you think you see may not actually be the reality."

She grinned. "Now *that* I can relate to. It's what I do with my camera. I'm going to give every red-blooded female in this country the illusion she has a chance with you."

"Ah, back to business."

Damn straight. Business was safer than the way he made her feel. "It's what makes the world go round. Now let's get a few test shots."

An hour later they were on their way to Reese's place.

"After we get your stuff, take me back to my uncle's office. I need to get my car. You can follow me to my place. I'll throw a few things together and we'll head to Carmel."

Reese nodded. "Sounds like a plan."

Frankie settled back into the comfortable captain seat. "You know, I think this is going to be huge. You and *Skin.*"

Reese nodded but remained silent.

"For copy, I'm thinking you can answer questions from readers. We'll set up an e-mail addy for you. Each issue until your reveal, you answer sexy questions." Frankie laughed. "Maybe you can find *your* fantasy woman."

Reese speared her a harsh look.

Warming to the subject, Frankie turned to face him. "Tell me."

He continued to look straight ahead, his concentration on the road ahead. "Tell you what."

"Your ultimate fantasy."

Reese shook his head and cast her a scowl. "You won't like it."

"Try me."

A half smile twisted his lips. "My ultimate fantasy is for once to have a woman I just made love to not want to set up house."

Frankie coughed, not expecting that. "Oh, puhleese. I doubt every woman who sleeps with you wants to have your babies."

He cocked a brow and looked at her. "You'd be surprised." Looking back at the road, he asked, "Why is that?"

"Why is what?"

"Why do women want to instantly nest? Why can't a woman just have sex for the fun of it? Live for the moment? Why does it always have to be more?"

Frankie shrugged. It bugged her that Reese spoke the truth. While she hadn't been a wallflower when it came to sex, and she always had a bevy of wannabes to choose from, she'd selected her lovers with extreme care and thoughts of future potential. After it became painfully apparent by her senior year of college that men were more interested in her last name than her personally, she'd sworn them off. Until Sean walked through her door. She really believed he was "the one." She learned painfully that he was not.

Frankie sighed and looked out the window. The sun was beginning to set. She was tired and wanted a good night's sleep. Somehow she didn't think she'd get it.

Her thoughts drifted back to Sean. Two years later she was still fighting for respect in the industry, and from the men in her family, as well as her own self-respect. The emotional ruin had taken longer. At least she could think of Sean now without the uncontrollable urge to rip his balls from between his legs and stuff them down his throat.

Even so, the fallout continued. Before Sean, she never second-guessed herself. Since Sean, it had become a habit. Hiring Reese was the latest example of her inner debate. She needed to stop it. She needed to just go with her gut and trust herself. Realizing her fists were clenched, Frankie relaxed them.

"What are you thinking?" Reese asked.

"I was thinking that most every pretty boy I've ever met has been arrogant and untrustworthy, and if for some reason I found myself waking up next to you in the morning, I could walk away from you as easily as from a bad cold."

"Bad colds linger."

She gave a laugh, a caustic edge lacing it. "Don't kid yourself, Reese. I can be every bit a man about sex. I'm not one of those cling-on types."

"So you caught your pretty boy in the sack, huh?"

"Hardly."

"And since he screwed you, you put us all in the same category."

"Butt out."

"Just don't let it affect our working relationship."

Frankie faced him. "Since when do you worry about a working relationship? All you've tried to do is get me out of my skirt."

Reese glanced at her and flashed a wolfish grin. "I don't need to get you out of your skirt to do what I want."

"There you go again."

He turned back to focus on the road. "Point taken. I apologize. I will from this point forward speak only about business. The last thing I want is to jeopardize my job, or whatever friendship we may develop."

Frankie opened her mouth to protest, to tell him joking around was okay, she liked it, from him, it made her feel—wanted. But she didn't. It was better this way.

CHAPTER FOURTEEN

Frankie walked ahead of Reese into his condo. Two men stood in the middle of the living room. On the floor a man rolled around like a trussed-up hog. It took her a moment to notice ropes around his ankles and tied to his hands behind his back. Another moment before she got a good look at his face. Was that . . . "Jimmy?"

The two men turned, their eyes intense and intimidating. Then she noticed their bodies, even more intimidating. What the hell? Her skin flushed and her lips formed a silent *O*, Jimmy forgotten.

Holy shit. The two guys in front of her could give Reese a run for his money. If he didn't fall in line, she'd offer one of these two—or hell, both of them—a contract.

Jimmy's muffled scream pulled her back to reality. Reluctantly she tore her gaze from the men to look down at her cousin.

"Why is he tied up? And why the hell is he here?"

"Hey, boys!" Reese stepped over a red-faced, grunting Jimmy. Frankie bent down to pull the sock out of his mouth. Reese caught her arm, holding her back.

"We came by to say hi and found this goombah lurking in your hall closet," the Adonis with the long black hair and slight Latin accent explained.

Jimmy squirmed against his ties.

"And we were just having a beer, deciding what we were going to do with him if you didn't show up soon," the hunk with milk-chocolate-colored hair and laughing green eyes said.

"Who the hell are you two?" Frankie demanded. She scowled, tapping her foot on the carpet and wondered why the hell her cousin was hiding in a closet in her model's house.

The tall, very dark one with deep hazel eyes that glowed like opals stepped over Jimmy and extended his hand to her. Trancelike, she took it. Long, firm fingers wrapped securely around her hand. She shivered. "I'm Ricco, an old buddy of Reese's."

The other one stepped over Jimmy, accidentally kicking him in the ass, and smiled, his dimples disarming her. She knew her mouth was open but she didn't care. He took her other hand, hanging limply at her side, into his big warm ones and brought it to his lips. After he kissed it a tad too long, he looked up at her and flashed a wolfish grin. "I'm Jase. I used to model with Reese when he was doing underwear ads for Sears."

Reese pushed them both away from Frankie, gifting them with an angry glare.

Ricco laughed and slapped him on the back. "C'mon, man, what happened to all for one and one for all?"

"You have your own if I remember correctly. Do you want to share?"

Ricco laughed and finished the bottle of beer in his left hand. "Nope, Alex would skin me alive."

"Then don't expect me to."

Frankie coughed, disappointed far more than she wanted to admit. "Damn. I knew it."

All three men looked at her. "You're too damned good-looking to be straight." She turned to Jase. "You too?"

Ricco spewed the beer in his mouth and wiped his mouth with the back of his hand. "Alexandra is my fiancée."

Reese and Jase laughed. Heat infused her cheeks. "Oh."

Jase stepped closer, took her hand again, and put it over his heart. The heat of his body warmed her fingers. "I'll gladly take this Neanderthal also known as Reese Barrett off your hands. Just give me the word and he's history."

Frankie played along. "I'm afraid I'm contractually obligated to him. We'd have to permanently off him."

"No problem. I know people."

The hair on her arms rose, and she pulled her hand away from Jase's chest, her jovial mood darkening. "Yeah, so do I."

The three men exchanged a look, and Jimmy screamed on the floor, the sock muffling the sound.

Frankie dropped down to her knees and took the sock out of Jimmy's mouth. "Why are you here?"

He sputtered and spit fibers from his mouth. "I was worried about you."

"So worried you had to hide in the closet?"

"I heard voices, and yours wasn't one of them."

She untied his hands, then his feet. He rubbed his wrists first, then his ankles, while he studied the three men who had turned away from him like he was no more threatening than a fly. "Don't even think about it, Jimmy," she warned, her voice low.

"Those guys ain't models."

Frankie thought the same thing. It was her biz to know who was hot and who was not. She'd know about Jase if he was legit. First chance she got, she was going to have Unk run Mr. Skin.

Reese turned his attention to Jimmy. "Rick's a promoter. The next time you're in Europe you'll see Jase's face plastered on every billboard from Spain to Russia."

Jimmy slowly stood. "Gimme my piece back."

Ricco shook his head. "No can do, Jimbo."

Jimmy was smart enough not to push it.

"I'll leave it here for Frankie to give you when we're gone," Reese said.

"You telling me to take a hike?"

Jase smiled tolerantly. "That's exactly what he's saying."

Jimmy glanced at Frankie. She shrugged.

The situation was uncomfortable enough without him. "Go on, Jimmy. I'll bring your gun to the office."

Once Jimmy exited the condo, Frankie turned to the three men, her feet apart, her hands on her hips. The men had bodies and faces any woman would drool over, but Jimmy was right, something about them . . . their characters were as hard as their bodies. "Who the hell are you guys?"

Reese walked past her and grabbed a beer from the fridge. "Would you like one?"

"I want answers, not alcohol."

"Ricco and Jase told you who they are and what they do. What else do you want?"

"The truth."

Jase chuckled. "Okay, Frankie, we'll level with you. I'm a woman trapped in a man's body and Ricky here is my lover."

"Jase, tell her the *real* truth," Reese said, his tone ominous.

Jase's features lost their humor. "Are you serious?"

Reese nodded, his face mirroring Jase's. Ricco stepped forward and put a hand on Frankie's shoulder. "You'd better sit down for this."

Finally. Answers. Frankie sat on the sofa.

His face solemn, Jase sat down next to Frankie and took her hands into his. "You have to promise not to repeat a word of what I tell you. If you do?" He looked at Ricco and Reese, then back to her. "I'll have to kill you."

Frankie saw the hardness in his face. The guy wasn't kidding. She swallowed hard and nodded. "I promise."

"Ricco, Reese and I are foster brothers who were captured when we were five by members of the planet Hogarth. They've just recently released us back to earth."

Frankie yanked her hands from his and stood. "Screw all three of you." All three men raised their brows and Jase and Reese grinned. And it looked like Ricco was fighting one and losing.

She strode down the hallway to the bathroom. When she came back into the living room, all three men were sitting at the kitchen table, beer in hand, laughing and making merry at her expense. Assholes.

She grabbed a napkin from the counter and scribbled her address on it. She threw it at Reese. "There's my address. Be there in an hour or you're fired."

She stalked past them to the front door and slammed it shut behind her. Hiking her bag over her shoulder, Frankie winced. She'd ignored the dull throb of it all day. Continuing to do so, she headed for the front gate. Halfway there, she pulled her cell phone out and called a cab. Then called her uncle. She frowned when she got his voice mail. He rarely had his cell phone turned on. He wasn't big on electronic leashes. *"I grew up without a remote or a computer,* cara, *I don't need a phone ringing in my pocket all day."*

"It's me, Unk. I'd like you to ask around about a Reese Barrett. I can get you his particulars later. Also, I had a little chat with my brother today. He said there was money missing from *Skin* and accused me of stealing it. I'm not sure what he's up to, but I wanted to let you know before you heard his accusations as a rumor. Ciao."

The door had barely slammed shut when Reese pulled out his cell phone and punched in a number.

"Yeah," a voice answered.

"The fox has bolted, put a tail on her."

"Done."

He flipped the phone shut and the three men looked at one another seriously, then cracked up in laughter.

Reese smacked Jase on the back. "That was good. I think Frankie bolted the quickest."

Ricco smiled. "They fall for it every time. But she's a smart one. You have your hands full."

"She has more than a handful," Jase quipped.

Reese's eyes narrowed. "Mine."

Jase threw his hands up and backed away. "I think the lady has a different idea, but I'll give you your shot. Then"—Jase cracked his knuckles and flexed his biceps—"the master will take over."

"When this case is over she's fair game."

Ricco quirked a brow. "You mean there will be leftover Frankie?"

Reese drained the rest of his beer. "I misspoke. I'll be off on my next UC. If Jase wants to pursue once this case is closed, I won't stand in his way."

Jase looked hard at Reese. "She doesn't do anything for you?"

Reese shrugged. She did something for him, all right. He was a constant walking hard-on. There was more to what she did to him than the physical, but that tidbit he kept to himself. "She's female, I'm male, on that level, yes."

Jase nodded. "She seems to be more than just female."

"She's got a temper."

"What else?"

Reese scowled. "Nothing else. I'm in it for the case. She's a means to an end. Stop trying to read something else into it."

"Sure, buddy, you always look at every female with lust in your eyes."

Reese shrugged the accusation off. Of the three, he was the reticent one.

"This is really a stretch for you, Reese, acting like Mr. Outgoing."

Jase laughed and grabbed another beer from the fridge. "Yeah, I'll hand over my Mr. Congeniality crown to you."

"Don't bother."

Jase glanced up at his buddy, a cryptic look crossing his face. "You falling for her act?"

"What act is that?"

"Miss Innocent."

"Hardly. Last night, she was either in the wrong place at the wrong time, or the right place and the shooter has bad aim. This afternoon she was walking across Post with her brother and they were both targeted for a hit-and-run. Again, either she's in the wrong place at the wrong time or the driver didn't move fast enough. I think it's too coincidental. I think she's the target."

Jase nodded and looked at Ricco before he looked at Reese. "We'll explore that, but I still say she's tit-deep in this."

Reese's cell phone beeped and he put it to his ear. "Yeah."

"The fox is being hunted."

"Got it." He clicked off the phone and looked hard at his cohorts. "Time for action. Frankie has an unfriendly tailing her."

Reese headed back to the spare room that served as an office and pulled his piece out from his desk's false bottom.

CHAPTER FIFTEEN

As she walked through the door of her town house Frankie stopped dead in her tracks. Shock registered. Fear flashed. Anger erupted. *Sonofabitch!*

Her brand-new sofa lay on its back, the fabric slashed to ribbons, the stuffing strewn all around. Her *nona* Fazzio's stained-glass Tiffany lamp lay broken and scattered across the shredded carpet. Paintings that had been in her family for years hung askew or were tossed on the floor along with the other carnage. Her hands shook. A deadly silence permeated her home.

Who did this? Who the hell broke into her house and violated everything she held sacred? Frankie dug her can of pepper spray out of her purse, wishing she had a gun instead.

Slowly she walked through the living room, glass and broken pottery crunching underfoot, to the equally destroyed dining room and then into the kitchen. Her china and crystal were shattered into millions of shards on the floor, the drawers pulled and dumped. The pantry door hung agape, the contents strewn everywhere.

Fury infused every cell of her body. Then Reese's words resonated in her mind. *"It's you they want."*

Even as the evidence lay before her, she still could not fathom why anyone, including Anthony, wanted her dead. For a long minute she stood silent, her gaze touching on the destruction, her eyes missing nothing. Every crevice, every corner, every layer was disturbed. Like someone was looking for something. What? Did someone think she had her father's will?

She stepped over the ruin in the kitchen and made her way down the hallway to her home studio. Her anger swelled. Her equipment was broken and thrown, her computer in pieces on the floor. Putting the pepper spray back in her purse, she set it and the camera bag down next to the splintered wood that was once her copy table. She bent down to pick up her old Nikon, surprised it was still intact. The treasured camera was one of the few things her father had given her. Sadness rushed through her and she wished she'd had a much different relationship with the man responsible for her birth.

She had gingerly set the camera on the window ledge and pulled her cell phone from her purse to call Unk when she heard the soft crunch of glass underfoot in the kitchen. She froze, terrified. Friend or foe? Her eyes darted around the room, already knowing what her brain knew. No way out and no escape route without being seen. She was trapped. No place to hide. The door to the closet hung awkwardly from one hinge. Impulsively, she darted through the doorway and upstairs to her bedroom and the cavernous walk-in closet.

She made the sign of the cross as she breathed a quick breath of relief. The door was secure, though open. She slipped inside and pulled the door almost all the way shut, keeping it cracked just enough to peek through and see the person who was going to pay with his life for destroying everything she'd worked so hard for.

Her heart beat like a kettledrum in her ears as she listened to the footsteps methodically go from room to room, stopping and starting. Realizing she left her purse downstairs in the office, she choked.

"Please, don't find it."

The footsteps halted at the bottom of the stairway.

"Breathe," she whispered to herself when she realized she was holding her breath, and then remembered the softball bat in the far corner of the closet. Slowly she backed up, feeling with her hand along the wall. She almost stumbled over a heap of clothes the shit disturber threw when he wrecked her closet. Squatting, she felt underneath the mounds of clothing. Just when she was about to cry in frustration, she touched the hard aluminum grip. Carefully she pulled it out from under the heavy mound of clothes. Her eyes adjusted in the darkness and she made out a blanket tangled around a pile of shoes. Setting the bat aside, she pulled the blanket up and draped it over the long hanger rung. Slipping behind it would offer small cover, but at least no one would open the closet door and see her standing there, a panicked mess.

Bat in one hand, Frankie tiptoed to the cracked door. Her gut lurched and she felt like she was going to throw up. The footsteps were entering her room. For a long minute there was no sound. She couldn't make out the person standing in her doorway; only a long shadow gave him away as he viewed the ripped sheets and guts of her mattress strewn over the room like snow in Tahoe.

Gripping the bat with her right hand, she slapped her left hand over her mouth to keep from crying out. The footsteps moved closer to the closet door. Did he hear the loud beat of her heart? Did he smell her fear? The shadow fell across the floor in front of her. *Oh, Virgin Mother Mary, please don't let me die. I promise to go to confession every Saturday.* Who was she kidding? Once a month.

The door opened, and light flooded the closet. Frankie screamed and swung the bat, pushing her way toward the hulk of a man in front of her. A dull grunt of pain as the bat hit solid flesh spurned her on.

She pulled back for another wallop; instead, the intruder tackled her low around the waist and pushed hard. Frankie screamed. In a flaying tangle of arms and legs, they landed on the guts of her mattress as she continued to whack him with the bat. Her hair caught around her face, obscuring her view, but her senses opened. Even blinded, she knew the strong woodsy scent of the man on top of her.

The bat halted midair. "Reese! You scared the hell out of me! Why didn't you call out?"

"Because, Miss Know-it-all, I didn't know one, if you were here, and two, if you were, whether someone had you at gunpoint. Now put that bat down."

Immediately she opened her fingers and the bat rolled out of her hand. Reese didn't seem in any hurry to remove his body from hers. Instead he leaned into her, smiled crookedly, and glanced around the room before settling those dark blue eyes of his back on her. "So, what is it you have hidden here?"

"I don't know what you mean. I was as shocked as you when I walked in here."

"Oh, I wouldn't say I was shocked. Surprised, maybe. It looks like whoever is after you has changed tactics."

"What do you mean?"

"It's obvious the person or persons who did this were looking for something. It wasn't a random scare tactic but a seek-and-destroy mission."

"Who are you?"

"The guy who's stuck with you and not liking it very much."

SKIN

She pushed his chest but he remained sprawled on her. "I thought you said you'd leave me alone."

He pressed his hips against her. "Feel that?"

"I don't feel anything except your hips."

"Exactly. *I. Don't. Do. Mafia. Princesses.*"

His hand slid up her bare thigh and pulled down her short skirt. Her skin warmed in its wake. "Even when they throw themselves at me."

"You're arrogant."

"You're stubborn."

Deep voices from the living room interrupted them. Frankie's body went rigid in renewed fear. Whoever ruined her house must be back. Reese put his finger to her lips and stood, hauling her up with him. He pushed Frankie toward the closet, then grabbed the bat from the floor.

"I hung a blanket," she whispered as Reese entered behind her and closed the door, leaving it open just a crack. The voices drew nearer.

In the darkness she felt his body heat. Gently he pushed her further back into the closet while he faced the door. She tripped over a mound of shoes and stifled a scream as he caught her, pulling her against him. She grabbed his arm for support and slid her other arm around his waist as he pulled her from the pile. The hard butt of a gun at his back surprised her more than his presence. A model with a gun? Who the hell was this guy?

The voices came closer, and she barely made out the words.

"Looks like someone had the same idea," a low, gruff voice said.

"Lightweights," an equally nasty voice responded.

"Whadya mean?" the first voice asked.

"You see a body?"

"Nah."

"Exactly. They screwed up. Lightweights."

"I didn't see no car out front. She ain't here. Looks like we won't be bagging one ourselves."

Reese slid his gun from his waist. Despite his quiet confidence and his gun pointed at the door, Frankie's heart hummed like a buzz saw against her chest. She was sure they could hear it. She pressed against Reese's back and wondered for the briefest of seconds if he felt it too.

She held her breath, straining hard to recognize at least one of the voices, but they were unfamiliar. Behind the blanket she could barely breathe, the closet was so warm. Frankie slipped her arms around Reese's waist and pressed her body against his, to draw on his strength and still her jittery nerves. Her knees wobbled and she felt the resurgence of nausea. She smiled when he ran a comforting hand across hers before disengaging her hands from him.

Holding his gun with one hand, he wrapped his fingers around the back of her head and whispered against her lips, "Don't make a sound." She nodded and he released her.

"Wanna give it a once-over before we go?" the first thug asked.

"Nah. It's the girl we wanted and she ain't here. Let's go."

The sound of heavy footsteps retreating from her room was the sweetest sound Frankie had ever heard.

"Let's head over to that magazine she runs."

"But the boss said—" the second voice interrupted.

"I want this—" the first one started to explain, and the voices faded down the stairway.

Still silent, she listened as the men made their way downstairs, their muffled voices giving way to murmurs as space separated them.

"What do we do now?" Frankie whispered.

Reese pushed her back toward the wall. "We wait for them to leave."

"Wait?" she hissed. "They're going to my offices."

"Yes, wait. And since you aren't there, no one will get hurt."

"You have a gun. Let's follow them."

Reese slid his weapon between his belt and back, then pulled her hard against his chest and kissed her. This time Frankie struggled. She pulled away from him. "I'm not going to stand in here while those thugs get away. Give me your gun."

"Keep quiet."

She moved past him and he grabbed her, spinning her around. She stumbled and he pushed her face first against the far corner of the closet. He was careful not to hurt her, but his patience had worn thin. He had a hankering to see the next sunrise. "As much as I'd like to go out there and play the Lone Ranger, there are two of them, one of you, and one of me. I happen to value my skin, and yours. So we wait."

"Let go of me," she said against the wall, the drywall muffling the percussion of it.

"You promise to be quiet?"

She pushed her ass against his swift-growing cock. He couldn't help it. Her perfume, her skimpy skirt, her smooth skin in the dark, warm confines of the closet. Every one of his thermo receptors was on high alert, and he had a real good idea how to keep her quiet, at least until the danger passed. But this was not the time for that. They had to keep alert to stay safe. If one of those thugs decided to come back upstairs and so much as opened the closet door, they would be a permanent fixture splattered on the wall. And judging from the muted sounds coming from downstairs, Reese figured the two guys weren't in any hurry to leave. They were no doubt looking for a few mementos they could pawn off for an extra buck.

The sudden trembling of Frankie's body triggered an emotion in him he'd buried years ago. She was scared to death but trying to act tough. The sudden urge to protect her at all costs flared bright in his gut. It wasn't, he realized, just a job anymore but his own personal quest. Someone wanted her dead, and he'd use whatever force was necessary to see that that didn't happen.

He inhaled sharply as the emotions collided. Her sultry scent tangled with his senses. His blood quickened, and he grasped for control.

The tension built as they waited, the closet getting hotter, him getting harder, her breathing coming fast. The slam of the front door announcing the thugs' departure made Frankie jerk against Reese. He jerked her back. Instead of releasing her, he held her closer, in no rush to go after them. He had something else entirely on his mind.

Frankie wiggled against him again and this time Reese groaned.

"You aren't the boss of me," Frankie said, her voice high, but with excitement, not fear. "Let's at least follow them. See where they go."

"No, it's too risky. We wait."

Frankie started to protest, but Reese had other plans. He sunk his teeth into the soft skin at the juncture of her neck and shoulder. Frankie hissed in a breath that shot to her toes. His hands slid up to her breasts. "I'm your fantasy playing out, Frankie. A stranger, in a dark corner. Danger lurking just outside." He felt her body shudder. Then she came undone in his hands. Her nipples hardened beneath his fingertips, the swell of the globes filling his hands.

She threw her head back, giving him open access to her throat. She tasted hot and spicy, a decadent blend of sex and sensuality. Her low moan encouraged him. While he kept one ear on the closet door, just in case their friends returned, every other sense was focused on the hot body writhing under his hands.

Determined not to trade any body fluids with her, Reese slid his hands down her waist to her thighs, rubbing her skin through the thin fabric of her skirt. He nipped at her throat, slipping his hands around and under her skirt to the voluptuous swell of her ass cheeks. He pressed his hard-on against her lower back. "Nice ass."

She moaned a response and Reese knew if he wanted to break the agreement, she'd allow it. He smiled against her skin.

He ran a fingertip up along the thin strip of material that served as the ass part of her thong panties. Her fanny squirmed under the pressure. "I want to slide my fingers into you, Frankie, and make you take off like a rocket."

She parted her thighs.

"You want that too?"

She didn't answer. He slipped his fingers around to her mound and just barely tapped her there. She gasped and pushed against him. He pushed with her, running a fingertip up and down the outside of the lacy fabric barrier shielding her hardened clit from him. Each time he trailed his fingertip across her, he increased the pressure. He'd make her beg for it.

His left hand massaged as his other hand moved upward to her waist, then to the clasp in the front of her bra, which he released with a flick of his fingers. She gasped as one full breast spilled into his hand.

"That is so sweet," he hoarsely said.

He nipped her throat and sucked her skin, pushing his groin hard against her back. Frankie braced herself against the wall, holding herself steady. Reese moved even closer to her. He felt every bit the Neanderthal at that moment. Possessive.

While that thought should have scared him into the next state, he chalked it up to the heat of the moment.

Reese pushed her shirt up, exposing the heat of her breasts, while his right hand played across her hard nub. Her breaths came hard and shallow, her hips moving against the rhythm of his hand.

"Please, Reese," she moaned.

"Please what?"

"Please make the ache go away."

With his fingertip he pulled the front of her panties down, then slid his finger up toward the pulsating nub, just barely touching her. "Like that?" he breathed against the back of her neck. He brushed his lips against the fine hair standing to attention, prompting more soft writhes of want.

"More," she panted.

He slid his finger deeper along the wet slit of her nether lips. "Like that?"

He felt her body tighten, her muscles bunch then release. "More," she pleaded. He heard her lick her lips. He wished it was lighter so he could watch the expression on her face. He slid his fingertips slowly up and down her slit, the soft sluice of her sounding loud in the closed confines of the closet. Her breathing quickened, her body hard and hot.

Reese wanted her like he never wanted a woman before. He clamped his teeth together. He would not cave and give her what she wanted—not . . . yet. Her warm, wet juices on his fingers invited him to put other, bigger things inside her. His dick hurt with the need to mark her. Under his hands he felt a soft, warm flush of perspiration erupt across her skin. Their hot breaths commingled, causing the heat and humidity in the small space to climb off the charts.

His keen sense of sound told him they were still alone in the house, and Frankie was about to blast off.

He slipped his middle finger into the deep, hot depth of her. Her moans filled the room. He pressed his left hand low against her belly and pushed his finger deeper into her.

Closing her eyes, Frankie threw her head back against Reese's chest, the sweet pressure of his thick finger inside her, tapping her sweet spot, excruciating in its sublimeness.

When he pressed against her womb, pushing deeper into her, she tried to dig her fingernails into the wall.

Moans of rapture escaped her throat with each thrust of his hand. In a quick movement Reese released her body, spun her around, and pressed her back against the corner of the closet. His big body moved closer. Her mouth gaped open, a silent plea for him to fill her.

He hiked her leg over his hip. Frankie rubbed the heel of her palm up the bulge in his jeans.

He filled her with his finger, and with the new position he hit her spot and she screamed. His mouth swallowed the noise and his tongue quelled the next one. Bucking wildly against his hand, Frankie hung on to his shoulders and rode out her orgasm.

His finger pressed and held her as she crested. As each wave crashed through her, her body twitched, and he silenced her moans of pleasure with his kisses.

Barely able to stand, she hung on to his shoulders, her pussy twitching in the aftermath of his lovemaking. Their hard breathing mingled in soft cacophony, and he kept his finger inside her. It occurred to Frankie that at that moment the only sound she could hear was their breathing.

Licking her dry lips, Frankie smiled in the darkness. Maybe she could return the fantasy.

Slowly Reese withdrew his finger from her. "No," she pleaded. She wanted more. She wanted all of him.

"Fantasy over."

A surge of anger flashed through her. Just that easy? That quick? Fantasy over? What was she, just something to pass the time? "It's not over until I say it's over."

In a quick fluid movement he pressed her against the corner of the closet, and in one swift and oh-so-sinful moment he slid a finger inside of her still spasming body. "Is that what you want?"

Before she could respond, he slipped another finger into her. She gasped, her hips jumping against his hand. Her body already primed, he brought her to another monster orgasm. As she cried out, new voices filtered into the closet. A new threat stood just feet away. Reese slapped his hand over her mouth to drown out her cries of pleasure.

"You hear that?" a vaguely familiar Italian-accented voice asked.

"*Si,* from the closet," another, more heavily accented voice said.

Frankie felt Reese remove his gun from his back holster. Adrenaline kicked in. She may have been writhing in the throes of passion just a minute ago, but now she felt for the bat.

The door slowly opened. Reese kept his hand firmly placed across her mouth, and for once she didn't resent his caveman action. As the door opened and light filtered in, she saw Reese's silhouette and the barrel of the gun aimed directly at the unfortunate who happened to fill the empty space.

CHAPTER SIXTEEN

The door opened wider, and Reese's finger caressed the trigger. Frankie held her breath.

"Hey, what the—" the first accented voice said.

Pfft. Pfft.

Frankie bit back a gasp, and the unmistakable sound of two rounds fired from a silencer sounded as loud as a thunderclap in the eerie silence. The dull thud of one body, then another followed. The second one fell against the door, slamming it shut. Darkness engulfed them. She felt Reese move toward the closed door, the muffled voices from the other side barely discernible.

"Looks like these boys won't be reporting back to anyone soon." It was the first voice from earlier, the one who was supposed to be going to her office. Frankie held her breath. Had they been watching?

"We gonna leave them here, or you want to clean up this mess?" the familiar second voice asked.

"Nah, leave them. Looks like they're from out of town. It'll send a message loud and clear to their boss."

Frankie crept up behind Reese, pressing her shaking body against his back. His hard warmth comforted her, and for some odd reason she felt if anyone could protect her from the bad guys, he could.

They both listened to the two retreating voices. After several long moments when no sound permeated the closet, Reese whispered, "I think they're gone." He felt for his cell phone and began to dial 911. Frankie grabbed the phone from him and flipped it shut.

"No cops, Reese."

"Bullshit. Your house is vandalized and we witnessed a double murder."

"Let's get out of here first and see who got whacked." Her soft, businesslike voice seemed as if it came from someone else.

"Who they are won't change my mind."

"Open the door."

That was easier said than done. It took both of them pushing in unison to get the door opened enough for Reese to stick his long arm out and roll the body away so they could step out.

The minute Frankie set eyes on the one nearest to the door, she gasped. "Tommy!"

She bent down and felt for a pulse. But the neat, dime-size hole right between his eyes told the complete story. Dead on impact.

"You know this guy?"

Nodding her head, Frankie moved down to his feet. She pulled back each of his pant cuffs, revealing one blue sock and one green sock. "Tommy 'Two Socks.' My brother's second cousin on his mother's side. I thought he went back to the old country." Or worse.

She stood and glanced at the other man, who lay facedown in the mattress stuffing, the back of his head splattered all over the headboard, or what was left of it.

Reese stepped over Tommy and rolled the other body over onto his back. He looked up at Frankie expectantly. She shook her head. "Never seen him before."

Reese scanned the room. "From the looks of it, I figure these two here did the trashing earlier, then left. The two guys who shot them came in looking for you, and left when they saw the place was trashed." Reese pointed the muzzle of his gun at the two dead guys on the floor. "Dumb and dumber came back and got whacked. The two unidentified must have been waiting outside for you to get home and saw these two yahoos."

At Reese's description Frankie shuddered. Someone not only thought she possessed her father's will, but they wanted her dead on top of it. Had she waited to come home, she'd be the one lying on her bedroom floor with a bullet hole in her head.

But who? She could not, *would* not believe her brother hated her so much to want her dead. And he wasn't stupid. Well, he wasn't the brightest in the family, but Anthony would not dare piss off Unk. And Unk would kill Anthony himself if he so much as suspected her little brother was behind her death. Who, then? She was convinced at this point it must be one of the other Bay Area families. But who? And why, for God's sake? And didn't they know they would face the wrath of Carmine Donatello? Perhaps they didn't care, maybe because Unk was on the list as well. She squeezed her eyes shut, not wanting to believe she was in the middle of her worst nightmare.

"Give me one good reason why I don't call the cops, Frankie." Reese pulled her back into the morbid present.

Frankie carefully collected her thoughts. "Because this is none of their business. I'm calling my uncle." She stepped past the bodies, ignoring Reese's shout for her to stop. She hurried down the steps of her trashed home to her studio, where she'd left her purse and camera bag.

Both were gone. "Son of a bitch!"

She turned to head back to Reese and found his wide chest barring her way. *"I'm* calling the cops," he said.

"My purse and camera bag are gone." Color drained from her face. "It had my cell phone and PDA with all my info on it."

Reese flipped his phone open.

"Give me your phone. I'm calling my uncle. He'll know what to do, especially with one of the guys being Tommy."

Reese raised a dark brow. "What does that say to you, Frankie? Your brother's cousin tossing your house?"

"What makes you so sure he tossed my house?"

"Two plus two equals four."

Frankie shook her head, her confusion over what had become her life confounding her beyond reason. "I—I don't understand. Tommy disappeared years ago. He—he—"

"He what?"

"My father caught him in bed with one of his ladies."

"So he disappeared?"

She nodded. It was par for the course with her family. You messed with a man's woman, you disappeared. "I thought he was dead."

"Why does he wear different-colored socks?"

"Tommy's color-blind. He could never match."

"I think Tommy still kept in touch with the family, your brother specifically, and he was here on your brother's behalf. What was he looking for?"

She studied Reese's earnest face. She almost fell for the look. Confiding in an outsider had cost her huge the last time.

"I don't know."

"You're lying."

Frankie shook her head and pushed past him. He grabbed her arm and pulled her hard against his chest. His warm breath fanned her cheeks. "There's nothing I hate worse than a lying woman."

"I'm not lying. And if I am? What's the big deal? This is none of your business."

"It's a big deal because I have no job if there is no you."

She jerked away. "So that's how it is?"

He softened his voice. "It's more than that. Let me help you."

"You can't help me." How could she make him understand the way it went down in her family without ratting them out? "No one can help me. Don't you understand? My family does things their way, and there's no way out of it until you're dead."

"You're wrong, Frankie. The world doesn't work that way. There are some good guys out there."

"If you mean the cops, you can keep them. They're worse than a sideways don. I'd rather be married to the mob than spend one night in bed with a cop."

Despite her words, his offer stopped her cold. No one, except Unk, had ever offered to help her with anything, well, not unless they wanted something from her. While Reese wanted to keep his job, she detected sincerity in his voice. And she did need help. Help finding the will, help keeping her shoot on schedule, and, most important, help staying alive.

"I'd rather be a poor model than a dead one. I'm calling the cops."

He started to dial 911.

"No! Damn you, hang up!"

Reese cocked a brow but didn't close the phone.

"Hang up."

"Only if you let me help you."

A million protests swirled through her head, but each one came back to Reese and his offer. It was time to take a leap of faith—and God help her if she was wrong about him.

She extended her hand. "You've just been promoted to body-guard."

Slowly he closed the phone. Reese took her hand and squeezed. "My rules."

"We'll see," Frankie said, then dropped his hand. "I need to get my camera from my office." She hurried back to the room and grabbed the Nikon from the sill, stuffed a few boxes of film into a spare camera bag along with a timer and minitripod, then hurried back to Reese.

Moments later, they were speeding down the freeway. "Take me to my office. I have credit cards there and clothes."

He shook his head. "No way."

He was right. She settled back into the comfortable seat and con-templated her position. The air racing in from the open windows blew away the last whispers of shock that clouded her mind; it also cleared the last shred of naïveté she possessed. It was time to take the proverbial bull by the horns and fight back. She smiled grimly. No problem. Sicilian blood coursed hot in her veins, and no one played as hard to win as Sicilians.

It occurred to her as she glanced around the cab of the truck that it wasn't the same one Reese had yesterday. "What happened to your other truck?"

"That was a loaner while this one was in the shop."

Made sense.

"But just in case, I'm going to call Ricco and Jase when we find a safe place and see if they'll swap with me."

"Safe place? I want to get down to Carmel, now."

He grinned and shook his head, the cool air blowing his hair. "My rules, Frankie."

"We don't have time to stop, I need to start shooting in the morning!"

"I need to make arrangements. That takes time, and in that time you can eat and get some rest. You look beat. We'll be in Carmel in the morning."

Frankie sat back in the seat and crossed her arms over her chest. She did not like being told what to do.

Instead of driving south to Carmel, Reese went through San Francisco, across the Bay Bridge, and down into the bowels of Oakland. Great.

He finally surfaced at the airport Hilton. When he offered her a helping hand out of the SUV, she brushed past him and stalked toward the hotel entrance. Just because she agreed to his terms didn't mean she had to like them. She half listened to his phone conversation with his "buddy" Jase. Once settled in the two-bedroom suite, Frankie ordered room service, then turned on Reese and let him have it. "I don't like your 'buddies' knowing where we are. While you may have reason to trust them, I don't. I want your word you won't tell them we're headed to Carmel. If for some reason whoever is after me finds them, they have ways of making men sing. It's for their protection as well as ours."

Reese's eyes twinkled.

"You think this is funny?"

"No, it's just nice to see you finally take this seriously."

She paced the main bedroom living room area. "Of course I take this seriously. I have from the beginning, I was just under the impression the bad guys wanted someone else dead."

A knock on the door startled her. Reese waved her toward the other bedroom. Drawing his gun, he moved to the side of the door. Frankie's heart pounded.

"Room service."

That was quick.

"Leave it in the hall," Reese called out.

"I need you to sign for this, sir."

"Slip it under the door."

A piece of paper slipped under the door. From an angle Reese bent down and snatched it up. He moved to the side out of direct alignment with the door, grabbed a pen off the desk, and scribbled on the paper. Then slid it back.

A muffled "Thank you." And the sound of the tray being pushed up against the door answered.

After several tense minutes, Reese, with gun still drawn, looked out the peephole. Satisfied, he quickly opened the door and pulled the tray in, then shut the door and double-locked it.

Frankie stood at the doorway to the separate bedroom with her arms crossed over her chest, eyeing this "model" with the Sonny Crockett moves. "I guess they taught you that at modeling school?"

He turned, sliding the gun between his belt and lower back. "No, MP school."

Unwinding herself, Frankie walked slowly into the room. Her mouth watered as the aroma wafting from the covered plates hit her nostrils. Despite her day, she was famished.

Reese opened the bottle of cab she'd ordered, poured her a glass, then dug into a rare steak. She noticed he drank water. "No wine?"

He shook his head, chewing the beef. "Nope, I need a clear head. You should go easy on it yourself in case we need to get out of here quick."

She narrowed her eyes again and stabbed at her chicken Caesar salad. Her mood had not soothed, and her suspicious nature ran rampant with thoughts.

Another knock on the door startled her again. She choked on a piece of chicken. Reese pounded her on the back and she held up her hand, signaling him to stop.

"It's Jase," a deep voice called from the hallway. Reese hurried to the door, looked out the peephole, then unlocked the door, swinging it open. Jase walked in, followed by Ricco.

Both men were dressed stylishly, and looked every part a *GQ* cover. They nodded in her direction; she ignored them and worked on her salad. She'd put her life in the hands of strangers and she didn't have a warm, fuzzy feeling about it.

The three men conferred quietly for a moment.

"I'm going down with Ricco to check out our ride," Reese said. "Jase will keep you company."

"Lucky me," Frankie muttered.

Jase cocked his head and gave her a sharp glare.

As the door closed behind Ricco and Reese, Frankie sat back, sipped her wine, and asked, "Who the hell are you guys?"

Jase shrugged and helped himself to a glass of wine. "Just your average hardworking Joes."

Frankie caught the same undercurrent of danger in this man as she did in Reese. It was evident in Ricco as well. But something different lurked behind Jase's guarded gaze. Was it scorn? "You three smell like cops."

Jase spewed his wine into his glass. Quickly he wiped the few drops on his pants with a napkin. "Lady, if I'm a cop, then you're Princess Diana."

"She's dead."

"I hear you might be soon."

Setting her glass down on the table, Frankie stood and began pacing the floor. Occasionally she threw a glare Jase's way. His body language spoke volumes. "What the hell did I ever do to you?" she said.

"I beg your pardon?"

"Contempt. I see it in your eyes."

He nodded and stood, then strode to the heavy curtain and pulled it slightly away from the window. "I don't like your type."

Feeling like a caged cat, and brewing for a fight, Frankie strode over to the arrogant man, more than willing to use him as her whipping boy. He was just what she needed to blow off some of the steam building inside of her. "And what type am I?"

"Coldhearted."

Shocked at the venomous tone, Frankie lashed out. She slapped him. Jase caught her hand and jerked her hard against him. He moved his face to within inches of hers. "And temperamental to boot."

"Nice to see I still rate, my friend," Reese said from the doorway, his voice ominously dark.

CHAPTER SEVENTEEN

Frankie gasped. Jase released her and threw Reese a tomcat grin.

"It's not what you think," Frankie sputtered, pulling away.

Ricco stood gawking behind Reese in the doorway.

"And what do I think it was?" Reese drawled. His eyes burned with anger and Frankie felt fear spike along her spine. The man before her was not one to toy with. He exuded a carefully controlled danger.

She shivered. "I, we—Jase—he was rude and I slapped him."

Reese turned his gaze to his friend and cocked a brow. Jase raised his brow and continued to grin, in no hurry to explain.

On the verge of slapping him again, Frankie fisted her hands. Her gaze swept from Jase, who stood like a bratty child who knew he was guilty, to Reese, who looked like he wanted to throttle *her,* and Ricco, who stood grinning like the village idiot who thought he had a clue.

"Screw all of you!" she shot, and headed for the bedroom.

"Just say when," Jase challenged.

"Fuck you," Reese said to his friend.

Frankie slammed the door behind her, and even though they couldn't see her, she flipped them off. She flopped onto the bed and fumed. What the hell was going on and why the hell was she stuck in this hotel room with three men she barely knew? Popping up from the bed, she began pacing the small room and considered her position in this crazy scenario.

Someone wanted her dead. It had to be an outside family. How far would they go? Shit, that answer was easy enough. Three times they showed how far they would go. And she had no doubt they would keep trying until they got it right.

But how to fight back? Was she supposed to be constantly looking over her shoulder, surrounded by bodyguards? No way. That would drive her to suicide. She should have paid closer attention as a child. She'd always steered clear of those conversations as an adult, but as a child playing in the large Carmel house, she had on several occasions overheard her father and uncle's conversations when they didn't know she was hiding in a nook in the room. By eight, she knew which capos did the dirty deeds and who called the shots. It was apparent to her very early on that her father was the quick draw, while Unk was the slow hand.

The muffled voices coming from the other room rose in anger. Good. Served them all right.

She flopped onto the bed again and didn't bother trying to decipher the muffled voices. Rolling onto her back, she rubbed the heels of her hands against her throbbing eyes. She had a massive headache all of a sudden.

The shock of what she'd been through hit her. Someone had trashed her home. Two men were shot and killed by two other men who, had they found her, would have sent her to meet her father. One of the dead guys was her brother's cousin. *Two plus two equals four.* Reese's words taunted her. She moaned and rolled over onto her stomach.

Think like Papa, Frankie, remove your emotions and look at the situation with a critical, objective eye.

Taking a deep breath, she exhaled slowly.

Okay, was Reese right? If Tommy was working for Anthony, did her brother really want her dead? Why? Did the will give her what he wanted and he knew it? But if that was true, who killed Tommy and his cohort? Were two sides playing the middle?

Anthony wouldn't be so bold. But was he hiding in plain sight? Or was there someone else who would benefit by his rise to the top?

Connie. Was she behind this? Playing Anthony as the fool? She would want that will as much as the next person. To claim what she thought she had coming to her or destroy the fact Papa cut her out? Was Connie so desperate to keep the power she had gained through her son that she'd kill her stepdaughter? Frankie pulled the spread tight around her shoulders, warding off a sudden chill. Connie was as driven as a viper. She needed to alert Unk.

She started when the door flew open.

"Didn't your mother teach you to knock?"

Reese's eyes flashed. "Don't talk to me about my mother."

Frankie knew she hit a nerve, and she felt the need to hurt him to put some emotional distance between them. She flung off the spread and slid off the bed, standing straight to face him. "Does Reese have Mommy issues?"

His face clouded and she realized she'd crossed a line. She didn't care.

His fists opened and closed at his sides.

"Did you piss your mommy off?"

"Shut up, Francesca."

"Oh, now it's Francesca?"

She looked past him to the empty living room. "Where'd your buddies go?" She moved to go by him but he grabbed her arm. "Didn't your mommy tell you it was bad manners to grab ladies by the arm and act the Neanderthal?"

He yanked her hard against him. His eyes darkened in rage. "I said shut up."

"No one tells me to shut up."

"Maybe it's time someone did."

"And I suppose you're making yourself that person?"

"Maybe I could call Jase back and he can tell you. You seem to get along so well with him." He stared hard at her for a long moment, then set her away from him.

"Go to bed," he said.

"No! I want to get the hell out of here."

"We both need some sleep."

Setting her jaw, she crossed her arms over her chest. "I don't need sleep, what I need to do is start my shoot. To do that I can't be holed up at the local Hilton."

"We sit tight. Your family or whoever the hell wants you dead is out on the streets now, listening for a whisper, anything to give you away. We sit tight here for a few hours."

The truth of Reese's words hit home. For the first time in her entire life she actually felt afraid of her family. But even though what Reese said made sense, she had a different slant. "I have a business I'm responsible for—I refuse to hide."

"You can't run it dead."

"No, I can't, but if I don't run it alive, there will be no business. No pictures equals no advertisers which equals no revenue which equals no *Skin.*" Realizing she was getting nowhere, Frankie changed her tactic. Lowering her voice to a more earnest tone, she said, "Look, Reese, no one knows what vehicle I'm in, no one knows I'm with you, I can't believe whoever it is out there gunning for me will find out if we leave this room right now and head to Carmel. The beach house is armed tighter than the Pentagon. I'll feel safer there. It's only a two-hour drive."

"You're a fool, Francesca."

Détente. "Are your friends coming back?"

He stepped up behind her.

"No."

She turned and faced him. Reese towered over her. The devil inside her goaded him. "That's too bad. Either one would make excellent backups." She turned and walked away, throwing her hair over her shoulder.

Reese followed close behind her, stopping just a few feet from the bar, where she bent over and opened the fridge. His feelings confused him. He didn't have a possessive bone in his body when it came to women—but something deep and dark reared its head when he walked in and saw her with Jase. His gaze slid down her round derriere, and his dick warmed. He could admit she turned him on like no other woman had. But what about her? Did he do it for her too? Would she heat up for him again or had her response to him earlier just been the excitement of the moment?

He decided to find out. He slid his hand over her rounded ass and she immediately straightened. "If it makes it easier, pretend I'm Jase."

Frankie turned around, a bottle of wine in her hand. She used her foot to close the door. She leaned back against the bar and smiled.

"Does that do it for you, Frankie? Another fantasy." He choked the words out. "You fuck one guy but think of another?"

She slapped him.

He grabbed her hand and squeezed until she cried out in pain. Her cry made him realize what he was doing. He let her go. Why did the thought of Jase, a man he considered a brother, buried to the hilt between Frankie's lush thighs infuriate him?

She turned from him and set the bottle down on the counter.

"If it *were* my fantasy, you're the last person I'd share it with."

"Why? Did I do such a lousy job playing out your last one?"

He watched her cheeks flush and her body shiver. Then he heard the catch in her breath.

"Are you jealous, Reese?"

"Hardly."

That was too bad; she wanted him to be. "Of course. How could I forget? It's just sex for you, no emotions."

"Exactly."

She stalked away from him, then turned to face him across the room. "Do you still want me?"

Reese's eyes burned hot. She felt his pull, unable to put her finger on exactly what it was. She could see he was fighting an internal battle. His pride, she guessed, still stinging over what he assumed was some type of interlude with Jase. Anger bubbled to the surface. It hurt that he thought so little of her. And being the Donatello she was, Vendetta was her middle name. Frankie chose at that moment to give him a taste of his own medicine.

CHAPTER EIGHTEEN

Frankie poured herself a glass of wine and slowly sipped it. Reese stood rooted to the floor. She smiled over the rim of her glass. Setting it down on the nightstand, she walked toward him, then circled behind.

Trailing her fingers across his broad shoulders, she leaned into his back. Pressing her breasts ever so slightly against him, she whispered, "Did it bother you seeing Jase touch me?" His body stiffened, so rigid that she thought he would snap in two.

His reaction empowered her. She wanted him the minute he walked into her office the day before, she wanted him when she caught him in the shower, she wanted him with every fiber of her being in her closet, and she realized, at that moment, she was willing to go to great lengths to have him. But on her terms.

Stepping around to face Reese, her legs slightly parted, Frankie dragged her fingers through her hair, then shook her head, allowing her hair to cascade down her back. She knew exactly how good she looked in her stiletto pumps, hip-hugging miniskirt, and form-fitting cashmere sweater. Setting her hands on her hips, she dragged her gaze across Reese's long form. His eyes burned bright, the only indicator he was a living thing. One foot in front of the other, her hips swaying suggestively, she sauntered toward him. Her lips quirked into a smile, her gaze dipped to his bulging jeans, and she caught her breath.

She stopped inches from him, her warm breath caressing his chin. She watched the throb of his jugular lurch against his tan skin. She stood up on her tiptoes and pressed her lips to his chin. Reese hissed in a breath but still remained immobile.

Frankie pulled her lips away but continued to balance on her toes. She pressed against his chest just enough to make the slightest contact. The meeting sent a hot flash straight to her core. Still, Reese didn't flinch. "You think you can resist me?" She laughed low, her voice husky and confident.

Sliding her palm up his belly to his chest, Frankie smiled and pressed her breasts more firmly against him. "Tell the truth, Reese."

When he didn't answer but continued to look straight ahead, she chuckled and pressed her lips close to his ear. "You didn't like coming in and seeing Jase so close to me."

Not expecting a response, Frankie continued her one-sided conversation. "Did you wonder if he touched me?" She slid her other hand up his chest to his shoulder. In a slow undulation, Frankie moved her hips against his thighs. His body flinched and she felt the surge of his cock against her belly. "Did it make you mad? Thinking I liked it?"

She slid her right hand slowly down his chest to his belly, then the heel of her palm along the full ridge of his pants. "You're so hard, Reese. Does it hurt?"

He groaned and she smiled, sinking her teeth into his jugular. His body surged, she could feel the tight bunching muscles against her, feel the heat of his skin seep into hers. Yet he kept his rigid stance. The unleashed power of his body as he sought to contain it excited her. The thought of pushing this man over the edge, of possessing control of his body despite his brain fighting it, thrilled her.

Frankie pulled her hands in a slow, unhurried slide from his body, then stepped back, air separating them completely. Her eyes lifted to his and she was met with a dark, brooding stare. The man didn't forgive easy. It didn't matter what really happened, it mattered that he was convinced he saw what he thought he saw. And she decided that was okay. Better, actually, because for him to crack and take her meant he moved past it. Reese was a man with pride as big as the state of California. Her determination to make him blink grew stronger.

She turned away from him, facing the bed. As she had done earlier, she dragged her fingers through her hair. She arched her back, her ass brushing the button fly of his jeans. She piled the heavy mass of her hair on top of her head, exposing her neck to Reese. She leaned back against his chest and wagged her fanny slowly back and forth against the hard rise in his jeans. She moaned softly, tilted her head back, and looked up to find Reese's hard eyes staring down at her. She closed her eyes and softly thrust her breasts out against the warm air. She bit her bottom lip and angled her neck so that her jugular lay exposed.

Her body lit up when she felt warmth engulf her from behind. Large hands slid down her back and Reese's body pressed against hers. Relief, mingled with a profound sense of craving, filled her. His mouth seized her throat. Frankie cried out, arching hard against the air. His teeth scraped down her neck, his tongue bathing it in moist heat. His hands slid up her waist, ravenously capturing her breasts, his hips digging hard into her back.

"Reese," she moaned, wanting every inch of him to mark her. His right hand slid down her waist to her thigh, then up beneath her skirt, his fingers like branding irons against her skin. Her legs spread of their own accord and with no precursor his finger dipped into her waiting heat. "Oh, God," she moaned, arching hard against his hand. Her body swelled and the sheer sensation of her body's reaction nearly did her in. His teeth sunk deeper into her skin, and her body thrummed in immediate, desperate response. She couldn't get enough of him. His left hand squeezed her breast rhythmically, his fingers teasing her nipple, his right middle finger fucking her hard, slow, and deep.

An orgasm swept up from nowhere and shattered inside her, the quickness and velocity of it leaving her breathless. Her legs wobbled and when Reese slid his finger from her she cried out, "No, please, don't stop."

"Do you want me to fuck you, Frankie?" he whispered against her ear. She arched hard, letting her body give the answer.

"Say it, or I walk right now."

Her libido grappled with her inherent desire to be in control. Again words failed her, and when she didn't say what she wanted he withdrew. "No!"

He stopped.

"Stay," she whispered.

He moved back, giving her his warmth. "Say it."

"I . . . want you."

"How?"

"Inside me."

He turned her to face him.

His eyes raked her face, making sure there were no doubts. She had none.

He picked her up and carried her toward the bar as if she weighed an ounce, then perched her on the edge of the counter. He spread her thighs with his hands and reached up and pulled her panties down her thighs. When they tangled around her knees he cursed and snapped them in half, then tossed them to the floor. His dark eyes held hers and he yanked his belt undone, then with one hand he unbuttoned his fly.

He pushed his pants and boxers down his thighs and Frankie gasped. His cock was rock hard and jutting proudly between them. He reached into his back pocket and pulled out a condom. He ripped the foil package with his teeth, spit the wrapper on the floor, then quickly rolled it on.

Reese pulled Frankie closer to the edge of the counter, closer to him. His jaw clenched and his eyes bore hot. Frankie slid her legs around his waist and he didn't waste one precious moment. He speared her and Frankie thought she'd died and gone to heaven. The full heat of him filled her to capacity and an incredible wave of emotion rolled through her. It was quickly replaced with the beginnings of an orgasm.

Her chest hurt and her breath came hard and forced, like she was drowning in a sea of erotically charged sensations. Reese inside her made her feel things she'd never felt before and for one panicked moment she was terrified. How could she let something this good go? Would she be able to or be reduced to one of those pathetic piles of female mush? It was too late now to think about it. She'd committed, and she would ride this wild ride with Reese as long as she could.

Slipping an arm around her, Reese pulled her closer, as if that was even possible. "Is that what you wanted, Frankie?"

"More," she demanded.

And more he gave her.

The temperature in the room had been warm to begin with, but now, in such close proximity and with her elevated blood pressure, the room felt tropical. Her lips suddenly dry, she licked them.

Reese's low growl close to her ear caused her blood to heat hotter.

His lips touched the base of her neck, the contact sending shivers racing across her skin. The contrasting heat and chill stimulated her higher. His hips thrust in and out, the pace frantic. Their bodies became damp with sweat, their skin sluicing sensuously back and forth, the friction almost unbearable.

Frankie hung on to his shoulders as he rocked her into an earth-shattering orgasm. She cried out his name, digging her nails into his back, wanting the intense feeling to crest over and over. Her body jerked against his and for the briefest of moments she felt suspended in the air, her nerve endings sizzling to the point of combustion. She opened her eyes and gasped. Reese's blue eyes had turned dark and stormy, the planes of his face rigid in desire. He slid a hand around her neck and pulled her up to his lips, and as his mouth took hers, his hips rocked hard into her and he came in a wild burst of energy.

Their wild undulation slowed, their hot, heavy breaths mingling with their sweat-soaked skin, cooling their overheated bodies.

Still inside of her, Reese pulled Frankie from the counter. With her arms and legs around him, he walked carefully with her in his arms to the bed. Then he flung her onto it. She screamed, the sudden loss of his body and heat shocking her system.

She lay sprawled on the bed, still in her heels.

Reese's chest heaved as he gasped for more air. The sight of Frankie's lush rosy body sprawled out on the bed in those mile-high heels sent his libido back to Go. Her skirt was hiked up just enough that he could see her pouty pussy lips, swollen and moist from him. He'd never wanted a woman again so fast. Hell, ever.

"It's hot in here," she murmured.

He pulled his jeans up and buttoned them.

"Where are you going?" Frankie quietly asked.

"I'll be right back," he softly said, then left the room. Ice. He needed to cool down and he had a dozen different ways he wanted to cool Frankie's sweltering skin down before he heated her up again. Reason intruded. They needed to sleep, then get on the road.

For a long minute Reese stood with the ice bucket in his hands, daydreaming of all of the ways he could cool her off.

"Shit!"

When Reese returned a few minutes later, Frankie lay reclined against the pillows. From the steady rise and fall of her chest, he could see her breathing had returned to normal. His pulse still raced. He didn't question his flash of anger when he walked into the room earlier and saw Jase touching her. He didn't bother to dig further inside himself and ask why for the first time in his life he felt the sharp prick of jealousy. He didn't bother to unravel the reasons his dick was constantly hard when he thought of Francesca Donatello.

No, instead he was a man of action, one who seized the moment. And he was going to seize every moment with the sultry siren lying on the bed before him while he could.

But not tonight.

He poured her a glass of ice water and handed it to her. He deliberately stood next to the bed, not trusting himself to go near her.

Frankie closed her eyes and took a long drink.

"Sorry about your panties."

Frankie's eyes opened and she handed him back the glass, a slow smile sliding across her lips. "I can get more."

Reese set the glass down on the nightstand. Frankie cocked a brow before moving over, allowing him room on the bed. "I won't bite you, Reese."

He kicked off his boots and stiffly lay down beside her. "We broke our rules," he said.

She smiled at him and resisted the urge to snuggle into the crook of his shoulder. "Rules schmules."

Reese chuckled and looked over at her. "And here I thought you were a nice girl."

"Ha, my nice-girl days are history."

"Nice girls are overrated anyway." Reese pulled her against his side, his long arm encircling her. He settled back into the pillows and closed his eyes. Frankie lay quiet, enjoying the way her body still pulsed, Reese's scent lingering between them, hers mixing with it, creating a sexy musk.

"Get some sleep," Reese said, his voice heavy with fatigue.

For long moments she lay quiet, contemplative, content, her cheek pressed against Reese's chest, the dull, steady rhythm of his heartbeat soothing. Soon his slow, steady breaths told her he was asleep. Typical.

She yawned and thought about his last words. Nice *was* overrated. If she played cutthroat like her father, she'd be well ahead in the game.

Her brows drew together in a scowl. Look what playing nice had gotten her. Shot at, almost run over, her house trashed, and a handful of wiseguys looking for her.

She fought back another yawn. Her body still twitched from the orgasm deluge. She stretched, her long legs sliding against Reese's longer ones. She thought that having him would end her ache, but . . . now she wanted more.

Hmm, how to get it?

As much as she wanted to linger in his arms in the aftermath of their sex, she slipped from the bed. She'd prove to Reese there was no moss growing on her either.

Reese woke to an empty bed. He scanned the room and found it empty. He bolted upright, the tangled sheets twisting around his legs, hampering his movement. He flung off the offending things and in a handful of strides stood before the closed door to the other bedroom. "I'm going to kill you, Francesca Donatello." He pushed open the door to the separate bedroom and stopped short at the threshold.

She lay sprawled in all of her naked glory, the white sheets twisted around her hips and through her legs. He took a minute to admire the honey-gold skin and the lush lines of her body. She had great tits, a tight ass, and lots of curves. Like a young Sophia Loren. His dick tingled. She surprised him last night, and she surprised him more now.

Why did it bother him to find Frankie gone from his bed? Had she had enough of him?

It occurred to him that this was what he always wanted the morning after. Solitude. No awkward morning-after conversation. No awkward lies about calling or getting together again. No tears or demands. He woke up and took off. It was what he did. But this time awkwardness be damned.

He contemplated her choice to wake up alone. He wanted her again. Now. Would she resent him intruding into her space? Her bed? He'd always made it a point not to bring a woman home to his place, that way he could just leave. There had been a few times when that didn't work out and he had to make coffee the next morning, always finding an excuse to send the flavor of the night on her way with a cup to go.

He didn't like morning-after sex. It said "I still want you." He didn't want anyone. His dick swelled. That may have been before, but right now he wanted Frankie again, and maybe even later.

He glanced at the illuminated clock on the nightstand: 5:03 a.m. Maybe a few minutes. He'd wake her up slow.

His body tightened as she moaned and stretched. He watched, mesmerized, as her nipples hardened before his eyes. Her soft moans grew louder, and he wondered what she was dreaming. She bit her bottom lip. He smiled and stepped closer, his body heat rising. The sheet hid her hand, but from the movement of the fabric he knew she was bringing herself to orgasm. He stepped closer and stood at the side of the bed.

He bent over, and just to help her along, he lightly tugged at the sheet. He smiled, his dick filling to capacity as her hand rubbing her clit came into full view. He liked the way her pussy looked. Her soft, dark hair was curled in moisture. Her long fingers swept rhythmically against her mound, and her hips pushed up toward the air. Her moans grew louder, more demanding, her thighs parted slightly, exposing her soft, pink lips.

His dick bucked against his jeans, and Reese couldn't ignore the pressure any longer. He unzipped his jeans and, following Frankie's lead, took matters into his own hands. His body lurched against the pressure as he wrapped his fingers around his dick, imagining they were Frankie's instead. He watched her face, the way her eyebrows drew together in concentration, the way her tits bobbed up and down with the rapid movement of her hand.

He pumped faster, the full force of his erection driving his rhythm. Frankie arched her head back, exposing the long column of her neck, her mouth open as she panted. He increased the momentum of his hand, squeezing tighter, wanting to bury himself deep into that pink glistening pussy of hers.

The sight of her turning herself on was wildly erotic to him. While he'd seen women do it before, none had done it so beautifully, so sexily as Frankie. His breath grew shorter, hotter, louder, hers mirrored his. Her fingers raced faster across her hard clit, the nub standing to full attention, a miniversion of his dick.

The urge to bend down and press his mouth to her hot mound nearly overcame him. He resisted. He wanted to see her come.

Frankie's body arched and she cried out. The sound of his name sent jolts of erotic electricity through him. He watched her hips buck and writhe as each wave of the orgasm ripped through her.

Reese resisted the urge to bring himself to orgasm. He stood still, rooted to the floor, and waited.

Frankie's eyes fluttered open. As she focused on his, they widened. Instinctively she grabbed for the sheet.

"No," Reese whispered, "don't."

She halted her attempt to hide herself from his eyes but the flush on her skin told him she was embarrassed.

"That was beautiful."

She closed her eyes for a moment, then reopened them, this time a flash of mischief lurking behind the hazel depths.

Her hands slid up her waist to her breasts, her hands cupping them. Generous portions swelled around her fingers. Her nipples peeked through. She squeezed and her hips responded, and so did Reese's hand still wrapped around his dick.

Her eyes locked with his. The tip of her pink tongue slid sexily across her lips. She threw her head back and closed her eyes, her right hand sliding down her belly to her pink glistening lips. She spread her thighs and spread her lips.

Reese shucked his clothes, then knelt on the bed, the musky scent of her sex wafting up to him. His nostrils twitched, the scent of his mate close.

He knew she felt the pressure of his weight on the mattress and she did nothing to stop him. He continued to stroke himself, his dick so full it hurt. He wanted to taste her again, to bury himself deep within her and ride her over one orgasm, then into another.

He loved her shyness, then the boldness she showed when she understood her sexuality. That it was okay to make yourself feel good and all the better when you could enhance another person's pleasure.

Unable to resist tasting her, Reese dipped his head toward her hips. Waves of sultry heat hit him in the face, her scent stronger. Her thighs parted further, and the heat of his breath reverberated off her thighs.

At the juncture of her thigh and pussy he bit her, taking her flesh and juices into his mouth, then sucking. Her hips jolted, and his lips traveled closer to the core of her. "You smell so sexy," he murmured against her swollen lips. "I want to eat you for breakfast." Like he was licking jam from a warm biscuit, his tongue laved the deep rivet that made her a woman. Strawberry-colored swells of her flesh glistened beneath his lips and gently he sucked the twins into his mouth, his tongue swirling, savoring the delicacy that was her.

Her cries of shock and pleasure drove him on. His hips pumped the air, his dick heavy with want. He wanted her hand wrapped around his cock while his face was buried between her legs.

Her hips jerked against him and she opened wider, giving her all to him. As she moved her hands back up to her breasts, one touched his dick. Reese pressed against her. "Take me, Frankie," he hoarsely said against her. She slid her fingers down the shaft of his cock, then slowly wrapped her fingers around him. His body shuddered and he groaned, pressing hotly into her hand.

Her hips responded, as did her hand. In a long, slow sequence she pumped him. Voraciously he licked and sucked her pussy. Frankie moaned, and her fist tightened around him. He felt her body flush hot, so close. He slowed his momentum. His fingers dug into the flesh of her thighs, and he steeled himself. He was so close to total explosion, but he wanted to last longer, give Frankie more pleasure, hear her call his name again as she came.

In slow, sensuous swirls, his tongue played with her clit, her thighs strained against his hands. The feast pushing them both to the brink. He sucked her clit into his mouth, flicking it with his tongue and sliding a finger into her hot, wet depths.

"Ah, God, Reese, that feels so—" Her cry of pleasure, combined with his moans of want, the slurping of her juices, and the slap of his balls against his thighs sent him reeling.

When she licked the head of his cock, his earth moved.

His body jerked against her mouth, and this time when he took her clit into his mouth, Frankie's body shuttered against his mouth. "Reese," she cried out, and the vibration of her orgasm hummed through him.

Her soft breath against the head of his cock was all he needed. He groaned and jerked hard as she milked him in a slow, sensuous pump. In a wild release he came, his seed coating the high curve of her breasts. Her hands continued a low slide up and down his shaft to the head of his dick, his semen adding lubrication, until there was nothing left in him. He collapsed on the bed next to her.

For several long minutes the only sound in the room was their labored breathing.

Reese rose up on an elbow and peered at Frankie. He liked his vantage point. Her steamy pussy still twitched, and her tits sat high and proud against her glistening chest.

"Sorry about that," he said, pointing to her glistening breast.

She wrinkled her nose as if just noticing his little gift. "Eww, thanks for that." She reached for a tissue on the nightstand.

As she cleaned him from her chest, Reese turned and watched and smiled.

Frankie threw the wet tissue at him and he dodged it. "Next time you do that, I'm going to smear it all over you."

Reese pulled the twisted sheet off the bed, then straightened it. He slipped in beside her. He rolled onto his side and traced a finger around a taut nipple. "So you're saying there will be a next time?"

She slapped his hand away and rolled over, presenting her back to him. "Just because I have sex with you doesn't mean you own the rights to me."

"I guess I'll have to find someone else to use all of those condoms on."

Frankie rolled back to face him. "Look, Reese, I'm not saying no more sex, I'm saying let's not make this any more complicated than it has to be, okay?"

Reese smiled and traced a finger along her cheekbone. "Sex is the most uncomplicated thing I know."

She nipped his finger when it traced her bottom lip. He smelled like her. She found it highly arousing. Holding the tip of his finger between her teeth, she wagged it.

"Hmm, maybe for a man—" The minute the words left her mouth she regretted them.

He smiled and moved closer. "Frankie, you disappoint me."

She pushed his finger away and moved back against the pillows. "I didn't mean it like that."

He moved where she had just been. "What did you mean?"

"Women have to worry about getting pregnant."

"We used a condom."

"You never know, it could break."

He nuzzled her throat and her skin warmed. "Always a possibility, but not in our case. But I understand what you mean. I promise to be very careful."

She sighed and decided she recovered enough not to look like a cling-on. "Glad to hear that."

"So does that mean I can get another condom?"

Frankie smacked him and rolled out of the bed. She grabbed the blanket at the foot of the bed and wrapped it around herself. "We need to get out of here."

Reese sat up. "We have another hour."

"I have a spread to do, and that means getting the hell out of here."

"In light of everything that's happened, I don't think Carmel is wise."

She hobbled toward him, cocooned in the blanket.

"I've seen everything you own, you really don't need to cover yourself."

She shook her head. "We need to get to Carmel."

He frowned. "I'm against it, we'll go to Santa Cruz for the beach shots."

"Your protest is so noted. But we're going to Carmel." Reese opened his mouth to protest but Frankie held up her free hand. "I have my reasons, and while I agreed to allow you to call the shots, this point is not negotiable. You'll have to trust me."

She flung off the blanket and stalked to the bathroom door. She opened it and threw him a saucy look over her shoulder. "There are two showers in this place, and I'm not sharing mine." Before she closed the door, she called back to him. "I need coffee."

• • •

Reese stood for a long moment and stared at the closed door. He didn't bother to contemplate going through it. Instead, he contemplated Francesca Donatello. She was quite a concoction. A woman who enjoyed sex but could turn off the afterglow like a man and get on with business. And he was sure that because of her adamancy the Carmel house held the key to both his business and hers. The sixty-thousand-dollar question was, would she trust him enough to tell him what it was?

He was a patient man. He shrugged as he padded his way to the other bathroom and plotted ways of getting information out of her and getting her undressed at the same time.

As the cold water sluiced down his body, Reese decided that going to Carmel was not a bad thing. Whatever Frankie was looking for down there would only help to serve the case. Besides, his team had been sitting on the "beach house" for a week. Zero activity.

Frankie hurried to answer the insistent knock at the hotel door. "Who is it?" she called, figuring it was Jase. Frustration erupted. She was going to tell that man just what she thought about him.

"Room service."

Ah, yes, coffee. Reese was more than just a pretty face after all. She was about to open the door, but she remembered Reese's precautions last night. At an angle she looked through the peephole. A nice-looking middle-aged man in uniform smiled as if he knew she was looking at him.

Satisfied, Frankie unlocked the door, swung it open, and screamed.

CHAPTER NINETEEN

Reese toweled off, contemplating the many ways he would get Frankie out of her clothes, keep her safe, and milk her for information.

Unlike Jase, he was convinced at this point Frankie was a target, not the trigger. Keeping her alive was paramount, and it would ultimately draw out the trigger man. He was convinced the person who killed Santini was also the same person who wanted his daughter next to him.

Her refusal to divulge information about her business or her uncle told him she had something to hide. He wished she didn't, but he understood her protectiveness of her family. He was working overtime in the charm department, portraying a character he was uncomfortable with but one he knew he must continue to play to get to her. If he could get her into bed a few more times, convince her he cared, he knew he could get the dirt. He needed her to slip up and drop information. And he knew she had lots of it.

He grinned. If she wanted location, he'd give her location. Bedding Francesca Donatello was no chore for him. No, she was a definite perk, and to his dismay, his natural reticent nature had taken a vacation. He liked verbally sparring with her, and he found himself actually looking forward to a woman's company.

He scowled. He wanted her to be as innocent as she appeared.

Holy shit! He vigorously rubbed the towel over his head, drying his hair. If Jase or Ty had an inkling how he felt, he'd be pulled off this case faster than he could read the bad guy his rights. Was he losing his objectivity? Just asking the question threw him off balance. He tied the towel securely around his waist. Frankie *was not* getting under his skin.

The minute he opened the door to the living room he knew something was wrong. The silence, followed by the unmistakable sound of rounds being fired through a silencer, and the distinct sound of bullets splintering wood, was his next FBI clue. He grabbed his piece from the bathroom counter, where he set it before he jumped in the shower. With only a towel wrapped around him, he moved as stealthily as a jaguar to Frankie's bedroom, where a man in waiter's garb stood at the door to her bathroom, shooting a pattern through the door.

Frankie's bloodied, bullet-ridden body flashed into his mind and he felt sick.

"Hey, wiseguy," Reese called. The guy turned around and Reese shot him once, right between his surprised eyes.

Reese stepped over the body and kicked in the door to find Frankie hunched down in the big sunken tub, bullet holes marring the marble. He grabbed her arm and she screamed, but quickly recovered when she saw it was him. "C'mon, sweetheart, we need to get the hell out of here."

She was already dressed, but he threw on his shirt and jumped into his jeans, then grabbed his boots and Frankie's hand and ran from the room. As they waited for the elevator, Reese decided against taking it. He grabbed her hand again and pulled her down the hallway to the stairwell. He yanked open the door and came face-to-face with two men who shouldn't have been there. He pushed Frankie back and kicked the front man in the gut, sending him tumbling backward with a loud whoosh into the smaller guy behind him. Reese slammed the door shut, jerked Frankie behind him, then ran back to the elevator. The door to the stairwell opened and the bullets whizzed past them. The elevator door opened and Reese jumped in, pulling Frankie behind him. Hitting the Close button, he slammed her up against the front right corner and pressed his body protectively in front of hers. The boys might get a shot off as the door closed, but flat up against the front panel, the trajectory of a clean shot would be nearly impossible, unless one of the wiseguys wanted to lose an arm when the door closed on it.

Frankie caught her breath and looked at Reese, her eyes wide with terror. "Why?"

Reese shook his head, watched the floor numbers go down, and jerked on his boots. "You've got something someone wants or you're in the way."

Chills rippled through her body. "I only have *Skin.*"

"Who wants it?"

"Anthony." She was a fool.

The door opened and Reese pushed Frankie back against the wall. He poked his head out with his gun drawn. At the early morning hour the lobby was empty. He grabbed her hand and ran with her through the lobby and out to the parking lot.

The two thugs in the stairwell raced out of the hotel just as Reese peeled out of the parking lot.

Frankie held on to the door handle, looking over her shoulder as the two jumped into a dark sedan. "They're following us!"

"Not for long."

He sped down the freeway ramp, blending into the oncoming traffic. He took the next exit ramp, drove under the overpass, and timed his merging back onto the freeway, going the opposite direction. As he merged, Frankie looked behind them. "They passed, and no brake lights."

Not taking anything for granted, Reese put the pedal to the metal and they headed east, taking the long way to Carmel.

"Why are you going east?"

"We're going to backtrack."

She didn't argue.

"Did you recognize any of those guys?" Reese asked.

Frankie shook her head. "No."

"Level with me."

"I am!"

"What's the big deal about *Skin?*"

"The big deal is it's a profitable magazine." She hadn't wanted to tell him about the missing will and the fact that if her father had kept his word, she owned *Skin* lock, stock, and barrel. Or about Anthony's accusations—her blood chilled. But what if there *was* money missing?

"How profitable?"

She scrunched her nose. "Profitable enough."

"Enough?"

"Yes, enough. We've been down a bit the last couple of years, but you're going to change that."

"Why is Anthony so interested?"

She shrugged. "Spite."

"He doesn't strike me as that type. Arrogant, yes, but spiteful? Doesn't he have other things to do, like run your father's businesses?"

Frankie thought about that. "I—I don't know. Right before Father was killed, Anthony started coming around the office."

"Maybe *Skin* isn't all it's cracked up to be?"

"What are you insinuating?"

"I don't know, you tell me."

She ran her fingers through her wet tangles. "Are you saying *Skin* is involved in illegal goings-on?"

He shrugged.

"No! My father promised. No family business. *Skin* is legit!"

"Maybe your father changed his mind."

"He gave me his word."

"Maybe Anthony wants to convert it."

She shook her head again. "There's too much to do with all of the other businesses. I don't know where he and Unk find the time. There aren't enough hours in the day for me just as creative director."

She thought of Unk and his many accountants and advisors. The family had many businesses, some legitimate. Her father tended the seedier side of Donatello Inc., the service side, if you will, and she naturally assumed Anthony would follow in his footsteps. So why would he have an interest in *Skin?* An interest so strong he'd kill for it?

"It doesn't make any sense."

"What about your uncle?"

She snapped her head up and narrowed her eyes. "What about him?"

"Maybe he wants *Skin.*"

"I'm going to tell you something, then understand this conversation about my family is over. Uncle Carmine has as much of a vested interest in *Skin* as me. We're a family, we share. There is no power trip going on here, at least not between my uncle and me. Maybe Anthony has a few issues with Unk, and his mother, Connie, but—"

"What kind of issues?"

She shook her head. "Never mind."

"Let me in, damn it! I can help you. Otherwise you'll wake up one morning next to your father."

She sat silent. She was aware. Painfully aware. And just as aware that she didn't want to tell this man, this person who came into her life two days ago and turned it upside down, a man who she knew had ulterior motives, that she was too busy trying to survive to pursue, that her family was the poster child for fucked-up beyond recognition, and that deep down she was humiliated by them and, worse, feared them.

She glanced at Reese and wanted to trust him, to tell him everything, to let someone else deal with this mess. But she couldn't.

"If you won't let me help, would you at least consider going to the cops and telling them what you know?"

She looked at him, incredulous. "Are you kidding? I go to the cops and I *am* as good as dead."

"They have witness protection."

"I know lots of dead people who went WP. No thanks." She crossed her arms over her chest.

"I know a place on the coast where we can lie low for a while and get some of those beach shots you talked about."

"I told you, we're going to my father's house. It's very secluded on Seventeen Mile Drive. It was closed up after Father's death. Only the caretakers are there."

"Who are they loyal to?"

"My father." And, she thought, herself. Mrs. Wilson had been there for all of her cuts and scrapes after the divorce. She trusted the older woman.

"We'll need to be ready to take off."

She nodded.

Frankie sat back in the seat. The Carmel house was the key to Papa's will. It was the last place she saw him, the place where they quarreled. Her heart hurt. She let out a long breath.

Reese didn't miss it. "You're going to need clothes and a camera."

She looked down at her bare feet. "And shoes." She smiled half-heartedly. "And panties."

Reese winked. "I don't mind you going commando."

"I can have Tawny wire me cash."

"She'd know where you are. I've got my wallet, don't worry."

A tumult of emotions collided in her head. She was with a virtual stranger. Well, not that strange, considering what she did with him, but she didn't know him, and yet she was running for her life with him.

"I need to call my uncle. May I use your cell phone?"

Reese started to say no, but he removed it from the clip on his belt and handed it to her. Luckily he'd left his belt in his pants last night with the phone attached. He needed a way to get in touch with his task force. At least with the GPS in his phone and in the truck, they had a bearing on them.

Frankie wished she had some privacy. She wanted to tell her uncle how scared she was, she wanted him to come get her, but she didn't. It would be showing weakness. Besides, she was a big girl, and, after all, the daughter of Santini Donatello.

"Hi, Unk."

"Francesca! Where are you?"

"I'm"—she glanced at Reese, who kept his eyes focused on the road—"with a friend. On location."

"*Cara,* the police were here. There were two dead men in your house. *Made* men. Anthony is threatening to put contracts out on anyone who won't talk."

"Who hired them?"

"I'm working on that right now. One of them was Tommy Two Socks. I thought your father took care of him years ago. I'm not sure who he's working for. When I find out . . ."

"I don't know what to do."

"Come home. I will protect you."

She glanced nervously at Reese. His hands clenched and unclenched the steering wheel. "I—I need to get some work done, Unk. I needed to get away, so it's a good time."

"Tell me where you are. I'll send protection."

"I don't need it."

"How can you say that? Two dead goons in your house! I believe now that the shot here at my office was meant for you. Anthony told me about the car incident yesterday. I never should have let you leave alone."

"I wasn't alone."

"Jimmy told me about your model and his friends."

"Did you find out anything?"

"Yes and no. Reese Barrett came up smelling too sweet. Like a buried cop."

If she had been shot point-blank by a wiseguy, it would have been less shocking than her uncle's words. Her chest tightened and she felt the urge to vomit. She was a fool. Frankie glanced at Reese, who acted as if he wasn't listening. *It's all about perception, Frankie.* The truest words Reese had spoken to her. How blind she had been. If he wasn't a cop, he was a fed.

Spots flashed in front of her and for a moment she felt faint. *Get a grip on yourself, Frankie. It's not the end of the world. You have the advantage now.* Her brain raced for an answer on how to proceed. A cop! She should have known. In hindsight all the signs were there. "Unk, I'll call you when I get settled."

She swallowed hard and asked her uncle another question. "Did you talk to Anthony about that accounting error?"

"I'm looking into it."

He didn't sound happy. Did he actually think she had disrespected the family by stealing from them?

"*Cara,* please, be careful and *don't trust anyone.*"

"I won't."

She hit the End button and handed Reese his phone. Without looking at her, he clipped it back onto his belt.

She refrained from comment and instead kept her eyes focused on the road ahead of her. A cop! Of course. She'd confront him when she had more control of the situation. She slanted a hard glare his way. He looked at her, his brows raised in question. Oh, he was good. Really, really good.

"What did your uncle say?"

"He said not to trust anyone."

Reese nodded. "It's good advice."

She glared at him. "Advice I'll take."

And she would keep the fact he was another lying man out on the table where she could see it. It made her job so much easier, and some of the sting lifted when she considered the one perk. Who better to protect her from her family than a trained professional?

Frankie retreated into her own private thoughts. She must have dozed off; when she woke they were just coming into Half Moon Bay and turning south on Highway One. Frankie shivered.

"What's wrong?"

"My father was killed just past the brewery."

Reese put his signal on to turn back onto the two-lane highway, and Frankie put her hand on his. "No, drive me there."

CHAPTER TWENTY

Frankie walked to the edge of the Blue Moon Brewery patio, perched on the top of a low cliff. She looked down at the raging surf.

"He came here for an espresso, just like he did every time he left Carmel." The breeze stirred her damp hair, and her soft scent flirted with Reese's senses. He resisted the urge to take her in his arms and kiss the top of her head. He shook his head, uncomfortable with the feelings her sorrow stirred. Instead, he flipped the switch and went into recon mode. He stepped up close behind her, letting the warmth of his body soothe her.

"Tell me what happened."

"It was early," she said, her voice barely audible over the surf, "the restaurant was closed. But Father knew the door code and let himself in like he'd done hundreds of times. Mr. Martini, the owner, owed my father. He loaned him the money to start this place." She laughed quietly. "Santo Gabriel to the rescue."

Reese reached out to her shoulder and touched her. It surprised him that the gesture came easy.

"Did Mr. Martini see your father?"

She shook her head. "No. He hadn't arrived yet. Father made his espresso and came out here."

"Who found him?"

"Jimmy."

That was news. "I thought Jimmy worked for your uncle."

Frankie nodded. "He does, but before that he was Father's bodyguard."

She leaned over the railing and pointed to a large, flat boulder sticking out of the side of the cliff about thirty yards down the slope. "You can still see the bloodstains on the rock." She shuddered. "They shot him in the back of the head like cowards, then dumped his body over this railing for good measure."

"I remember reading about it." Reese put his hands on the railing on either side of Frankie and pressed his chest against her back.

He smiled when she didn't stiffen. His grin widened when she relaxed into his body. "I doubt he suffered," he said, his lips touching her hair, her clean scent titillating. As it always did when she was so close, his body responded. His blood vessels swelled and his skin warmed. He wanted more of her and idly wondered if he could ever get enough.

"That's what the coroner said."

She turned and leaned back against the stone railing. The morning light raining over the restaurant roof shone in her face, and she had to squint to see him. The breeze toyed with a stray lock of her dark hair.

Reese pushed it behind her ear. "I'm sorry, Frankie," he said.

She nodded. "Me too. He wasn't a bad man."

Reese would beg to differ but held his tongue. "How did your mother take it?"

Frankie laughed. "No love lost, they've been divorced for years."

"Anthony isn't your brother?"

"Half brother. His mother maneuvered my father good."

"No love lost, huh?"

She shook her head. "Not an ounce. I mean Anthony is okay for the spoiled man-child he is, but his mother, as my mother would say, is 'common.' "

At least, Reese thought, Anthony's mother stuck around.

"What about you, Reese?"

His intimacy alarm went off. He released his grip on the railing and stepped back from her.

"Oh, no you don't." Frankie grabbed his shirt front, pulling him to her. "You ask an awful lot of questions, now it's my turn."

He stopped his retreat and inwardly cringed. "What?"

"Tell me about your mother, your family."

His muscles tensed and anger clouded his brain. "I don't have any family."

"What happened to them?"

He shrugged and tried to step away again, but Frankie's grip on his shirt tightened. "Tell me."

"They're dead."

"What happened?" she murmured.

"Not sure about my mother, but after my sister died my father mentally checked out."

"Do you see him?"

"No."

"How old was your sister when she died?"

"Twelve."

"I'm so sorry."

Reese stood rigid, his jaw tight, barely able to contain the pain and guilt that tore at his gut.

"Do you miss your mom?"

Reese shook his head and this time stepped back with enough force to break her grip. "No."

He looked over his shoulder and around the empty balcony. Despite the fresh morning air and the salty breeze rolling off the Pacific, he felt uncomfortable, exposed. "We need to hit the road. Lightning has been known to strike the same place twice."

For once she didn't argue with him.

Reese felt reasonably sure they weren't being tailed by unfriendlies. He knew one or more of the task force men would be following in their wake, the GPS device in his cell and also in his truck a constant beacon. Frankie had quieted and for once her fight seemed to be gone. He felt for her. She was alone in the world right now, running for her life and with no one to turn to but him, a stranger who in the end could send her up the river if she was guilty of a crime.

For the first time in his many undercover cases, Reese questioned his tactics. It all boiled down to him using Frankie as a means to an end. An end that would take a bunch of bad guys off the streets for a long time. Did the end justify the means?

Reese had given too many death notifications to shocked parents because their kid OD'd on drugs the Donatellos sold on the street. So many lives wasted, the dirty money used to garner more drugs, more prostitutes, more violence against society. Yeah, the end justified the means. And as in all things in life, there was collateral damage. He glanced at Frankie and his gut twisted. He was just sorry that in the end, she would be caught in the crossfire.

He gripped the steering wheel tighter. He needed more information, and in her current mood she seemed receptive.

"I'm hungry." His stomach growled to confirm his words.

Frankie nodded, the gesture barely perceptible. "There are plenty of little cafés along the coast. Just pick one."

A few minutes later Reese pulled off Highway One and into the parking lot of a nondescript little café.

He came around and opened the door for Frankie and guessed from her down-turned lips and the dark circles under her eyes that she was tired and unhappy. Hell, no wonder. She'd been through the ringer. He let out a long breath. And he was about to squeeze some more.

He took her hand and led her up the sidewalk. For the second time that morning, she didn't flinch when he touched her outside of bed. The echoing sound of the waves crashing the beach across the street coupled with the cries of the circling gulls echoed Frankie's mood. He scanned the perimeter of the small building for the third time as they approached the structure.

"Is the food any good here?" he asked.

She shrugged absently. "I don't know."

They were seated immediately. The hostess gave them menus and asked if they would like something to drink. They both opted for coffee.

Several minutes later Reese ordered enough food to feed her entire father's side of the family. Frankie ordered toast.

"You should eat, Frankie," Reese chastised.

She shrugged and looked out the window toward the ocean. Her long hair stirred as a breeze blew through the open screen window, a single strand catching across her lips. Reese reached over and brushed it away, his fingertips lingering on her bottom lip. "I know this is hard for you, Frankie. I give you my word, I'll do whatever I can to protect you."

Her reaction surprised him: her eyes narrowed and she slapped his hand away. "Do us both a favor, Reese, and stop lying to me."

He withdrew and eyed her hard. "What is that supposed to mean?"

"It means we talk only in truths. And here are mine. You signed a contract to strip where and when I tell you. I'm holding you to every clause. I also agreed to allow you to stick around to protect my ass. When we get to Carmel, I might ask you to help me with something else, and you will either agree or not. If you agree, you'll do it without questions or subterfuge. I don't want any complications with you."

The waitress approached with a laden tray and filled the table with Reese's many plates. "Why won't you talk about him?" Reese stabbed a hunk of sausage and put it in his mouth. He eyed her as he slowly chewed. He took a swig of his coffee, swallowed, and said, "He must have burned you bad."

Instead of eating, she looked out the window, her jaw set, her body language clear. "Mind your own business."

It didn't stop Reese. "Did he humiliate you?"

Frankie turned to him, her eyes narrowed, her nostrils flared, her color high. She looked incredibly fuckable at that moment, and Reese's body reacted.

"Why the fifty questions?"

"You're my meal ticket, I don't want to make the same mistake as the guy before me." He cringed as the words came out. He didn't mean it the way it sounded.

Frankie's eyes widened and her jaw clenched. "So I'm nothing but a meal ticket to you?"

"You're more than that." And it wasn't a lie, damn it.

"Oh, that's right, I'm also your sport fucking partner."

He leaned forward, covering the space of the small table. Frankie sat back in her chair and crossed her arms protectively over her chest. He traced a finger along her forearm to her hand, trailing a circle around her knuckles. He sniffed the air; her unique natural scent blended with the spicy salt of the sea, flirted with his nostrils. "I'll never forget how sweet you smelled this morning." He watched her cheeks flush deep red.

She snatched her hand away from his lingering fingers. "Don't touch me again."

"C'mon, Frankie. Admit it, we fit."

Frankie's demeanor didn't change. Her brows slammed together and the muscles under her jaw twitched.

"I'm not the bad guy."

"You're a man, that's enough."

"Aw, c'mon, Frankie, be nice to me."

Her lips twitched. She shook her head.

"Maybe you just need to sit back and relax, let it ride and see what happens." Reese plucked a strawberry off the mound of cream on his waffles. When he bit into it, it sluiced. He licked the pooling juice with a slow, lascivious swipe of his tongue. "That was you this morning, Frankie, sweet, red, and juicy."

"Stop it," she whispered. And despite her sour mood, his words excited her. Everything about him excited her.

He dipped his finger into the cream on his plate and spread it across the glistening flesh of the strawberry. His blue eyes sparkled like sapphires when he looked at her. He licked the cream long and hard from the flesh of the ripe fruit. "That's what I'm going to do to you the next time I get between your legs."

Frankie squirmed in her chair. Reese popped the strawberry into his mouth and chewed slowly, his gaze never wavering from hers. He plucked another one from the bowl and dredged it through the cream. He leaned forward, a smile tugging at his lips, and wagged the cream-covered strawberry beneath her nose. "I dare you."

She smiled despite her dark mood.

"Tell me about the prick who broke your heart."

Frankie shook her head and gazed out the window. Suddenly Sean didn't matter. She turned and looked hard at Reese. "I was duped. He got me into bed, promised me the world, asked me to marry him, and then sold me out." There, she said it. And for some reason saying it out loud took some of the sting out of it.

She watched Reese for a reaction. He didn't move a muscle. His face remained impassive.

"That guy was an idiot."

"I know that now. I think I was more upset about what I thought I lost than the actual loss of him."

"I never make promises I can't keep." Reese raised the strawberry to her mouth and rubbed the cream-laden tip across her full bottom lip. "I promise you, you won't get bored with me."

She smiled and licked the creamy strawberry. Reese grinned, his teeth shining in the bright morning light. She bit into the fruit, the juice sliding down her chin. Reese moved his chair closer. Bending his face to her, he whispered, "Woman, you drive me crazy," then licked her chin.

His warm tongue swiped across her skin. "The feeling is mutual."

Reese pulled back and smiled. "Good, for once we agree."

Despite the situation she found herself in, Frankie ate with a new gusto, her spirits considerably lifted.

With her belly full, and the smooth suspension of the SUV, Frankie bit back several yawns. "Get some sleep, I'll wake you when we hit Monterey." She nodded, and before she realized she had slept, Reese was shaking her awake.

She sat up with a start. Glancing at the dash clock, she realized she had slept for two hours. "Thanks for letting me sleep."

"You were dreaming."

She furrowed her brow. "Sean . . ."

Frankie racked her brain. She didn't remember specifics, but she knew her dreams were not wishful regarding Sean. Probably reliving the shame and pain. And though she was over Sean, it still stung at times.

"Why are you angry?" she asked.

"I'm not."

"Yes, you are. The muscles in your cheek are all twitching and you're gripping the steering wheel so tight your knuckles are white."

He shot her a dark scowl.

"See? And now you're looking at me all mean."

"I'm not angry with you, Frankie. I just can't stand guys like Sean." Or the fact that she'd spent the last three days with him, and it was that asshole she was dreaming about.

"Me either."

"Then why the hell did you agree to marry the schmuck? Didn't you see it coming?"

She blanched with shock at his accusation. "You've never made a mistake?" she shot back.

It was his turn to blanch. He'd made more than a few. One killed his sister.

He shook his head.

Sitting next to Reese, his anger bouncing around the truck cab, Frankie felt her emotions collide. This man drove her crazy. One moment she felt like maybe they had a connection, then, *bam,* in the next breath he shattered it, beating her up for a mistake. She sucked in a deep breath and slowly exhaled. None of it mattered, she realized. Unk's words surfaced. The only connection she could have with him was between her camera lens and his body. She realized she'd begun to have feelings for him. Bad, Frankie. Real bad. He was dangerous on so many levels, and she was not up for more heartache.

She glanced covertly at his handsome profile. The muscle in his jaw still twitched and she was sure she was responsible for it on some level. For that she was glad. He could suffer right along with her. Her eyes narrowed. She decided to give him a chance to come clean with her.

"Are you a cop?"

Reese scowled at her. "I've already answered that question."

"Answer it again."

"No."

"No, you aren't going to answer again or no, you aren't a cop?"

"No to both."

Frankie sat back and crossed her arms over her chest and her legs at the knees. She frowned. If he was a cop, did that mean he wasn't held to the contract he signed? If he was a cop, and this whole deal went south, did she even want him as her centerfold? She glanced at him, and her belly rolled. Yeah, she wanted him. And come hell or worse—her family getting in the way—she was going to have his sexy naked ass and abs on every magazine stand in the country. "I want your word, no matter what, even if you turn out to be someone else, you'll honor the contract."

Reese did not hesitate with his answer. "I give you my word." Of course, it could be completely worthless. She was willing to take a chance on this man.

"If you're lying to me, you'll regret it."

He shot her a narrowed glare. "Are you threatening me?"

"I'm just stating a fact."

He turned his attention back to the road and the twitch in his cheek flared with renewed vigor.

After a long, drawn-out minute, Frankie said, "I need film and clothes."

"We'll stop in Monterey."

"No, take One into Carmel." She smiled smugly at him. The boutiques she had in mind would set him back a few dollars. "I prefer the shopping in Carmel. Then we'll go back to Seventeen Mile Drive to my father's house."

Reese set his jaw. "I only have so much cash on me."

"Then I suggest you get your plastic out. I'll pay you back when all of this messy family business blows over."

Reese grunted. It was the first of many. Frankie had no qualms about plunking down two hundred bucks for a pair of jeans, and she liked variety. She bought three pairs that looked the same to him. While she tried on clothes, Reese went outside and checked in with his team. No activity around the Carmel house, not even a drive-by.

Frankie bought sweaters, a jacket, shirts, shoes, and finally film. Out of necessity, Reese picked up a few things for himself. As he dumped the bags into the back of his truck, she announced, "We'll need food. Pisotle's is around the corner. Best deli in Carmel. Lots of goodies."

Now, food Reese could relate to. Despite his large breakfast, he was hungry again.

. . .

After loading up a small shopping cart with enough food to feed a small army, Reese strolled down the impressive wine aisle. Frankie shook her head. "Don't bother, my father has . . . had an excellent selection in his wine cellar. You'll find anything you want at the house."

He nodded, paid the ridiculous tab, and loaded the SUV.

Despite going back to the place she last saw her father alive, Frankie felt excited. She gave Reese instructions to the entrance of Seventeen Mile Drive. The western sun had begun a slow descent over the Pacific. The light show in store would be amazing. A kaleidoscope of oranges, reds, and pinks would blend into a swirling cheerful mesh of color to later blend with violets, then blues, then finally black. Her photographer's eye was dying to catch the stunning transformation.

"I want to get a few dusk shots on the beach before we do anything," Frankie said.

Reese only shrugged.

"Turn at the next driveway on the left," Frankie said, looking at the road again. She'd nearly missed the turn, as her thoughts were focused on Reese. As he turned into the wide driveway, they were met with solid steel gates. Frankie hopped out of the truck and strode to the large metal box embedded in a stone foundation. She slid back the metal lid to a code pad and keyed in a code that opened the main box, which exposed another keypad, this one considerably more involved. It had colored buttons as well as numbered buttons. She deftly entered the necessary code and the heavy gates lurched, then swung slowly open.

Frankie hopped back into the truck and they continued down the wide, tree-lined drive, the gate closing in a low rumble behind them. Reese whistled when they pulled up in front of a Gothic monstrosity. It reminded him of the Tahoe house of Michael Corleone in *Godfather II.* The place went on for miles.

"Nice place."

"I grew up here. My father called it Casa di Falco."

As they walked up to the front door, it occurred to Frankie she didn't have the key. "The caretakers' cottage is in the back. The Winstons will have a key."

Reese turned back to the truck. He held her door open, waiting for her, and he noticed several cameras inconspicuously mounted in the surrounding trees.

"This place is tighter than the Pentagon," Frankie assured him. It gave him a modicum of comfort. Frankie hopped in. Reese closed the door, then got in himself.

They drove down the driveway, past the main house to a densely wooded side yard. To the right, a large formal pool with fountains beckoned. If it was warmer, a swim might not be a bad idea. Reese wondered if it had a hot tub. He parked the truck in front of an actual cottage. Frankie stepped out and went to the front door and knocked. Reese expected Peter Rabbit to answer. No one answered.

Reese followed her out of the truck. "Peter Rabbit go out?"

Frankie smiled and shrugged. "Probably." She tried the doorknob, and it turned. "I don't think they'd mind if I came in for the key."

She walked into darkness. Only a few shards of filtered sunlight made it through the trees and into the entryway. Dust motes stirred in her wake. "Mrs. Winston? Mr. Winston? It's Francesca."

Silence. "I came for the house key." The great room that served as living room, dining room, and kitchen was tidy, but it looked like no one had been in the house for some time. Why?

"Strange," she said to herself.

Reese walked up behind her. "Strange how?"

"It looks like they haven't been here for a while. And I know they were here two weeks ago."

"I'm not getting a good feeling about this, Frankie. Let's get a place in town and come back later."

"*No,* I need to be here."

He cocked a brow, then scowled. "There's plenty of beach around. Why here?"

"I'll explain later." And she decided it didn't matter if he was a cop and privy to the details of her father's will. In fact, it was a plus if he was a cop. Then it was a safe bet he wasn't out to kill her. She'd take advantage of his training and experience as long as she could.

She stepped to the back of the great room to a battered rolltop desk. She pushed the lid up, pulled open one of the drawers, and plucked out a key.

She dangled it in front of Reese. "See? With this and the alarm code we'll be fine."

"Is it unusual for them to be gone?"

"Maybe. It looks like they've been gone for a while."

"Vacation?"

"Not the kind you're thinking of."

Reese shook his head. "Frankie, your family is scary. How do you live constantly looking over your shoulder?"

"I never have." She chewed her bottom lip. Had something happened to the Winstons? "Things are different since my father died. The old ways are gone."

"Just like that?"

"No, it's been coming. It's probably why Father is dead. He was old school. He didn't like the new ways."

"What is the new way?"

"You wouldn't understand."

"You'd be surprised what I'd understand."

"Look, my family is what it is. I make no excuses for them."

"Then why are you afraid?"

"I'm not afraid."

"You're a lousy liar, Donatello. And stupid if you're not scared."

"My family wouldn't hurt me."

"Maybe not the old guard, but like you just said, times are different."

She swallowed and nodded. She couldn't say it out loud, not to him, not to anyone. Especially herself. "Let's get down to the beach before we lose our light."

"That's fine, but I'm taking some of the groceries, I'm hungry."

Frankie headed down the short hallway and said over her shoulder, "There's wine in the pantry there and a corkscrew in the drawer next to the sink. Grab a couple of glasses from the cupboard."

He grinned. She stopped and turned completely around to face him. "No hanky-panky, I have a job to do, and just in case you forgot, so do you." She wheeled around and headed down the hallway, returning a few minutes later with an armful of blankets and towels. "I don't think the Winstons will mind."

He grinned again, this time wider. His blood warmed the minute she told him to grab a bottle of wine. Maybe she had work on the brain, but he had something else entirely on his. Not only was she vulnerable emotionally to him right now, but he needed to get all cop thoughts out of her mind. And what better way to do that than shucking his clothes at sunset on one of the greatest places in the world with a beautiful woman who couldn't take her eyes off him?

CHAPTER TWENTY-ONE

Frankie navigated the steep trail down to the white and black sands of the beach below like a mountain goat. Reese followed, carrying a picnic basket he'd found in the pantry and then loaded with wine, meat, fruit, cheese, and bread. He was salivating more over the delectable ass taunting him like a bone in front of a hungry dog than the salami and cheese in the basket.

It took a good ten minutes to navigate the trail, and once they touched the bottom, Frankie turned and smiled. The breeze blew her hair back, her nipples puckered beneath the white fabric of her white cotton shirt, and the sun's bright rays haloed her like a vixen saint. Reese caught his breath. She was beautiful, and he realized at that moment he wanted more from her than sex. For the first time in his life he was willing to step outside of the exile he'd placed himself in since the death of his sister. The notion shattered his resolve with the force of a wrecking ball. It was impossible.

Frankie laughed and grabbed his hand, pulling him out of his stalled stance and down the beach. She tossed the blankets under a leaning cypress and pulled him closer to the crashing waves. "Strip!" she called, and laughed at his surprised reaction.

She continued to pull him, her hand in his, warm and trusting. He tensed, and she must have felt it. She stopped and looked up at him, the sun illuminating her curves. He wanted to smash his mouth against hers, strip her bare, then take her in wild abandon there on the sand.

"What's wrong, Reese?"

He pulled her toward him, but she dug her heels into the sand. "No time for that."

She turned and yanked his arm, dragging him toward the surf. "I need you to strip then walk into the water, dive in, then turn around and come wading out, smoothing your hair back real slow, like a male version of *The Birth of Venus*."

When she let go of his hand, she pulled her Nikon from its case, and quickly loaded it, he realized she was serious.

He groaned and rolled his eyes. Scanning the private beach, he was grateful for at least that. He shucked his boots, then his shirt. As he was unbuttoning his jeans, she called over the breeze. "Hurry up." She jogged toward him and unhooked the first three buttons of his jeans. His dick responded to the touch of her hands through the denim.

She looked up at him and grinned.

When he hesitated, she pushed him. "Hurry, we're losing light."

Frankie watched as Reese jogged down to the water. She admired the hard play of his muscles across his back and the rhythmic symmetry of his glutes, thighs, and calves. She couldn't wait to see the front of him all wet and glistening. She kicked off her shoes and followed. When he stood knee-deep, he turned around. "It's fucking cold!"

"Stop whining and dive."

He stood defiant, his brows drawn low over his blue eyes. She eyed the sinking sun. She had maybe thirty minutes and was hoping she'd get one or two decent shots. She couldn't control the lighting; she was flying on pure instinct. "Now."

He turned and dove. She followed him into the low surf, stopping when it hit her knees. Like an orca, he surfaced several yards from her. She focused, and the minute he turned she began her magic. Reese didn't need to be told twice what she wanted. As he stalked toward her, his hard body glistening, his muscles rippling under the glow of the setting sun, her female parts warmed. She slowly backed up as he came forward, his gaze locked on her lens.

"Slower. Yes, that's it, close your eyes and throw your head back. Oh, yes, perfect, now dig your fingers into your hair. Excellent, now slowly, open your eyes and walk toward me."

His eyes morphed dark and even through the lens she could tell his intentions. He waded toward her and she backed up, her shutter opening and closing at a maddening pace.

"Shit! I ran out of film." She bolted for her bag and yelled over her shoulder. "Don't move!"

The breeze stirred up, for each second the sun sank, so did the temperature. When she finally had her camera reloaded, Frankie realized she had lost the lighting for the surf shots. But not for a few quick poses of Reese lying all sexy on the beach. "On the sand, lie down and let the surf come up to your thighs," she called, jogging toward him.

"It's fifty degrees!"

"So cry about it."

Reese lay down on the sand. Frankie smiled, bent down, and grabbed a small handful of wet sand. She smeared it across his chest and stood back, allowing a low wave to ripple up to his chest. From his expression, she could tell he was not amused. "Drop the scowl! Just a few shots, then we'll get you all cleaned up."

She was as good as her word. With the usable lighting all but gone, she offered her hand to Reese. He took it, but instead of letting her pull him up, he yanked her toward him. She screamed, holding her camera up in the air. He wrapped his wet arms around her waist and rubbed his wet hair all over her chest.

"Reese!" she squealed, holding the camera away from the deadly salt water. "My camera!"

He rolled over on her, her arm still high in the air. He picked her up and walked out into the water. She shrieked, kicking and screaming.

"No more subzero water shots," Reese said. His face was grim but there was a sparkle in his eye.

"You signed a contract. Anytime. Anywhere."

He dipped her toward a rising wave. She wrapped her arms tighter around his neck.

"Okay, okay!"

He laughed and twirled around. "Don't forget it."

"I won't, now put me down."

He walked from the water onto the beach. "All in good time," he said.

Despite his wet, sandy body, Reese's body heat seeped into her damp skin. She'd be a fool to let go, she told herself; it was chilly now that the sun had all but set and the evening breeze was rolling in.

Reese walked with her cradled against his chest to the cypress tree, where the basket and the towels lay. When he set Frankie down, her long, soft curves slid down his hard, damp body. He immediately reacted.

Frankie leaned into him and felt his erection. She jerked back, her eyes wide. He pressed closer to her when she couldn't help but look down. His swollen head winked at her. "Don't you ever stop thinking of sex?" she asked, dragging her eyes regretfully from his very male part and up to his grinning face.

"You make it difficult to think of anything else."

She smiled. She liked his answer. "There's a shower just up the way, near the fire pit." She grabbed a towel and wrapped it around his broad shoulders, noticing the goose bumps on his skin, then gathered up the other towels, her camera bag, and the blankets. "Follow me, and I'll show you."

They approached the open shower stall tucked into the craggy side of the cliff, the fire pit with a gas starter, and the table and chairs scattered around for intimate conversation. "Nice setup," Reese said.

"I've been coming down here since I was a kid. Some of my best memories are from here. My mother insisted we have the bare essentials. There was nothing worse than spending the day on the beach then not being able to rinse before indulging in the fire-roasted marshmallows and ghost stories."

She showed him where the light was for the shower. While he rinsed off, she threw a few pieces of the stacked driftwood next to the pit on the grate, turned on the gas starter, and within minutes had a roaring fire.

She opened the picnic basket and realized she was famished. She expertly uncorked the bottle of cabernet Reese had picked out and admired his choice. One of her favorites.

"Pour me a tall one," Reese said, his deep voice close.

Frankie gasped and looked up to find him three feet from her and wearing only a towel. She swallowed hard, her eyes dropping to his waist and the rising fabric. "I think you should get dressed."

"My jeans are still on the beach."

Pouring the wine, Frankie looked toward the beach and in the muted light could discern a dark mound on the sand. Her gaze swept back to Reese slicing the salami and cheese. "Just don't forget them."

Reese winked. "Be sure to remind me." He looked out over the ocean. "This place is incredible, Frankie."

"It beats a tenth-floor walk-up."

She handed his wine to him and set about slicing the fruit. She didn't want to look at him, she knew he would look too good to resist, and her defenses were down. As much as she wanted to curl up in his lap and have him tell her everything would be all right, she couldn't. Her survival depended on her not weakening, and that included investing even a scant bit of trust.

With the food prepared, she placed the basket between them and reclined on her side, facing the fire. A quiet silence filled the space between them. Reese sipped his wine. "This is nice," he said, and she knew he meant the wine.

She nodded.

Suddenly she felt vulnerable, and shy. She'd been as physically intimate with him as she had ever been with a man, hell, more than with any man. Even Sean.

Absently she chewed on a slice of apple and brie. Sipping her wine, Frankie looked out over the glimmering Pacific. A half-moon hung suspended, as if it couldn't make up its mind whether it wanted to come or go. The cast gave just enough light to see the beach and the soft waves lapping against the sand.

The fire crackled and embers shot into the air, the sound startling her.

"It's just wet wood," Reese said, his voice calming.

He sounded close and she looked at him. He had moved the basket aside and was only a few inches away. The fire played across his bare chest and the towel hung loosely around his waist. She had the uncontrollable urge to press him onto the thick blanket and kiss him senseless. And when she'd had enough of his lips, she wanted to crawl up his chest and in a slow, agonizing slide impale herself on his full cock. She moved back, away from his pull.

"What are you thinking, Frankie?" he asked, moving closer as he swept a fluttering lock of her hair from her face.

"Wouldn't you like to know?"

"From the look in your eyes, I'd say I was dessert."

"Not quite."

He cocked a dark brow, the gesture giving him a devilish appearance. "Tell me."

"More like the main course."

"I can fill you up so you're not hungry anymore." He slid his hand around her neck and pulled her toward his lips.

She wanted it, bad. "I can't do this, Reese."

"Do what?"

"Kiss you."

"Then I'll kiss you." His lips brushed hers and shock waves rocked straight to her core. Just a kiss lit her up like a bonfire. Dangerous.

"Reese," she murmured, her lips brushing up against his. His warm breath smelled sweet, like the grapes he'd just eaten and the soft oak of the cab. "Please, I—" She couldn't say it. She couldn't say if they kept at it like this, she might fall in love with him. She closed her eyes, wishing with all her heart they were two people in a different place and a different time. In so many ways they were on opposite sides. She was on one side of the camera, Reese on the other, her

family was less than upstanding, and he was probably a cop out to
put them all behind bars.

The realization had a sobering effect. "I can't have sex with you."

"You already have."

"It was a mistake."

He laughed, the sound soft and throaty. The percussion of it ran
along her cheeks, making her hotter.

"I don't think so. Sex like that is never a mistake."

She pulled away. "I wouldn't know."

He moved back and sat up. He made himself a sandwich and she
watched him. He was addictive, and if she wasn't careful, she just
might overdose on the man and die, or wish she had when he
betrayed her.

Frankie grabbed her wineglass and took a hearty gulp.

Reese chewed slowly, a contemplative look on his face.

"I've never wanted to keep a woman to myself like I do you."

Her heart flipped, then flopped at his confession. She knew for a
man like Reese it was a huge confession. "I'm flattered." Was he
being honest or just stringing her along? She eyed him cryptically.
She didn't know for sure, but she liked to think that maybe there was
some truth to his words regardless of his motives.

She finished the wine and set her glass in the open basket. "We
should get going back to the house."

When she moved to stand, Reese grabbed her hand and pulled
her down to him. "Relax, and come here for a minute."

Reese watched her eyes widen like a frightened doe. "I won't hurt
you, Frankie," he whispered. She swallowed and he inwardly
cringed. Lying had always come easy to him while undercover. Not
so easy this time.

She nodded. "I want to believe you."

"Try."

She nodded again. "No sex."

He grinned. "Let's play it by ear."

This time she grinned and pulled away and stood. "Sure."

The climb up the trail was considerably more work than the climb down, especially in damp, sandy jeans. Reese couldn't wait to get a real shower and into dry clothes.

"Let's go into the main house," Frankie said. "We can clean up and I have a few more ideas for shots."

"Don't I get a break?"

"Stop whining."

As they crested the path to the back of the house, Reese slowed his step.

"Let's be careful," he said.

"No one knows where I am. I didn't tell anyone." Besides, Connie and Unk had already gone through the house, and those that needed to know, knew the compound was impregnable.

"Would anyone suspect?"

"No." Except her mother, and she didn't count. Lucia would never work against her only child.

Reese scanned the dark stone walls of the shadowy house. Despite sitting on the edge of the ocean, where sunlight bathed it daily, the house sat dark and brooding on a high bluff. In the darkness large windows along the east side absorbed the moonlight, their glass foreboding. High stone walls surrounded the property, and surveillance cameras watched from strategic placement among the tall Monterey pine. So why wasn't he hearing an electric hum?

His suspicion rose. "When was the last time anyone from the family was here?"

He watched a shadow fall over Frankie's face. "I'm not sure. I know Anthony and his mother have been here and my uncle. I don't know when the Wilsons left."

They made their way toward the back of the house, where Frankie pushed the top of a large rock near a sliding glass door. A lid slowly opened, exposing a coded box. She pressed in a code that slid back to reveal a panel. "That's odd."

Reese stepped closer to look at the panel of LED numbers and letters along with several colored buttons and program dials. Very sophisticated. "The alarm isn't set," she said. Which meant Connie, Unk, or the Wilsons forgot to set it.

"Let me go in and check out the house first."

"No, let me set the sensors. It'll let me know from here if there are any bodies in the house."

"Bodies?"

"Not dead, the sensors pick up body heat."

She fiddled with a few dials, entered a code. "Nothing, not even a squirrel."

"Could it be the sensors aren't working?"

"Anything is possible. Let's go in. Do you have your gun?"

Reese raised a brow. "I don't normally—"

"Knock it off. Do you have it?"

He nodded and pulled it from the picnic basket.

"Good, let's get going."

Although it had been closed for almost two weeks, the dark house smelled musty, old. Frankie shivered. Like death. Although as a child the house scared her, since she'd outgrown her childhood fears, she had always felt safe. Now she felt like an outsider. She knew her father loved the place—she had too—but now she found it sad and depressing and would always think of her father's harsh words spoken in his library. *"You are dead to me."*

Reese touched her shoulder, jolting her out of her daydream. "What happened here?"

She smiled sadly and turned on the light to the large mudroom. "My father loved this house. He preferred to run business from here than in the San Francisco offices." She led the way into the cavernous kitchen. Copper pans hung from black wrought-iron hangers, stainless steel appliances gleamed under the soft dusk light. A large chopping block table with a wide stainless steel sink dominated the middle of the room. The faint scent of garlic and fresh herbs permeated the room. "Father loved to eat."

"I love to eat."

His words sent shivers stampeding across her skin as she remembered his mouth on her that morning. Had it been just this morning when she woke to find him so aroused in her bedroom? Had it been just this morning when he sent her off into space after he put his mouth between her thighs and made a meal out of her? Her body flushed hot. Mentally she shook herself, pushing all thoughts of Reese and his seduction away. She needed to concentrate; her life depended on it.

Frankie showed Reese the alarm setup, and in the process reset all of the preliminary alarms and activated the cameras.

After an extensive search of the house, it was obvious there were no unwelcome guests. No Winstons. Not even a squirrel. Where the caretakers were, she had no clue. She couldn't blame Mrs. Winston if she quit after the horrible shouting match she overheard between Frankie and her father. But still, it wasn't like them to abandon the grounds.

"Let's get our clothes from the truck and clean up," Frankie said.

Reese grinned his wolfish grin. "Show me the way."

CHAPTER TWENTY-TWO

Frankie showed Reese to a room next to her old room. They agreed to meet in the hallway in twenty minutes. They would pack everything except their new toothbrushes and put them into the SUV, then they would get to work.

She took the quickest shower of her life, wanting to get on with business. She slipped on a pair of black hip-hugger terry cloth jogging pants and a white-button down terry midriff. Camera in hand, she paced the hallway outside Reese's door.

She stared when his door opened and he stepped out of the room, showered, shaved, and clad in a white-button down chambray shirt tucked into very tight acid-washed 501s. Damn, he looked good enough to eat.

Frankie hiked her camera bag over her shoulder and said, "First we're going to do some recon."

He cocked a brow.

"Don't play coy. You know that word."

He opened his mouth to protest, but she turned and told him not to waste his breath.

Reese followed her down the wide staircase and then down to the north wing to her father's office. She quietly opened the heavy oak office door, then leaned back against the paneled plane. Rich aromatic cigar smoke lingered in the room. Her father loved a good cigar, and the ones he smoked didn't bother her, not like some of the cheap ones she'd smelled. The light scent of fine brandy mingled with the cigar aroma made her eyes fill with tears. She loved her father. And she missed him. He wasn't the poster child for Dads "R" Us, but he was her father and in his way she knew he loved her.

Swiping a tear from her cheek, Frankie took a big breath and resolved to find the document. She glanced at Reese, who stood silent in the doorway. She was grateful for his silence.

Setting her camera bag down on the desk, she moved to stand behind her father's massive mahogany and brass desk. Sliding a hand along the smooth edge, she blinked back another onslaught of tears. She looked up to find Reese had not moved, but his eyes were soft in understanding. "I need your help," she said.

"Anything."

She smiled and swiped her moist eyes. "I must find my father's will. It's paramount to my family's survival."

Reese nodded.

"This desk and office has all kinds of false bottoms in the drawers and side panels. I want to be careful and not destroy anything." Taking a deep breath, she asked Reese point-blank. "If you were a will, and didn't want anyone to find you, where would you hide?"

"How about in plain sight?"

"Good idea, and something my father would do."

"If you don't mind me asking, is there no one in your family who has a copy?"

"The one my brother's waving around is bogus."

Reese nodded. "What does your brother stand to lose if the new will turns up?"

"*Skin,* this house." Father had told her since she was the only one who appreciated it, the house should rightfully go to her. But that was a long time ago.

"Are you kidding me, Frankie?"

Her head snapped back at his incredulous tone. "Kidding you how?"

"Here we've been tossing around names of people who'd like to see you as fertilizer and you drop this on me? Anthony gets your magazine and this house, which would go for what? Fifteen, twenty mil? Are you that blind, or just dumb?"

Standing straight up, she clenched her hands, strode into his space, then jabbed an index finger in his chest. "Look here, mister, I'm neither blind nor stupid, and for what it's worth, you don't know my brother, I do, and despite the fact he's a spoiled mama's boy, and despite what he stands to lose, and despite the obvious, in my heart I don't believe he's out to kill me." Taking a deep breath, Frankie continued, "And *if,* and that's a big if, Anthony is behind this, my uncle would skin him alive strip by strip and throw them all into the bay for the sharks to eat, and don't think Anthony doesn't know it!"

Reese shook his head and wiped his hand across his face. "You know what? Let's for the sake of argument say everyone, including me, wants a piece of you. Now what do you do?"

"Tell you all to get fucked."

Reese grinned. "I'll get fucked all right, but first, I'll help you. Now, did Daddy have a favorite piece of furniture or book or toy he might slip this elusive will into?"

"He spent most of his time here, but his favorite place in the house was the atrium."

"Do you think he hid it in a tree?"

"No, smart-ass, it's here in this house, and even though I'm sure his widow and my uncle have gone through it, I can feel it's here, I just don't know where."

"And how many other people do you think will figure out it's here?"

"Everyone knows this place has the tightest security money can buy. Besides, if they were going to come look, they already would have. If we get company, we'll know the minute someone tries to come onto the property."

"I suggest after we do what we have to do here, we find somewhere else to go for a few days and lie low."

"That was my plan."

Reese reached out and touched her shoulder. "It's going to be okay, Frankie."

She nodded, her damp hair falling across her eyes. She swiped it away. She wanted to believe him, to wake up and have the nightmare be over. His fingers pressed reassuringly against her skin. She felt a little crack in her shell and thought how nice it would be to trust him. "I know." And she planned to make it okay, with or without Reese.

He sensed her discomfort, so he looked around the room. "His office is as good a place as any to start."

They dug in. After almost two hours of pulling out books, files, furniture, and paintings, they came up empty.

Frankie sat down in her father's studded black leather chair and blew her hair out of her face. "I give up." She felt dusty, dirty, and disappointed. Damn! She so badly wanted something to go right.

Reese squatted down in front of her. "Who would have a copy?"

"If anyone, Aldo Geppi, and he's dead."

"Nice family you have."

"Leave me alone."

He stood. "Let's go check out the atrium."

Frankie grabbed her camera. "Plan on showing some skin, it's a great place to get in some shots. But first I want to get some out by the pool. The night lighting is incredible."

"I see how it is. I'm just skin, bones, and muscles to you."

She smiled despite her fatigue, her body suddenly revving up at the opportunity to see Reese undress again. "Carpe diem, baby." And she swept past him.

"I'd like to seize something else."

As they opened the door from the kitchen to the back of the house, Frankie stopped, her feet planted on the threshold. "It's raining."

"I can see that."

Not wasting any time, Frankie closed the door and locked it, then grabbed Reese's hand and pulled him behind her. "Follow me."

As they wound their way back to the front of the house and then down a long, dark hallway to the south wing, Frankie smiled in front of a set of large double doors.

"Here's the next best thing." She opened the doors to reveal an indoor forest, complete with waterfall and swimming lagoon.

Reese smiled and entered the atrium-solarium-pool room.

"My favorite place on the entire estate. My father's too. From the time I was a little girl I could always find him out here reading." She pointed to an old cane-back recliner propped up against the steamy glass wall. "He would sit out here and smoke a cigar and feed the birds. Anyone who wanted to see him had to put up with the humidity and the birds flying around."

Reese looked at the palms and ficus growing naturally from the mounds of earth lining the deep blue water of the lagoon. The waterfall made soft, soothing sounds.

Frankie looked up to the glass ceiling and tall trees. "The birds are up there somewhere. There are open vents for them to come and go. They're quiet now because it's nighttime."

Reese knelt down and trailed his hand through the water. "It's warm." He grinned up at her and stood, unbuttoning his shirt.

"Not so fast, cowboy. I want to set this up just right."

She slid her father's chair out from the wall, pulled out the swing arm, and set her equipment on it.

"I'm thinking of you naked under the waterfall. No, no, wait. In your jeans, shirt unbuttoned, water sluicing over your shoulders and down your chest."

Reese kicked off his boots and socks, then unbuttoned his shirt. Frankie nodded and attached the appropriate lens. She turned on several sunlamps. With the rain hitting the windows, clouding them up, and the angle of the sunlamps, a sultry feeling took over the room. The humidity was high, the temperature higher, and Frankie warmed up to her work. She pushed away thoughts of her father, and people trying to kill her.

Reese stepped into the shallow pool and waded toward the eight-foot waterfall.

"Hey," Frankie called.

Reese turned and quirked a dark brow.

"I want you to warm up. Imagine you're undressing your fantasy woman. I want to see it in your eyes, feel it through my lens."

He scooped up a handful of the warm water and splashed it across his chest. Soaked, the white fabric clung to him like a second skin. "Since my fantasy woman is standing in front of me, let me show you." He stepped closer.

She smiled and focused the lens. "Tell me, Reese. Tell me what you want to do to me."

He smiled slowly, a shameless gleam in his eyes. "Lots of things, but first?" His hot gaze dipped to her breasts, then slowly back to her lens. "First, I'd splash you with water and watch your nipples harden under your shirt." He flicked water at her, and she jumped back.

"Careful of the camera." She grinned but moved closer. Her nipples didn't need water to stiffen. She felt the tingle beneath her bra. His gaze dropped to her chest again.

"Looks like I didn't need water."

Slowly she shook her head, keeping her eye to the lens. "Closer." Her voice squeaked, and she flushed. She sounded like a schoolgirl.

Reese reached out an index finger and traced a circle in the air several inches from her right nipple. "Then I'd trace your tits with a wet finger, and feel you get harder under my fingertip." He stopped a foot from her, and even though the room was steamy, she felt his body heat across the space.

"Next I'd unbutton your shirt, button by button, while I licked and sucked your lips. With my free hand I'd grab your ass and thrust your hips against my hard-on."

His hand lowered to the rising mound beneath his unbuttoned pants. His breath hitched when he touched himself, and Frankie caught her breath. His long, tan fingers splayed across his groin and his hips rocked ever so slightly.

"You'd drop to your knees, wanting to spring me, but I'd pull you back up and slide your shirt off. It would float away on the water, your bra would follow. Then I'd take you under the waterfall, letting the warm water slide over your tits. I'd suck on them at the same time." He moved backward toward the falls, his eyes never leaving her lens. "You'd tell me how much you loved my body and wanted to touch, but I wouldn't let you."

"Why not?"

"Because that, my sweet Francesca, would be giving you what you want, and I can't allow that."

"You're mean."

"You have no idea how mean I can be." He slapped his hands together, the sharp crack startling her. "I think I'd like to punish you."

"Punish me?"

"Yes, punish."

"Why?"

He smiled and backed closer into the waterfall. "Because you're spoiled and deserve it."

"I've never been spanked by anyone, not even my father. What makes you think you're man enough?"

"Try me and find out for yourself."

Without thinking, Frankie kicked off her sandals and stepped into the lagoon. The warm water swirled around her calves, and she caught herself. "I just might."

Reese disappeared behind the rolling curtain of water. For several long moments he didn't emerge.

"C'mon, Reese." Frankie laughed out loud when he stuck his foot out and wiggled his toes.

"I need some encouragement," he called from behind the water.

Frankie set the camera down on a rock on the edge of the pool. Quickly she unbuttoned her shirt and tossed it onto the water, watching as the current took it toward the fall. Reese's hand sprang out from the curtain of water and snatched it. That was as far as she would go to get him hot and bothered. Anything further and she wouldn't trust herself.

"Okay, Reese, your turn."

She grabbed her camera and focused. Reese emerged from the water, pulling his shirt off, rivulets of water cascading down his muscular chest. "You're getting really good at this. Now run your fingers through your hair. That's it, now shake your head. That's it, slower, Reese, now take a deep breath."

His rippling muscles beneath the smooth tan of his skin mesmerized her, but what took her breath away was the intensity of his blue eyes and their unwavering gaze. He looked like he was eating a favorite meal, and she was it.

"Lock your thumbs in your belt loops, yes, like that." Her camera shutter worked at a furious pace, the swooshing open-and-close sound a lullaby to her ears. "Now pull down, slow, yes, inch by inch."

"Come here, Frankie," Reese said, his voice hoarse.

"No, I'm not ready for close-ups yet."

"I am."

"Patience is everything, Reese."

He continued to pull his wet jeans down his thighs, the water causing the fabric to drag. She waited with bated breath for him to spring free. "Harder, Reese," she whispered.

He pushed the fabric down and his cock sprang out. "Beautiful," she said, and began to slowly work her way toward him. "Cover yourself."

Instead he stroked his shaft. "Come here, Frankie, and touch me."

Shaking her head, she halted. "No, Reese. I want to get the shots, not play."

He pulled up his pants.

"Stop!"

He buttoned them. "We both want something from the other. I'm willing to negotiate."

"That's not fair, you signed a contract."

"So sue me."

Frankie cocked her head and put her free hand on her hip. Reese looked good enough to eat, standing so nonchalantly in front of the waterfall, the humid temp and sound of the sluicing water intensifying the effect of his muscled planes. But there was more to this man than his good looks. While his magnetism was tangible and she realized she wanted him again, she wanted to know more about this reticent man. What did he think? What made him tick? "I have an idea," she said.

"I bet you do."

"Let's play truth or dare."

Reese scowled, the gesture brief before his eyes sparked and he smiled. "I'm game."

Frankie put her camera to her eye and focused. "Truth or dare?"

"Dare."

"I dare you to pull down your jeans."

Reese didn't hesitate.

"My turn," he softly said.

Frankie swallowed hard and licked her lips, her shutter opening and closing wildly as she angled her shots.

"Truth or dare?" he asked.

"Dare."

"Unhook your bra."

She set her camera aside, and slowly her fingers trailed down to the front clasp and pulled it back, revealing the swell of high, firm breasts. Reese's breath hitched and Frankie smiled.

"I like it when my models listen to me." Reese grinned as he threw her words back at her. Then he traced a fingertip across a nipple, instigating it to full pucker.

When she made the effort to cover herself, his hand stayed her, his fingertips brushing across her flesh. It was Frankie's turn to gasp. The warmth of his hand stirred her. She closed her eyes for a brief second and bit her bottom lip. He had a terrible effect over her, and her weakness for his touch scared her.

"Truth or dare?" she whispered.

"Truth."

Her skin shivered in excitement. "How did you get that scar on your face?"

"I fell."

"How?"

"One question at a time."

"Not if I'm not satisfied."

He moved closer, his breath warm against her cheek. "I always satisfy."

"Tell me."

He drew back and darkness clouded his features. "My father hit me so hard I slammed into the edge of the kitchen table."

Frankie gasped. "How old were you?"

He closed his face, now void of emotion, but his eyes burned hot. "Fifteen."

She reached out to him in a comforting gesture, but he flinched from her. "I don't need your pity."

She set the camera aside and ignored his chilled demeanor. He crossed his arms over his chest and his dark brows drew ominously down over his flashing eyes. "Pity is the last thing you'll get from me." She touched the scar. His jaw clenched and she felt something clench inside her too. She thought it was her heart. "Mr. Tough Guy."

She moved closer to his face, her finger softly trailing the scar. She pressed against his chest and on her tiptoes, she kissed the scar where it turned downward to his throat. His jugular pulsed strong against her lips.

"I guess we both have screwed-up families," she said.

Reese ran his hands up her ass to her waist to her shoulders. Clasping them, he pushed her away from him. "My turn now. Truth or dare."

"Truth."

"Do you want me?"

"Want you how?"

"Inside you."

Frankie swallowed hard. Reese smiled harder.

"If you don't answer truthfully, I get to dare you."

"How will you know if I'm lying?"

"I'll know."

"I—dare me."

"Chicken."

"Dare."

"I dare you to take off your clothes."

Without a word Frankie stripped. Her sultry skin glowed under the light. Reese got harder.

He moved closer, the warm water swirling around him. In a surprising move, he sunk to his knees less than two feet from her. "You're so pretty and pink, Frankie. I want to fill you up."

"My turn," she whispered. "Truth or dare."

He looked up. "Dare."

Her eyes locked with his. "I want to see you masturbate again, like before, but for me this time."

Slowly he rose to his full height and without breaking their gaze he unbuttoned his jeans. This time he didn't just push them down to his thighs; instead, he took them off, flinging them to the stone side of the pond. His dick jutted into the air, full and demanding.

He wrapped his right hand around the thick shaft and began to slowly pump. The temperature spiked. Frankie smiled and began the same slow, rhythmic movement against herself.

"My turn," he hoarsely said.

She nodded, her excitement as she watched his big hand wrapped around that beautiful cock of his her only concern at the moment.

"Truth or dare."

"Dare," she panted.

"I dare you to come before me."

Biting her bottom lip, Frankie inhaled sharply. She settled back onto the slope of the beach entrance to the pond and lay in the water. The buoyancy bounced her hips up above the surface. She pushed up on her elbows, her lips spread, and smiled at Reese. "If you come first, I get two truth-or-dares in a row."

He nodded, his eyes blistering in their sharpness, his hand slowly pumping his shaft. Frankie lay back. Slipping her right hand back down her belly, she dipped the tip of her index finger between her slippery lips, then trailed it up to her straining clit. "I wish that were you, Reese."

His hand squeezed his cock and his hips thrust toward her. "Me too."

In a slow swirl she rubbed her hard nub, the sensations her own touch wrought almost as good as if it were Reese's hand between her thighs. She began to mimic his slow rhythm but, unable to halt the rising waves of sensation, increased the pressure and pace. Her body drew taut in the water, her toes pointing toward Reese, her hips pushing the air above her hot box.

"Faster, Frankie," Reese hoarsely said.

She didn't need much encouragement; the sensation welled and she couldn't stop if she wanted to. Open mouthed, she licked her lips and increased the tempo, her fingertips moving faster and faster across her pussy, her clit straining, every sense heightened. When the crest reared, she gasped and her body went completely rigid. Then the orgasm hit, washing over her one intense wave at a time. Her hips bucked against the rippling water and despite the quick, hard release, she wanted more.

Her pussy throbbed even as her hand slowed, then stopped. She felt her swollen lips, so sensitive to her touch but wanting something more, something stronger.

Reese.

Watching him increase the momentum of his rhythm, she felt compelled to touch him herself. She sat up, reached out, and put her hand over his hand. He started, his eyes boring into her.

"Let go," she said, and moved closer, replacing his hand with hers.

She thought he was as big as he could get, but he swelled fuller beneath her hand. He groaned softly and pushed hard against her.

"Finish what you started," he demanded.

Grasping him with her right hand, she cupped his heavy balls with the other and gently massaged them as she moved her fist slowly up and down the length of him. She wanted to spread herself for him and mount him, to rock him into the next universe.

Her pussy constricted and her hand increased its tempo.

He reached out a hand to her breast and bent down, taking a nipple into his mouth. The heat and intensity of his mouth almost caused another orgasm.

She arched against him and they moaned together, his breath hitching as she ground her hips against her fist and his cock.

"Faster, Frankie," Reese said against her breast, his teeth tugging on her nipple.

The sweet pain drove her wild. She pushed against him, her fist pumping wildly. His hips rocked against her, and his right arm slipped around her waist, pulling her even harder against his body. The slapping sound of their humid skin hitting against each other excited her further. She threw her head back and watched his hooded eyes watch her. He bit down on the soft flesh of her throat.

"Oh, God," she gasped.

Reese pulled a hank of her hair, pulling her back head, forcing her face up to his. Her body arched in a backward C, and he pressed harder against her throbbing clit. Their momentum climaxed at the exact moment. Reese came against her belly, his warm seed shooting up between them. He groaned and jerked hard against her, still holding her hair in his hand. He sunk his teeth deep into her exposed neck and she screamed, the primal act and the ensuing pain more exciting than anything she had ever experienced.

Like animals they panted in each other's breaths, their bodies naked, slick with sweat and come. She grabbed his shoulders to keep herself erect. Slowly his fist unwound and he let her go, but kept a strong arm around her waist, still holding her tightly against him. Their breaths blew hot in each other's faces, and Frankie licked her dry lips.

"Truth," Frankie panted.

Reese flexed his cock against her belly.

"Okay, truth."

"Was that the wildest thing you ever did?"

"Yes."

CHAPTER TWENTY-THREE

Reese admitted the truth. It surprised the hell out of him. He wasn't a Boy Scout by any stretch of the term, and although they hadn't actually had intercourse, latent primal urges overtook him. He'd never been so physical with a woman.

"Did I hurt you?" he asked, pulling away from her.

She shook her head no, but when he glanced down at her neck, bruises where he'd bit her already stewed. He traced a fingertip along the bite marks. "I'm sorry. I've never had the urge to chew my partner before."

Frankie laughed and touched her fingertips to the tender spot as well, brushing his fingers in the process. He didn't pull away. Neither did she. "It's okay."

He watched fire spark in her eyes as she felt the swollen flesh of her throat. "You liked that, didn't you?" he asked.

He grinned when she blushed. "So, Frankie likes it rough?"

"I never thought I did, but with you, it seemed . . . right."

Always thinking of the shot, Frankie snatched the camera from the ledge. "Your semihard state is perfect for what I want. Come lie down here against the slope. Yes, just like that. The waterline is perfect, you can just"—she clicked off a few shots—"see the full root of your cock."

He flexed his hips and the head of his cock bobbed against the water. "No. No head shots yet." She laughed at her pun, then frowned. Film over. Quickly she scrambled from the water and loaded a fresh roll. Reese kept his pose. He seemed relaxed for the moment and contemplative in the water. Her body still throbbed, every one of her senses still lit. She wanted the full effect of that man inside of her turning her inside out.

"Truth or dare?" She prayed he wouldn't figure out she lost the bet, and he'd go for the dare.

Reese's head snapped up from his resigned pose. He eyed her skeptically, then slowly smiled. "Which one do you want me to pick?"

Her brain debated his question. Reverse psychology or shoot straight?

"Truth."

"Dare."

She smiled. Men could be so predictable sometimes. "I dare you to let me set a timer on a tripod and photograph us."

He cocked a dark brow. "Doing what?"

She bit her bottom lip and chewed on it for a thoughtful moment. She was going way out on an emotional limb here. If he rejected her, she didn't know how she would handle it. Taking a deep breath, she went for it. "Making love."

Reese snorted and pushed up from his supine position. "Making love? Don't you have to be *in* love to do that?"

She scowled and felt embarrassed. It wasn't like she was declaring herself or something.

"Poor choice of words. How does hot, sweaty, no-holds-barred sex grab you?"

He crossed his arms over his chest. He wasn't making this easy for her. He stood naked as the day he was born and contemplated her offer of sex on film as nonchalantly as if deciding what he wanted from a breakfast menu.

"Offer withdrawn."

She turned to get out of the water, which suddenly held no more allure, and the humidity, now too stifling.

He grabbed her hand and pulled her back. She stumbled in the water, losing her balance. He scooped her up against his chest, his cock rising in a hard hello.

"I can't let you think you have me wrapped, Frankie."

She relaxed in his arms but swatted him. "I'm a woman first, an artist second. And sometimes the two meld. Like now. I want to capture our passion on film."

"What happens when we break up?"

"Since we aren't anything but employer and employee, we'll be nothing but professional when that time comes."

"What if I don't want it to come?"

Frankie pulled back and stared at him. "Get serious. Our worlds don't mix."

He released her and sighed. "You're right. Besides, your family knocks people off."

His comment jolted her back to the reason they were there. Not for the first time, she desperately yearned for a normal life, one uncluttered, one where she could wake up every morning and not have to wonder what shenanigans her family was up to, and not always have to look over her shoulder. Although she was a "mafia princess," as Reese had labeled her, she wanted what most women wanted. A life devoid of wondering if she'd wake up dead. Someone to love, a few kids to raise in a safe, loving environment, and a career that satisfied. Basic.

She cocked an eye toward Reese and smiled to herself. There was no doubt in her mind. They could produce some of the best-looking children the earth had ever seen.

Egads, there was that ridiculous image again. Frankie mentally kicked herself. It was time to change gears.

"Let's get into some dry clothes, eat, then go toss my father's room."

"What about the hot monkey sex?"

"Later."

He scooped her wet shirt from where it snagged on a rock and handed it to her. When she grabbed it he yanked her toward him, and she slid into him. His long arms encircled her waist and he smiled down at her.

Her hazel eyes looked almost green in the low light, and her cheeks flushed rosy.

"You are the most intriguing woman I've come across in a long time."

"Hmmm, how long?"

He was bending his head to kiss her when the low beep of the perimeter sensor went off. Frankie's body tensed. "Someone is on the property," she said, her voice high. What seemed like an instant later, light flashed through the misty glass windows.

"Shit!" Reese pushed Frankie down into the water, killed the soft ground lamps nearest them, and followed her. Only their heads remained above water. "I'm not sure if those were headlights or flashlights."

Reese moved forward, his head popping up from the water like a periscope. From his vantage point he could see nothing. If they stayed they were sitting ducks. He moved back to Frankie and whispered, "Stay low and stay quiet, and don't let go of me." He took Frankie's hand and crept from the pond, pulling her behind him.

Frankie halted, resisting his tug on her hand. "I can't leave here, Reese. Not yet."

He turned. Damn it, she picked a lousy time to defy him. "If we don't leave now, you'll be here permanently."

"We can hide."

He shook his head vehemently. "Don't argue with me. We're out of here."

"But—"

He pulled her hard against his chest. "Listen to me. I don't care how many hiding spaces this place has, we need to get out of here, out of California. You need to trust me on this. Otherwise you're dead." He watched the turmoil in her eyes, and each second she wasted deciding if she could trust him or not was a second closer to a dire end.

She nodded. "I trust you."

"Good, now let's get the hell out of here."

They slipped from the pond and tugged on their soggy clothes. Frankie grabbed her camera, stuffing it in the bag, and followed close behind Reese. They both left wet footprints in their wake.

"This way," she whispered, pulling him down the hall and up the wide, winding stairway. "We can use the butler's elevator to go down when they come up."

Reese nodded and just as they were halfway up the staircase, voices infiltrated the wide entryway. They hurried to the landing.

"Bobby says the tags came back as a rental," a voice clearly said. She recognized it as one of the two who had shot the second set of thugs in her house. "He's working on the who."

"I know it ain't those old folks who used to live in the back," his partner said.

Dark laughter filtered up to the landing, where Frankie huddled against Reese's back. He squeezed her arm reassuringly.

"We scared them off good."

Frankie pulled Reese's arm toward the elevator. Reese hesitated. As much as he wanted to get Frankie out of there, he wanted to hear what the goons were saying.

"Where the hell is that Judas bitch anyway? We don't come back with her this time, the boss is gonna have our nads in a press."

Frankie inhaled sharply, digging her fingers into Reese's arm.

"Maybe that's her car out there or someone who knows where she is. Who'da thunk, a chick ripping off her own family."

"It's those young Turks. They got no respect."

The footsteps came to an abrupt halt.

"Hey, looks like water here on the floor."

"Footsteps."

Reese grabbed Frankie and ran with her down the hallway. "Last door on the right," she whispered above the loud, thudding footsteps coming up the stairway toward them. As Reese slammed the door behind them, shots rang out, a bullet lodging in the woodwork only inches from Frankie's head. She screamed and ran with Reese to the corner. She opened what looked like a closet door but was actually an elevator door.

"I locked the door," he said. "It might get us a few extra seconds."

He pushed Frankie into the elevator and climbed in behind her. Closing the door, he hit the button from the inside. The elevator lurched upward before it began to lower at an agonizing snail's pace.

The sound of splintering wood echoed into the elevator car, followed by a final thud. Shit. The door was down. Reese grabbed Frankie's arm.

"Over there!" one of the thugs yelled.

Reese shielded Frankie with his body. The elevator thumped to a halt, stopping a half foot higher than the door on the floor below the goons.

Reese kicked the door open. "Quick." He pushed her toward the opening. She gave him a wild look, then stuck her head and chest through. He lifted her at the hips and she slid through. Just in time, he dived into the opening after her and heard bullets whizzing into the elevator.

The liquid fire of a speeding bullet shaved down his back. Gritting his teeth, Reese let his adrenaline do its job. He felt no pain after the initial contact and knew the hit was superficial. He'd managed through worse and survived.

He pushed past Frankie and they took off through the back kitchen door, racing for his SUV.

Frankie yanked open the passenger door, threw in her camera bag, and dove in behind it. Reese was already starting the engine as she jerked the door closed. He slammed into reverse, the gears grinding hard, then gunned it. The vehicle was speeding backward as two men ran out from the kitchen door and stopped directly behind them. Not missing a beat, they started firing.

"Down!" Reese yelled. Frankie's head hit the dashboard, then she curled up into a ball on the floorboards. Reese kept his foot to the pedal. A loud thump was followed by a scream. He gritted his teeth in a smile. Yeah! The last man ran in front of the truck and started firing again. Reese pulled the emergency brake and swung the steering wheel around, gunning the truck. Despite the seriousness of the situation, he grinned. He loved it when the full one-eighty worked so well. Just like in the movies.

He gunned the engine again and put his hand on Frankie's head. "Stay down!" Then they busted through the closed metal gates of the estate.

He pulled his cell phone from his belt and hit a button.

"Guido," a voice answered.

"I need a fueled plane at the Monterey airport, like yesterday. I'll fly."

"I copy."

He ran his hand across the top of Frankie's head, her damp hair warm. "You can get up now. No headlights. Yet."

He knew it was just a matter of time.

"Where are we going?"

"To my place." When Reese said it out loud, he knew the demons he'd find there would be almost as dangerous as the ones he and Frankie faced here in California.

"Where is that?"

"Where no one will find you."

CHAPTER TWENTY-FOUR

O nce the shock of being shot at again began to wane and the small jet they were in took off into the night, Frankie yelled over the roar of the engines, "Do you juggle too?"

Reese shook his head. Several hours later, in the first inkling of dawn, they landed on a small airstrip in what appeared to be the middle of nowhere. Snow dusted low foothills, and what looked to be pine trees dotted the landscape. She had no idea where she was and knew virtually nothing about the man who brought her here. Yet she felt safe, and for the first time in a very long time, she allowed the pressure to excel to take a backseat to her will to survive. Letting go of that baggage lightened her considerably.

She looked at Reese as he took his headset off and checked the cockpit panels one light after another until only a low green glowed.

He moved past her and opened the hatch, grabbing the bags they brought from the truck. Turning, Reese extended his hand to Frankie, who shivered in the cold night air. She took it. "Let's get into the pilot house and see if we can find some coats."

On the ground she looked around. A low light illuminated the small building that she surmised doubled as the pilothouse and control tower, but there were no vehicles in sight.

"Where are we?" she asked.

Reese looked over at the rough mountains and the light dusting of snow. For a long moment he stood silent. "Home."

The two-story building was unlocked. With familiarity Reese crossed to the door at the back of the foyer and opened it, pulling out two heavy wool coats. He handed her one and put on the other one.

"Won't the owner mind?"

"No."

Frankie refrained from asking more questions. The hard set of Reese's jaw left no opening. She had the uncomfortable feeling that although he might be home, he wasn't happy about it.

He steered her through the small tidy building to a back door. As they exited she saw an old truck parked on the back side of the building. Wyoming plates. Running his hand up along the inside of the right front wheel well, he pulled out a key. Two minutes later they were on their way, headed east down a long, desolate country road. Umber-colored plains spotted with pines surrounded them.

"Someone could go stir-crazy out here," Frankie said.

"It happens a lot." His grim tone, like his set jaw, left no room for conversation.

After twenty minutes they pulled onto a decent highway. They drove another mile and he turned onto an asphalt road; wide metal gates stood open in welcome. Unlike the dark, foreboding presence of the ones at Casa di Falco, these gates were slatted with twisting black iron, and two silhouettes of horses faced each other at the meeting point of the gates. Above each horse's head was a scrolled letter *B.*

Reese drove down the neat white plank fenced road. The sweet smell of horses tickled Frankie's nostrils. She loved horses and missed her riding days, when she was a little girl and pretended she was Audra Barkley on *The Big Valley.*

After more than a mile, a house emerged from the dark morning air. As they approached, Frankie smiled. This was no little ranch house, but a large, sprawling abode. She could barely make out the shadows of other, larger structures in the background. A soft light shone in the large front window of the house.

"Nice spread," Frankie said.

Reese grunted.

"Your house?"

"My father's."

"Oh." The father who smacked him around. Great. She was going from her family, who wanted her dead, to his family, who wanted to maim.

"We have more in common than I thought, Reese. My family shoots at me and yours maims. I'm never having kids."

He pulled the truck around the full circular driveway, stopping in front of the house. Almost reluctantly, he put the truck in Park and killed the engine.

After a long minute he looked over at her and smiled grimly, not making any move to leave the truck. "I'm with you on that one. Too much bullshit for them to deal with."

She nodded, glad they agreed on some things. He still made no move to get out of the truck.

"Are we going to get out of here or stay and freeze our butts off?"

"In a minute."

She watched his features and intuitively realized he was afraid. Instinctively she moved her hand over his, realizing he was gripping the steering wheel. "What else happened here, Reese?"

Unblinking, he continued to stare at the front door.

"Reese?"

Shaking himself, Reese opened his door, then walked around to open hers. "C'mon," he said, holding out his hand to her. Their eyes locked and she took it.

He walked stiffly beside her down the short sidewalk to the wide porch and stopped at the front door. He looked down at her.

She squeezed his hand. "Knock."

He did. Although there were no lights except the front room light, Frankie sensed this was once a house of joy. Now it radiated tension.

After several more knocks and no answer, Reese let out a long breath and let go of her hand.

"How long has it been since you were here?"

"Fifteen years."

The unmistakable sound of a shotgun racking caught their attention. Frankie gasped, grabbing Reese's arm.

"No trespassing!" a gnarly voice shouted from the side of the porch.

"Midas?"

"Holy shit," the old voice muttered.

Reese hurried down the wide wooden steps to the hunched figure standing at the corner of the house, illuminated by the slow rising sun. "Midas, it's Reese."

"Boy? You finally come home?"

"You old codger, how the hell are you?"

Frankie's throat constricted, and her heart tugged. Reese's voice sounded happy, carefree, almost like he was a boy again.

Instead of taking the old man's extended hand, Reese wrapped him in a bear hug, lifting him off the ground.

"Boy, you finally come home," Midas repeated.

Reese set the old man down. "For a while, Midas. Maybe. If my old man allows it."

Midas stepped back. "You ain't heard?"

Reese shook his head. "I haven't spoken to him since I left fifteen years ago."

The old man made a gravelly sound in his throat. "He nutted up, been over at the old folks home in Jackson for a decade or more."

"What happened?"

"I guess his old ticker got broke one too many times."

"Not for me it didn't."

Frankie flinched at the acid in his voice. Ah, the old Reese returns.

"Ya always thought ya knew everything."

"I can read people, and you of all people know there wasn't a rock I could hide under in this state to keep him from me."

Midas put his hand on Reese's shoulder. "You got it all wrong, boy."

Gently, Reese put his hand over the older man's. "It's history. It doesn't matter. Nothing can be changed."

"You can go to him—"

"Midas," Reese said harshly, then he gentled his tone. "What's done is done."

The old man coughed and looked over his shoulder at Frankie. "You gonna bring that filly down here and introduce me or did you forget the few manners your mama taught you?"

Reese hurried back to Frankie and took her hand, bringing her to the old man. "Midas, this is—ah, Frankie, my friend."

Frankie smiled and would have loved to say "Yes, the friend who has been taking nekkid pictures of your boy." Instead she said, "It's nice to meet you, Mr. Midas."

The old man made a funny sound like a laugh that came out as a wheezed cough instead. "No mister about, it's just Midas."

"Okay, Midas."

Frankie glanced at Reese. Despite his happy face, she knew by his tense arm against her side that he was wary, not of the old man but of the situation with his father. Maybe her predicament was part of it too. Or maybe she just wanted to think so.

She turned back to the old man. "Is Midas your given name?"

"Naw. Miss Thelma, Reese's mama, gave it to me. She said I could tame the wildest mustang by just a touch of my hand. Which is a lie."

"Now who's lying, old man? You have the touch, don't deny it."

Frankie squeezed Reese's hand before letting go. "I bet back in the day it worked for the ladies too, huh?"

The man chuckled. "I could have given this stud here a run for his money. But not now. Hell, even as a youngun the girls come sniffing from miles around for this boy." Old brown eyes danced in remembered humor. "We're lucky no Daisy Dukes showed up after you took off with a babe, huh?"

"Enough, Midas. We're tired, and hungry."

"C'mon, then, I'll let you in through the back. I got enough pro-visions for us all. 'Sides"—he turned a sly eye on Reese—"that Angie Thomas comes out here every day to work her horses. I bet she'd be happy to cook for you." He flushed. "I mean for you both as long as you stay here."

"Angie?" Reese grinned. "I thought she would have taken off for the big city. It was always her dream."

"That dream included you, boy. Ain't the same any way you slice it without you around here." Midas gave Reese a quick hug. "I'm sure glad you're back."

"It's only temporary."

"Why? The bloodline is still strong, I made sure the place kept going."

"Another time, Midas. We're tired."

Frankie followed the two men inside, her steps sluggish. She wanted to sleep for days, and when she'd wake up her father would be alive and she wouldn't have goombahs trying to kill her. Midas offered food; she yawned and shook her head. She just wanted blissful sleep.

Moments later she flopped onto the bed in the room Reese showed her. Her eyes still open, she realized if she rewound her life it would not include Reese. Suddenly the here and now wasn't so awful with him in it—if she managed to survive it.

She dragged herself off the bed, moved to the window, and pushed back the drapes. Her eyes went to the small lit house in the distance. She watched Reese slowly walk toward it. Midas's place, she surmised. She watched the wide set of Reese's shoulders sag just a fraction and wondered what ghosts haunted him here.

She yawned and took stock of her room. Nothing special. Just your basic nondescript guest room. Midas had mentioned that Angie housecleaned twice a month to help pay for her boarding fees at the ranch. Great, Frankie thought, an old flame to deal with. She couldn't catch a break.

As she undressed, she realized she didn't have anything to put on. Though she'd brought most of her Carmel purchases, none of them included sleepwear. Well, she could go commando, even though she hated doing that in a strange house, or go on a search mission. She doubted Reese would mind. And if he did? Tough.

Slipping her shirt and pants back on, she followed the hallway light to the room next to hers. She opened the door. Cool air and darkness hit her face. She felt along the wall until she found a light switch and flipped it up. Warm light filled the room. A little girl's room. Blue ribbons and trophies adorned the walls and shelves. A multitude of stuffed animals held court among frilly pillows on a hand-sewn calico quilt.

Curious, Frankie stepped closer to the bed. A framed picture on the painted white nightstand caught her eye. A picture of a girl, maybe ten, sitting on a pony with a handsome teenage boy standing next to her. Reese. He was a heartthrob then. Both beamed ear to ear. Picking up the picture, she touched her fingertip to Reese's smile. She wanted him to smile like that for her.

She wanted to wipe away his brooding disposition. She wanted him happy.

As if it burned, she put the picture back on the dresser. What the hell was she thinking? Reese was one of those men who didn't stay anywhere long, a man who didn't allow feelings or people to attach to him.

She backed out of the room and decided she'd had enough of Reese and his family for the night. She'd clean up and sleep au naturel.

Reese stood at the head of the stairway and watched Frankie close Missy's bedroom door. For a long moment he stared at the closed door, his feet refusing to move forward. Raw emotions he'd tamped down for years surfaced, exploding in his brain. His heart constricted and he felt the agony as fresh and hot as if he were fifteen again. Taking a deep breath, he pushed past the pain like he had done for years and walked without looking at her door to his own room.

After he showered, Reese lay in his bed with his hands behind his head and stared at the ceiling, the rays from the rising sun pouring into his room.

Despite Midas's words, words from a wishful old man, Reese had no desire to see the man who had adopted him. And he refused to give his mother, the only blood relative he knew of, a second thought. She'd made her choice all those years ago and she could kiss his ass.

His thoughts went to the woman in the room next to him. He had the unusual urge to go to her, take her in his arms and hold her. Missy would have liked her. Both of them so similar in spirit.

He squeezed his eyes shut, the guilt and the pain too much for him to bear. It was his fault Missy was dead, and he would take that knowledge to his grave.

A slight noise caught his attention. His door slowly opened. He rolled over and grabbed his gun. A silhouette halted in the doorway. "Reese?"

He set his gun back on the nightstand. "Are you okay, Frankie?"

"I'm lonely."

His heart squeezed for the briefest instant before his brain, that trusty protection mechanism, wrestled the emotion from him. Reese slid to the side of the full-size bed, his back against the wall, and pulled down the spread, holding it up invitingly.

It was the invitation she needed. Without a word she slipped into the bed, her naked body wrapped only in the sheet from her guest room bed. She felt Reese's surprise at her pajama choice and smiled to herself. As much as she wanted him sexually, she wanted his arms around her more, reassuring her all would be right with the world when they woke.

As if sensing her mood, Reese pulled her close against his chest, where she snuggled her head and closed her eyes.

• • •

Bright light speared her eyelids and she stretched. Yawning loudly, Frankie bolted upright in bed. Wyoming. She was in Wyoming at Reese's home. No, his father's home. The two thugs shooting at them last night pressed forward in her consciousness and she shivered. Wrapping the sheet tight around her naked body, Frankie couldn't help a smug smile. She'd slept like a dead person. If Reese had touched her, it was his secret. Her body warmed and she frowned. She knew from experience he woke up with a hard-on; why hadn't he exercised it?

A loud whinny from the back of the house gave her her answer. She hurried to the window to see a tall, shapely blonde wrapped around Reese as pretty as a bow on a present. Frankie growled. When Reese slipped his arm around the hussy's waist and pulled her close, giving her a full kiss on the lips, she hissed.

She hurried to her room and threw on a pair of new jeans and a form-fitting aquamarine sweater. She'd have to settle for her tennis shoes; the other ones were still in the truck. Quickly, she washed her face, brushed her teeth, and pulled back her wild hair into a neater wild mass, then dabbed on lip gloss and mascara.

The wonderful aroma of breakfast halted her mission to disengage Reese and what's-her-name. She told herself she didn't care. A covered plate sat on a warmer, and when she took the lid off she almost had an orgasm. Blueberry griddle cakes, warm syrup, sausage patties, and fresh compote. Grabbing the plate, Frankie loaded it, then sat down at the kitchen table and made quick work of the meal.

Just as she savored the last bite, Reese walked through the back kitchen door with that woman still wrapped around him. This time she looked more like a strangling weed. His grin waned when he saw her. The blonde could have chilled a snowman, her stare was so cold.

"I didn't think you'd be up yet, Frankie."

"I thought you city girls didn't get up till noon," the blonde said in an annoying hick accent.

"Yeah, well, this city girl can chew you up and spit you out, so knock off the crap chatter."

The blonde—Angie, Frankie surmised—blanched, wide-eyed, and dropped one hand from Reese's arm. But not the other.

Pushing back from the table, Frankie stood and Reese beamed. She grabbed the plate and looked Reese square in the eye. "I'm so happy you find humor at my expense." She rinsed the plate off in the sink, her movements jerky. "And far be it from me to remind you, we have work to do."

Reese nodded.

"Anything I can help with?" Blondie asked.

Reese laughed. "Not this time, Angie." And he unwrapped the rest of Angie from his body.

Frankie set the rest of the dishes in the sink, turned back to the couple, brushed past them, and went out the back door. She was clueless as to her destination; she just needed to be away from Reese. The urge to dig her nails into his back was overwhelming, and her inability to control that impulse, sent her into flight mode.

Reese disturbed her emotional balance at a most basic level, and she didn't like it. The thought of sharing Reese instigated a surge of violence she'd never experienced before. She wanted to scream, her frustration was so overwhelming. Her hands opened and closed into fists at her sides. At that moment she felt more vulnerable than if she were standing naked in Golden Gate Park. The sensation made her stomach churn and she fought the urge to vomit. This was not good. She didn't sign on for this shit.

She ran a hand through her hair, took several deep cleansing breaths, and followed the scent of horses to the long, low barn. The fresh country air smelled good. Her pulse rate slowed. She liked the crispness of the air and the way it cleared her head.

She was at heart a one-woman man. Apparently Reese was a multiwoman man. Her insides rolled, and her hands fisted again. She was making herself physically ill. What was more distressing was that while she'd formed some twisted emotional attachment to the man, he hadn't to her. She was basically forgotten. She had gone to him last night, lonely and yearning for contact. She'd hoped he would reach out to her in the way men did. With their bodies. Instead, she woke alone and untouched in his bed. While she hadn't wanted more than what he gave her—a safe, warm place to sleep—she knew enough about men to know what was on their brain pretty much nonstop. So why had he shunned her?

"Stupid, the answer is tall, blonde, and standing back there in the kitchen."

Frankie picked up her pace. When had she started to have feelings for Reese? And for the love of God, why? He was just a pretty face, a nice cock, a good lover. He was pretty amazing, actually.

She strode through the open double doors to the barn, determined to get an emotional grip on herself. The swooshy sound of horse tails and soft nickers filled her senses. Immediately her mood softened. Just being around horses soothed her. She'd never lost her passion for the beasts or for riding. But it had been years since she sat in a saddle, galloping along the beaches of Half Moon Bay with her mother. She made a mental note to find a horse and ride regularly when she got home.

The late-morning air had a slight nip to it, but the sun shone brightly, promising warmth. Lazy dust motes swirled idly around the wooden beams of the pitched roof.

"Mornin', Miss Frankie."

Frankie smiled as Midas came out of a stall, a hoof pick in his hand.

"Good morning, Midas. Thank you for that wonderful breakfast."

He moved a piece of straw from one side of his mouth to the other. "No thanking me. Reese done cooked it. The boy always did like those blueberry pancakes. Missy liked the banana ones."

"What happened to Missy, Midas?"

He moved the piece of straw back to the other side of his mouth and shuffled his feet, his head down, finding the floor interesting. "She died."

Frankie opened her mouth to speak but Midas continued, "Reese don't like to talk about it, so it's best you don't mention her."

"How did she die?"

"Like Midas said, I don't like to talk about it."

Frankie whirled around to find Reese standing only a few feet behind her, his dark features stormy in the bright sunlight.

Her jaw clenched. Taking a deep breath, Frankie cooled her temper. Reese was entitled to his own demons. God knew she had her own. She focused a professional eye on her subject.

In the kitchen she'd immediately noticed his rugged handsomeness. The way his ass filled his tight Wranglers, and the way his chest busted out against the doeskin-colored chambray shirt he wore open at the collar. The worn leather boots he sported finished the look. Immediately her photographer's eye conjured up pictures of him half naked on a horse, bareback . . . and . . . her skin flushed warm . . . him riding her bareback.

He snapped his fingers in front of her. "Earth to Frankie."

She shook herself out of her lustful daydream and smiled at him. "We have work to do. I know how to ride, so let's saddle up and you show me around. The more scenic the better."

"It's nearly winter in Wyoming."

"Yep, and unseasonably warm. Let's get going."

She turned to Midas. "I can ride, but it's been a while, so some gentle old soul will work just fine for me."

"How do you know we have a horse for you?" he asked.

"Um, the brass plaque on the barn door that says Bronson Quarter Horses." Her brows furrowed. "Who *is* Bronson?"

"My father's name."

"Then it's yours as well? What about Barrett?"

"It's my stage name."

It made sense. Lots of models used pseudonyms. Maybe that's why Unk couldn't get much on him. That was good news. Maybe he really was who he said he was. But she doubted it.

CHAPTER TWENTY-FIVE

Riding a horse was like riding a bike, Frankie thought, lifting her face to the sun. Once in the saddle, she felt like it had been only a day instead of years since the last time. She knew she'd pay the next day, but she enjoyed the feeling of freedom she always felt when riding. The chestnut mare, Rosie, was gentle but spunky.

Reese's black stallion, Zorro, rolled his eyes and shook his head at Rosie. Unlike Reese, who looked ahead at the horizon and never at her. She frowned.

As usual when something bothered her, she focused her thoughts on her work. Her camera and a tripod, along with several rolls of film, were stuffed in her backpack. Reese's saddlebags held several blankets to use for props. The sun shone brightly, warming the chilled air. Reese wouldn't freeze while she filmed him. She could Photoshop goose bumps, but penises reacted badly to the cold.

Zorro sidled up to her mare. After a sharp command from his rider and a firm rein, he calmed to a more controlled walk.

"Control your mount, mister," Frankie said over her shoulder, her nose up in the air. "My daddy told me about men like you."

Reese urged the stallion closer. His hard features softened and she could practically see his morose mood roll off him. When his left leg brushed against her right leg, she stopped wondering about his mood. The thrill of the contact was instant, and as much as she liked it, she wished she didn't. She craved Reese like she craved caffeine. "Well, little girl, my mama told me to stay away from your type."

"And what type might that be, sir?"

"The siren type."

Frankie laughed. "There is nothing siren about me." She never considered herself beautiful, maybe exotic in an odd way, certainly not everyone's cup of tea. Her dark features were strong, not the classic girl-next-door features of the blonde she met this morning. She could see Angie as every man's fantasy woman.

"For someone who has an artistic eye, you sure sell yourself short," Reese said.

"What are you saying?"

"Fishing for a compliment?"

"No, I just don't understand what you meant by that comment."

"Your look. It's exotic, you remind me of a young Sophia Loren."

She raised a brow. He nodded. "Everything about you is lush. Your lips, your eyes." He grinned. "Your ass."

When she opened her mouth to respond he cut her off. "Your tits. You have great tits, Frankie."

She felt a flush scroll from her breast to her forehead. "Stop it."

"Can't take a compliment?"

She shrugged. "No, it's not that."

"Then what?"

She shrugged again. "I was an early bloomer. By the sixth grade I was in a D cup, and well, I was teased. My father insisted I wear baggy clothes and told me God was testing me."

"Testing you how?"

"By giving me so much, it was up to me to keep the boys away."

"That's ridiculous."

"It was his way of keeping me chaste. Catholic guilt is strong voodoo. If planted properly and nurtured, it can screw you up for life."

Reese grinned. "I can see by the way you dress you got over the guilt."

"What's that supposed to mean?"

"You dress to accentuate what you have."

"I don't flaunt it."

His eyebrow quirked. "If you say so."

"I don't!"

"Who are you trying to convince?"

"I'm not trying to convince anyone, it's the truth. Besides, you go around looking like you just walked out of *GQ*. How do you afford that on a cop's salary?"

Reese shook his head. "Nice try. It's my job to look good. I'm a highly paid professional, and I get lots of designers who pay me to wear their threads."

"Yeah, Wrangler and Levi's."

"I just haven't shown all my stuff."

"I think I've seen just about all your stuff."

"You like it?"

"It's okay."

"Just okay?" His brow quirked again.

"Okay, your cock is *lush*."

He laughed. "I'll take that as a compliment, although I can tell you didn't. I meant you're lush in the best of ways."

"Sure. A nice way to say I'm fat."

"Fat isn't a word I'd use to describe you."

"No, lush." She urged Rosie to pick up the pace. "I've never been the tall, slender type. I look at pasta and it sticks to my thighs."

"You have great thighs."

"Hmm, well, thanks, but I see you more with the tall, skinny blonde types. Like your friend, Amy."

"Angie. And she definitely has her assets."

Frankie's ire rose. "Maybe I'll get a few shots of the two of you. She'll translate well."

"What about us?" His voice dropped, and although they were coming upon a rather swift running stream, he spoke low. The deep timbre of his voice stroked her as effectively as his hand.

She caught his meaning immediately.

"I haven't forgotten, but out here we don't exactly have privacy."

"I can make her go away. And Midas said he was going over to his sister's for dinner. She's in Jackson, a good hour's drive. How about the barn later tonight?"

The thought sent waves of warmth through her. She smiled. "I guess we'll play it by ear, then."

"Yeah, see what comes up."

Before Frankie could make a snide comeback, they entered a wide clearing. "This is beautiful," Frankie gasped.

Several huge oaks made up a natural umbrella over a small inlet of the stream. Sunlight glistened like dancing jewels off the clear blue water. As she drank in the soothing landscape, Frankie realized the trees stood on the other side of the stream, which looked less than lazy. She peered up and down but didn't see a bridge. "Is it safe?"

When Reese failed to answer, she turned in the saddle to ask him again. He sat ramrod stiff, his eyes far away but focused. A small twitch worked his left jaw.

"Reese, what's wrong?"

His skin paled and he pulled the reins back. Zorro stomped, then backed up. "This is a bad spot."

He turned Zorro and urged him into a canter that quickly turned into a wild gallop. Frankie chased after him for a few minutes, then slowed. The stallion's stride far outpaced the mare's.

He disappeared over a hill. She pushed down her worry. But when she crested the hill she found the meadow below empty, and her breath shortened. Where was he?

A dark form crested another hill past the meadow and her breath gushed out in relief. At least he was going in a straight line. She continued after him at a leisurely canter. His mood changes since they arrived in Wyoming confused her. She wished he would open up and tell her what bothered him. Instead, he had become more morose.

When she finally caught up to him, Zorro stood tied to a tree and Reese lounged against a thick oak, chewing a piece of grass.

She liked the setting, but not the company. "What's bugging you?" she asked.

Perspiration glistened on his face. Before he could answer, she'd switched gears, seeing him through the mind of a camera as well as of a woman. "Do some jumping jacks to keep your skin all slick like it is. When I tell you, take your shirt off."

She hurried to set up her camera. When Reese didn't do what she asked, she frowned. "C'mon, Reese, I want the hot, sultry look. You and Zorro. C'mon, these shots will be incredible."

He scowled. Instead of doing jumping jacks, he pulled a blanket out of a saddlebag, sat down on it, and did a few sit-ups. She smiled. "That'll work."

Once he slicked up, she told him to stop. "I want you like you were when I rode up, against the tree, the grass in your mouth. Yep, just like that." She reached down and unbuttoned his shirt a few buttons, her fingertips lingering on his sultry skin. "Perfect."

She stood back, focused, and began her shoot.

After several shots she lowered her camera. "Reese, I need you to go someplace else. This isn't working."

He stood and shrugged. "Where?"

"Not physically, emotionally. Whatever is on your mind is coming through in your eyes."

His features tightened.

Damn. She knew he'd react like that but she had to try. "Sometimes it helps to talk about things."

"Like you do?"

She put her hand on her hip. "Don't turn this around."

"Why not? You want something from me you're unwilling to give yourself."

"The difference is my stuff is personal and has nothing to do with our contract. Something is obviously bugging you and until you deal with it or go somewhere else in your head, it's affecting my shoot, which affects my bottom line."

"I'm not a trained monkey, I can't turn on and off for you."

"You are a trained monkey. We have a contract, and I need you to perform, *now.*" The minute she said the words she regretted them. She knew she was pushing him away, and she didn't understand why.

He spit the grass from his mouth and buttoned up his shirt. "Well, lady, this monkey is done for the day." He strode past her.

She grabbed his arm. "You can't do this! I have deadlines." Again she knew her words were wrong, but damn it, he couldn't just stop now.

He spun her around and grabbed her by the forearms. "Is that all this is to you? A means to an end, a deadline?"

"*Skin* is my priority."

"What if I quit?"

She felt the blood drain to her feet. "You wouldn't do that. We have a contract." She swallowed hard and reached out to him.

He pushed her arms away, turned his back to her, and strode back to Zorro. "So sue me."

Every organ inside her hardened. She put the camera down on the ground and ran after him. She had nothing but *Skin*—he was her only hope to hang on to it. "Reese! You can't quit! Everything hinges on this shoot."

He untied the reins, his expression grim. "Find another monkey."

"Don't do this to me!"

He turned, his eyes narrow. "I'm done, Frankie."

"Fine, Reese. Fine. Running away from me isn't going to change what you're running away from here." She went back to pick up her camera. She'd done it again, allowed a man to fuck up everything when the stakes would make or break her. She was at the edge, looking down into a black hole that had become her life, ready to throw her hands up and say to hell with the world. Sadness for them both engulfed her. "I never had you pegged for a coward."

Without another word she carefully packed her camera. She glanced back at Reese. He stood at the side of his horse, staring angrily at her.

"I'm going home," she announced. She couldn't stay here with him. Her father's words, *hormone-induced stupidity,* rang in her ears. She'd done it again. Fool that she was.

"You can't go home."

She gathered the reins and turned her back to him to mount her horse. "I can and I will."

For the first time since she was a little girl, Frankie felt the uncontrollable urge to cry, to cry in frustration, to cry for herself. She'd worked so hard for this, and now when her entire world was turned upside down and inside out, the one person who she had put a little faith in, the one who had protected her, saved her life, was in effect taking it. But not in one fell swoop; he was killing her slowly. She could get another model, but it wouldn't be the same. And really, could she just walk back into her office and feel safe?

She needed to call Unk, she needed his protection. She needed to confront Anthony. She shivered. She needed to find her father's will.

She felt Reese behind her. "If you leave, you die." His voice was softer. She felt the change in him but was afraid to hope.

She turned around and wiped the tears from her eyes. "I can't control fate, Reese. If my fate is to die at twenty-eight, then so be it."

"Now who's the quitter?"

"Don't talk to me about quitting. It's obvious from what little I've heard since I came here that you quit on your family fifteen years ago."

His jaw stiffened. "Shut up."

"Shut up?" Emotion poured through her like a burst dam. "You bring me to God knows where, tell me I can't go home, then break a legal contract that all but breaks me? I'm not going to shut up!" She balled her fists and punched him in the right pectoral. She reared back for another hit, but Reese grabbed her fist and yanked her hard against him.

His mouth swooped down on hers. She slammed her palms against his chest and pushed away from him. "No. Not this time. You want sex, go get it from your blonde girlfriend. I'm done with you!"

She couldn't remember being so angry at anyone in her life. She'd been humiliated by Sean. She'd been frustrated by her father, and Anthony would make a nun swear, but never had she felt so frustrated and furious and hurt at a single individual as she did right now at Reese. She told herself it was because he was backing out, leaving her with her career in ruins, but she knew in her heart it was more than that. She'd come to trust him. He was her self-appointed protector, and now she felt betrayed.

She turned to mount Rosie.

"I don't get you, Francesca," he said, his voice barely perceptible.

His words and tone hit her emotional wall hard. It took every drop of willpower she possessed not to turn around and take another chance. Could she? Did she have the heart for another emotional crash landing?

"No one does," she said.

"Do you get yourself?"

The question caught her off guard. She turned around but looked down at the ground. She answered truthfully. "Not really." She didn't get much these days. Just when she thought she knew what she wanted, her family tried to kill her.

"What do you want?" he asked.

Her head snapped up and she looked him in the eyes. "Respect." *To live. To not have to look over my shoulder every time I step outside. To share my life with someone I trust, who even if I screwed up royally wouldn't want to drop me like last week's news.*

"You have that in the industry."

"I have it only by way of my family name."

"Why did you go to work for your father?"

She let out a long, frustrated breath and backed up against Rosie. Why did this man continually challenge her? "To show him I had something to contribute. To prove to him I was a team player."

"Are you?"

She narrowed her eyes and jerked back her head. "What do you mean?"

"Are you playing on your father's team or getting back at him?"

"Getting back at him for what?"

Reese shrugged. "All the years of neglect."

"Look, Father wouldn't have won any Father of the Year awards, even with Anthony. He was what he was. I accept that."

"Then why work for him?"

"I thought it was what I wanted. To work for my father. To make him proud of me."

"Was he?"

She swallowed hard and slowly shook her head. "Not in the end."

"What happened, Frankie?"

"We disagreed about a lot of things."

Reese moved closer and pushed a tendril of dark hair from her cheek with his fingertips. "If you could be anyone or do anything, what would it be?"

She shrugged and patted Rosie's withers. "I've always loved horses. As a little girl I watched reruns of *Big Valley* with my mother. She loved Heath." She looked up and squinted against the sunshine. "I wanted to be blonde and beautiful like Audra, and marry Heath."

"She lived on a ranch. He was nothing but a cowboy."

"Yes, but she was so sophisticated. She had the best of both worlds. And what's so wrong with cowboys?"

"My mother thought she wanted that life too, cowboy and all. Turns out she didn't."

She watched the shadows cross his face. "What happened?"

He shrugged and unbuttoned the top button of his shirt. His eyes locked with hers and he unbuttoned the next one. "She left."

This time when Frankie reached out to touch Reese, he let her. His muscles flexed hard beneath her palm.

"Do you miss her?"

"No."

"If I had children, I'd walk through fire for them."

He unbuttoned the third button and opened his shirt. Her hand slid up his forearm to his bicep. "Do you want children?" he asked.

He lowered his head and her hand slid up to his shoulder. The controlled power of the man excited her. "Yes," she whispered. "Do you?"

"No."

"Why not?"

His lips pressed against her throat and a jolt of excitement racked her. His touch stirred something deep and primal within her. It scared her as much as it excited her. She didn't stop whatever ploy he was up to. First, because she wanted his touch and to follow the path wherever it may lead, and second, in this sexy and compliant mood, she could get some great shots.

"I'd be a lousy father."

Before she could reply, he lightly bit her jugular and held it between his teeth. Her back arched. His warm, wet tongue laved the length of her neck. Her nipples spiked and she slid her hand between his shirt and chest. The heat of his skin surprised her. She rubbed her fingertips across his flat nipple. It immediately rose to her touch.

His arm slipped around her waist, bringing her closer against his chest. "We'd make beautiful babies, you know."

Frankie gasped in surprise, and Reese inwardly cringed. What the hell did he just say? And for the love of God, why?

Not wanting to discuss or think about any underlying meaning, he kissed her hard, his mouth plundering her to silence. He wanted her. He wanted her now; he wanted her tomorrow, and maybe even the day after that.

He pulled her over to the blanket he had laid out and lay her down. "I want you, Frankie. Here. Now."

His hands dove into the thick mass of her hair; he rubbed his face into the silky softness of it and inhaled her scent. He couldn't remember another time when he considered the scent of a woman. Not her perfume but her true essence. "You smell good." He rubbed his nose down her throat, then kissed her at the junction of her neck and shoulder.

Frankie's body swelled beneath his and he pulled her closer in a fierce embrace. He marveled at her complexity and her tenacity. At the same time he saw through her layers. While she pretended to be the hard-ass her family expected, she was nothing more than a scared little girl in a world that lied to her, rejected her, and now wanted her head. Protective feelings pushed their way to the surface of his consciousness. He would, Reese decided at that moment, protect her not only from her family but himself as well.

They were both in too deep. His hands trailed from the small of her back to her breasts. Their full ripeness overflowed in his hands. He'd always considered himself an ass man, but Frankie's tits were, in his opinion, the eighth wonder of the world. He pushed up her sweater and bra, his mouth hungry for the taste of her. She cried out as he roughly took a nipple in his mouth and sucked hard, his fingers fondling the other.

A wild sense of urgency overtook him, like some wild, untamed thing took possession of him. He wanted her raw and passionate, on the prairie, like his Indian ancestors had taken their women. He pushed her shirt over her head and snatched off her bra. With one hand he unzipped her jeans and pushed them down her legs. She helped by kicking off her shoes. Her panties didn't have a chance. He ripped them off her.

He unbuttoned his pants and shoved them down just far enough to release his swollen dick. Then he pushed her down on the blanket and plunged deep into her hot wetness.

"Frankie," he moaned against her lips as he filled her to the hilt. Her hips rocked up to accommodate him and her long legs wrapped around his waist. He knew he was going to come too quick, and he couldn't help it. Taking her was all he wanted. He'd make it up to her later. Tonight.

He thrust deep, hard, once, twice, a dozen times, his hips bucking out of control like a loco bronc. His body, mind, and soul were possessed with only one aim. The age-old ritual of mating. The chill in the air was nonexistent, Frankie's hard gasps of pleasure barely registering.

Long pent-up emotion, emotion he didn't know he harbored swelled. His hips drove into hers, his vision a cloudy haze, his only coherent thought was the woman beneath him who stirred up old hurts and his desire to take her, to send her over the edge to mark her as his.

He exploded inside of her. Frankie cried out. Her legs fell away from him, and her arms tightened around his neck as he drove into her like a battering ram, his seed continuing to spew. He'd never had an orgasm last so long and hard. Just when it peaked, Frankie clasped her thighs around him, her inner muscles pulling him deeper, milking him of every ounce of fluid he possessed. Her back arched and she bit his shoulder, her teeth sharp. He plunged deeper, the pain of her action driving him crazy. Their sweat-slicked bodies slid and slapped, and Frankie threw her head back, her mouth gasping for air as she came in one hard-hitting orgasm.

The minute Reese came back to earth, he pushed his chest up. Still inside her, he scanned her for damage. "I'm sorry, Frankie, I don't know—"

She pulled his face down by the ears and kissed him hard. When she let him go she smiled, her lips swollen. She licked them. "Did you hear me say stop?"

On his hands, peering down at her, he shook his head.

"Then shut up." She squirmed out from under him and quickly dressed. When he began to pull his jeans up, she stopped him with her hand. "Jeans only, and leave them unbuttoned—hell, take them off all the way, I'll get a blanket to drape over you. I want aftermath pictures.

"You're always working, aren't you?"

She smiled over her shoulder as she pulled another blanket from the saddlebag. "Ya snooze, ya lose."

Reese lay back against the blanket. "And you can never lose, can you?"

She nodded. "You get me, Reese, I'm glad." She tossed him the blanket. "No hard feelings?"

He draped the soft flannel blanket across his lap. She nodded in approval at the full outline of his penis under the thin fabric. Though it had waned, it would still give most guys a complex.

"No, but don't get all over me when it comes back to bite you in the ass."

She focused her camera a few steps away from him. "What do you mean?"

"I play to win too."

"Lie back." She positioned the blanket to cover most of his cock, only exposing the few full inches of his root. "Put your arms up behind your head." She focused. "Perfect, now close your eyes." She zoomed in. "When I tell you, open them slowly, and look at me like you want me."

CHAPTER TWENTY-SIX

Frankie focused in on Reese's sexy hooded look. Her eyes dropped to the rising blanket. "You're hornier than a sixteen-year-old virgin."

"Stop looking good enough to eat and maybe this old boy will calm down some."

Frankie laughed, enjoying his compliment. "Sorry, sir, I have work to do. Maybe later, I'll see if I can squeeze you in."

His cock reared and he growled. "You'll do more than squeeze me in."

"So tell me what you're going to do to me tonight in the barn?"

His eyes sparkled and his lips turned up into a mischievous smile. "I'm gonna take you from behind like a stallion does a mare."

She squatted next to him. Pressing her hand against his chest, she pushed him back until he was flat on his back. "Turn slightly to your right. Good, now put both your arms over your head. Yes, wow, Reese, your body just screams 'fuck me.' "

"Fuck me, then."

His cock stirred beneath the thin flannel of the blanket and she stepped back and caught it in several frames.

"I'm afraid I can't publish pictures of me riding that lush cock of yours."

"How about *me* riding it?" The throaty female voice behind the horses startled Frankie, but Reese remained composed. Angie sat mounted on a pretty dark bay mare no more than twenty-five feet from them. Had she seen them just a few moments ago? Frankie flushed, angry.

"This is a closed set, Amy."

"It's Angie." She nudged her horse closer. Frankie turned to Reese to stop her. She found him pulling his pants on, watching the woman approach. Frankie's temper cranked up a notch to boiling.

Although Reese had his pants buttoned up, he allowed the woman access to her "closed set." Fury, frustration, and embarrassment clouded Frankie's vision. Her earlier feelings of violence resumed and she knew if she didn't get away, she would do something really stupid. She glared at Reese. She couldn't force him to want only her, and she'd be damned if she'd share him on any level. At odds with how to deal with her out-of-control emotions, she did the only thing she could. She ran.

Frankie backed away from Reese, shoved her camera in her backpack, mounted Rosie, and put her heels to the mare's flanks.

She didn't look back, not even when the hot sting of tears blurred her vision. Was she destined to always be second best when it came to men? First her father, then Sean, now Reese. She didn't hear Reese until Zorro was almost on top of her and Rosie. He grabbed her reins, slowing Rosie to a stop. He was dressed only in his jeans; he hadn't bothered to grab his shirt.

"Don't, Frankie," he said.

She wiped back the sting in her eyes. The breeze picked up, whipping her loose hair against her cheeks. "If you think I'm going to sit there and watch you and that woman make goo-goo eyes at each other, especially after we—" She hiccuped a breath. "You're mistaken."

"I wasn't."

"Right."

"Angie and I go way back. We're friends."

Frankie rolled her eyes. "Do I look like I need special ed?"

"No."

"Then don't expect me to believe that line of bullshit."

His lips quirked at the corners.

"See!"

"Look, I won't deny she's attractive and we had a thing before—but I'm not interested in her."

She grabbed the reins from him. "I know how men are, Reese, you don't have to make excuses."

He maneuvered Zorro around in front of Rosie. The stallion's bulk stopped her from leaving. "Just how are we?"

"Always craving the excitement of another woman, never content with the one you have, even if it's just casual. Always looking for something better and more exciting."

Reese leaned over his saddle, slid his arm around her, and plucked Frankie from Rosie's back, setting her in front of him. "You're exciting enough for me, I don't want anyone else."

She pushed against his chest. "For the moment."

"What else is there?"

"The moment after."

He kissed her. When he released her she let out a long breath. He was doing it to her again. Making her want him.

"Seize the moment Frankie, there might not be a moment after," he said, his voice husky.

His words sunk in fast. She nodded. She'd live like she was dying.

Frankie and Reese walked from the barn to the house. She felt the stretch of her inner thighs from the unaccustomed exercise on the horse and from Reese.

"I'm going to need supplies," she said, turning her mind back toward Reese.

"Supplies?"

"To develop my film."

"Can we send it out?"

She stopped and looked at him. "Hardly. I don't want to take a chance some clerk will report me for lascivious content."

"Didn't consider that. How about if you give me the list and I have Midas pick up what you need?"

"That'll work. I really don't feel like driving anywhere. I like the tranquility here."

Reese looked at her strangely. "That'll only last a few days, then the cabin fever will set in."

Maybe. She looked at him just as strangely. He didn't know her well. Or maybe he did. "Maybe," she said. Maybe she didn't know herself.

She steered clear of Angie when she came riding back. Even when Reese headed back to the main barn after a quick lunch where she knew Angie lurked, Frankie kept her cool. She ignored the pangs of jealousy that gnawed at her. She could not change another person's desires, only her own. It was easier saying those words than living by them.

• • •

"Hey, wiseguy, got any news for me?" Reese asked on the barn phone.

"Lots. You secure?"

"As I can be, I'm calling on a land line."

"Okay, good, here's what I have. Anthony is tearing San Francisco apart looking for his sister. He's crying foul and swearing he'll kill whoever damages a hair on her head."

"Interesting."

"It gets better. He had it out with his uncle last night. The old bastard accused the young Turk of embezzling over six million dollars. Had the cooked books to prove it. Said if the old man knew, he'd come back from the grave and slit the punk's throat. Anthony insisted it was his sister thwarting the old man."

"Judas bitch" echoed in his ears. Reese's skin warmed. No, Frankie wasn't like that. If he had been hit in the gut with a baseball bat, he couldn't have been more stunned by his revelation. Was he making excuses for her?

Shit!

"If he's so sure she cheated him out of the money, then why does he want her safe?"

"I think he wants to do the deed himself."

"Frankie doesn't have the money."

"What makes you so sure?"

"She doesn't have it in her."

"You're getting too close to the crack, man."

Reese shook his head in denial. It wasn't like that. He hadn't lost his objectivity. He swiped a hand across the stubble on his chin and wondered if he was being honest with himself.

He recalled the two thugs at the Carmel house, the same two who took out the out-of-towners, and the conversation he'd overheard. Someone was misdirecting. He'd always been a gut guy. His gut told him Frankie wasn't involved. Regardless of what he over-heard and Jase's innuendo.

"No, I'm not. I have a hunch. The old man knew who was rip-ping him off and he must have confronted them or made noises about it. That person killed him."

"I have it different."

"How?"

"Didn't his only daughter and he have it out the day before he died? Word is he disowned her, told her he was changing his will. Immediately."

The hair on the back of Reese's neck spiked. "I know they argued."

"Yeah, well, a Loretta Wilson crawled out of a crack this morning scared to death, demanding a signed witness protection contract before she said a word."

Reese's gut twisted painfully. "And?"

"We gave it to her. She said Donatello and his daughter had a knock-down, drag-out fight the morning before he died. The daugh-ter told the old man he was dead to her."

"Shit."

"Yeah, I feel your pain, man."

"I can't believe—"

"Dude, we have the accounts, even though she buried two of them. They double back to her. She had motive, means, and oppor-tunity. Who else knew the old man was traveling without his usual goons to the restaurant that morning? And who else could get that close to him to off him?"

"Then who is trying to kill her?"

"Nobody."

Reese's blood ran cold through his veins.

"She set it up to look like her brother, so her uncle would take care of him. Carmine almost did. According to the Wilson woman, the old man was going to change the will, leave it all to his son."

"I don't buy it, too many close calls."

"Really? Let's take it apart. First she gets winged in the arm at her uncle's. She could easily have set it up. Tell her shooter where and when, then make it look like what it looked like. Next, she has someone trash her house, then, to make sure those guys keep their mouths shut, she hires more guys to off them."

Reese's scowl deepened. "What about the car?"

"What about it? She knew what was coming, she would have managed to get out of its way if Superman hadn't shown up."

"So I guess she called those two bozos who showed up at the Carmel house and instructed them to shoot at her."

"Bingo. Same with the hotel shooter. How convenient—and not even a knick. It's just a matter of time before someone shows up there."

"She doesn't know where she is."

"The hell she doesn't. I'll bet you my new house she's already sent the signal. Mark my words, buddy. Goombahs will show up, coz she'll get the word out."

Reese stared, unseeing, at the knots in the wood of the small office he stood in. Inch by inch his brain absorbed Jase's words. Looking at this objectively, void of emotion or libido, every puzzle piece fit.

"And there's one more thing."

Reese took a deep breath. "What?"

"Tawny, the secretary, came forward about an hour ago. We're waiting for her lawyer to show up, but she says she can prove big sister tried to kill little brother. Apparently, she has a recorded phone conversation."

Reese's blood chilled. "I have some work left to do."

"Watch your back, man. She's dangerous with a capital *D*."

"Right." Slowly Reese replaced the phone in its cradle. He felt sick to his stomach. His gut screamed no, it wasn't true, but his brain, the one that had analyzed hundreds of cases, told him every piece of evidence pointed at Frankie. Glaringly so. What better way to get back at the person who shunned you privately, who put your brother first, who never bothered with you? And what a perfect way to take out the sibling that garnered all of the attention? Pit him against the new head of the family, the loving uncle, the one with all of the power, and make him look like the bad guy.

He punched the wall, the wood splintering beneath his knuckles. He barely flinched as sharp pieces dug into his skin. "Son of a bitch! How could I be so damn blind?"

He punched the wall again, this time feeling pain. It resonated to his heart. He gritted his teeth. At least when his mother deserted him, she was honest about her reasons, shitty as they were. Francesca manipulated everyone and everything around her. He sat down in the rickety old chair and hung his head. His innards twisted in agonizing pain. When, he asked himself, did he begin to have feelings for her?

"Fuck." He stood. He'd fallen hard for a cold-blooded killer. And what was worse, now he wanted to hurt her, like she hurt him. Worse than that . . . he still wanted her—despite the mounting evidence.

Jase was right. He'd lost his objectivity. He'd gone soft; he let his dick think for him and then his emotions followed blindly behind like a damn puppy on a leash. He should pull himself off the case right now—but the thought of that stung deep. He couldn't.

And so he did what any person in denial did. His heart interceded and he rationalized this situation.

Maybe there was a way around this. If she came clean. Maybe if she was granted leniency, she'd tell him the truth. He shook his head. No, there would be no clemency for premeditated murder. What if she turned state's evidence? The courts could be massaged.

A sudden thought came to him. Maybe she was in fear of her life, maybe the old man tried to kill her; self-defense was pardonable. There was still the hit out on her brother and the embezzlement.

For long moments Reese tried to convince himself that if he told Frankie how much he cared, she'd come around, and if she turned state's evidence, the DA would cut her a deal.

No. No damn deal! Reality hit him hard in the gut. How could he have been so blind? Feeling like he'd been hollowed out like a jack-o'-lantern, he turned to leave the room.

"Hey, cowboy," Angie purred, blocking his exit. His shirt hung around her bare shoulders. She must have picked it up when he went after Frankie. It was all she wore at the moment.

"I'm not interested."

She rubbed her hand down the length of his fly and pressed her substantial breasts against his bare chest. "You were earlier. I saw how you stared at me."

He was a lot of things earlier, including the schmuck he still was. Anger flared. Damn Frankie for playing him like a fool. He gave Angie a second look. He forced a smile. "Maybe I am after all."

He pulled her back into the office and slammed the door shut with the heel of his boot. Then he slammed her against the wall he'd punched. Her fingers worked fast. She had his pants unbuttoned and her hand pulling him out before she let him change his mind.

"Reese," she panted, "I've missed you for so long. Why didn't you come back for me?"

He couldn't come back for himself, how could he for her? Besides, there was no one to come back to. His mother ran off, he killed his sister, and his father disowned him. Sadness welled in his heart. Sadness for a family lost, and he realized sadness for what would never be with Frankie.

He grabbed Angie's hand from his dick. Gently he pushed her away and pulled up his pants. "I'm sorry, but I can't."

He buttoned his pants and stepped past her.

"Is she that good, Reese, or am I that bad?"

He turned to look at her, emotions he couldn't put a name to roiling within his chest. "Neither."

He walked to the tack room and crossed to the sink. Angie's cloistering scent clung to him like a weed. He turned on the water, stuck his head under the faucet, and let the icy water numb his brain.

Throwing his head back, he let the water run down to his chest. His shirt lay on the wooden horse beside him. He smiled wanly. At least Angie wasn't a screaming bitch about it. He mopped his face and chest dry with his shirt. When he opened it up to put it on, he laughed. The back was ripped in half. Okay, so she was a woman scorned. He slipped it on anyway, grateful for the modicum of warmth it would give him on the short walk to the house. The house where a murderer played caring photographer.

He walked out to the open end of the barn and stood and watched Angie get into her truck. Her eyes caught his and he stared back. She'd make some man a fine wife. He just wasn't the man.

He'd always wondered if he was forever ruined for marriage because of what happened with his mother and sister. Frankie left no doubt now. His lifestyle suited him more than he cared to admit.

Undercover work provided him a place where he would never lay down roots, only a temporary stay. He'd always prided himself on not becoming involved on an emotional level in his cases. So much for his arrogance in thinking no one could get under his skin. He'd thought his feelings were dead.

He looked up at the house and watched the upstairs curtains to the guest room sway. So, she was watching, was she? In a monumental effort, he pushed the emptiness from his heart and painted on a smile. He had a charade to continue and he hadn't earned his nickname "Ice" for nothing.

Frankie stepped back from the window. Her hands shook as she watched Angie step out of the barn. The blonde looked up at the house and casually smoothed back her long hair before securing the top button of her shirt. As she tucked her loose shirt into her jeans, Frankie grabbed her hands, twisting them to keep them from shaking. Reese emerged from the barn several minutes later, his hair wet, shrugging on his shirt, the shirt he left behind, the shirt Angie obviously gave him in the barn, *after* their little tryst. It didn't take a PhD to figure out what happened.

Emotions collided so violently in her chest, she felt as if a three-hundred-pound man had sat on top of her. She watched Reese watch Angie get in her truck and the longing look they gave each other before she drove away. When Reese looked up at her standing at the window, her heart squeezed so hard she thought she was actually having a heart attack.

"Oh, my God!" she cried. When had she fallen in love with him?

Reese entered the house half expecting Frankie to mouth off about what he suspected she witnessed and her own drawn conclusions. As much as he wanted to hurt her back, he had to keep his cool. The case was far from closed. He'd continue what started as a charade, enjoy the benefits, then go in for the kill.

Silence met him as he walked into the kitchen. He was glad for it. He wanted to shower, he wanted time to collect his emotions before he came face-to-face with Frankie. He knew he'd never be able to look at her the same again. Little by little he closed his heart to her. He told himself she was a criminal of the highest order. A murdering bitch.

As he was about to strip, the sound of racing hoofbeats startled him out of his thoughts. He hurried to the window to see Frankie riding Rosie bareback in a mad dash toward the trail they had taken that morning.

His vision blurred. Time pulled him back fifteen years.

"Missy!" he yelled, then raced down the hallway and down the stairway in a blind panic.

CHAPTER TWENTY-SEVEN

The ends of her long hair whipped across Frankie's cheeks, stinging her sensitive skin. Tears blinded her vision. Huge sobs racked her chest. She cried like a little girl who was lost in a big department store. And that was how she felt. Lost. Alone. And terrified.

In the past week she'd come to depend on Reese, to trust him. "Stupid!" she screamed at the wind. Rosie's ears twitched back and forth, her gait steadily eating up ground. Frankie headed toward the same trail she and Reese took that morning. She had no idea where she was going, only that she wanted to get away from other humans. Humans did hurtful things to each other. Humans were selfish and self-serving. She was tired of trying to be what everyone wanted her to be.

When would she do what she wanted for herself? She laughed harshly. She'd indulged in Reese, and look what that got her. Who the hell was she kidding when she told herself she could indulge all she wanted and not get emotionally involved? Stupid. Stupid. Stupid. The minute another woman wagged her tits in his face, he was off. What the hell was it with men and always wanting more?

She crested the hill and the small, tranquil clearing she had admired earlier unfolded before her. Long, lazy afternoon shadows crept across the blue water of the inlet. Invisible birds chortled an afternoon greeting in the high branches of the trees. The rush of the stream water had slowed. She could easily cross now. And then what? she asked herself. Stay out here and freeze her ass off? She looked longingly over her shoulder, wishing Reese would ride up, tell her she was mistaken, that no other woman mattered.

She choked back a laugh when off in the distance what started as a black speck turned into a man on a black horse. Zorro. And Reese. No, she wouldn't slow for him, she wouldn't fall for his lies again. She faced forward and urged Rosie on. The mare took her time wading through the chilly water, enough time for Reese to catch up. Just as she cleared the other side, Zorro lunged into the water. Frankie kicked the mare into a gallop.

"Frankie!" Reese yelled. She didn't look back. She hunched low over the mare's neck and held on as Rosie took off as if the hounds of hell bit at their heels.

"Frankie!" Reese called, his voice shrill, the sound of desperation in it.

She ignored it, kicking Rosie's sides again. The mare's powerful haunches carried them up the slight embankment, where they crested.

She realized they were moving too fast down the other side of the embankment, Frankie knew that if they continued at their current pace, they would roll. She pulled back on the reins but the mare had taken the bit into her mouth, refusing to stop.

Rosie galloped headlong down the hill. Panic filled Frankie's senses. Reese's voice called her name again, behind her, this time closer. She held on tight, the leather reins biting into her palm.

The mare stumbled just as the earth flattened out. In the blink of an eye Frankie's life flashed before her, and she had more than a few regrets. As the mare dug her hooves into the hard earth, Frankie catapulted from the saddle. As if in slow motion, Frankie tumbled over Rosie's withers. She saw the sky, the sun, and the trees.

Then. Blackness.

"Frankie!" Reese screamed as he jumped from Zorro to run to the unmoving form lying on the ground. Rosie whinnied and backed up as Reese raced toward her fallen rider.

"God, please, not again."

He slid on his knees as he dropped to the hard earth at her side. Desperately he felt her jugular for a pulse, and although she was out cold, her pulse beat strong. He breathed a sigh of relief. Gulping for air in an effort to catch his breath, he trailed his finger slowly over her scalp, looking for bumps or cuts. As he passed over her head for the second time, finding nothing of significance, his breath steadied. Her chest rose and fell evenly.

Her long black lashes lay thick, a dark blanket over her creamy, smooth skin. Her cheeks glowed a rosy pink. Her nostrils flared slightly and her full lips parted, her pearly-white teeth peeking out from behind. Such a waste.

His heart thudded heavily against his chest wall. He brushed the dirt from her cheek, and wished with all his heart she wasn't the killer she was.

For the second time in his life Reese wished he could change fate. That day, he told Missy the truth about their mother. This day, he learned the woman he was falling in love with murdered her father. He swiped a hand through his hair and sat back on his haunches. Shit, he didn't even know what the hell love was anymore.

His chest tightened. He'd run every conceivable scenario through his brain, trying to convince himself Frankie was innocent. And even though his heart told him it was ludicrous, the evidence added up too neatly. And after he couldn't deny the evidence, he'd even tried to justify a way in his mind of taking her and running away. Going somewhere where they could live together, where the world would never find them. But as much as he wanted her in his life, he couldn't, wouldn't go against what he believed. His convictions.

She was a criminal and it was his job to put her away.

Midas always told him it was a man of character who stood for something and one who lacked character who fell for everything. Reese could never live with himself if he ran off with Frankie.

He choked back a dry laugh. Like she would even want him. She was good. The best. And also the hardest lesson he'd learned as an adult. One he would never forget.

She moaned softly. He bent down and kissed her lips. He drew back and her eyes fluttered open.

"Are you Prince Charming?"

He wished he was. That would make her Cinderella, and they'd live happily ever after.

"No, babe, just a guy."

She reached up to his cheek and touched him. "What happened?"

"You fell off your horse," he said, and brushed a leaf from her hair.

Frankie closed her eyes and moaned again. "I knew I shouldn't have . . ." Her eyes flew open, then narrowed.

So, she remembered. He sighed. It would have been perfect if she had amnesia. How could a jury convict her of a murder she couldn't remember? Wouldn't matter. As long as they had the proof, she'd be on death row in less than a year.

Frankie pushed his hand away. "Don't touch me."

"Why not?"

She rolled her eyes and winced, then squinched her eyes shut. "Your girlfriend might have a problem with it."

"I don't have a girlfriend."

Her eyes flashed open, accusing. "Well, then, your whatever Amy is."

"Frankie, I haven't touched Angie since we were in high school."

"You're lying."

"I don't lie to you." He inwardly cringed.

"Are you trying to tell me you haven't lied to me since we met?"

He paused a second too long before he answered. "Yes."

"You're lying again."

He shook his head. "I'm not lying about Angie."

"It doesn't matter. Nothing does."

The breeze picked up a lock of her hair and he brushed it from her eyes.

"It matters to me that you believe me about her, Frankie."

With his help, she sat up. She rubbed the back of her head and looked slowly around. "Tell me why you don't like this place."

He felt the blood drain from his cheeks. The last thing he wanted to tell her was the truth. *But,* his reason said, *if you tell her the truth she will feel closer to you, more trusting,* and that, he decided, would equal information. It was time to take off the gloves and play for keeps.

"My sister died here."

Frankie gasped. "How?"

"I killed her."

He almost smiled at her shocked expression. Didn't killing your own father rank up there with killing your baby sister?

"What happened?"

Every muscle in his body tensed. The ugly scene played out like it was yesterday. He didn't think even for a conviction he could replay it in his head and talk about it.

"I don't like to talk about it."

"Surely, Reese, what happened was an accident. You could never kill someone you loved."

He smiled grimly. "You'd be surprised what I'm capable of."

She looked hard at him. "I suppose in the heat of the moment we can all do things we wouldn't normally do."

"Sometimes it comes down to survival."

"Does your father blame you too?"

He felt his face freeze. He rose. "I don't speak to him."

"Maybe you should. Clear the air."

"If your father was still alive, would you clear the air with him?"

Anger flashed across her face, then blankness. "I was dead to my father. When he made that abundantly clear to me, the feeling, at least at the time, was reciprocated."

"That about sums up me and my father."

"At least you have a chance. Your father is still alive."

"No more chances, Frankie, I can't erase the past."

She nodded and softly said, "You're right, the past cannot be fixed."

Gently he helped her up, her words echoing like a death knell in his ears. While he still struggled with his father's rejection, Frankie dispassionately dismissed hers. Coldness infiltrated his heart.

Reese watched her try to get her bearings. It took her a moment to get her sea legs. He grabbed her arm and steadied her. "You can't ride alone."

He gathered Rosie's reins and drew Frankie toward Zorro. "C'mon, let me help you up."

She didn't argue. After he got Frankie safely mounted, he hopped up behind her. She sat rigidly in front of him. He bent his lips to her ear. "Relax, I won't bite."

He wrapped his left hand around her waist and pulled her against him. He smiled when she relaxed against his chest. She was so good at her act he almost fell for it—again.

He wanted to be angry, he was angry, but a deep sadness took a tighter hold. Just when he begins to feel again, he gets played. His right hand, holding the reins to both horses, tightened into a fist. He worked it open and closed. His left arm inadvertently tightened around her waist.

"Oww," she complained.

The urge to lash out at her became overwhelming.

"You know, Frankie, we're more alike than you might think."

She turned slightly and looked up at him. "How so?"

"We're both oldest siblings. Our fathers could give a rat's ass about us. We're both in the same business, just on opposite sides." He almost laughed at that one. It was so true. "And—" he nuzzled her throat with his nose, inhaling her unique scent—"we really dig fucking each other."

Knowing she was going to die by lethal injection didn't hamper his dick. It swelled at the thought of diving deep into her. He loved the way her pussy smelled, all hot and musky, the way it got slick with anticipation, the way her muscles milked him dry.

He loosened his hold on her waist and brushed a thumb against her hardening nipple. He nibbled her earlobe and felt her body shiver. "Yeah, even if you denied it, your body tells the story." He bit down on her earlobe and she cried out. "There are just some things, Frankie, you can't hide. Eventually you get found out."

His hand crushed her breast and she arched against him. "I forgot, you like it rough." He pushed his hips against her back, digging his erection into the small of her back. "I like rough too, the rougher the better."

She turned halfway around, her lips parted, the spark in her eyes challenging. She slid an arm around his neck and pulled his lips down to hers. When his arm clamped harder on her breast, she pushed harder against his chest. Her teeth cut into the tender flesh of his lip. Reese growled and jerked his head back. He licked the blood from his bottom lip. "You're going to pay for that." He cupped her head in his hand and crushed his mouth over hers. Her soft whimpers spurred him on. He wanted her to feel something genuine for him, even if it was pain. He wanted payback and he would get it through her body.

He released her, and she panted hard, her warm breath penetrating his shirt. When she raised her mouth to him again, he yanked her back by a hank of her hair. "No, Frankie, this time it's on my terms."

The ride back to the ranch house was silent. Frankie's pride wouldn't allow her to demand Reese put an end to the hot throb between her legs. Her pussy screamed for his touch and yet she couldn't bring herself to beg. She had a modicum of pride left.

Frankie was off Zorro before they came to a complete stop. As she headed for the house he called to her, "You have two hours. Then I'm coming for you."

His words sent a thrill through her so electric Frankie thought if she so much as touched herself, she'd come right there in the dirt. A vision of Reese's sweat-slicked body dominating her, making her beg for him, flashed before her. Totally surrendering to the man would be the ultimate turn-on.

After taking a couple of aspirin for a dull headache, no doubt initiated by her tumble, Frankie tried to take a nap. Her mind refused to quiet, so she took a long, hot shower. It was all she could do in the shower not to touch herself. She wanted to give it all to Reese. She wanted him to take it. *After* she made him wait.

She showered then pain-stakingly rubbed lotion over every inch of her skin, blow-dried her long hair and applied a light round of makeup. While she didn't have much to choose from in the clothes department, she decided one of Reese's button-down denim shirts would be a nice change. When she padded down the hall into his room, she noticed how silent the house was. Had he showered? Was he even in the house? Finding the shirt she wanted, she put it on. No bra, but she decided she'd make him work, so she put on a pair of thong panties.

Glancing at the clock, Frankie noted two hours and ten minutes had passed since she had seen Reese. Where was he?

The sun had long sunk behind the craggy mountains. Low lights illuminated her way downstairs to the kitchen. An open bottle of cab aired on the counter. Obviously someone had been inside since she went upstairs. She smiled and poured herself a small glass. Her stomach quivered and her body simmered with anticipation.

Another ten minutes passed and she looked at her empty glass. She poured another one, and instead of feeling all warm and fuzzy, she was angry.

She wasn't some sex-starved bimbo waiting for Reese to snap his fingers for her to drop and spread her legs. She opened the door to the back porch and looked over at the barn. His truck was parked where he had left it the night they came in. The barn doors were open and a low glow of light illuminated the building. Where was he?

She stepped off the porch and walked toward the barn. With the exception of the low nickers of the horses, there was no sound. At the end of the wide aisle a soft light crept from under one of the large enclosed stalls, a slight rustling sound coming from within. She walked toward it.

CHAPTER TWENTY-EIGHT

"Reese?" Frankie called out. Several low nickers from the four-legged residents answered her. Suddenly she felt foolish for wanting him so bad *and* looking for him. Was he playing games? She'd had enough of being jerked around by men.

She almost turned and left the barn, but the heat between her thighs spurred her on. Reese excited her like no other. She wanted him, plain and simple.

She reached the double stacked door of the last stall, pushed open the door, and caught her breath.

Softly illuminated by several enclosed lanterns was what she could only call a love nest. An array of blankets covered what she surmised were several bales of hay pushed together to form a bed of sorts. The thick blankets would not only keep the hay from poking and scratching but also add comfort and warmth to the chilly air. Propped up against the far wall of the large box stall was a wide mirror. And sitting on a tripod next to it, a digital camera. Her skin warmed. The thought of them on film titillated her beyond reason.

And he knew that. But caution curbed her excitement. Her fantasy would be corporate suicide if those shots ever got out of her hands. On an impulse, Frankie turned to get her camera, somehow feeling less exposed with her own equipment.

A large, dark body filled the doorway, startling her.

"Where you going, Frankie?" Reese asked in a low, husky voice.

Her fear morphed into excitement. "Where do you want to take me?"

Reese grinned and walked into the stall, closing the doors behind him. Her eyes raked him from head to toe. He wore a lightweight camel-hair sweater, snug-fitting blue jeans, and black ostrich-skin cowboy boots. His legs went on forever, stopping at the bulge beneath his button fly. She licked her lips.

"Wherever you want to go."

He moved into her space and she backed up a half step. His eyes flashed wickedly and she sensed a change in him. He reminded her of a predator, sure of his prey, sure that she could run, sure that she could hide, but confident he would find her and devour her and she would be powerless to stop him.

He continued into the stall, and she continued backward until the smooth plank of the wall stopped her. She heard a soft click and knew the camera was shooting.

"Turn that off," she said.

"No." He moved in closer.

"You can't—"

He pressed his finger against her lips. "I can do whatever the hell I want and there isn't a damn thing you can do to stop me."

Frankie hiked back a gasp. He was so intense, so direct, so sexy in his power that her knees wobbled in excitement.

He pushed her none too gently into the corner of the stall. The straw caught beneath her feet. He grabbed her arms, keeping her from falling.

"Afraid?"

She shook her head. "You don't scare me."

"Really?"

Grabbing a handful of her shirt, he yanked her against him. "Does anyone scare you?"

She swallowed hard and nearly choked, her throat suddenly dry. "No."

He laughed and cupped the back of her head with his right hand. He pulled her roughly toward him. "I guess with your last name there aren't too many people to be afraid of."

"Except those guys who keep shooting at me."

He smiled grimly. "Yeah, except those guys."

"Why do you say it like that?"

"Like what?"

"Like I'm lying. You were there."

"Yeah, I was."

He slid a hand down the front of her shirt, resting it on her left breast. Her heart pounded wildly beneath it.

"For someone who isn't afraid, your heart is beating fast."

"So?"

He searched her eyes for the truth and he found only lies. Her hazel eyes were almost emerald green, the golden flecks around her irises bright. Her nostrils flared slightly, like a bitch in heat. His hand closed firmly around her breast.

He lowered his lips to her cheek. "I want to fuck you until you scream for me to stop."

Her body arched into his, her nipple poking the palm of his hand.

Frankie slid her hands up his arms, lingering on his thick biceps. "And I want to get it all on film," she said.

"It's rolling."

"No, my camera."

"We use the digital, it has a large-capacity card. I set it for every thirty seconds."

"You think of everything, don't you?"

He gave her a half smile. "Not everything."

She cocked an eye at him, then pushed away. "Where did you get it?"

"I borrowed it from Midas. The man should have stock in Radio Shack, he has so many gadgets."

"I keep the chip—no duplicate pictures."

Reese grabbed her hand and pushed her back toward the covered bales of hay. "No more talking." When she moved to protest, he pressed her down onto the soft blankets. "Uh-uh, Frankie. We both get stills."

"Reese . . ."

He straddled her, grabbed her shirt into each of his hands, and yanked it apart. She gasped as buttons flew across the space, silently landing in the straw and blanket fabric. She raised her hands to cover herself. Reese halted her effort. "No, Frankie, I want to watch your nipples harden."

He ran a fingertip across one nipple and nodded as it instantly responded. He smiled devilishly and pulled the rest of the shirt from her body. Before she was aware of what he was doing, he wrapped the sleeve around her right wrist. She frowned. What? Then he picked up her other wrist. She realized what he was doing and tried to jerk away. He laughed, sure of his strength, wrapping the shirt around her left wrist and pulling both wrists together. "No!" She struggled, but her hips pressed against his.

"I'm in charge now, Frankie, you're going to have to trust me."

"I—can't."

He twisted the fabric, tightening it. "Can't let me tie you up or can't trust me?"

"Both."

"Your loss."

He held her bound hands together over her head, and when she protested again he sucked a nipple into his mouth, teasing it with his tongue. She hissed and closed her eyes, arching against his mouth. Heat spread through her limbs, racing to her apex. He took her nipple between his teeth and gently rolled it. His free hand slipped behind her neck and he pulled her up, exposing the soft flesh. His mouth traveled up to the swell of her breast, and he nibbled her. His teeth scraped lightly against her sensitive skin and she moaned.

"Harder," she demanded.

Reese growled and moved up higher, his left hand clamping around her throat, his teeth laving her jugular.

Slowly the pressure of his fingers increased, and she could hear the pounding rush of her blood in her neck, feel it force its way through her jugular. His thumb rubbed the length of her vein and his teeth sunk into her skin, his lips hot and moist around it. Her body arched harder against him. She wanted penetration; she wanted it hard, fast, and rough. The fantasy of giving up complete control, of having a man totally dominate her, made her wet.

In her business she called the shots with men; they always sucked up to her. Reese was taking what he wanted and for the first time in her life it was what she wanted too. It did involve a level of trust. She trusted him to know her boundaries.

Reese grabbed a lead shank hanging from a hook on the stall wall and looped it around the fabric binding her wrists, then fastened it back to the ring. His eyes locked with hers when he stepped back to look down at her.

"Your tits are begging for me."

She nodded. They throbbed, heavy, overly sensitive. One of the most sensitive areas on her body and Reese stimulated her to the point of combustion.

"When was the last time you were properly fucked in living color?"

"Never."

"Tell me what's so exciting about seeing yourself getting fucked."

"Everything."

She licked her lips, straining against the ties. He hadn't moved toward her but stood next to her and looked sideways at the mirror, where they both watched her breasts pierce the air when she arched and writhed.

Reese walked to the other side of the bales so that he looked directly into the camera and could see both of their images reflected there.

"Watch, Frankie," he whispered as he knelt down beside her. She turned her head and caught his gaze in the mirror. A flush stampeded across her skin, leaving goose flesh in its wake. Reese laughed low. "Can't wait, can you?"

She twisted, her wrists pulling against the fabric binding. Reese slid a large hand over the small of her back, his gaze never leaving hers in the mirror. Stretched out as she was, the indentations of her ribs stood out. His fingertips traced each one, beginning at the one nearest her waist. His fingers brushed the bottom swell of her right breast and she strained, the points sitting up high.

"Your tits are magnificent."

Not taking his eyes from hers, he lowered his mouth to the back of her rib cage and ran his tongue the length of her back. She strained against the ties, wanting to turn, to feel his mouth clamp down on her breasts. His lick turned into a kiss and his kiss into nibbles. The waistband of her jeans stopped his downward trail. His hand slid around to her hips and Frankie trembled. Her thighs parted.

"Not so fast," he whispered against her skin. His hand slid around to the front, to her fly and lower. Then he pressed his open palm against her mound. Frankie moaned and jerked against the pressure.

"Reese," she moaned, "take my pants off."

His mouth trailed to her neck, nibbling, teasing, tormenting. She couldn't arch high enough, demanding in her bound state he touch her more thoroughly.

Reese had his own ideas. His hand rested on her mound, rubbing slowly, painfully slow across her, and when he bit into the soft flesh behind her ear, Frankie felt like she was going to faint. Her nether lips swelled, her pussy throbbed, moisture made her ready. Reese's hand moved faster and more firmly.

Her hips twitched in rhythm. His right hand slid beneath her shoulders and around to cup her breast while his hand swept her into an orgasm. His lips never left her neck.

Wide-eyed, her mouth gaping for air, Frankie watched Reese play her body, the thrill of watching herself come at his hand more intoxicating than any drug. She gasped and pulled hard against the binding, the fabric tightening, but she needed to; the pressure building up in her body needed release.

"Now, Frankie," Reese hoarsely demanded against her neck before he sunk his teeth into her flesh. She screamed, her orgasm opening her up like a rose blooming in fast forward. Her hips jerked against his hand, and his finger tortured her nipple.

She closed her eyes, savoring the delicious racking sensations coursing through her body. His hand slowed, his lips loosened, his hand on her breast relaxed. She wanted more.

Reese moved away, and Frankie opened her eyes, feeling exposed. "Untie me."

He shook his head no and reached down to the corner behind her head. She heard the uncorking of a bottle, then the slow, sluicing pour of liquid. Reese held up a glass of deep red wine and took a long sip. He held it out to Frankie. She lifted her head and he tipped the glass for her to sip. When she pulled her head back, he trailed the bottom of the glass down her jaw and throat, then between her breasts, where he tipped the glass; warm wine sluiced between her breasts, then down her sides. She jerked against the bindings.

"Sorry," Reese whispered. "Let me get that."

He set the empty glass in the straw and licked what was left from her skin, being sure to get each straining nipple. Frankie twisted, wanting to give his mouth more of her, but he toyed with her, giving her just enough of his mouth to leave her wanting.

She almost cried in relief when she watched his hand slide down to the top button of her jeans. She raised her hips, offering him help he didn't need. "Not so fast, Frankie."

"Yes, fast, please, Reese."

His hand stopped and his eyes caught hers in the mirror. "Please," she said, "hurry."

"Hurry?" His fingers unbuttoned the second button, and he slipped a finger between the fabric and her skin. "Your skin is on fire, Frankie." He traced a short path of kisses along her throat. "I bet you're wet too."

He slid his fingers back to her belly, and she whimpered. He unbuttoned the third button, and then the fourth. "One more button, Frankie, one more button to your hot button."

He slipped his hand down her belly, touching her soft, damp curls. The tip of his middle finger tapped her hardened clit and she gasped. "Oh, Reese."

His breath blew hot against her skin. "You are so hot and so wet, I could slide right into you."

She pressed her hips against his finger. "Inside, Reese."

Reese focused on the here and now, not the future. Here and now was Frankie—hot, bothered, and sexier than any woman had a right to be. The future? He pushed thoughts of it out of his brain. Tonight he would pretend they'd ride off into the sunset tomorrow.

He slid his hand down further, finding her lips warm, swollen, and wet. He inserted his fingertip into her and moaned as she hissed in a deep breath. Her scent wafted up to his nose and Reese tamped down his urgency to strip her and take her from behind. His dick swelled to capacity and he found it more than difficult to keep his pace slow.

He wanted to devour her, to consume her, to ingest her, and then do it all over again. Her scent called to him, and his lips trailed down her belly, lingering at her belly button. Her smooth, silky skin was addictive, her hip bones cradles for his hands. He pushed her pants down further, exposing more of her. He rubbed his nose across her soft, downy fur, inhaling her sex. Frankie's soft, sexy moans brought his blood to boiling. He pulled her jeans down to just above her knees, her pussy glistened with desire. He blew hot breath across her hard nub.

She gasped, gulping for air. "Reese." Her hips twisted, her back arched, her body writhed.

His tongue lapped lightly at her clit. "How bad do you want it, Frankie?" he whispered across her damp curls. Her body twitched; he looked in the mirror and found her eyes riveted to him. He smiled and in a long, deep lap he dug his tongue into her. It was what she craved. She cried out and her hips shook.

"Oh, God, Reese," she moaned, "I need more now."

"How much more?"

"All of you, please, don't torture me."

He pulled her jeans down a bit further. "How is this?" he softly asked, sliding a finger slow and deep inside of her. Her vaginal muscles clamped around him, pulling him deeper inside.

"That feels so good."

"I know."

He slid his finger in and out in a slow, seductive rhythm, the soft slurp of her juices exciting him. He laid his head down on her belly, his lips just inches from her pussy. He caught her eyes before he buried his face between her thighs.

A sharp, hard orgasm ripped through her, and Frankie felt like an invisible force had grabbed her, picked her up, spun her around, then slammed her into earth. She wanted to open her thighs and give Reese more room, but her jeans at her knees kept her immobile.

When he slid in a second finger and sucked her clit, she came undone. Wildly she bucked against him. Her hands had gone numb, and for the first time in her life she felt completely and utterly out of control.

Wave after wave of pleasure ripped through her body, and she still wanted more, it wasn't enough. She wanted a connection with him that only intercourse could give her. As she twisted away from his mouth, his fingers slid from her. "I want you, Reese, not your fingers, not your mouth."

He sat back and caught her eyes in the mirror. Her long body drew taut in her excitement, tits firm, high, and lush. In all of his years of whoring, in all of his years of womanizing, in all his years of bed hopping, he couldn't remember being so attracted to a woman as he was to Frankie. She exuded sex and she wanted him. Her dark eyes beckoned him, promising him the ride of his life. Or the ride to end his life.

Reality hit him square in the chest.

Roughly he pulled her pants down to her ankles, then yanked off her shoes; her pants followed. She licked her lips in anticipation.

He jerked his shirt over his head and kicked off his boots. His eyes held hers as he unbuttoned his jeans. He didn't take them off, only pushed them down to his thighs.

Roughly he slipped his arm beneath her waist and twisted her over so she was face-down in the blankets. She cried out, surprised. He pulled up her hips, settling his hands on each side of her hips. The smooth, round curve of her hip bones fit his hands perfectly. He spread her thighs with his right knee.

He spread her cheeks with his hand and turned her hips up, her pink, wet lips glistening in the lantern light. He glanced at the mirror to see his dick jutting up hard at her ass. From between the thick strands of her hair, he knew she watched too. He bent over her, his dick sliding up between her ass cheeks. She moaned and pushed back. He swept her long hair from her face and trailed his fingertips down her throat to her breasts. She arched her ass, rubbing against him.

"Reese," she pleaded. Taking her hips into his hands again, he reared back and rubbed the tip of his cock against her swollen lips. She pushed back and caught him. He groaned and fought the urge to thrust deep into her.

He ran a finger down her spine and withdrew his dick from her. She moaned and pushed back against him. Like a guided missile his cock dug into her. This time deeper. He hissed in a breath and pulled back. His eyes locked in the mirror with hers and he saw in their depth, a challenge to make him succumb.

Frankie rotated her hips in a circular movement, her cheeks brushing against the head of his dick. She slipped a leg back, locked it around his thigh, and pushed back harder against his cock. The head slid up her ass, and with the lubrication she gave off, the head of his dick slid into her.

She gasped, "No, Reese, too much." She pressed her hips forward, trying to unhook her leg from his thigh, but he grabbed her harder, steadying her.

He knew he was too big to go deeper. But he kept the head firmly inside to give her something, but more to keep him from plunging deep into her pussy. He wasn't ready for that—yet. He slid a hand around the soft curve of her ass. She pushed back against him and gasped as he went deeper into her. His finger slid up to her clit and he dipped into her hot box.

"Is that what you want?"

"All of you."

His finger delved deep into her and she straightened up on her knees as he hit her sweet spot. Her orgasm was instant. His finger rode her out and his cock went an inch deeper. He closed his eyes and gritted his teeth. He withdrew from her, and she cried out.

He steadied her thrusting hips with his hands, luxuriating in the velvety heat of her skin. She slid her leg back again, and while he tried to get his desire under control, she seized the moment. Her slick labia slid along his shaft and she pulled forward just enough to tip his cock. She spread her thighs wider and caught the head at her opening. As he surged forward just for a taste, she clamped her thighs tight around him and pushed backward, impaling herself on the length of him. He gritted his teeth and gave in to the sublime feel of her velvety heat.

"Frankie," he moaned. He gathered her tighter to him and with his hands on each of her hip bones, he sank himself as deep into her as he could. He felt her muscles quiver, her womb vibrate. Her skin sweltered.

Frankie watched the hard play of muscles along Reese's long arms as he pulled her toward him, holding her close as their bodies became one. His tan skin glowed bronze in the low light of the lantern, and the sight of his power possessing her made her heart ache. Her body arched against his, and she began the slow, rhythmic dance of passion.

When his eyes opened she paused. His fierce stare unnerved her, his power excited her.

"Move, Reese, slow and deep."

He did, and she took every inch of him in and out in the slow, long, deep thrusts. She could see in the mirror he fought it, each thrust a thought, a conscious decision, one that his body made, not him. Frankie closed her eyes and pulled him along with her, giving him no choice but to go with nature. She felt it the minute he made the switch. His fingers dug deeper into her hips and he held her closer, and his thrusts came deeper, more languid, savoring.

She met him thrust for thrust, skin to skin, heart to heart. She was in too deep to do otherwise, and she knew in her heart he was too.

Reese's eyes closed and she watched the play of emotions cross his face as their bodies parried and engaged. It was all she could do not to lose herself in the moment, but she wanted to watch him as their bodies met, then separated: the curve of her hip, the thrust of his cock, the sheen on their bodies, the way her body pulled him in only to give him up, then take him back, deeper, hotter, faster.

Frankie moaned, aroused by the visual of his cock thrusting in and out of her, their bodies hot and healthy, mating; the sublime sensation only he could deliver crested. A smooth sheen of perspiration erupted and Frankie cried out. Her body quivering, her womb constricting wildly, her release complete.

"Jesus, Frankie," Reese groaned as his body followed her to the ultimate fulfillment.

CHAPTER TWENTY-NINE

For a long moment they remained as one, their heavy breaths blowing steamy into the cool air of the stall. Frankie's breasts heaved as she drew in deep breaths.

Reese slid a large hand down around the curve of her ass and squeezed her.

"Untie me," she said, her voice hoarse. She swallowed again to coat her dry throat. Reese reached over her and released the shank from the hook. Frankie slowly pulled her arms close to her body and moved away from Reese, his still full cock slipping from her. She gasped and felt empty. She rolled over onto her back and brought her hands down in front of her.

Reese sat back on his haunches, eyeing her warily.

"What?" she asked.

He shook his head and yanked her hands toward him. Too drained to fight his surly action, she allowed him to untie and unwrap his shirt from around her wrists.

"I thought guys were always nice after sex."

He grunted and lay down alongside her. Wrapping the blankets around them, he edged closer to her, but not enough so that their bodies touched.

She rolled on her side, facing him. "What's bothering you?"

"You."

"Me?"

"That's what I said."

"Well, clue me in."

He shrugged. "I don't like being lied to."

She smoothed her hair back from her face. "That makes two of us."

His eyes narrowed.

"And since it's obvious we don't trust each other, let's not dwell on it," she said.

"Just like that?"

She sighed. "What do you want from me, Reese? A confession?"

He remained silent.

"What do you want me to confess?"

"The truth."

She shook her head and pushed away from him, pulling another blanket around her shoulders. "Can you be specific?"

"Tell me about your father."

She stiffened. "There's nothing to tell."

"Yes, there is."

"Tell me about yours."

It was his turn to scowl.

"See?" she said. "Some things are better left unsaid."

"What happened between you and your father?"

She felt her chest tighten and her eyes warmed. "When he didn't go for my idea to convert *Skin,* I told him I was going to go to my uncle for support. He accused me of betraying him. I didn't back down. He told me I was dead to him. So I told him he was dead to me."

"Who killed him?"

"How did your sister die?"

His jaw drew taut. "My sister is none of your business."

"Neither is my father yours."

She moved to leave their warm cocoon, but Reese curled long fingers around her arm and pulled her back. "Stay."

She turned back to see his face. It was a difficult mask to read. His eyes glittered angrily but she knew he wanted her there.

"You don't like to be challenged, do you?" she asked.

"Not really."

"You're a control freak, Reese. If you can't have your way, you try to muscle it. And then if that doesn't work, you coerce."

"Did I coerce you?"

"Yes, you did. But as it happened, I wanted it."

He pulled her close to him and finally she could feel his body heat. "Yeah, you did."

"Okay, so that's two of my fantasies you've made come true. You're going to get yours in the morning."

He raised a brow.

"Remember? You wanted to wake up after sex and find the woman gone, no demands?"

"You can't leave."

"I can and I will. I'm tired of running. It's not my style. I'm going to find my father's will, and then I'm going to confront Anthony."

"You're not leaving."

"Do you want Midas to die? Or even your friend Amy?" She wouldn't be responsible for their deaths. Or Reese's.

"They will never find you here."

"They always find their mark."

"The only way they can find you here is if someone tells them. I'm not going to, and Midas and Angie have no idea what's going on."

She pulled away and he pulled her back. "It doesn't matter. I'm leaving. I'm not running anymore."

She yawned and realized she felt exhausted.

"Go to sleep," he said. "We'll talk about it later."

She closed her eyes and shook her head but allowed him to pull her into the crook of his arm. She settled against his shoulder, and the last thought as sleep consumed her was how good their sex smelled.

Frankie woke later to the feel of Reese's long, hard body beneath hers. Slowly she opened her eyes and realized by his deep, even breaths he was asleep. She traced a finger across the scars on his chest and wondered for the hundredth time how he really got them.

She stretched and yawned, and as her thigh brushed against his cock it swelled. She smiled and an idea took hold. Very carefully she slid up toward the lead shank still attached to the ring in the stall wall. For a moment she wondered how she could manage to immobilize Reese without waking him. The thought of him writhing crazily beneath her, completely under her power, sent her skin warming and her pussy constricting.

Carefully she wrapped the braided cotton around his wrists, then tied it off in a loose square knot. The minute Reese pulled, it would tighten. She smiled. She learned one thing from her family. There was nothing sweeter than a vendetta well served.

She debated on finding another lead shank and tying up his feet. Instead, she hurried from the stall to the small office and used the bathroom, where she cleaned herself up a little. She smiled as she hurried back through the cold air and into the stall. She noticed there was a camera bag in the corner by the tripod case. She opened it to find another picture card. She changed it out and reset the timer. When she looked across the small space to Reese she met his dark penetrating gaze.

"Untie me," he said, his voice low, deep, and dangerous.

She grabbed a loose blanket and wrapped it around herself. "No."

"Francesca, do it now or pay the price."

She sauntered up to him and smiled. "By the time you get yourself out of this mess I'll be long gone."

He scowled and pulled against the rope. Frankie secured the lightweight blanket around her and tied two ends over one shoulder toga style. Then she took the camera from the tripod. "Now, let's see what shots I can get."

He pulled against the rope again, his biceps bulging.

"Oh, that looks so good, Reese. Maybe I'll have a taste of you before I go."

"Don't touch me."

She laughed out loud. "Don't say the prospect doesn't interest you." She moved in for a close-up.

He answered with angry eyes. She pulled the blanket further down his chest. "Looks like you just might be a tad bit intrigued, cowboy."

Her eyes swept down the length of his belly to the rising blanket. "I have to go to the bathroom," he said.

"Oh, I think"—she pulled the blanket down a little further,

exposing his patch of hair—"it might be a little bit more than that."

Reese growled a warning, one she ignored. She continued to get her shots. When she pulled the blanket from him she did it slowly, dragging it across his raging hard-on. He sucked in a deep breath and she laughed low. "Does that feel good?"

He shot her a vicious glare, and for a moment she hesitated. The raw emotion on his face was priceless. She'd apologize later, but she reminded him of his contract. "You agreed to anytime, anywhere."

She turned and put the camera back onto the tripod, then set the timer.

She walked to the foot of the bales and pulled the blanket the rest of the way from Reese's body. "You have the most incredible body of any man I've ever seen." She moved to his side and touched a finger to his chest, tracing the longest of the scars there. "How'd you get that?"

"From the last woman I killed after she tied me up."

She pressed her lips to it. "I hope you aren't so violent with me."

"Untie me and I won't be."

She traced a finger down his belly to his groin. "I'm sorry, can't do that, Reese, I need the shot." She slid her open hand palm first down the thick heat of his erection, and he reared against her hand. "Yes, you see? You do like it."

She wrapped her hand around him and he groaned. "This will be the last time you take a picture of me. I quit." He hissed as she manipulated him to staggering proportions.

She squeezed his cock in her hand. "After these, I'll have enough pictures of you."

She pressed her lips to his chest and felt the sharp lurch of his heart against her mouth. "You know you want me."

"I want you to untie me."

"I can't do that. You need to know what it's like to be powerless, to have no say."

"Why?"

Her lips traveled lower, and she nibbled on his hip bone. Deftly she slid out of her makeshift toga. "Payback."

"A sexual vendetta?"

She licked the wide tip of his cock and Reese's hips left the blankets. Then she took him in her mouth, knowing there was no way she could get all of him in, but she gave it her best shot.

Reese's body stiffened and he cursed her. She ignored him. Just as she worked him up to overflow, she stopped. Her pussy throbbed so thickly, she felt like she was going to come right there.

She took his cock between her full breasts and fucked him that way. He watched, his eyes narrow slits, his jaw set. His hips moved boldly against her full flesh.

"Jesus, Frankie," he hoarsely whispered as his thrusts increased in tempo and power. Without warning she pulled away from him. Crawling up him, she scratched his chest with her nails and pushed him closer to the edge.

"Sit on my face," he demanded. She crawled further up his chest. The cool air wafted across her steamy pussy and she couldn't wait to feel his mouth torment her. She grabbed the round handle the lead shank was attached to and held on as she straddled his face and lowered herself to him. His hot lips clamped onto her nether lips and she cried out.

She thought about loosening the tie so he could slip a finger deep into her, but she refrained. She needed him tied up when she left. Her emotions were messing with her mind and she knew there was no future with this man unless she cleared the air with her family first.

His tongue drilled into her, then laved her tightened clit; his teeth nibbled and his lips suckled her deep into his mouth. An orgasm erupted and she bucked against his face, her juices releasing into his mouth. He continued to ravage her and the orgasm continued to rip through her one electrifying wave at a time.

Back arched, her tits thrust into the chilled air, her nipples tight, Frankie wanted all of him.

She pulled back from his mouth, her body twitching and quivering as the vestiges of her orgasms waned.

She looked at him, his lips glistening with her all over him.

"Untie me."

She shook her head and slid down him, indulgently filling herself with him. The contact was magic. His cock was a lightning rod to her pussy, the contact explosive. He thrust high up into her and she cried out. He pulled hard at the rope, his jaw set. His legs twined with hers and he set the pace. He showed her no mercy.

"Reese," she gasped, "please."

He pulled harder at the rope, and the wood splintered. His furious thrusts nearly split her in two; she tried to gauge him but his furious pace was unrelenting. His legs clamped around hers and she was his prisoner. The hard look in his eyes scared her. She was no longer in control. "Please, Reese." Tears heated her eyes. She didn't want his anger, she wanted his tenderness.

The wood broke all the way and Reese was free of the restraint of the wall, although his hands were still tied. In a quick movement he rolled her over onto her back, still inside of her. She screamed. His blue eyes flashed like polished sapphires. He pulled the knot loose with his teeth and in an instant he was no longer restrained. Panic rose inside her chest and she felt his cock flex inside of her. The thrill of his control of her and the fear she felt at that moment nearly triggered another orgasm.

His hand slid to her throat and he wrapped his fingers around it. "What now, Frankie?"

She had no words. She closed her eyes, the emotions so raw inside her it hurt. She felt a warm tear slide from the corner of her eye and cursed herself.

His hands loosened around her throat. What he did next surprised her. He kissed away the tear. Gently he took her face into his hands and kissed her lips. Slowly he opened her mouth with his tongue, gently probing. Her chest constricted. Never had anyone been so gentle with her, and after what she did? Another tear slipped from her closed eyes, followed by another.

"Shh, Frankie, shh, it's all right." He consoled her, her arms slid around his neck, and she kissed him back deeply. Her hips quaked and his pressed against hers, neither asking nor taking.

Powerful emotion swelled in her chest, infusing her cells. She wanted him now more than at any other time. She wanted his love. "Make love to me, Reese."

He kissed her again and smoothed back her hair. His hips moved slowly at first, but as she met him thrust for thrust the momentum increased. His lips trailed from her lips to her eyes where he kissed away her tears, then down her throat. She wrapped her arms tighter around his neck, rubbing her cheek against his shoulder, never wanting him to let her go. He called out her name as he came. She followed a second later, their bodies undulating in perfect motion, their rhythm one.

For several long moments they lay silent, catching their breath, their fingers, arms, and legs entwined.

"What just happened?" Frankie softly asked.

He smoothed her hair back and looked at her tenderly. "I think that was called making love."

She smiled and snuggled closer to him. "Reese—I'm sorry."

"For what?"

"For calling you a trained monkey. For everything. I haven't been exactly honest with you."

She felt his body tighten. "About what?"

"Um, well, it isn't my usual practice to have sex with my models, as you know."

"Go on."

"And, well, I used our attraction to get shots out of you."

"Just business, huh?"

She smiled again. "Yes, but, well, if it hadn't been you, I wouldn't have. I couldn't." The words "I care about you" choked in her throat. She didn't want to scare him out of bed.

"Fuhgeddaboudit."

"Have you?"

"What?"

"Been honest with me?"

"Yes."

"Then would you trust me enough to tell me about your sister?"

He let out a long breath. "She died fifteen years ago."

"How?"

"She took off on her horse after I gave her some bad news. She fell and broke her neck." Pain twisted his face and his eyes wavered from hers.

"Oh, my God, Reese, how horrible." She sat up. "Surely you don't blame yourself?"

He nodded. "I gave her the news."

"But it was her choice to run off."

"No, Frankie, I lashed out at her in my anger. She was fucking twelve years old! I should have protected her. Instead it was my hand that pushed her."

"And your father blames you?"

"Rightfully so."

"I don't believe it! You were fifteen, how were you to know what would happen?"

"I knew she wasn't stable. I wanted her to stop asking questions."

"What news did you give her?"

"I told her the truth. Our mother didn't love us enough to hang around."

"She deserted you?"

"Yeah, ranch life wasn't for her. She up and left one night while my father was in Cheyenne. The old man blamed me, said I was too much work and he regretted ever adopting me."

Frankie gasped. He laughed. "Don't feel sorry for me, Frankie, I'm not worth it. My biological father didn't stay around long enough for morning sex. It was me and Mom for years. Until she met Sam. He was a good man, but he was also a man of the land. Mom always took to the cities. They met in Dallas. She was working a quarter horse convention, and he was buying a stud to start his line. He promised her a place to live and his love, she promised him she'd try. After Missy was born she changed. Missy was a colicky baby, and my mother was different. I think now she might have had a touch of depression that never left. Me and Sam took over raising Missy and Mom just kind of blended in with the woodwork. She was just never the same. She up and left one day, said she couldn't do this life anymore."

Frankie smoothed back his hair, her heart breaking for the family. "Missy kept crying, blaming herself. I finally had it one day and told her to grow up, it wasn't her, it was our mother. Mother was selfish, and it was time to move on. Missy jumped on her pony and took off. Sam yelled at me to go get her. When I got to her it was too late."

"Oh, Reese, I'm so sorry. But it isn't your fault. Girls do stupid things all of the time. How were you to know she would react like that?"

"I don't know. I always had a temper, my parents always told me it would get me in trouble, and it did."

"No, no, it isn't that way. You can't control everything, or everyone, only yourself."

"It's history."

"But you love it here."

"I stopped loving this place the day my father hit me and told me never to come back. That I was as dead to him as Missy was."

She gasped. "My father said the same thing to me."

His eyes narrowed. "What happened?"

She swallowed hard. "I don't know." Her eyes filled with tears. "He hurt me, Reese, and God forgive me, but I struck back by defying him."

"I can help you, Frankie."

"No, you can't. No one can."

He gathered her into his arms. "Trust me."

She turned watery eyes up to him. "I have to do this myself."

She fell asleep in Reese's arms, and long after the camera stopped, Reese stared at the ceiling of the stall. The lights dimmed in the lanterns, the batteries losing juice.

Had Frankie admitted she killed her father or was she innocent? If she was guilty, then there was no reason fighting her idea to go confront her brother. Maybe that was a setup to take him out too. Jase's words echoed in his head. *"Mark my words, buddy. Goombahs will show up, coz she'll get the word out."*

It had been two days and no sign of soldiers. Could Frankie be innocent? Stealthily, Reese slipped from the warmth of Frankie's body and the blankets. He quickly dressed, then headed for the office, closed the door, and made a call.

"Wiseguy," a voice answered.

Reese smiled. Jase's version of a goombah was good.

"Did you get a statement from the secretary?"

"Nah, her lawyer is holding out, but we're working on it."

Reese felt a momentary sense of relief. "I think we've got this wrong."

"How so?"

"No goons in these parts and I just can't buy into your theory."

"Ah, I see, you got some more and you want to keep getting it."

"Look, if she killed her old man, I'll find out. I've got her primed, the next time I fuck her she'll sing." Reese cringed at his crudity. It was necessary if he was to keep up his front with Jase. The last thing he needed was for Jase to report back to Ty that he was too close to the crack. He'd be yanked off the case so fast everyone's heads would spin. He needed more time. If she was a killer, he'd arrest her, but if she wasn't?

"Get fucking, man, 'cause our eyes and ears tell us war is about to break out."

"I'll pump her for as much as I can get, but I want your word you'll keep quiet to Jamerson, I don't want to get pulled."

"You got it, man. I'll give you twenty-four more hours, then we pull her in."

"I need more than twenty-four hours."

"It's less now, get humping, man."

"Fuck you, Jase," he mumbled before slamming the phone down. He opened the door and came face-to-face with Frankie. She slapped him across the face so hard that for several seconds he heard little birdies.

"You're nothing but a dirty lying cop!"

CHAPTER THIRTY

"Frankie—"

She punched him in the chest. "I hate you!" Pain speared her hand. Her adrenaline spiked, the hurt ignored.

She punched him again. "I hate you!" she screamed at the top of her lungs, so loud her throat strained and horses whinnied nervously. She turned to run from him but he caught her arm. She spun around so fast it surprised him. "Don't you ever touch me again! Do you understand? *Never!*"

She yanked her arm from his grasp and ran back to the stall. Emotions collided like a multiple-engine train wreck in her heart. It was always there, right in front of her, she just refused to deal with it.

Humiliation, anger, frustration, and a profound sense of loss smashed together, one on top of the other, into a heap of what her life had become. Hot tears stung her eyes. She could barely see what she grabbed. She managed to navigate the small space and find her clothes. Hastily she dressed, not wanting to stand naked before him for a second longer. She grabbed the camera. She felt Reese step forward. A low, guttural sound like a wounded beast emanated from deep within her. She dared him with an icy glare to try and take it.

He stepped back. Clutching the camera to her chest, Frankie hurried past him.

When she entered the house, the kitchen door slammed shut behind her. She started, but not before she was grabbed from behind.

"Got you now, *cara.* "

Reese took his time leaving the barn. Despite Frankie's threats to leave, there was nowhere for her to go. He had the keys to the truck and Midas wouldn't be back until later. If she called for help, by the time anyone arrived he would have her packed and gone.

His shoulders sagged in resignation.

Frankie was right. They needed to go back. Running got them nowhere. It was time to take the tiger by the tail.

He stood in the empty stall, his gaze resting on the rumpled blanket of the makeshift bed. If these walls could talk. A multitude of emotions racked him. Guilt, anger, sadness. A profound sense of loss. And just as powerful, regret. Regret for what might have been. What could have been. What wasn't.

The last straw was his conversation with Jase. She didn't need to hear that. It wasn't meant the way it sounded. As much as the evidence pointed to Frankie, he didn't want her sad, or angry. He knew what his side of the conversation sounded like, and if he was honest with himself, it was true. He could use sex to get info out of her. And he had. He cringed. He hadn't been honest with her.

He steeled his resolve. She hadn't been honest either, in fact she downright lied. *Did two wrongs make a right?* he asked himself. It sure as hell did when it put a murderer behind bars.

He let out a long breath. Why, then, did he feel hollow inside? He looked at the empty tripod. Thinking about what they captured on film, his body warmed. Not at the interval when he had Frankie tied up and at his mercy. No, what turned him on was the memory of their tender lovemaking, when she hung in his arms and cried. He'd felt the emotion pour from her. All his anger, his wanting to hurt her back for hurting him had evaporated. When he'd reciprocated, it felt more right than anything in his life.

He needed to talk to her, to make her understand he had a job to do. Yeah, right before you arrest her.

Shit!

He walked out of the barn. Exhaustion consumed him. He wanted to throw a bedroll on the back of his saddle and ride Zorro out to the linemen's cabin on the north side of the ranch, stare at a campfire for a week, come back to reality, and be all right with the world. But it wasn't his style. He'd never run from anything in his life. Except the memories here.

He smiled sadly. Frankie was right. He'd held his demons in too long. He needed to let go. He sighed and entered the house. Curiously, the door was ajar. Maybe not so curious. He bet Frankie slammed it so hard it bounced open from the velocity. He rubbed his chest. The woman had a punch.

He glanced out the open door. The sun was just rising over the eastern foothills. He knew what he had to do before he left this place. He had nothing to lose, and maybe something to gain by seeing the man who raised him.

Dragging his feet to the landing of the long staircase, he looked up, the door to Frankie's room only half visible. He wanted to go up, to say he was sorry, but he resisted. It was too late for that now. The hollowness inside him ate at his gut like a vulture on carrion. He turned back from the staircase and moved into the large family room. He stood in the empty silence, feeling more alone than he did fifteen years ago.

Frankie knew she was in a car. The steady hum of the engine beneath her body warmed the floorboards. She groaned and rubbed the lump at the base of her skull. She opened her eyes and saw only black, but immediately felt something tied around her head. Blindfolded.

"Don't even try to get outta here. I have no problem giving you a matching lump for the first one." The heavy New York accent was unfamiliar to her.

"Who do you work for?" she demanded.

"None of your business."

"Where are you taking me?"

"On a airplane ride."

She tried to stretch out against the bindings. Her back cramped and she moaned. "Whatever your boss is paying you, my uncle will double it."

He laughed, the sound anything but amusing. "Hear that, Jimmy boy? She's gonna pay me with all that money she stole."

Frankie went rigid. "Peanuts? Are you here?" she cried out, the implications if he was confusing her beyond reason if it was him. The New Yorker's guttural laugh sent shivers down her spine.

"Jimmy!"

"Be quiet, Frankie, it'll all be over soon," her cousin said from in front of her.

"Not you too," she cried. "Not you too." Was no one who they appeared to be?

"Shut up. Before I shut you up," the New York wiseguy said.

Frankie chose to keep quiet, the sense of hopelessness permeating her every pore. For Jimmy to be in on her demise meant her uncle was too. She felt light-headed. No. Not Unk. He loved her like the daughter he never had. Jimmy must be working his own angle. With Anthony. She sobbed once, then clamped her mouth shut.

As she tried to work every angle, every twist, every turn of the recent events in her life, she came up clear on two things. Reese used her in the worst possible way a man could use a woman, and not only was her brother after her, but he'd elicited the help of Jimmy Peanuts. Her father's bodyguard and now her uncle's. She gasped as a thought blindsided her. Had Anthony ordered the hit on their father? And had Jimmy carried it out?

Jimmy was the first of Father's men to arrive at the brewery; he was the one who doled out the hazy details. And now he worked for Unk. Was Unk next, after her? Was Anthony methodically weeding the family of potential problems so he could rule his underworld unfettered?

Was *Skin* that important? Why? Her frazzled brain continued to add. The money. Those thugs in the Carmel house had said "Judas bitch," obviously referring to her. Who set her up? And was that why her father was so angry at her? He thought she stole from him?

Who was skimming?

Her head throbbed, it was too much to comprehend.

The sudden halt of the car woke her, and she had no idea how much time had passed. The blindfold was so dark and so tight, she couldn't tell if it was light out.

The door opened and cold air hit her in the face. "C'mon, sweet cheeks." The New York thug pulled her roughly from the vehicle, and she stumbled. Her legs gave way and her knees hit concrete. He hiked her up and the sound of a plane engine in the near distance caught her attention.

After she was hustled up steps, she was shoved down what she surmised was an aisle. A narrow one, by the way her knees hit the ends of seats. She was pushed down and quickly belted in.

"I have to go to the bathroom," she said, and it wasn't a ploy.

The thug grumbled, unbelted her, and hiked her up. He pushed her forward. After several steps her face hit into a wall, or door. He pulled off her blindfold and she blinked against the bright light in her face.

An ugly, unfamiliar face greeted her. "In there," he said, pointing to a door two feet away.

She held up her bound hands. "I'm not a man."

He yanked at the rope. "If you was you'd be dead by now."

As the rope came off, he pushed her back into the bathroom. "Make it quick, we're about set to go."

As she came out of the bathroom, she looked toward the main area of the jet. She stopped in her tracks.

Anthony sat in one of the single seats and smiled dangerously.

"Hello, big sister."

She was shocked speechless. Reese had been right when all of her instincts told her Anthony wouldn't go so far.

"I won't have Sal tie you up again if you promise to be a good girl."

Her anger mushroomed. "Anthony, what the hell is going on?"

"You tell me."

She'd never seen him so composed, *so* sure of himself. He'd always been cocky, but that was false bravado, this was deeper now, an innate sense of self he'd never shown her. And it unsettled her. Frankie shook her head. Nothing could surprise her now. She sank down into the seat across from him, trying to get a grasp on what the hell was going on here. While she and Anthony had never been close, she never thought he hated her so much to put a hit out on her. "I'm not sure what you're fishing for, Anthony, but other than the fact I've had too many encounters with goombahs and bullets recently, there isn't much to tell."

"What about you and that cop? What did you tell him about family business, Frankie?"

"You knew he was a cop?"

"I know everything."

"Why didn't you tell me? You could have saved me so much—" She bit off what she was going to say.

"You never could read men, Frankie. You're too trusting. Not a good trait to have in this family."

"So because a cop duped me, you're trying to kill me? Because you think I'm ratting out the family?"

"I've never made bones about my feelings for you, big sister, but putting out a hit?" He leaned forward and continued, "I'm a big boy now. I'd kill you myself."

"How did you find me?"

He smiled. "You should know by now we have eyes and ears everywhere and when those eyes and ears need a nudge, cash works wonders."

"But—"

"I had a hunch you'd run to Carmel. You never were smart that way, Frankie. So imagine my surprise when I find two dead out-of-towners in the driveway and your clothes in your bedroom?"

"But how did you know I was in Wyoming?"

"The janitor at the Monterey airport overheard the flight plan. When we started asking around, he was happy to share when he heard the price for any information. He had a memory, that one. Showed us everything. It didn't take Sally and Jimmy long to find out the airstrip you came in on is owned by your cop friend's father. Getting the address was a piece of cake."

The captain popped out of the cockpit. "Buckle up, folks, we're cleared for takeoff."

"Why all the trouble to find me, Anthony?"

"I want Father's will," Anthony softly said.

"I don't have it.'

"Then, until it shows up, and if you want to stay alive, I suggest staying close to me."

Frankie looked at her brother for a long time, unsure of his meaning. Did he mean to off her once the will turned up? "What happens when the will turns up?"

He smiled grimly. "The whole world changes."

Reese fought the raging turmoil in his head and heart that pushed him to an emotional low. He looked up the stairway toward the woman who tore him up. Several times he stepped up to the landing, wanting to go to her. To talk, to demand that she put all the cards on the table and give him the entire truth about her father.

He thought how he kissed away her tears before they made love, how she cried in his arms. He took the steps three at a time to her room. He didn't know what he was going to say or what he was going to do, but the powerful feelings in his gut told him she needed to know, for what it was worth, that he cared. He opened the door and stopped short.

It was empty and his instinct told him she hadn't returned to it when she left the barn. While he'd loitered in the barn, had she managed to leave the ranch? How?

He scowled. Where the hell was she? He moved to the window and pushed back the curtain. He stepped back and looked closer at the room. Nothing disturbed. It looked like she hadn't even been in it. He hurried down the stairs to the kitchen. Slowly his eyes scanned the room. There in the corner of the floor—the camera. "What the hell?"

He picked it up; he could almost feel Frankie's energy on it. He walked to the door and opened it. He stepped out onto the porch, his eyes scanning every inch. As he walked down the plank steps he stopped. His blood ran cold. There, on the ground, peanut shells.

"Fuck!"

He hurried back into the house and grabbed the phone. He dialed Jase's cell.

"Yeah," Jase answered.

"They have her."

"Who has who?"

"Frankie. Carmine's men took her from here, the ranch."

"Calm down, buddy, and think about it."

"Think about what? She's gone—kidnapped."

"Gone, but not kidnapped."

The full meaning burst in spectacular Technicolor in Reese's brain. There was no denying it now. "She found a way to let them know where she was," he slowly said, not wanting to believe the words he'd just spoken. Every shred of his denial dissolved.

"I'm really sorry, buddy. It's why I love 'em, then leave 'em.

It had been Reese's modus operandi as well. So much for taking a chance. He'd never do it again.

"It's time to make our move, Reese."

"I'll be back in town in less than seven hours."

CHAPTER THIRTY-ONE

"Why are we in Monterey?" Frankie asked Anthony as they deplaned and loaded into a waiting limousine.

"We're going back to the Carmel house."

"Why?"

"Because that's where Father's will is, and we're going to find it."

"I've been through that place and so has Unk, and I bet your mother paid a fortune to have it tossed top to bottom. It's not there."

"It has to be."

"So what if we find it? Then what?"

"Payback begins."

"I won't help you unless you tell me what's going on. I want to call Unk."

"We'll call Unk when the time is right."

Frankie looked out the window and the landscape that whizzed by her. If she reached out it would elude her, just like her options.

From beneath lowered lashes, she observed her bother. His dark eyes sparkled, his gaze locked on her. "You'll regret this, Anthony."

"Not as much as you will."

Frankie blanched at the venom of his tone. With calmness she didn't feel, Frankie sat back in the soft leather in the back of the limo and thoughtfully stared at her brother. His quiet confidence had disappeared, replaced with nervous energy. His fingers constantly drummed the seat edge.

"Who was the man with Jimmy who kidnapped me?"

"Kidnapping is such a harsh term, Frankie. Let's just say he brought you to me."

"He's out-of-town. Why?"

His eyes narrowed. Avoiding her direct stare, he looked out the window.

"The two dead guys in my townhouse were out-of-towners."

"Consider me resourceful."

Frustration mounted. Why was Anthony being so vague? She pushed back hard into the leather seat. As they drove through the open gates to the estate, fresh memories of her time there with Reese launched into her mind. A warm shiver skirted along her flesh, and her stomach tightened. A damn cop! Fucking her while trying to pump her for information. Son of a bitch, how had she been so stupid? "You only see what you want to see, Frankie," her mother always told her. Hadn't Reese told her the same thing?

It was so much easier to believe in a person's integrity instead of always suspecting duplicity. Even after Sean, she just couldn't quite dismiss humankind as the unsavory, distrustful lot her family tried to convince her they were. If she ended up coming out of this mess alive, she vowed never to trust another human being as long as she lived.

Her new motto would be: Expect nothing—suspect everyone.

She pushed Reese from her thoughts. The New York man opened the door for her. She slid out off the backseat when he gave her a polite but deadly smile. He'd snap her neck with just a nod from Anthony.

When she didn't move fast enough, New York pushed her forward. "You look like you're going to the guillotine, Frankie," Anthony said.

"I wonder why?"

As they entered the house, Frankie's brain went into rescue mode. Her only hope was Unk.

"We'll divide the house in half," Anthony said. "Jimmy will work with you and Sal with me."

Hope lit inside her. Jimmy always had a soft spot for her.

"No ideas, Frankie. Leave Jimmy alone and just do the job. Until that will is located, I guarantee you, your ass is grass."

As they went their separate ways, Jimmy materialized from thin air. He gave his cousin a narrowed glare. "Don't try anything, Frankie. I don't want to hurt you, but I will."

Setting her jaw, Frankie nodded. "I see how it is, Jimmy, and don't think for a minute I won't forget any of this."

She stalked past him and climbed the stairs to the guest bedroom at the far end of the south wing. When she entered it, she realized it was the one Reese had used when they were there. She quelled her rising emotions. "I have to use the bathroom, Jimmy," she said over her shoulder. And, she thought, the telephone in it.

Unzipping her pants, she sat on the toilet and picked up the phone. As quietly as she could, Frankie dialed Unk's cell phone. After several rings it went to voice mail. "Unk, I'm at the Carmel house with Anthony."

Just as she hung up the phone, the door opened.

"Jimmy!"

He flushed a deep shade of red and closed the door. Thank God the phone was at her side, out of Jimmy's sight.

After Frankie washed her hands she came out of the room and scowled. "That was just rude."

"Sorry, wanted to make sure you didn't call anyone."

Frankie stiffened and began looking for the elusive will.

Several hours later, hungry, tired, and with too much time to think about things she shouldn't be thinking about, Frankie met Anthony and Sal down in the atrium.

Exhausted, she sat down in her father's cane-back recliner.

"Any luck?" he asked her.

"No, it's futile. If there was a will here, it's gone."

Anthony began to pace the stone floor. "I have to find that will!"

"Is having everything of Father's so important to you, Anthony?"

He stopped and stared at her. His eyes narrowed and he morphed into the spoiled little boy she had always seen him as, yet now there was true malice behind his expression.

"That will holds the truth."

"Speak it in plain English. What is more important than you owning the world?"

"Proof Unk killed father."

Frankie gasped, shocked to the core. She stood. "You're crazy! They were brothers."

Anthony's eyes narrowed to slits. "And the proof that you sanctioned it."

Now she knew he'd lost it. The minute she opened her mouth to defend herself, shrill laughter filtered into the room from the hallway.

Frankie twisted toward the noise. Connie.

"I always knew you were a conniving little bitch like your mother," she said coming into the room to stand next to her son. Anthony was her mirror image, with shorter hair and a penis. Connie smoothed Anthony's hair from his face. "That's why I always kept my Anthony away from you. Santini knew too, and agreed with me." She smiled at Anthony. Frankie ignored the almost incestuous way Connie beamed at her son. "I came as soon as you called. Did you find it?"

Slowly Anthony shook his head.

Frankie was still reeling from Anthony's accusations.

"Anthony, what are you talking about? I didn't sanction anything. And for the love of God, why would I?"

"The embezzlement, Frankie. The millions of dollars in your accounts."

This was a nightmare getting worse. "What accounts? I have my piddly-ass savings and checking accounts."

Anthony laughed and pulled a gun from the small of his back. He aimed it directly at her chest. Frankie swallowed hard.

"Really? I've seen the statements. I have to hand it to you. You were smart, burying them in your mother's maiden name. But technology today is an incredible thing."

"You're crazy." What else could she say?

Connie cackled. "What deal did you cut with the feds?"

"I didn't cut any deal! I'd never betray the family," Frankie cried.

"Liar," Connie said.

"I'm not lying!" She turned to her brother. "Anthony, you're wrong, I didn't kill Father. I loved him."

"You told him he was dead to you."

Words she regretted in more ways than one. "I was angry and hurt."

Anthony shrugged, unmoved. "As the cops would say, big sister, you had motive, means, and opportunity."

"I didn't kill him! If I did, then who has been trying to kill me?"

"I don't know. Who else have you pissed off?"

His response stopped her cold. Up to that point, although he denied it on the plane, she assumed he was lying to string her along. But now, under the heat of pressure . . . "You mean you didn't put a hit out on me?"

"He doesn't have the stomach for it, Francesca," Unk said, coming in from the hallway.

Connie shrieked and hid behind her son.

Two goons she didn't recognize followed in behind him, both with semis trained, one on New York Sal, and the other on Anthony.

Sal cursed loudly, then charged, and one of Unk's men capped off a round. Shots echoed in the atrium. Frankie hit the stone floor. Connie pushed Anthony into the lagoon and Unk's boys made hash out of Sal. Jimmy bolted into the room, gun drawn. He slid to a halt when he saw the occupants.

Frankie scurried up and ran to her uncle, who took her into the circle of his arms. "Unk!"

"*Cara mia,* are you all right?"

His warm cigar smell enveloped her in its safe scent. "Yes, but I don't understand any of this. Why does Anthony think you killed Father?"

"Because, 'Cesca, your shit-for-brains brother isn't as stupid as we all thought."

Frankie gasped at the new voice. "Mama?" This was getting too bizarre. "What are you doing here? How did—?" The how didn't matter, what mattered was her mother was here for her—finally.

"*Puta!*" Connie spat as she dragged her drenched self from the lagoon, Anthony helping her. They both stood drenched at the edge, water pooling at their feet.

"Lucia," Unk purred. "What a pleasant surprise."

Frankie looked at the man who was more of a father to her than her own had been, then back to the woman who gave birth to her. Of all the players in the room, her mother, dressed as always in chic Chanel and sporting a matching leather portfolio, looked as unperturbed as a saint.

Frankie made a move to her mother, but Unk's large hand restrained her. "Stay here with me, *cara*. Just for a moment."

"Leave her out of this, Carmine," her mother's stern voice demanded.

"Lucia, come now, I mustn't neglect the family's interests."

"And what would those be, Uncle," Anthony asked.

"Preservation. Without a current will, I retain control of the family, and I'll do things a bit different." Unk laughed. "You see, Anthony, your father was old school, he kept the family business too close, too legit. No hard-core drugs, no arms, no business with countries that don't have the same religion as us. In short, he had no vision."

"And you did?"

"Yes. The family has diversified over the past few years, and very profitably so."

"And part of that includes my sister cooking the books at *Skin* so you could siphon off profits to the tune of millions to launch your new enterprises?"

"I didn't cook the books!" Frankie said.

Anthony shook his head. "Stop lying, Frankie. The trail leads right to your computer."

"I—"

"In Frankie's defense, you can thank Tawny for that," Unk offered.

341

"Tawny?" Anthony, Frankie, and Connie said in unison.

Carmine nodded, a smile tugging at his lips. "She has proven to be quite the little spy."

Frankie stood, shocked to the bone. "You killed my father?"

"*Si, cara,* and I was also the one who told him you were skimming money. I'm sorry, it was necessary. The fool believed me. He knew how close we were."

Frankie felt the hot sting of angry tears. "You son of a bitch." And it occurred to her from the evidence against her, Reese also suspected her of her father's death and embezzling. He was a cop. How could he not?

"Why?" she asked, her voice tight.

"Why do you think, Francesca? Control. The only way to achieve that is to erase those who stand in my way."

"Did you kill Aldo Geppi?"

"Of course, and destroyed the notarized will your father had drawn up the night before he died."

Frankie looked at her mother for strength. Her mother's deep brown eyes held compassion in them but there was something else. Whatever reason her mother had for showing up, she was not ready to reveal it. Lucia nodded slightly, urging Frankie to keep going. She looked at her brother and for the first time in her life felt an emotional connection to him. They'd both been played by Carmine all these years.

Frankie turned back to the man she had loved like a father. Her gut twisted painfully. She just wanted him to curl up and die. "How long have you planned this?"

"Since you were born. I'm a patient man, *cara.* And now it's paying off." He nodded to his nearest thug, who did not hesitate to train his gun from Anthony's head to his heart.

Connie shrieked and Lucia's voice, calm and direct, cut through the tension. "You forgot one minor detail, Carmine." She stepped further into the room.

Carmine stiffened next to Frankie. "I think not, Lucia."

Lucia set the portfolio down on a nearby table and unzipped it. She pulled out a sheaf of papers and held up what appeared to be a legal document. "Sonny made sure there was more than one notarized document."

Frankie, Connie, and Anthony gasped in surprise.

"Bogus. Why would you have a copy?" Carmine asked, his hand tightening around Frankie's arm.

"Because my husband sent it to me, knowing he could trust me with our daughter's interests, just in case something happened to Aldo." She smiled confidently and gave Frankie an apologetic look. "I would have produced it sooner, 'Cesca, but he sent it to my old address. It took a little time for it to get to me."

"He's not your husband!" Connie spat.

Lucia smiled, saccharine. "We'll get to that minor detail, Constance, but first, would you like to know how the last will and testament of Santini Marco Donatello reads?"

"It's of no consequence," Carmine said.

Lucia laughed, the sound light. "Oh, but Carmine, it is." She flipped the first page and began, "To my daughter Francesca, I leave you my regret for believing your uncle, my brother Carmine, and my regret for not making you more a part of my life. I hope you can forgive me. I also leave you full control of *Skin,* to do with as you please, but remember to always, despite your uncle's nefarious nature, uphold the family name. I also leave you the deed to Casa di Falco, and all items on the grounds and within the house."

"This is my house!" Connie screamed, stepping forward. Two gun barrels turned on her. She halted, her eyes wide.

Standing in shock, Frankie looked at Anthony. And so did her mother. "I'm afraid, young man, Sonny was not only duped by his brother in the end, but by Carmine and your mother in the beginning."

"Shut your mouth, Lucy," Connie warned.

"What do you mean?" Anthony asked.

Frankie's stomach roiled. It couldn't get worse.

Lucia looked at Carmine, a smug smile twisting her lips. "Would you like to tell your son or should I?"

Frankie gasped so hard her chest hurt. She felt like she was going to throw up. She looked at Anthony, whose face lost all color. Connie screeched. "You're a lying bitch. It's why Sonny had your marriage annulled."

Lucia smiled and from the look, Frankie knew what the next shock was going to be. "My marriage to Sonny was never annulled." She let the words sink in before continuing. "The archbishop didn't feel there were grounds, especially with a child involved."

"Liar!" Connie screamed.

Lucia shrugged. "No, but you can blame Sonny for this one. I didn't realize it until I received the paperwork in the mail this morning."

"So, my brother sent you everything?"

"Yes, I guess he knew I would always have Frankie's best interests at heart and set the record straight. He also sent copies to the San Francisco DA and to one of his judge friends."

So Anthony wasn't her brother at all.

Frankie looked up at her uncle's tight jaw. "You're Anthony's father?" That meant that Connie— Frankie looked at her. She stood damp and pale, and there were no words necessary to confirm what her mother had said. Frankie's heart went out to Anthony, she expected him to look defeated but instead he looked—relieved.

"How did Santini know the DNA results were bogus?" Carmine casually asked.

"The clerk you paid off to falsify the report got a conscience."

Carmine nodded, his manner seemingly unconcerned. "So, now it appears there will be a slight change in my plans." He nodded to the two thugs. "However, my plans for all of you remain the same."

CHAPTER THIRTY-TWO

"Wait!" Frankie yelled, her voice reverberating against the slanted glass ceiling. She turned to her uncle, no fear in her heart, only anger as the last of the devastating realizations hit her. "Was the car meant for me and Anthony?"

Carmine nodded. Frankie didn't need to ask about the other attempts. It was understood.

She turned and squarely faced her uncle, and slapped him with everything she had across the face. A collective gasp rang out around her. But Unk remained stoic, unmoving, a white imprint of her hand flaring on his cheek.

She spat at his feet. "You disgrace me and our family name. How dare you! How dare you and that woman"—she pointed at Connie—"cuckold my father and allow him to raise your bastard! How dare you lie to him and steal from him! Have you no shame, no honor?" She moved closer to him, her anger mushrooming. "How dare you lie to him, about me, his only child!" Hot tears swelled in her eyes. "How dare you so cavalierly destroy lives!" She swiped at her cheek. "And for what? Money? Control? Power?" She spat, this time in his face.

She turned to Anthony. "Cousin, should you survive this treacherous man, *Skin* is yours. I want no part of it." She turned back to her uncle; fury stamped his features. "You won't get away with this, Uncle, you can't kill us all."

As he opened his mouth to speak, Frankie lunged at him. He wasn't much taller than her and her effort caught him by surprise. They went bowling backward. In the slow motion of the action, she heard gunshots, screams, and bodies hitting the ground.

Carmine grabbed her neck, rolling over onto her, his weight keeping her immobile. His fingers wrapped tightly around her throat, cutting off her air supply. Her brain waves slowed and she asked herself what Reese would do.

She grabbed Carmine's hands and pulled his hands from her neck just enough to give herself the breath she needed. His eyes narrowed to slits. Then she closed her eyes, said a prayer, and head-butted him in the nose. A warm spray of blood sprinkled across her cheeks. Carmine howled and let go of her. She heaved him away from her and rolled to her side. It took her a few seconds to get her breath. Scurrying to her feet, she turned and ran straight into a hard, unmoving chest.

"Frankie!"

Reese?

He grabbed her to him before pushing her behind him. Reese leveled his gun and aimed at Carmine, who was up and coming at them like a wounded bull. "Another inch and you're a dead man," Reese said.

Carmine slid to a halt, his wide eyes darting around the room. Blood ran freely from his broken nose, and at that instant Frankie saw him as the monster he truly was.

A swarm of federal agents and local cops filled the room. Frankie recognized Jase and the other one, Ricco. Her mother ran to her. Frankie held her arms out in welcome as her gaze swept the room. Connie lay in Anthony's arms, a bloodstain spreading at her shoulder. Jimmy lay on his back, looking at the ceiling, blood blossoming from the gunshot wound on the left side of his chest. One of Carmine's goons floated in the lagoon, the other held his bleeding arm and growled at the fed handcuffing him.

" 'Cesca, *bella,* you are okay?" Lucia asked.

Frankie choked back a sob. "How did you know I was here?"

Lucia's dark eyes softened and swept across the room to Frankie's cousin on the floor. "Jimmy called me. He was loyal to the end, 'Cesca."

Frankie's heart swelled and she couldn't bear to look at her dead cousin. She owed him her life.

The enormity of what just happened and the emotional roller coaster of her life and the last week with Reese had taken everything she had.

She could only nod, unable to form a word.

It was over. All of it. And what was she left with? Nothing.

"Frankie?" a familiar voice said from beside her. Its deep timbre once stirred her senseless. Now it left her cold.

With tired eyes she looked at Reese. "You thought I was up to my neck in this?"

"I didn't want to believe, but my intell—"

"Stop it! I don't want to hear your excuses." She looked around the room, and her eyes clashed with her uncle's; he was now standing handcuffed in the corner. "You'd better kill him along with the others, because I refuse to testify if it means I have to look at your face ever again."

She turned from her mother and walked over to Anthony, who had moved away from his bitch mother. "I meant what I said. *Skin* is yours. Do whatever the hell you want with it."

She wheeled around and walked out of the room, out of the house, down the long driveway, and off the property. And she kept walking. Even when she heard Reese's calls to her to stop, she kept walking.

Angry tears blurred her vision. Every last person in her life who meant something to her, except her mother, thank the Holy Virgin for her, had used or manipulated her for their own gain. And the worst of it all was the damn son of a bitch she'd fallen in love with.

Was there something about her that bred distrust or that screamed "fuck me over"? She was sick of her family and sick of her life. She'd take her little bit of savings and settle somewhere where no one had heard the name Donatello. Better yet, where the word spaghetti was a foreign word. Someplace where she could lick her wounds and heal. Someplace far away where there were no people.

Maintaining her pace, Frankie glanced to her right. She stopped at the view of the churning blue Pacific, and for once didn't think of a camera. The picture meant nothing to her.

Stiffening as a car pulled up behind her, she refused to look and see who it was.

" 'Cesca," her mother called. "Get in. I'll take you away from here."

Three weeks later

"Father?" Reese said to the man staring out the window.

The old man's hand resting on the cane-back chair flinched.

Reese hid his shock. In fifteen years the man who could single-handedly run a quarter horse ranch had shriveled up into a shell of a man. Watery brown eyes looked up at Reese as he came around to look the old man in the eye. A gnarled hand reached out toward him and Reese swallowed hard when a single tear ran down his father's cheek.

Reese took the hand and squeezed it. "How have you been, Father?"

The old man nodded and opened his mouth as if to speak, but he coughed. Reese held his hand and waited for the spell to pass.

"Son," he said, his voice raspy, as if little used.

"I'm here."

The brown eyes bored into him. "I'm sorry."

Reese patted the old man's hand. "Me too." And for so many things.

His father stared out the window and smiled a slow, sad smile. "It was my fault your mama left. I promised her excitement. I promised her the moon. I couldn't deliver."

"You can't take the blame for her actions. It took me a long time to realize it wasn't us, Dad, it was her, we were never enough. I'm sorry for you we weren't." He knew the feeling well. He wasn't enough for Frankie. She'd made the same choice as his mother. To live a life without him.

"Missy didn't understand," his father said.

"No, she was too young. I thought the truth would make her see, clarify things."

Sam squeezed his son's hand. "It wasn't your fault, boy. I reacted out of my own frustration. You were right to tell her the truth." He coughed, then cleared his throat. "Soon I'll see her. But I want you to know the ranch is yours. Old Midas has been holding down the fort, waiting for you to come back."

Reese sat, stunned by the news.

The old man coughed and shook his head. Tears welled in his tired eyes. "You belong to the ranch, it will always be there for you, don't forget it."

"I won't."

Three months later

After months of wallowing in self-pity, anger, regret, and too many tears to count, Frankie felt as empty as the Grand Canyon. Her heart physically hurt. She missed her father and the man she'd always thought was Unk. She missed her cousin Anthony. It seemed so odd to think of him in that way, but slowly she got used to it. She missed her camera, she missed that damn ranch in Wyoming, and more than anything or anyone she missed Reese. To the point of physical pain.

Reese tried several times to contact her. She refused to talk to him or see him. Jase came by once and she refused to see him too. Ricco gave it a shot and was shot down. A man named Ty Jamerson came by with his fiancée on Reese's behalf. She told them all to take a hike.

All the while her mother kept a watchful eye on her and honored her every wish. But not without commentary. " 'Cesca, you're losing too much weight."

Frankie would shrug and respond, "So what? I have a few pounds to spare."

" 'Cesca, your color is terrible, go out into the sun, it's good for you."

"I don't like the sun."

" 'Cesca, come see the rabbits, take a picture."

"I don't ever want to pick up a camera again."

" 'Cesca, a package for you."

"Leave it on the table."

It was then her mother took a stand.

Lucia brought in a package addressed to her. She thrust it in Frankie's face. "Open it."

"No."

"There might be something good in it."

"I don't care what's in it."

"Then I will open it."

"Be my guest."

Frankie just stared out the window.

"Oh, looks like pictures. With a card."

Frankie flinched.

Lucia opened the card. "It says, 'a picture is worth a thousand words.'"

Frankie's blood pressure spiked.

"I'll open this envelope and see what they are."

"No!"

Lucia chuckled. "So there is a person in that body." She set the envelope down next to her daughter. "I'll bring you a nice glass of Chianti."

When she returned a few minutes later and put the glass down next to Frankie, Lucia reached for the envelope. "I'd like to see those."

Frankie grabbed it. "No, Mama."

Lucia smiled and took the chair next to her daughter. "Francesca, I love having you here, but you're almost thirty, and you need to go out and make your mark on the world. Anthony wants you back at *Skin.*"

"*Skin* is a lie."

"You believed in it once."

"I believed in a lot of things once."

"What do you want, *mia amore?*"

"I don't know."

"I think you do. Maybe those pictures will help you realize it." Lucia stood. "Drink your wine."

Once her mother left the room, Frankie's gaze locked on the envelope. She knew what was in it, and she didn't want to see images of her and Reese.

Her ire piqued for the first time in months. How dare he do that? Send her their sex pictures? After he used sex as a means to pump her for information? How low could a person go? He made her fall in love and all for a job. To get information to put her in jail.

And he would have too!

She ripped open the envelope.

For a long moment she held it in her hand, not wanting to look but unable not to.

She slid a small grouping of pictures into her hand. She caught her breath, the sensations from that night engulfing her as if Reese was beside her, touching her skin. She closed her eyes. She could almost smell him.

Opening her eyes, she looked at the picture in her hand. Her gut somersaulted and emotion swelled in her throat. She lay sleeping on the bed of blankets Reese had made for her. He gently stroked her hair. She looked at the next picture; in this one he kissed her lips. The next he gazed lovingly at her.

Frankie sat back in the chair, resting her hand in her lap. When had he taken them?

She raised her hand and her skin flushed warm. The picture showed her body's response to his touch. Her breasts were plump, her nipples beaded hard, the fine hair on her arms raised.

The next picture showed his fingertips brushing against her nipple. The next showed them making love in a slow undulation. The tender look in his eyes and the way she remembered his slow, sinuous rhythm forced emotion she had been denying to well.

The last picture was of Reese gently kissing her tears away.

Either he was a great actor or he meant it, or maybe some of both.

"Looks like two fools in love," Lucia said over her shoulder.

"Mother!"

"Francesca, why are you here?"

She had no answer.

One month later

Sam called up to Reese from the kitchen, "You need to get that, son, me an' Midas are busy."

Reese didn't hurry down the stairs. But he smiled at his father's voice. It got stronger every day. The demons they both lived with the past years were slowly disappearing. While he was glad to have his father back, an even bigger hole, the one in his soul, remained empty.

He had tried everything to get Frankie to speak to him, even going to Scottsdale with Lucia's help, but Frankie refused to see him.

When it became painfully apparent she wanted nothing to do with him, he took a leave of absence and retired to the ranch and what was left of his family.

He couldn't blame her for not trusting him. Hell, he wouldn't either.

The persistent knock at the front door to the sprawling ranch house disrupted his thoughts. Must be someone responding to the ad he put in the paper.

He opened the door and his heart dropped to his feet. Even though a wide-brimmed Stetson obscured her face, her scent hit him broadside.

From her leather boots to the denim duster she wore, Francesca Donatello's curves betrayed her.

She held a folded newspaper in her hand. When she pushed the hat back and looked up at him, his heart melted. His smile pulled so hard at his lips, it hurt.

"I hear you need a ranch hand, mister. I'm here to apply for the job."

"What experience do you have?"

She stepped up closer to him, her eyes never leaving his face. She pulled the duster back, revealing her full naked breasts. "I hear the guy who runs this place likes his women nekkid."

"Who is it, son?"

Frankie yipped and wrapped herself back in the duster. Reese grabbed her by the hand and pulled her into the house, closing the door behind him with his boot.

"It's the mother of your future grandchildren."

"Whoa, not so fast, cowboy," Frankie said as he scooped her into his arms and kissed her so hard she lost her breath.